THE CRITICS LOVE AMANDA SCOTT!

DANGEROUS ANGELS:
". . . an exciting Regency romance filled with two great lead characters, a tremendous cast, and a brilliant story-line. If you haven't read the prequel, DANGEROUS GAMES . . . it is strongly recommended that you do so."

—*Affaire de Coeur*

DANGEROUS ILLUSIONS:
"Amanda Scott captures the Regency with a sharp pen and her dry wit, portraying the glamourous appeal and the sorrow of the era to a tee. A true treat."

—*Romantic Times*

BAWDY BRIDE:
"Ms. Scott captures your interest with the very first sentence and then proceeds to weave a spell around your heart. . . ."

—*Rendezvous*

BORDER BRIDE:
"BORDER BRIDE is a provocative and seductive mix . . . hours of reading fun."

—Catherine Coulter

IT WAS THE LAST THING HE EXPECTED. . . .

Rothwell concealed his astonishment with difficulty. For the life of him, he could not think what his brother James was doing dragging a disreputable female into Rothwell House library.

"I suppose your reason for bursting in upon me in this fashion is an important one?"

The young female's eyes flashed, and he saw that they were a singularly greenish shade of hazel. She had scrubbed her face and hands, but her gown was as filthy and bedraggled as that of any street wench.

"Lord Rothwell, I cannot allow you to continue to speak of me as if I were a drab off the street. I'll have you know I am no such thing."

"Dear me," Rothwell said, raising his eyeglass and peering at her through it in sudden suspicion that she really wasn't what she seemed. She was not at all in awe of him, for one thing, and spoke as if to an equal. She was, therefore, either demented or of gentle birth. "I believe I have misjudged you, young woman. You speak rashly, but you speak in educated tones."

"I am very well educated, sir, though I cannot see what that fact has to do with the point at hand."

Rothwell found himself studying her more carefully. Her face, animated by anger now, was an exceedingly pretty one, and though she was small of stature, her figure—which he could surmise easily enough despite her deplorable clothing—was slender and delicately curved. The greenish eyes sparkled, her chin tilted up defiantly, and her full lips parted, revealing even white teeth.

"James, tell me in plain words, where did you find her?"

"In the magistrate's court at Bridewell."

"Good God." He saw her flush deeply and bite her lower lip, and found himself wondering what it must taste like. Mentally chastising himself for a fool, he reined in his errant thoughts abruptly and said, "Tell me the whole, James, *without interruption!*"

HIGHLAND FLING

Amanda Scott

Zebra Books
Kensington Publishing Corp.

http://www.zebrabooks.com

ZEBRA BOOKS are published by

Kensington Publishing Corp.
850 Third Avenue
New York, NY 10022

First Pinnacle Printing: February, 1995
First Zebra Printing: October, 1997
10 9 8 7 6 5 4 3 2

Printed in the United States of America

To Jim, with love

AUTHOR'S NOTE

The correct British and traditional Scottish spelling for the House of Stewart, according to *Chambers's Biographical Dictionary* has been used in this story. Confusion sometimes arises because Stuart became the "correct" spelling briefly when Mary, Queen of Scots, married Charles, Lord Darnley, whose family spelled the name in the French manner. Mary was Bonnie Prince Charlie's great-great-grandmother.

J

The white half-moon floating above the shadowy bulk of Carn Odhar was the sort Lowlanders call an aval moon. Highlanders, on the other hand, called it MacDrumin's moon, because it gave that canny gentleman sufficient light for his purpose without shedding too much for safety on activities that might draw the interest of prying English authorities. As the hour approached midnight, the little moon disappeared from time to time behind scudding fat clouds, reappearing moments later to cast a silvery glow over the mischief afoot in the Great Glen.

The wind putting the clouds to flight, though it brought a crisp chill to the air, hinting at colder nights to come, failed to sweep low enough to banish the thick mist rising from Loch Ness, but every once in a while an errant gust cleared an opening and allowed moonlight to sparkle briefly on shining ripples of black water before the mist closed in again.

In one such moment the moonlight caught movement on the eastern shore of the loch, when ten shadowy figures emerged from the thick growth of pine trees edging the steep lower slope of Carn Odhar near the shoreline. Although clouds soon obscured the moon again, splashes and murmuring voices could be heard, followed by thuds of wood on wood and against metal, hastily muffled. Then all was still except for the gentle lapping of water against the shore and the hush of breezes soughing through the treetops. For a moment even breezes and water were still, as if to aid those who listened for betraying sounds from a lurking enemy.

Maggie MacDrumin, standing stiffly erect, every nerve aquiver in her small, delicately curved body, scanned the distant shore for movement and strained her ears for the slightest sound of human presence there. As she pulled her wool mantle tighter to ward off the chill, she even felt her nose twitch as if it might somehow smell out danger, though in truth, she detected no more than the tangy aroma of pine needles, the dampness of the rising mist, and the musky odor of nearby horses.

Her tension was reflected in the postures of her companions, particularly the thin young woman beside her. Kate's pale plaited hair—lighter and finer in texture than Maggie's thick honey-gold tresses—looked silver in the moonlight, and her eyes, huge in her pixie face from lack of proper food, grew wider and even more wary when she caught Maggie's gaze upon her.

"I dinna like standing aboot in the open like this," Kate muttered tersely, her lapse into Highland accents revealing uncharacteristic nervousness, since she generally took care to pattern her speech after Maggie's. "Seems fidging unnatural, and I tell you true, Mag, this business of the laird's be like tae land us all in Inverness Tolbooth afore the nicht be o'er."

"Do you good to learn the consequences of mad

folly, you daft wench," the chief of the MacDrumins muttered as he loomed out of the shadows behind them. A man of middle height in his late forties, Andrew MacDrumin of MacDrumin, ninth laird of that ilk, was nonetheless powerfully built, and though presently he wore his powdered periwig and a voluminous mantle, even in the shadowy moonlight he projected an air of unmistakable audacity.

When Kate grimaced, he grinned at her, showing the gap where an eye tooth had been knocked out four years before at the bloodbath known as Culloden. That lost tooth being his only injury, he had managed to escape the field and lead the tattered remnants of his clan, by way of the devious mountain paths he knew so well, to the relative safety of Glen Drumin, and to do so with such speed as to thwart all attempts by the authorities later to prove his direct involvement in the uprising. Though suspicion was rife among the English, no Highlander would admit without equivocation that the MacDrumin personally had taken part. Now, looking at Kate, he demanded gruffly, "Do you think I know naught of folly myself, lass?"

"Nay, my lord," Kate retorted. "I believe ye ken more of such business than most men do."

" 'Tis true, I do," he agreed, his eyes twinkling in the moonlight, "so you'd best believe me, Kate MacCain, when I say you're a sight safer in the business you be part of this night than in the madness you've been stirring up these past several months and more, for I speak naught but the simple truth."

Kate lifted her chin but did not voice her defiance aloud, and Maggie hid a smile, knowing that had it been anyone else who dared to reprove her, Kate's volatile temper would have exploded like a keg of gunpowder. Few persons, male or female, young or old, cared to stir MacDrumin's fury, however. Even the devilish Campbells and cursed English gave him wide berth once his anger had been aroused.

Maggie focused her gaze again on the distant shore but saw only the massive moonlit walls of Castle Urquhart rising out of the mist. The ghostly landscape around them seemed uninhabited.

"Don't squint, lass," MacDrumin muttered, "or you'll wrinkle your bonny face. They'll be there right enough, so now then, the pair of you, into the boat you go."

"But I was going to row over with Dugald," Kate protested.

"Well, you're not," MacDrumin said, "for your cousin Dugald can no more make you mind than he can fly. I want the pair of you skittersome, unruly females safe under my own eye, and that's all I'll say about it. Steady that boat with your oars, lads," he added, his voice carrying easily through the night. Then, holding a hand out to help Kate, he said, "Mind the kegs now, lassies; and, you men yonder in the other two boats, mind you stay close to us, and we'll protect our cargo as if 'twere rubies and gold."

Maggie heard laughter in his voice and saw several of the others smiling. She sighed. This was no time for humor.

Moments later, aside from an occasional night bird's call, the only sounds were the oars plunging into the water followed by dripping splashes when they emerged again. The occupants of the three long, narrow boats were quiet now, and so eerie did they all look to Maggie that it was as if they were but black shadows skimming through the silent mist. Rowers and passengers alike kept at least one eye cast toward Castle Urquhart, for they all knew that no permanent obstacle barred their path across the mysterious, un-fathomed black depths of the loch so long as they held a straight course toward the shadowed ruin.

"I hope the monster sleeps deep tonight," Kate murmured with an audible shudder in her voice.

Maggie chuckled softly. Despite the many tales she had heard, she put small faith in the mythical monster that supposedly lurked below in the deep, narrow chasm containing the loch. "The only monsters afoot tonight," she said, "are English excisemen, whispering plots with their Campbell and MacKenzie toadies."

"I'll have no profanities spoken in this boat," Mac-Drumin said sternly.

"I didn't! I said only—"

"You spoke of the blasted English," he snapped. " 'Tis as bad as a damn any day. Och, but I spit on them, and on their wicked, evil laws. Bad enough that without cause they did take a man's land that's been in his family for centuries and gave it without so much as a by-your-leave to one of their own, *and* have tried to undermine a proper chief's authority amongst his own people, but then to demand rents he canna raise, nor his people either—" He paused, drawing breath in between his teeth. "Och, but 'tis not the time to talk of such foulness. Indeed, if things come to pass as they ought, there'll soon be no need for talk at all."

Kate said softly, "Aye, for when his highness—"

"Och, lassie, whisst! Even a whisper carries far over water, and 'tis only a mile now. You mustna speak so plain."

Maggie, seeing uncharacteristic dismay in Kate's face, said, "Words will not carry so far, Kate, only sounds." Then, turning to her father, she said quietly, "We MacDrumins must soon make our loyalty known in London, sir. The more men who support him there, the more likely his mission will succeed this time."

"Agreed, lass, but if you're thinking that I ought to go myself, you'd best think again. For me even to stir southward whilst they watch me so close would be as good as a grand announcement of things to come. To go to London would be witless. Mayhap, if I had a son, he could go, or if I could spare your cousin Colin . . . but nay." He sighed. "Even Colin would draw undesirable attention."

Maggie bit her lip, annoyed as she always was when her father bemoaned his lack of a son. Not that he had ever really held her gender against her. He had even obeyed the law enacted nearly a century before—and by a Stewart king, at that—that required him to send his eldest daughter (if he had no son) to be educated in the English manner. As a result, she had lived the greater parts of six years in Edinburgh, spending only her long vacations in the Highlands, and had expected to remain one more year to make her entry into society as the daughter of a mighty Highland chief. The Uprising of Forty-five had ended that plan, for after the early Jacobite victory at Prestonpans, MacDrumin had deemed it prudent for her to return to the Highlands to be out of harm's way. Edinburgh having remained staunchly Hanoverian despite the presence in the city of the true Stewart heir, the Jacobite victory had only made matters more unstable for the Highlanders who happened still to be living there.

Maggie had not regretted her return, for Glen Drumin was her home and she loved it there. By comparison, Edinburgh had always seemed an unfriendly place filled with people who preferred peace to principle, people only too willing to bend a knee to the distant Hanoverian king and to forget the loyalty they

owed to the Stewarts. Highlanders were not so fickle.-
The western shore was near now, and there was no
more murmuring, only the steady dip and drip of oars
and the occasional muffled thump of wood in the
wrapped oarlocks. The first boat crunched onto the
shore, followed directly by the other two, and men
leapt out to drag them out of reach of the gently
lapping water, for they were well aware that Ness, like
other lochs, ebbed and flowed with the distant sea
tides.

With the boats safely beached, the men moved
swiftly to deal with the kegs; however, no sooner was
the first one upended on the shore than a host of
armed men erupted from nearby shrubbery and a deep
voice thundered, "Hold where you are, MacDrumin!
'Tis Fergus Campbell, bailie, here with official excisemen holding commissions from the Lord High Constable in Edinburgh. Tell your men to throw down
their weapons at once, you scoundrel."

Instead, MacDrumin shouted, "At them, lads! 'Tis
a trick, by God, for it can be naught else! Out of the
way, lassies, whilst we teach these thieving ruffians the
folly of trying to steal goods from the MacDrumin!"

His men obeyed instantly, bellowing the fierce Mac-
Drumin war cry as they leapt to engage the enemy with
fists and clubs. Reacting just as quickly, Maggie
grabbed Kate and pulled her well away from the
fracas, scarcely daring to take her eyes off MacDrumin
while she did so, for fear he would be killed.

Kate wailed, "They'll be murdered, the lot of them!
What was himself thinking, Mag?" Bending swiftly,
she snatched up the hem of her skirt, but Maggie,
instantly divining her intent, grabbed her arm again
and jerked her upright.

"No weapons, Kate! You know the English law

forbids any Highlander to go armed. That means womenfolk, too, you lackwit. You would endanger us all!"

Letting her skirt fall back into place just as Mac-Drumin knocked two heads together with a crack that could be heard above the rest of the din, then flung the pair aside to leap to the aid of another of his men, Kate said scornfully, "Endanger them? 'Tis not myself who endangers them, Mag. The laird must be crazed to take on a Campbell and his tame excisemen. Our lads canna win."

Nor did they. Although the eight MacDrumin men defended their casks with such vigor that more than one enemy head was broken, at last they stood silent, glaring defiantly at the party of excisemen and at the man who, despite being a Scotsman and a Highlander like themselves, was clearly the enemy leader.

Burly, dark-haired Fergus Campbell stood with his feet apart and his hamlike hands on his hips, smirking at them, his triumph clear. "Now, then, where be your ponies hidden, MacDrumin?"

"What ponies are those, Fergus, my lad?"

"Them that was meant tae carry these blasted whisky kegs o' yours to Inverness, you auld heathen."

A muttering stir of anger could be heard from the captured men, but MacDrumin, tilting his periwig slightly askew in order to scratch his head, said only, "You seem mighty brave with all your wee men lined up behind you, laddie mine, but if you think I'd be smuggling whisky with my daughter and her pretty friend along for the fun of it all, you are making a rare grand fool of yourself."

Campbell snarled, "Devil take you, MacDrumin, you'd smuggle whisky with your ailing mother hiding it under her skirt for you!"

"Mayhap I would, lad, but that prospect has naught to do with the present occasion, so if you ken what you mean to do next, you had best proceed with it. I know of no ponies hereabouts, and since my word is vastly more dependable than your own, you would be wise to accept it and not keep these sweet lassies idling about in the cold to no good purpose."

Campbell snorted in derision, but after a brief colloquy with his companions, he ordered the excisemen and their assistants to load several of the kegs onto their horses, leaving the rest on shore, under guard, until more horses could be fetched from the Highland capital to retrieve them.

The distance to Inverness was less than ten miles, but since they had to walk, it was after two o'clock in the morning before they reached the town. When they came to the great stone prison known as the Tolbooth, and Campbell made it clear that his intent was to house the entire lot of them inside, MacDrumin said gently, "That must be your decision, I agree, but you might bear in mind, lad, that my daughter has been raised a lady and a common jail is no place for one of her ilk. Her friend, too," he added with a twinkling look at Kate, "would be most out of place there. Won't like it much myself, come to that, especially since I've done naught to deserve such barbarous treatment."

Campbell slapped a nearby keg. "Naught, eh? We'll just see that, come morning, when these casks will be opened in the presence of the High Sheriff as the law requires. You can tell his worship then just how ill-treated you all have been."

One of the Englishmen, who had been gazing speculatively at Kate and Maggie, moved up to Campbell and whispered in his ear. The Scotsman shot a grim look at the women and nodded with visible reluctance. Then, turning back to MacDrumin, he said, "I have no authority to house your daughter and her friend elsewhere, but my companions agree that the Tolbooth is no proper place for them. I can lock you all in one cell together until morning, away from the other prisoners, but that will have to suffice."

"Aye, it will at that," MacDrumin said cordially, "and I thank you kindly, Fergus Campbell, for your rare compassion."

Campbell shot him a suspicious look, but MacDrumin met it with bland innocence. Moments later, the ten Highlanders were alone in a single dark chamber that was infrequently and dimly lit only when parting clouds revealed a scattering of stars through the small barred window high in one wall.

"Can we talk, Papa?" Maggie asked softly.

"Of a certainty, lass, but say naught that you be not full willing for enemy ears to overhear."

Beside them, Kate made a growling sound. "Whoever that is who just put his hand on my leg, take it away this instant or I'll feed what's left of it to my dogs after I have cut it off."

"No mischief, lads," MacDrumin said sharply, "and as for you, Kate MacCain, if you have the means by you to carry out that wicked threat, keep it well hid, for even I cannot protect you if the damned English suspect you've a weapon on your person."

A masculine voice interjected a hasty apology. "I didna ken it were you, lass. I'd no ha' touched ye else. I vow, 'twas nae more than a brush as I shifted m'self on this hard floor."

"Sleep, all of you," MacDrumin said. "We shall need to have our wits about us come the dawning."

Maggie was as sure as she could be that she would

not sleep a wink, for the stone floor was not only cold but damp and there was no place else to sit or lie down. Her father pulled her toward him, however, and with her head against his broad chest and his mantle and her own covering her, she dozed and then slept. When she awoke, she saw by the gray dawn light that Mac-Drumin still dozed, his periwig tilted rakishly over one eye; but others were stirring, and one man gasped in shock when he awoke to find Kate sleeping with her head resting comfortably on his stomach.

"Och, what'll I do?" he demanded in a hushed tone.

"Gang softly, Angus," whispered the big one called Dugald. "Here's me fecket. See can ye slip it under yon vixen's head in place o' yersel', or I fear 'twill be the last dawning ye'll see."

Gratefully, Angus accepted the jacket, and while Maggie held her breath, stifling equal amounts of amusement and apprehension, he moved with exaggerated delicacy and care to shift Kate's head to a less compromising location.

"What the devil?" Kate sat bolt upright, glaring around in fury as the man scrambled away. "By the rood, Angus," she snapped, "I'll snatch ye baldheaded, ye brazen—"

"Nay, nay, lass," MacDrumin said, laughing. " 'Twas none of his doing, so whisst now! 'Twas yourself who sought a pillow softer than the stones upon which to rest your bonny head."

The others were chuckling now too, although none dared to laugh as hard as their chief did.

Kate looked from one face to another, and though the chuckles quickly faded, their amusement was still plain. She fixed her gaze inquiringly upon Maggie.

"Aye, Papa's got the right of it," Maggie said, grinning. "You put your own head on poor Angus's stomach. I only wish you might have seen his face when he first awoke and found it there."

Kate smiled. "So long as he knew his danger, that's all right then. Peace, Angus, I swear I won't eat you."

"Well, that puts my mind tae rest," he said with relief, glancing at the youngest lad, who was climbing onto Dugald's broad back to peer out the high, barred window. "What's o'clock, Rory?"

"Nigh onto eight, I make it," Rory replied.

It was well over an hour later before someone came to hail them before the high sheriff, a plump middle-aged gentleman wearing the full robes and regalia of his office, who peered down at them from his high bench, his round face looking pale beneath his full-bottomed, heavily powdered wig, his blue eyes small but shrewd behind wire-rimmed spectacles.

"MacDrumin, is that you?" he demanded when the chief stood before him.

"Aye, your worship," MacDrumin replied cheerfully, adjusting his voluminous green-and-black-checked mantle and twitching the sleeves of his saffron-colored shirt into place as though he meant to settle himself for a comfortable visit. "And how does your worship fare these days, and all?"

The sheriff looked at Campbell, and when Maggie's gaze followed his, she had all she could do to maintain a calm and ladylike demeanor, for the very sight of Fergus Campbell angered her. A thickset man six feet in height, he possessed a cocky arrogance that made her want to prick him with a pin to see if he would yelp like other mortals. His crisp brown hair, ruddy cheeks, and hazel eyes might have made him a handsome man had he not maintained such an air of superiority. And all, she thought, because he and his clan, having chosen to betray their own people to side with the royal forces, had then taken full advantage of that treachery after the royalists had won at Culloden.

In the intervening years, various Campbells had committed untold rape and murder upon their own neighbors, but that was no new thing. Their perfidy at Glencoe sixty years ago, when in cold blood they had murdered the hospitable MacDonalds as they slept, was still a bitter memory throughout the Highlands. In Maggie's opinion, Campbells were the lowest of the low—worse even than the thieving MacGregors. Seeing Fergus Campbell look at the sheriff now with that annoyingly triumphant smirk in his eyes made her want to hit him.

The sheriff said, "What's the charge against him, Campbell?"

"Why, that he has been smuggling whisky, your worship, as we ha' brought the goods along tae prove. Caught him red-handed, we did, in the wee hours of the night, a-rowing his cargo as quiet as a wee mouse across Loch Ness. Owing tae information received, however, we was on the lookout and took him and his lot without loss of a solitary man, though they fought hard with yon wicked cudgels and did bodily harm tae more than one. Had they been able tae overpower us, no doubt they'd ha' killed us all."

The sheriff looked steadily at MacDrumin. "Is that so?"

" 'Tis true enough that we fought hard," MacDrumin said, "but what else were we to do when a pack of thieving rogues leapt at us out of the bushes and attempted to steal our lawful property?"

"Have you paid the required duty on that whisky then, sir?"

MacDrumin's eyes widened. "And, pray now, your worship, what whisky would that be, if you please?"

Amanda Scott

Fergus Campbell snorted. "What whisky, he says. What whisky indeed? Ha' ye forgotten so soon then, MacDrumin, that we brought yon kegs along wi' us the nicht?"

"You have all the characteristics of a popular politician, Fergus Campbell," MacDrumin said grimly, "a horrible voice, bad breeding, and a vulgar manner; but what I recall, laddie mine, is that you forced us to leave most of our cargo on the shore of Loch Ness, where most likely it will be spoiled by midday today."

"Aged a few more hours is all it will be," Campbell said, jeering as he turned. "You, there at the back of the room, roll up them kegs now. We'll let his worship see for himself this so-called lawful cargo, and if the MacDrumin canna produce papers tae show he's paid the required duty for making his whisky, he'll be taking up residence in yon Tolbooth for a good long while."

The kegs were rolled up beneath the sheriff's high bench, and when the first was upright again, a man with a pry bar opened it, freeing a smell sour enough to make Maggie wrinkle her nose. Others nearby reacted with similar disgust, and with a startled look of dismay, Campbell leapt forward and peered into the keg.

"Herring!" Turning on the man who had opened it, he demanded, "Where the devil did you come by this keg, man?"

"Why, 'tis one o' them we captured in the nicht, Fergus Campbell. Ye ken that yerself, for it's got your ain mark upon it. There." He pointed to a red slash on the side of the keg.

The sheriff said, "Is that indeed your mark, Mr. Campbell?"

"Aye," Campbell said grimly, shifting his furious gaze to the innocent-looking MacDrumin.

Maggie schooled her features to ladylike hauteur, not daring to look at Kate.

"Herring, is it?" the sheriff said.

MacDrumin nodded and sighed deeply. "Aye, your worship, and quite worthless now, as anyone can tell by that nasty smell."

"But why," the sheriff asked reasonably, "did you not tell Campbell and his gaugers that your kegs contained only herring?"

"Tell them?" MacDrumin looked indignant. "And when, pray tell, was I given a chance to speak a word to yon great lout, Fergus Campbell, or indeed to any of them? Fell upon us out of the night, they did, like thieves trying to steal our lawful goods, then forced us and our innocent lassies to march behind them afterward like common felons. Never once did they ask what was in the kegs. And since when, I ask your worship again, is it a crime for a man to defend his own property from brutal attack?"

The sheriff shifted his stern gaze to Campbell. "Since when, indeed? Mr. Campbell, have you aught to say to that?"

"They carried weapons, your worship!"

"Had they pistols, dirks, or axes?"

"Nay, only cudgels, but—"

"Then they broke no law, did they, Mr. Campbell?"

Campbell grimaced, exchanging glances with several of his men. "Nay, your worship, but I would warn . . . That is," he added hastily, catching the sheriff's flintlike gaze, "I would strongly suggest tae Laird MacDrumin that in future he take more care when he travels in the dark of night, for 'tis mighty difficult at such a time tae tell friend from foe."

"Aye, lad," MacDrumin said sweetly, "and isn't that just what I said myself? But, begging your worship's pardon, who is going to repay me now for all my spoiled herring?"

Maggie, hearing Kate gasp, struggled to conceal her own astonished delight at this additional effrontery on her father's part, but one glance at the expression of outraged fury on Campbell's face turned delight to apprehension.

Austerely, the sheriff said, "That, I think, must be a lesson to you, MacDrumin, for Mr. Campbell was but doing his duty and I do believe that you might have made more of a push to identify your goods. You and your men can go, Campbell, but though I will not order you to repay his lordship, you too must take more care, for you have done him an ill service by so grievously misjudging him. Still and all, I will make it plain to him before he leaves that he must in future identify not only himself but his goods."

There was silence until the disgruntled excisemen and Campbell had gone and the door had been shut behind them. Then the sheriff shifted his keen gaze once more to MacDrumin.

"And the whisky, Andrew," he said gently. "Did the whisky make it safely to Inverness?"

"Aye, your worship, that it did, taking the eastern shore of the loch whilst we occupied Campbell and his wee playmates on the western side. Your own share will have been delivered to your back doorstep this morning before dawn. Och, but I wish it were possible to have had a picture made of yon Fergus Campbell's face when he found himself staring eye to eye with that barrelful of herring! 'Twas a rare and splendid sight, that was."

The sheriff frowned. "Have a care, Andrew. Their

suspicions rise a wee bit higher every time you twist
their tails like this. 'Twas bad enough when they suspected you of plotting against the present royal family.
Take care lest they lay siege to Glen Drumin in hopes
of ferreting out your stills."

"But Campbell has looked, your worship, and more
than once. As I keep telling him, there be nary a still
for him to see."

"Keep it that way. You, by the door," he added,
raising his voice. "Look out and be certain that no one
is loitering nearby." When the man had looked,
shaken his head, and shut the door again, the sheriff
said, "What other news have you, Andrew?"

"He's to visit London midmonth," MacDrumin
said, lowering his voice. "Our Bonnie Charlie will not
come again to the Highlands, they tell me, unless he
can first be assured of support from those damned
capricious English Jacobites. Since the blatherskites
refused to join him the last time, the thinking in the
Great Glen and elsewhere, as you know, is that this
time the business must *begin* in the south. However,
once again, France has promised us full support when
the rebellion gets under way."

"We saw how little such promises were worth in
forty-five."

"Aye, we did, but memories are short and wishes
strong."

Maggie, moving nearer, said, "I have been telling
him, sir, that we must make a push to discover what
passes with his highness in London and to assure those
who might help us that we stand ready to join them the
instant they make plain their intent."

The sheriff nodded thoughtfully. "We do have lads
in London with their ears to the ground—and a few
lasses, too," he said, smiling at her. "Indeed, mistress,

I warrant news comes to us from England at a speed that would astonish German George had he but the least notion of it, so I cannot agree that your father ought to go south, if that is the course you have urged upon him."

" 'Tis true," MacDrumin said, nodding, "and so I've told her, but she's got this maggot in her brain that we'll not get the whole truth if we cannot hear it from one of our own. Not," he added with a sigh, "that there might not be a wee bit of sense in the lass's argument when all is said and done."

Kate had moved up behind Maggie. "What of Angus or Cousin Dugald, my lord? Could one of them not go?"

"Nay, lass," MacDrumin said, his gaze sweeping over the two young men. "We've a need for someone who can move in the first circles, for that is where he will learn the most. What's more, with young Ian and your auld mother and gran to look after, you've more need of Dugald and Angus here than we have for them in London. But enough chatter. We are not so safe, even here and now, that we can afford to rattle on about such things without great care. We'll be off now, your worship, if it's all the same to you. You've my deepest thanks for this."

"I accept your thanks," the sheriff said, "and your excellent whisky as well, you rascal."

"And welcome," MacDrumin said, grinning, "though 'tis a pity you couldna see your way clear to making yon Campbell pay for the herring. We could have used the gelt."

"I thought it unwise to infuriate him further. Are the herring truly all spoiled?"

"They should be, and the kegs as well—which is much worse, of course—for they've been sitting amongst the pine trees these four days past, waiting on a proper moon, whilst our Fergus hid harmlessly under a bush each night and peered at the loch."

They left the sheriff chuckling and made their way to the south end of town, where they were met by friends who had been expecting them. Mounted at last and fed, they made good time along the eastern shore of Loch Ness to the trail leading to Glen Drumin, nestled deep in the heart of the Monadhliath mountains.

As she rode, Maggie thought back to their brief conversation with the sheriff and knew her father had been tactful for once when he had so gently refused Kate's suggestion that either Angus or Dugald serve as their envoy to London. Neither man would do. Whoever went to meet Charles Edward Stewart—their own Bonnie Prince Charlie—must be someone who could meet him in polite company, for although he would travel incognito, he would scorn this time to travel as a commoner. He had surely had enough of that after Culloden, during the months he had been forced to hide out in the hills, protected by Highlanders who slipped him from hut to hut and cave to cave, often right under the noses of the soldiers who searched for him, before his escape to France.

She thought again of her cousin Colin as a possible emissary, and dismissed him. He was still young, only a year older than she was, and seemed even younger, despite the fact that at eighteen, he had been old enough to fight at Culloden and come home with no more than a sword scratch.

Glancing at MacDrumin, she saw that he was smiling again, no doubt congratulating himself on the success of his latest venture. She wished she had as much confidence in his illegal activities as he did, but she could not believe it would be long before his entire operation was unmasked and the English locked him away. Fergus Campbell was a dreadful man; worse, he was a tenacious one. The thought terrified her, for she knew not how she or the rest of the clan would survive without MacDrumin's leadership.

Life had been difficult the past four years since Culloden, for the relentless hunting down of Jacobites and their fugitive prince had resulted in months of terror followed by savage reprisals, the banning of all weapons, the outlawing of proper Highland dress, and the English garrisoning of all Highland fortresses. The English had even outlawed the bagpipe, calling it an instrument of war. Small wonder, she thought, that the Highlanders had turned increasingly to whisky as the answer to their problems. Chiefs who, like her father, had returned to their lands after Culloden had soon realized they were no longer patriarchs but merely landlords or stewards. Clan lands had been divided arbitrarily into tenants' lots too small to support their occupants, who were in any case in no position to pay rents.

Had the wicked English not been determined to change the entire system, the MacDrumin clan might still have continued to function as it had in the past, with those who made shoes for the clan continuing to make them in lieu of rent, and those who wove cloth, tended cattle, or farmed the clan's more fertile acres continuing to do their bit as well, providing the clan with a thriving economy and the manpower to guard it. But MacDrumin had not been allowed to make the choice. Because of his known Jacobite sympathies, his lands had been forfeited and awarded to an Englishman, the mighty Earl of Rothwell, who lived in London and had never so much as set foot in the

Highlands, and who no doubt never would set foot there unless he, like others of his ilk, decided to turn his Highland acres into a sporting estate to be visited as and when the spirit moved him. In the meantime, English factors, supported by the odious bailie Fergus Campbell, collected his rents and posted them to him in London.

That was not the way things ought to be, but in Maggie's opinion there was only one way to change them. If no one else could go to London, she would go herself. She was not, she thanked heaven, as volatile of temper as her father or Kate MacCain, but she did know how to get her own way when she set her mind to a purpose. And never had she believed in one more strongly than she believed in that of Bonnie Prince Charlie. MacDrumin and the others, surrounded by enemies as indeed they were, and likely to find themselves in the direst of straits at any moment, needed help desperately. If necessary, she would find their hero in London and drag him, and his army, all the way back to Scotland with her own two hands.

JJ

Edward Carsley, fourth Earl of Rothwell, leaned back in the leather winged chair. Smoothing an imagined wrinkle from one lace-trimmed golden-brown velvet cuff with a perfectly manicured fingertip, he said languidly to the dour elderly man standing with apparent if unexpected composure before his desk, "Did you not hear me, MacKinnon? I said, his majesty the king has granted you a full pardon. You can go home to Kilmorie."

"Aye, I heard you, my lord." Ian Dubh MacKinnon of MacKinnon, painfully thin, his face pale from three years' captivity in the Tower of London, stared calmly back at him.

"Is that all you have to say?" Rothwell glanced at the third man in the room, but although a glint of amusement lurked at the back of Attorney General Sir Dudley Ryder's clear blue eyes, he remained silent, watching the old Scotsman.

MacKinnon said evenly, "Did I ken what it is you wish me to say, Rothwell, mayhap I could oblige you, but as it is—" He spread his hands.

"Good heavens, man, we know that you fought at Culloden and took part in the meeting of chiefs on the following day. We know, too, that when the pretender Charles Stewart finally reached MacKinnon country on the Isle of Skye, he was given shelter and entertained to a feast on your land the evening before you and your nephew John conveyed him to the mainland, where you continued to accompany him for at least twelve days."

The old man's chin lifted. "In the Highlands, a gentleman refuses welcome to no man who seeks it. Mayhap Sassenach hospitality is less generous. I've certainly small regard for what little of it I've experienced in your Tower of London."

"As the matter was recounted to me, MacKinnon, that damnable feast took place in a dark, extremely *in*hospitable cave."

MacKinnon shrugged. "Mayhap that is so, my lord."

"Dear sir, I take leave to remind you that you were put on trial for your life, found guilty on all counts, and ought to have been sentenced to death for your transgressions. Instead of which, because of your advanced age and obviously mistaken sense of chivalry, you were merely imprisoned for a time and have now been pardoned. Do you not wish to express at least a modicum of gratitude to his majesty for his gracious mercy?"

"Oh, aye, certainly," the old man said. "You may tell German George for me that, had I my own wish in the matter, I should serve him in precisely the same way he is serving me, by sending him back to *his* own country!"

After a tense silence, Rothwell signed to Ryder, who opened the door and called for a guard. The earl said gently, "Is there anything you wish to retrieve from your Tower room, MacKinnon?"

Looking surprised, the Scotsman replied, "Aye, I've some books I'd like to take away, and a few other odd trappings."

Rothwell nodded. "Then you will be taken back there long enough to collect your gear, after which you will be given sufficient funds to take you back to Skye. Not in grand style, I'm afraid, but by stage to Bristol and then by packet up the coast. And, MacKinnon, I'd not advise you to linger in London."

"I have no more wish to linger than you have to provide me hospitality. I'll be off by the first coach."

He moved to follow the guard when Rothwell said, "There is just one thing more, MacKinnon. Do you know aught of one Andrew MacDrumin of MacDrumin?"

The old man paused, and for a moment Rothwell thought he stiffened, but when he turned back his expression was calm. "I have heard the name, of course, for it is a proud one in the Highlands, but Glen Drumin is east of the Great Glen, you see, so I cannot say that I know him. To ask me such a question is much the same as asking a man in Bristol if he knows one from Oxford."

"I see. Thank you. You may go."

When the door had shut, Ryder chuckled. "That old reprobate. Butter wouldn't have melted in his mouth, but did you see the look on his face when you asked if he had belongings he wanted to claim? I daresay he expected us to order him clapped up again after his impudence, though he recovered quickly enough. 'Oh, aye, my lord, I've some books,' says he. Well, by now my lads will have turned that room of his inside out, so if he had anything worth discovering, we shall soon have word of it."

"My thanks for allowing me to be the one to give him the good news," Rothwell said with a faint, mocking smile.

"You were the one who pressed hardest for his release, after all, and oiled the wheels of the mill. When you choose to ally yourself and your fortune with one faction against another, Ned, the outcome is generally predictable and your rewards are usually more tangible than this one was. It was the least I could do."

"My stepmother could not have said that better, if your meaning is that you would have liked to do less."

"It is no great secret that I disagreed with you about releasing any of the leaders of the uprising. After all, it is my duty to keep as many damned Jacobites as possible locked up."

"One sometimes gains much by a show of mercy, however."

"I leave mercy to heaven, Ned, and to politicians."

Rothwell stood up, shaking out the deep lace shirt ruffles that had inched up beneath the turned-back cuffs of his full-skirted coat. "What do you think of this rig?" He opened the coat, showing off his heavily embroidered gold satin waistcoat and revealing the elegantly jeweled hilt of his new smallsword. "Lydia nearly had this satin made into a petticoat before I could send it to my tailor. I tell you, it is as much as a man's life is worth these days to have new fabric delivered to his house."

"Your stepsister is a delightful minx," Ryder said, smiling, "and as beautiful as she is, I doubt that you will have her on your hands for long. As for your pretty waistcoat, you know how little heed I pay to such stuff, so do stop behaving like a damned fop.

That may serve you with others, but having known you for twenty years, since our first days together at Eton, I am quite immune to it and well aware that the jewels on that weapon of yours are of less value to you than the fine Italian crafting of its blade. Do you think MacKinnon really will leave London at once, or will he linger to take part in the forthcoming events?"

"He'll leave." Rothwell moved to the fireplace to gaze into the glass above the mantel. Ryder was correct in suggesting that he was not so obsessed by fashion as he pretended to be, but the pose amused him. It was a habit he had developed years before, to seem to focus his attention upon his appearance when he wanted to think. He paid no heed to his image in the glass now, for not only were his chiseled features, pale complexion, thin-lipped mouth, gray eyes, and the heavy dark brows that nearly met over his aquiline nose perfectly familiar to him but his well-powdered locks were perfectly in order, and since he scorned to use the aids to complexion that many of his fellows dabbed upon their faces, there was nothing to be altered. Instead he looked past his reflection to that of his friend's lanky, relaxed form, and catching his eye, added, "MacKinnon's a canny old devil and knows full well that your lot will keep a sharp eye on him. He'll not jeopardize his colleagues' safety by drawing undue attention to their activities, though he cannot have the slightest notion that you've got friends with Charlie now just as you did five years ago, keeping you apprised of his every move."

"As a matter of fact," Ryder said, "our best man's back in England, and we've no one else with the prince who's nearly as reliable. Seems Charlie's thinking of paying London a secret visit, and our man thought he would do better to be in place here well beforehand.

He won't be of much use to us in any event, I'm afraid, because his family spends much of the year in London, and he writes that he might have difficulty eluding them if he tries to go creeping about the city with Charles Stewart."

"He writes? Have you not spoken with this paragon?"

"I don't know who he is. He began writing us some time ago, and his accounts proved accurate, but he's never given his name."

"How very odd," Rothwell said. "Still, I doubt that Charles and his Jacobites can outwit your people. In the past, they have proved to be rather foolish, though I confess I did underestimate MacKinnon. I'd no notion any Scotsman would prove to be so well educated or so sure of himself, but he's clearly a gentleman."

"I shouldn't be surprised to learn that he'd done the grand tour with your father and mine," Ryder said dryly. "Certainly, he's a deep one. What possessed you to ask him about MacDrumin?" Before Rothwell could reply, he snapped his fingers and said, "Never mind, I have it. The MacDrumin land was your reward for your bits of gracious assistance during the late trouble, was it not? Were you hoping MacKinnon would give you information to help you collect your rents? I'm told that many of the new English landlords have had undue difficulty in that regard."

"I haven't." Rothwell turned from the mirror. "My rents arrive with admirable regularity. In point of fact, I am told that my factor finds it necessary to visit only one of my tenants, the MacDrumin himself, in order to collect them."

Ryder chuckled. "I'd call such exemplary behavior damned suspicious, Ned. Like as not, the old boy is smuggling Highland whisky, since I cannot think of anything else that would produce such a regular income in these troubled times. God knows, land in the Highlands is rarely fertile enough to raise anything but a few cows or sheep. Many English landlords cannot house or feed their Highland tenants, let alone collect their rents. Moreover, those remote glens have more than their share of smugglers. They know very well that they are supposed to pay duty on any whisky they produce, but to a man they refuse to do so. Perhaps I ought to order my lads to look into the goings-on in Glen Drumin."

"Not unless you want some of your more imaginative exploits at school made public, dear boy," Rothwell said with a direct look. "I need those rents. You've no notion how expensive Lydia has become, especially since my stepmama is determined to marry her off to a wealthy peer of the realm—and that in the face of Lydia's latest and most absurd preference for a quite ineligible friend of her scapegrace brother. Moreover, I've had to order more satins and velvets for myself, so as not to forfeit my well-merited reputation for sartorial splendor during the upcoming Season. Would you beggar me, Ryder?"

"It would take much more than the loss of your Scottish rents to do that," Ryder said, shaking his head, "but I am perfectly willing to leave it alone for now. No time to devote to it, in any case, till we've settled with the young Pretender. What is it about that man that wins him so many followers? I have never comprehended his attraction."

Rothwell shrugged. "An aura of romance, I suppose, and a strong dose of wishful thinking. It certainly cannot be his beauty. He looks more Polish than English, poor lad."

"That is scarcely surprising, since his mother is Polish, but it ain't his looks that concern me. The reason he is said to be bound for London from Antwerp is that he is obsessed with this notion of his to restore the Stewarts to the throne, and 'tis said he's already ordered twenty-six thousand muskets delivered to his followers here, so who is to say he will not succeed in taking the city this time around?"

Rothwell's smile was weary. "Unless he has learned wisdom these past four years—and we've no reason to think he has—he is the same thoughtless upstart he was in forty-five, when he was so anxious to establish his authority that he constantly brushed aside the excellent advice of older, more experienced men."

"I'll grant you he cannot bear opposition," Ryder said. "It's that fact added to the fact that his only thought in life is to restore the Stewarts to the throne that concerns me. He is not alone in his objective, Ned. He has a host of followers."

"True, but not all of them are in full agreement with the objective, my friend. Recollect MacKinnon's attitude, if you will. That old man still thinks of England as a foreign country fifty years after unification, and has no interest in the English throne. He wants a Stewart, but on the throne of an independent Scotland. Charles Edward Stewart yearns to rule London."

"But that is just what I fear. Don't you remember what it was like before, with all London in a panic from the moment the Scots attacked in the north? The whole city quaked while our army advanced to meet them."

"And it all came to naught," Rothwell said easily, "just as it will this time. People were frightened then because they believed the uprising was instigated by the French king, with whom, as you will recall, we were still at odds."

"Well, there was some truth to that."

"There was indeed." Rothwell picked up his gloves and began to put them on. "Will you come home with me? My stepmother is entertaining tonight, and I should be glad of your support."

"Lady Rothwell wouldn't," Ryder retorted. "Not only does she not admire politicians on the best of days but my unexpected presence would upset her numbers at table."

"It is still my table, I believe," Rothwell said, his voice as soft as velvet. He reached for his tricorn and walking stick.

Though most men who knew him would have shifted ground hastily at hearing that tone, Ryder said calmly, "You need not twitch your temper at me, Ned, for it don't impress me at all in such a case as this one. I know it is your table, and I do not doubt that you would insure my welcome there, but her ladyship wouldn't like it, and I do not care to be at outs with her."

"Angling for my sister, Ryder? She won't have you."

Ryder flushed. "I am far too old for Lady Lydia, and even if I were a fellow for the ladies—which I am not—I am amply aware that my suit would not be well received at Rothwell House."

"Don't be an ass. I'd accept it in a moment. Do you want the chit? By God, I shall make you a present of her, and welcome. Go and purchase a special license at once, I beg you, and we shall see to the matter before dinner."

Ryder laughed and began to gather his things in preparation to depart. "You are absurd, Ned. I have far too much to do to burden myself with a wife and family. Moreover, did you not say a moment ago that Lydia is already enamored of someone?"

"A mere puppy, not yet dry behind the ears. Having no doubt reduced his sire to penury by enjoying a lengthy grand tour, upon which he appears to have learned nothing worth knowing, he now lives with James in that ridiculous house of his on the bridge."

"Another artist?"

"No, a parasite. For all he's the son of a marquess, I doubt he has tuppence to rub together, but he is handsome and possessed of excellent address. A Trinity man, I believe."

"I see how it is," Ryder said with a grin. "You agree with Horace Walpole that Trinity's a nursery of nonsense and bigotry."

"Do not speak to me of Walpoles. Even the most harmless amongst them sports a damned dangerous tongue. Now, blast your eyes, do you come home with me?"

"I shall walk with you, if you like, but I cannot linger at Rothwell House, for I am due in Whitehall within the hour. Indeed, the only reason I accompany you at all is that I hope you will be so generous as to lend me the use of your barge."

"It will be at the stairs now, I believe." He raised an eyebrow. "I wonder if my dignity will suffer if we walk so far as that. Perhaps I should send some fellow to summon a chair."

Since the distance from the Parliament offices to Parliament Stairs was less than a hundred yards, Ryder chuckled. "You will survive the walking, my decrepit friend, more easily than the poor chairmen would survive carrying you. Just don't topple off the heels of your pretty shoes."

Rothwell extended a large foot, displaying a silver-buckled black shoe. "It is not the shoe you must admire, my dear, but the elegant clocked stockings that encase my noble legs."

"Come along, Ned, before I forget that you are not the pompous Jack Straw you delight in pretending to be, and say something that will actually stir that damnable temper of yours."

"Nonsense, I have no temper. I am but a simple, placid fellow, the gentlest of mortals."

"And I am the King of England."

"Dear, dear," Rothwell complained, "not another one. We've had far too many spurious claimants to the throne already."

Opening the door, Ryder bowed slightly and extended a hand in pointed invitation.

Amused, Rothwell stepped past him, then waited in the dimly lit corridor while he locked the door. The office they had used was on the upper floor of a converted chapel of St. Stephen's Church, near the chamber that served as Britain's House of Commons. The door to that room was open when they passed it, and Rothwell glanced inside, thinking, as he had so often before, that it was much too plain for its purpose, too much like a Dissenters' chapel in some provincial town. Wooden wainscoting covered the frescoed walls, and the great tracery window at the far end, once embellished with the finest stained glass, had been replaced in the previous century with three round-headed windows. Iron props with disproportionately large Corinthian capitals supported the balconies, their blatant ugliness reminding him of the single occasion when his half-brother, James, had deigned to accompany him to view the buildings where the laws and destiny of Britain were debated.

James had been singularly disappointed, his artist's

soul cringing at their smallness and insignificance. Even the House of Lords, on the upper floor of an irregular-shaped building slightly to the south of St. Stephen's, had failed to impress him. Rothwell, who spent much of his time there each year, particularly from January until June, personally thought the House of Lords regal by comparison to the Commons. But even the superb Flemish tapestries that lined the walls, illustrating the Armada and presented to England by Holland in the days of Queen Elizabeth, had failed to please James. The most he would say was that the gilded throne with its red velvet canopy, surmounted by the Royal Arms, was nicely set off against the tapestries' delicate colors, and that, with the whole scene lighted by the hundreds of candles in their chased silver sconces, and the peers of the realm wearing their red velvet robes of state, the total effect would be impressive. He had never, however, expressed the slightest desire to reproduce that scene on canvas.

Rothwell and Ryder emerged into Old Palace Yard from St. Stephen's by way of a dark and irregular passage much like the approach to a stage door, and made their way to a second passage leading from the top of Abingdon Street down to the Thames and Parliament Stairs, where Rothwell's bargeman had insinuated his craft through a myriad of others to the nearest position.

Settling themselves on two of the barge's four comfortable seats, the two men sat back, each silent for a time with his own thoughts. Once the barge drifted to the center of the river, Rothwell could see Westminster Hall with the Abbey towers behind it, and as they slipped beneath Westminster Bridge—nearly finished now and due to open in less than three months—his thoughts returned to MacKinnon of MacKinnon. Little did the old man realize the machinations that had been necessary to secure his release. One had to admire his pluck, however, for he had not lost a jot of his dignity in prison.

Shrill feminine laughter rising above the usual noises of the river drew Rothwell's attention, and he saw several maids hanging out windows of the houses in Dorset Court, exchanging remarks with watermen near the shore. Ahead, beyond the timber and stone wharves that provided materials for the rapidly expanding City of Westminster, the low stone walls and semicircular bastions of old Whitehall Palace still survived along the riverside, though the magnificent palace to which they belonged had long since perished in flames. Between the wall and the beautiful old Privy Garden, in what was now the most fashionable residential spot in London, lay a medley of mansions of all shapes and sizes, built on the ruins of the palace and inhabited by noblemen and gentlemen of the first quality and the nicest tastes. Most were intimates of the king and held appointments at his court.

As the barge passed Todd's Wharf and began angling nearer the shore, the first of these great houses loomed above them. Belonging to the recently deceased Duke of Richmond, it looked more like a series of houses, for its parts were connected like a staircase lying on its side. The whole assemblage was fronted by a huge iron-railed stone terrace that overlooked the river.

Rothwell House, next door, was the most imposing house on the Whitehall front, for it was the only one built symmetrically. All the others, erected on the very odd-shaped lots granted their owners after the Great Fire of London had claimed the palace, looked as if they had been cramped and crunched into place merely to fit their unusual lots, which indeed had been the case.

The barge moved past the old Privy Garden stairs, closed and useless since the building of Richmond House, and glided silently to the foot of the wide private stone steps shared by the duke and Rothwell. As Rothwell stepped from the barge to the landing, he said to the brawny young bargeman, "Take Sir Dudley to Whitehall Stairs, Oliver, and then take your orders from him for the rest of the day. I shan't require you again before morning."

"Begging your pardon, my lord," Oliver said diffidently, "but my Lady Lydia ordered the barge for three o'clock, and it be well past that hour now."

Rothwell smiled wryly. "I will speak to her. I daresay she will decide that she does not need you now after all."

Ryder raised a mocking eyebrow, but Rothwell chose not to acknowledge it and said only, "If you change your mind about dinner, my friend, I can promise you will be made welcome."

"Thank you," Ryder said. "I wish now that I could accept, for I believe the fireworks might well rival those his grace of Richmond provided last spring to celebrate the Peace."

Still smiling, Rothwell shook his head, but as he turned to mount the steps, he heard Oliver say naively, "Be that true, Sir Dudley, sir? Will there be fireworks tonight? Last May, when his grace set the night afire, 'twere a splendid sight! Why, there was thousands gathered here to see it, and any number of folks fell right into the river, so excited did they get."

Ryder's reply was inaudible to the now grinning Rothwell, and by the time he had unlocked the tall wooden gate at the top of the stairs, the barge was moving swiftly away on the current and their voices had been lost among the other noises of the waterfront. Passing through the gate, Rothwell entered a high-walled passageway, at the end of which were two doors in the side walls facing each other. The one on the left led to Richmond House terrace, the one on the right to Rothwell House, and since these were the river entrances to two great houses, each was guarded by a liveried and powdered footman. The two young men, warned by the sound of his key in the lock, stood stiffly erect until the one on the right moved to open the door for him.

Straight ahead was another door, leading to the ground floor of the house. Had his stepmother not been in residence, Rothwell would have used it, since a service stair nearby led right to his bedchamber. But Lady Rothwell would not only have thought such an unceremonious entry to his own house unseemly; she would have commented upon it at tedious length. Therefore he mounted a second flight of stone steps to the terrace and entered the house through double French doors beneath an imposing portico. This entry took him straight into the grand saloon, a wide, elegantly furnished room with a high gilded and painted ceiling and twin marble chimney pieces at each end. Two maroon-and-gold-liveried footmen wearing formal, powdered tie-wigs stood ready to take his hat, stick, and gloves.

"Frederick, where will I find the Lady Lydia?" he asked the older of the two.

"In the long gallery, my lord, looking at pictures."

Only a long habit of concealing his thoughts kept Rothwell from raising his eyebrows at this information. Not only had his bargeman's words led him to think his flighty half-sister would be watching anxiously for the return of the barge, but her interest in the paintings and family portraits that lined the long gallery had hitherto been nonexistent.

Turning toward the central stair hall, he paused and added as an afterthought, "Is Lady Rothwell in her sitting room?"

"No, my lord. She has begun to dress for dinner. She said to remind you that your guests will begin to arrive before six."

"Thank you," Rothwell said, hoping his relief that he would not immediately encounter his stepmother could not be heard in his voice. Stray shafts of late afternoon sunlight glinted on the polished East Indian mahogany bannister of the stairs that swooped invitingly upward in a graceful spiral, lighted from above by windows encircling the high dome. Rothwell went straight on to the main entrance hall on the Privy Garden side of the house, then turned right and passed through his bookroom to the long gallery at the north end of the house.

Lady Lydia Carsley, a willowy young woman in her eighteenth year, her long curls as black and glistening as polished obsidian, stood by a window that provided an oblique view of the river but gazed toward a door at the far end of the room. She jumped when he spoke her name, and whirled in a rustle of panniers and petticoats to face him. Her dark brown eyes widened in her pretty, oval face.

"Ned, 'pon rep, how you startled me! I felt sure you would come to me through Mama's sitting room."

"You were wrong, my dear."

"Lud, 'tis of no account. I'm excessively glad to see you."

"Are you? I bring you bad news. You may not order up my barge whenever the fancy strikes you to do so.

In point of fact, I forbid you to use it at all without my express permission."

She waved his words away with a gesture. "Oh, I knew when Oliver said he was to fetch you at Parliament Stairs that there was no use thinking I might have time to visit James today. For that is all I was going to do, you know. I give you my word."

"Only James, Lyddy? Not his lamentable companion as well?"

She shrugged eloquently. "Well, of course, if Lord Thomas had chanced to be at home . . ." Encountering his hard gaze, she faltered, then added hastily, "I do not know why you must be so cruel. The poor man cannot help being in love with me, you know, and he has such affecting sensibilities. Why, he even tried to end his life when I failed to wear a posy he had sent me."

"So I heard," Rothwell said dryly. "A pity he didn't use a rope instead of one of your hair ribbons, my dear. The silly clunch must have known the ribbon would not bear his weight."

"He did *not* know," she retorted indignantly, "and he was utterly unconscious when James found him. Indeed, he was lucky it was James who did, too, because of course James knew precisely what to do for him, which someone else might not."

"He is certainly lucky I did not find him."

"Yes, he is," she said tartly, "for you do not know nearly as much about reviving people and helping them as James does, because he has learned a great deal about such things from his friend Dr. Brockelby. Indeed, had James not been nobly born, he might have liked to become a doctor himself."

"His birth didn't stop him from becoming a painter," Rothwell pointed out.

"A *Court* painter," Lydia said quickly. "Even Mama does not think that is such a bad thing to be, for he will very likely make a great deal of money someday."

Rothwell was tempted but decided there was nothing to be gained by telling his half-sister that she and her mama were laboring under a slight misconception. Instead he said, "James's noble pride certainly does not keep him from coming to me whenever he runs out of money. Is that what stirred you to this notion of visiting him today, Lyddy? Did he send for you?"

"No. In fact . . ." She hesitated, and to his surprise, a glint of mischief lit her eyes. "Ned, do you recall the last time James was here—before you two quarreled and he stormed out of the house—when Mama was showing us the family book?"

Rothwell grimaced. His stepmother was inordinately fond of regaling her friends and family with the fact that both she and her late lord were descended from Edward I by his two queens. When a fashion developed for having one's pedigree professionally detailed, Lady Rothwell had instantly ordered theirs done, and the entire lineage had been duly painted in a book. The primary illustration was nothing so common as a genealogical tree either. Instead she had devised a pineapple plant sprouting out of a basket on which King Edward's head was painted. All the intermediate arms were painted on the leaves, and the fruit had been sliced open to reveal busts of the late earl and herself flanked by smaller portraits of their offspring.

Remembering, Rothwell said, "Ridiculous stuff."

Lydia chuckled. "You only say that because James's portrait is much more flattering than your own."

"Mine is scarcely even visible," he reminded her, not mentioning the much more painful fact that his

mother's picture had been omitted. "The thing looks
like an afterthought."

"It probably was one," she agreed, "but Mama
could scarcely leave you out altogether, since you are
the present earl."

"And since I paid for her pretty book."

"Did you? Yes, I suppose you did. But Mama is so
taken up now with genealogy that she bored on and on
to James when he was here that day, and you know
how he is when his sense of the ridiculous is stirred.
Look." She gestured toward the wall behind him, and
Rothwell's gaze followed the gesture.

Two new portraits had taken pride of place among
the many covering the gallery wall. The first, showing
a voluptuous female reclining against a tree and smiling seductively at a snake dangling from a nearby
branch, with an apple in its mouth, was labeled *Eve de
Carsley*. Its mate depicted a slender, extremely foolish-
looking male, his privy parts hidden by a convenient
bit of shrubbery, who gazed up in bewilderment at a
stern-looking face formed in dark thunderclouds surrounded by lightning bolts. That portrait was labeled
Adam de Carsley.

Rothwell stared at the pair for one long, pregnant
moment, then burst into laughter so hard that he soon
had tears streaming down his face, and had to hold his
aching sides.

Lydia watched him with a crooked smile and did
not attempt to speak until he had stopped laughing.
Then she said matter-of-factly, "It is very funny, of
course, but what are we to do, Ned? That is what I
meant to ask James today, for you must see that we
cannot leave them there. Mama thinks he stopped by
whilst you were out today only to bring her more
distillation of nightshade for her complexion. She

would be utterly mortified if any of her guests saw these pictures. Why, she has invited Lady Townshend and the Countess of Portland to dine tonight."

Stifling a last chuckle, Rothwell straightened and said, "I'll take care of them, Lyddy. Don't trouble yourself."

"Very well. But, Ned—" She looked directly at him. "You will keep them safe, won't you? They are very well done."

He reached out and pinched her chin. "I will, puss. I think they are magnificent. Should you not be dressing?"

She smiled. "It does not take me two hours to dress, sir, but I will leave you now. I have letters to write." And, still smiling sunnily, she turned toward Lady Rothwell's sitting room.

"Lydia." When she glanced back, he said gently, "No letters to Lord Thomas Deverill—"

"As if I would!" She tossed her head.

"And no more flirting with Oliver," he added grimly. "I do not want to have to dismiss the lad for allowing his head to be turned by a saucy minx who ought to know better."

She tilted her head curiously. "Would you really turn him off, Ned?"

"Instantly and without a character."

"Oh." She thought for a moment. "That would hardly be fair to him, sir."

"No, it would not. But it would be necessary."

Nibbling her lower lip, she turned away more slowly this time, and he was sorry to see the light fade from her expression, but he hoped she would take his warning to heart.

When she had gone, he glanced back at the two portraits and grinned. There were times when he liked his irresponsible but undeniably talented half-brother very much indeed.

Ringing for a footman and giving orders that the two pictures should be rehung in his own bedchamber, he went back to the bookroom, where he was soon poring over a map of Britain in an attempt to discover if his newest and most distant estate was really as far from the Isle of Skye as Bristol was from Oxford.

III

London, September 1750

Had the rattle of iron coach wheels on the cobble-stone streets not been enough to make Maggie want to cover her ears, certainly the acrimonious bickering between the coachman on the box and her companion, leaning precariously out the coach window to shriek insults at him, would have been more than enough.

"Fiona, sit down and be quiet," Maggie said, raising her voice in an attempt to make herself heard above the din. It was useless. Street cries mingled with the argument between the two, underscored by the clatter of wheels and hooves, and her coach was by no means the only one racketing along the crowded street.

She was in London at last. In fact, once the reluctant MacDrumin had at last been persuaded to let her travel to England, the arrangements had been made quickly and her journey had been swift. Indeed, if she was not mistaken, today was Friday, the eleventh of September, and Bonnie Prince Charlie would arrive in London within the week. Safely tucked inside her corset, crackling at times against her ribcage when she moved, were the messages she carried from numerous Highland leaders, to present to the prince.

She had feared her journey would take much longer, for as if to recover his sense of dominance after her arguments had worn him down, MacDrumin had flatly forbidden her to spend so much as a single night at a public inn. Instead he had arranged for her to be passed like a secret parcel from one Jacobite family to another, and had told anyone expressing interest in her travel preparations that his daughter was bound for Edinburgh to visit friends. Maggie had enjoyed her trip and had learned a great deal, although not all of the news she received had been welcome.

In the homes she visited in Scotland, support for the prince had seemed unexpectedly weak, but she remained certain that once his banner was raised again, Scottish Jacobites would rally to his cause; however, the further south she traveled, the less sincere had his sympathizers seemed. Though they enjoyed having "secrets" and never failed to hold their wineglasses over their water glasses when toasting the king—thus toasting the king *over the water* and not German George—these were but gestures and promised little true support. Moreover, and much more dismaying, was the fact that the ladies she met were far more loyal to the Stewart cause than their menfolk were. The men had been more apt to warn her of the dangers of her journey than to applaud her purpose. Nevertheless, everyone had been genuinely excited to know that the prince intended to slip secretly into London to meet with his supporters there.

Hearing another shriek from her companion, Maggie reached over and unceremoniously yanked Fiona back down onto the seat by her skirt, saying sternly, "Mungo knows where to go, Fiona. You only confuse him when you shout at him like that, and you make a dreadful spectacle of yourself besides."

"But he will gang awry, Miss Maggie, as sure as check, for Mungo be a man wha' canna find his ain stockings twixt his feet and his boots in the purest dawn light."

"He has only to find Essex Street," Maggie said, "and since we know it ends at the river Thames, that cannot be so hard."

"London be a mickling large city," Fiona said grimly.

"But a civilized one, by the look of it, and bright and clean withal," Maggie said, gazing out the window and remembering that the greater part of London had been rebuilt some eighty years before, after the Great Fire. The red and ochre brickwork of the buildings they were passing had grown mellow with time, but neither houses nor public buildings were yet so soot-covered as their counterparts in Edinburgh.

The coach had entered the city from Hampstead along Gray's Inn Road, and most of the residential streets she saw were pleasantly uniform in appearance from end to end. More architectural variety occurred in shopping streets like Chancery Lane and Holborn, where new shops had popped up among more ancient buildings and where even the latter appeared to have been fitted with up-to-date fronts. Gaily colored signs hung over every shop, to guide illiterate coachmen, and along with the colorful coaches, sedan chairs, and the vivid costumes of the pedestrians, they created a delightfully cheerful scene.

The streets were cobbled with small, round stones, as were the footways at all but the most important thoroughfares, where there were flagstones. Fascinated by all the activity, Maggie saw a boy riding astride his father's cane as if it were a horse, and a man playing a flute on a street corner. When the coach slowed near an intersection, a playful struggle erupted between a pretty girl and two lads trying to steal kisses from her, and Maggie laughed to see her snatch off one tormentor's wig, revealing his shaven head, then dash away with both lads in pursuit. Fiona clicked her tongue at such saucy behavior, just as if she herself always behaved with impeccable propriety.

A gingerbread seller at the corner rang a bell to call attention to her delicacies, and the aroma of hot gingerbread wafted above other, less pleasant smells as the coach turned from the wide road into a much narrower one, where Maggie saw a man drinking wine from a bottle and a woman leaning against a building, suckling a baby, apparently unconcerned by jostling passersby. The crowds that only moments before had looked jolly and gay now seemed rougher, of a different class altogether, and when Maggie saw two street louts leering at her, she sat back quickly against the squabs, shaken and a little alarmed.

"That daft Mungo ha' taken the wrong turning," Fiona said sharply. "I'll tell him tae turn right aboot and gae back."

But before she could put her head outside again, Maggie yanked her back. "No, don't," she said. "Do nothing more to call attention to us. I don't like the way those men are looking at us, and Mungo must have realized as quickly as we did that he has mistaken the turning. We'll soon be at the end of this dreadful street, and surely the next will be more like all the others we have seen before now."

However, instead of finding themselves in a more pleasant residential street, like those they had seen earlier, they discovered that the next road was even narrower and more dismal than the last. It was darker, too, although Maggie soon realized that the effect was caused by jutting upper stories of buildings on either side that nearly met overhead, cutting off most of the sunlight. The coach was drawing notice from more passersby now, and the looks she encountered were not friendly. She wanted to shout at Mungo to get them out of there, but she was certain she would be wiser to draw no more attention to herself.

Feeling panic stir when men began to crowd around the coach, jeering and banging on the wooden sides, she remained stiffly upright on her seat, looking neither right nor left and praying that Fiona would have the sense to do likewise. Sorry now that she had not heeded Fiona's warnings, Maggie knew she ought at least to have made Mungo repeat his instructions to be sure he had them clear in his mind. She could hear him now shouting at the men to stand back, but not one of the ones pressing so near and peering in the windows at her heeded him.

The coach slowed more and more, then stopped altogether and began rather sickeningly to rock back and forth.

"They'll ha' us over," Fiona shrieked, grabbing Maggie's arm. "By St. Andrew's cross, mistress, what are we tae do?"

Wishing she carried a weapon like Kate's, or better yet, a loaded pistol, Maggie pressed her lips together, determined not to shriek her terror aloud like Fiona but to retain at least a semblance of her dignity. Her mind raced, for she knew they stood in grave danger, but she found it nearly impossible to think clearly. So many people surrounded the coach now that the light was all but cut off. Then the window nearest her shattered in an explosion of glass, and a leering face pressed toward her.

Angrily, she snatched up a small satchel from beneath her feet and hit the man, trying to push his face away, but he snatched the bag and disappeared. On the other side, the coach door opened and hands began grabbing at Fiona and then at her. The older woman struck out with her fists and kicked anyone she could reach, but she was being dragged bodily from the coach.

Maggie grabbed at Fiona's skirt, trying to keep her from being pulled from the dangerously lurching coach, but then she felt her own arms grabbed.

"No!" Fighting desperately to protect herself, she could do nothing more to help Fiona, who was wrenched mercilessly from the coach and swallowed by the crush. Maggie fought like a cornered badger, but soon she too was jerked from the coach and flung into the crowd. Kicking and screaming, terrified and beyond reasonable thought, she felt hands pawing at her breasts, at her face, her bottom, and even between her naked legs, until suddenly she was falling, choking, unable to breathe, into blackness.

When she came to her senses, she was lying, bruised and battered, on the filthy footway, and the street was oddly silent. Feeling sick, she tried to sit, tried to order her dazed thoughts to recall what had happened. She could not seem to concentrate. Leaning against the wall of the nearest building, she held her aching head and waited for her dizziness to ease. When she could make herself look around, she saw that the area was not entirely deserted, but no one appeared to be paying any attention to her, and there was no sign of her coach or of Fiona or Mungo. Remembering her messages and feeling frantically to find them still safe in-

side her corset, she drew a deep breath and shut her
eyes again in profound relief.

A hand touched her shoulder.

Shrieking, Maggie jerked away, hit her head against
the stone wall, and nearly blacked out again.

"Be easy, girlie," a scratchy but discernibly female
voice said. "Them pesky louts oughtn't to have hurt
such a pretty gel as yerself, but it could ha' been a sight
worse did they not all run off wi' yer coach, and no
doubt ye'll be fit as a fiddle in due time. Have a nip
from me bottle now, and ye'll soon be feeling much
more the thing."

The woman's accent was strange, but Maggie understood enough to believe she meant only kindness.
Still, the smell of cheap gin right under her nose nearly
led to her undoing. Turning away and swallowing the
hot, sour taste that roiled into her throat, she struggled
to attain a more respectable position and looked at her
would-be savior, wishing she could think clearly.

Dressed in tattered black rags, the person she saw
was definitely female but member of a class Maggie
knew little about. In the Highlands, the poorest of folk
generally looked respectable, and even those who liked
their whisky overmuch never reeked of the stuff like
this old crone did. Above the smell of cheap gin wafted
the even more repulsive odor of a long-unwashed and
no doubt diseased body. When the bottle was pressed
to her lips again, Maggie nearly vomited.

Collecting herself, she pushed the bottle away and
muttered, "No, thank you." Her throat felt as if it
were coated with sand, her breasts hurt, her gown was
in tatters, and the knot on the back of her head ached
unbearably, but with the woman still staring at her,
clearly waiting for her to say more, she exerted herself
enough to add, "Perhaps I might have some water."

"Bless her." The woman glanced around and added, as if to an audience, "Water, she says." Her laugh sounded like a witch's cackle. "Ye dassn't drink the water here, girlie. Tastes of what floats in it." Cackling again, she reached into the road, scooped up a handful of steaming horse manure, and waved it under Maggie's nose. "D'ye like that?" When Maggie recoiled from the stench, the crone tossed the mess away, cackling again and holding her sides until she realized that gin was spilling out of her bottle, and clapped her filthy hand over the lip.

Maggie watched, fascinated, when the woman lifted the bottle again to drink, but she paused with it still inches from her lips, wrinkling her nose distastefully. Peering myopically at the dirty bottle, she grimaced, grabbed a handful of her skirt, and used it to wipe the opening before drinking. Then, after taking a long pull of the contents, she looked at Maggie again. "What ye looking at, girlie? Ain't ye never seed no one take a drink afore? Ye'll get used to such an ye linger here-abouts."

Drawing a steadying breath, Maggie said as calmly as she could, "I have no wish to linger. Do you perchance know what became of my servants and coach?"

The woman chortled. "The dead don't linger neither, girl."

"Dead!" The word echoed through her mind as if it were bouncing off hollow walls in a darkened room, but it did not seem to disturb her. She said simply, "They cannot be dead."

"Oh, aye. Put up a grand fight, didn't they? The woman, a-screeching and a-carrying on like a banshee about what they was doing to her, so they was bound to hesh her up, and the man . . . Well, he didn't fight so much, 'cause his head were broke open when they toppled yon coach 'n he come down headfirst on them stones. Sure ye don't want a slug o' me gin, dearie?"

Maggie, her sensibilities numb now, shook her head, then wished she had not when new waves of painful dizziness struck her. Closing her eyes, she waited until they had passed. She was having difficulty collecting her thoughts. "What . . . what became of my coach?"

The woman shrugged. "Dunno, mistress, but ye oughta be that grateful them louts forgot about yerself a-laying there. Coach were there one minute, gorn the next, and them with it. Worth a pile of money, it were, and such dassn't linger long on streets in Alsatia. Dead bodies neither," she added thoughtfully.

"Alsatia?"

"Aye, that's where we be, right enough."

"Nonsense, we are in London."

The woman cackled again. "Lord love ye, dearie, but o' course we be in London. Alsatia b'ain't no-wheres else." Looking around at her make-believe audience, she added, "Poor girl be touched in the head, I'm thinking."

Maggie struggled to stand up, holding onto the wall for support. Her head still swam, but her legs felt steadier than she had feared might be the case. The woman was much her own height, and now that she looked eye to eye with her, she realized she was not as ancient as she had first thought her to be.

"Please, what is your name?" she asked.

"They calls me Peg Short."

"I am Margaret MacDrumin," Maggie said politely.

"Scotch, then?"

"Yes, I am Scottish." She watched Peg Short warily,

knowing that acknowledging her heritage might prove dangerous, but Peg only nodded wisely.

"Aye, so I thought from the name, but ye talks so pretty, I warn't sure. S'pect them louts didn't leave ye no money, mistress. How will ye eat?"

Not only was her money gone, but Maggie discovered that the thieves had also taken a ring her father had given her on her sixteenth birthday. Neither observation seemed to distress her, and it occurred to her only now that she had scarcely blinked at being told that both Mungo and Fiona, servants—nay, good friends—whom she had known her entire life, had perished at the hands of the ruffians who had attacked her coach. That she was not sobbing with grief seemed most peculiar, but she had not the slightest inclination to cry. She had no particular desire to do anything, except perhaps to lie down and go to sleep.

That would not do at all. Clearly, her mind had been affected in much the same way as when she had learned of the defeat at Culloden and other dreadful events that had occurred—thanks to the English and certain Scottish traitors—in the time since then. It was certainly not the first time she had observed that her mind tended to take on a sort of protective casing when she was particularly distressed. It would be better for her, she thought, if the odd calm that overcame her at such times would only make it easier to think, but that was not the case. In the thoughts that flitted through her mind without reason or meaning, only one was clear. She did not want to stay where she was.

"I must get to Essex Street," she told Peg Short.

Peg's eyes widened. "Essex Street, is it? And just who might ye be knowin' in that fine neighborhood, girlie?"

"My arrival is anticipated at the house of the widow

Viscountess Primrose," Maggie said. "Do you know where that is?"

"Aye, mayhap, but why should I help ye? Ye've naught to give old Peg in return for 'er kindness, that's sure."

"No, but Lady Primrose will reward you if you will but convey me safely to her house. If you cannot take me so far, perhaps you will just help me get out of this neighborhood. If I can find a safer street, perhaps I can hire a chair—"

"Lord love ye, mistress, but no honest chairman would take ye up, looking like ye do, even if ye had gelt, which ye don't."

Maggie bit her lip. Peg Short was right. "Then what is to become of me?"

Peg looked upward for a long moment as if she sought counsel from the heavens. Then, looking shrewdly at Maggie, she said, "Be it worth ten bob to ye, then, to find Essex Street?"

"Yes, it would be, and I am certain that Lady Primrose will pay you even more if you will see me safely to her doorstep."

Peg looked carefully to right and to left, as if consulting with her imaginary friends, then appeared to make up her mind. "I'll do it," she said. "Can ye walk, mistress? For it b'ain't no good expecting me to carry ye."

Repressing her own doubts, Maggie assured her that she could walk and forced herself to keep up as Peg led the way through what were surely the worst parts of Alsatia. Trying to keep her eyes straight ahead of her, so as not to call attention to herself, Maggie was certain her ragged clothing must help her blend in with the inhabitants. She looked no better than Peg.

After what seemed an eternity, they emerged onto a

wider street, more like the ones the coach had passed
along before taking the fatal turning, and Maggie
began to take hope. She was exhausted and by no
means sure she could much longer keep up the pace
Peg set, but she was determined to follow until she
dropped. At least now she felt safe again, though the
footway was much more crowded than before.

Peg, just ahead of her, brushed against a stocky
gentleman, and Maggie had to swerve to avoid running right into him. A moment later, Peg stopped in
her tracks, bent swiftly and straightened, then turned
back to Maggie, holding a fat purse in one hand.
"That man," she said, pointing toward the one she had
jostled. "He done dropped it, mistress. D'ye run after
him and give it back. Quick now! Me old legs'll never
catch him."

Maggie stared at the retreating back of the gentleman, wondering how on earth Peg expected her to run
after him when she could scarcely walk without col-
lapsing. But when she turned to tell Peg she could not
do it, the woman was nowhere to be seen. Instead,
standing right in front of her was a very large, very
angry man wearing a low-crowned, wide-brimmed
slouch hat, a voluminous drab cloak that looked like
a discarded coachman's greatcoat, light breeches and
stockings, and black boots. He held a cudgel in one
hand but grabbed her right arm tightly with his other.
Then, tucking the cudgel under that same arm, he took
a wooden bell out of a pocket in his cloak and began
to wave it overhead. With the rattling sound to punctuate his words, he bellowed at the top of his lungs, "A
thief, a thief! Gentlemen, look to your purses! She's
took a fat 'un from some'un."

Too terrified even to struggle, Maggie saw the
stocky man stop, pat his clothing, and turn around, his

expression shocked and furious. "I say," he shouted, "that's mine she's taken!"

"Then you'll be knowing how much is inside it, sir."

"I certainly do know, my good man. There is all of five pounds inside it."

Her captor put away his rattle and, keeping a sharp eye on Maggie, opened the purse. Clicking his tongue, he said, "There be all of that, sir, which be a good bit more than the forty shillings required to hang the wicked wench."

"But I did not take his purse," Maggie said, trying to retain her dignity and knowing she failed miserably. "Who are you to dare to detain me, fellow?"

"I be a constable's watchman, that's who I be, wench, expected to keep the king's peace in London town. And who do ye think ye be, to be talking so high and mighty to yer betters?"

"I . . ." Seeing the number of people who hovered curiously nearby to see what would become of her, Maggie felt the shredded remnants of her courage disintegrate. The last thing she wanted to do was to announce her name so publicly. Looking desperately from Peg Short's victim to the watchman, she said finally, "I did not take that gentleman's purse. If you will only let me—"

"Aye, wench, o' course ye didn't take it. The thing just flew out of the gentleman's pocket and into your hand."

"No, of course it did no such thing, but I did not take it. There was a woman with me, Peg Short, who picked it up off the footpath and handed it to me." But even as she said the words, she knew that was not what had happened, that Peg had stolen the purse and had thrust it at her in order to make her own escape.

The watchman winked at her. "Not much of a liar,

are ye, wench. Best ye polish that tale up a mite afore ye tell it to his worship." Taking her arm again, he said, "Come along now."

"But where are you taking me?" Maggie cried.

"Why, to Bridewell magistrate's court, o' course," he told her. "Lucky ye be 'tis a Friday, or ye'd sit in a cell for a few days first. His worship holds his court but once a week. Ye might scrub yer face a bit," he added, looking her over with a critical eye. "Happen he'll be swayed more by a pretty face than by yer silly story and decline to hang ye after all."

It was the second time he had mentioned hanging, and Maggie shuddered. "They won't really hang me!"

"Oh, aye. If ye were male, his worship would no doubt order ye strung up in irons outside the city afterwards, as a warning to them what enters to mind our laws 'n all."

She remembered seeing such grotesque sights along the Hampstead Road. The punishment was a peculiarly English one, and she had been appalled, but Fiona had said practically that such sights must deter highwaymen, which was no doubt their purpose.

Suddenly, at thought of Fiona, tears sprang to her eyes, and a moment later, she was sobbing hysterically. Fiona and Mungo were really dead, and as if that were not dreadful enough, she was all alone, and the damnable English meant to hang her.

The watchman, unimpressed by her tears, merely tightened his hand on her arm and dragged her along the street behind him until her knees buckled and the world went black again.

The next time she opened her eyes, he was carrying her in his arms and they were passing through an arched stone entrance into what she feared must be Bridewell Prison.

"If ye've come to your senses, ye can walk," her captor said sternly, dumping her unceremoniously onto her feet again and steadying her with a bruising grip when she swayed precariously.

The stench assailed her nostrils, and she wrinkled her nose distastefully and pressed her lips tightly together.

"Aye, it stinks, don't it?" he said. "Hard to think it were once a royal palace. Given to the city, it were, some two hundred years ago, for a workhouse and correctional institution." He grinned as he carefully pronounced the last two words, adding, "Ye'll be corrected here, right enough. Been here afore, wench?"

"No, of course I have not."

"Don't rightly see how there be any 'o' course' about it," he said, pushing her ahead of him. "Most pickpockets, nightwalkers, vagrants, strumpets, and other idle folk as get took up for their ill lives ends up here, not ter mention such like incorrigible and disobedient servants as finds theirselves committed by Justices of the Peace. Look there." He pointed to a crowded, open yard, its iron-barred gate held ajar by a burly jailor carrying a ring of huge keys. "That's where ye'll spend what time ye got left on this earth, a-beating hemp or being beaten yerself." He leered at her as he added, "Mebbe the judge'll be payin' some lucky watchman fourpence to give ye a good whipping afore he orders ye locked up."

Maggie could see that the yard, open to public view, was filled mostly with women, some in tatters, others in shabby but brocaded gowns. There was one man in a pillory at the rear of the yard, and a few others scattered amidst the women, but it was the women who held her attention. Some were clearly hardened criminals, others almost children. A guard with a stick threatened a young one who paused in her work to look at Maggie, and the girl hastily wielded her mallet again. Maggie shivered.

"See the whipping post yonder, wench? If his worship don't order ye stripped naked and whipped immediate—which is what pleases the spectators most, o' course—like as not it'll be done there in the yard on the day afore ye're hanged." With these cheerful words, he shoved her ahead of him, through a pair of open double doors, into a large and overcrowded chamber.

Maggie stopped, swaying, when the blackness threatened to overcome her again. The noise and the smell were overpowering, and the fear that had begun with her arrest now seemed to rob her of the ability to think about anything else. Never in her life had she felt so terrifyingly alone. The courtroom was nothing like the only other such chamber she had set foot in, and if the magistrate sitting behind the high bench reminded her at all of his counterpart in Inverness, it was only because they wore the same black robes, full-bottomed powdered wig, and wire-rimmed spectacles. Nothing else was the same, for this man was thin and harsh-looking. He glared down at the man presently before him.

"As a vagrant in this city, you are condemned to be whipped on your bare back until the blood runs down to your heels. If I see you here again, I will order a hundred lashes." The gavel crashed down, the defendant's legs buckled, and two grim-faced jailors dragged the poor victim away.

Maggie began to tremble and could not stop. If the horrid judge ordered her whipped on her bare back, the messages she carried would certainly be discovered. The watchman pushed her again, and she stumbled up the aisle between the rows of pews set out for spectators. A man near the aisle on one of the forward benches, who was drawing, glanced up at the one being dragged from the courtroom, then sketched again rapidly, as if he would catch the entire scene on paper. The thought that anyone would come to such a place merely to draw pictures of the wretches sentenced by the court made her feel ill, but she could not take her eyes from him. At last, determined to recover her dignity, she lifted her chin and forced herself to look away, only to encounter the magistrate's flintlike gaze.

"Next case," he declared in a cold, unfeeling voice.

Maggie glanced over her shoulder at her captor, but he shook his head. "Jest find yerself a seat on that front pew, wench. There be others ahead o' ye, fer which ye should be grateful."

She could not bring herself to ask anyone to make room for her, and stood by the front pew until the watchman snapped at the two women sitting nearest her to cozy up a bit. As Maggie moved to sit down, she encountered the gaze of the man with the drawing board. Glaring at him, she looked swiftly away again and sat down, hating the thought that he might dare to draw her likeness.

Time crawled by, and each case that preceded hers added to her fears, for the magistrate sitting that day was clearly not a man well-acquainted with mercy. Time and time again, he ordered his poor victim thrown into prison until such time as he might expeditiously be hanged, and in more than one case, he ordered a public whipping to take place the day before the hanging. So far, the only encouraging sign was that he had not ordered anyone's punishment to take place immediately, in the courtroom.

Maggie kept her eyes firmly fixed on the point where the high bench met the floor, but she was constantly aware of noises behind her. Feet shuffled, people coughed or sneezed, and there was incessant murmuring and muttering. Several times, above the rest, she heard the sound of paper being shifted.

At last, when the call came for the next case, the watchman touched her arm, urging her to stand. Maggie obeyed, quaking, her knees weak, wondering how on earth she could save herself.

The formidable magistrate said icily, "What is the crime in this case, watchman?"

"Theft, your worship, more than five pounds taken."

The cold gray eyes shifted to Maggie. "Have you anything to say for yourself, young woman?"

"Yes, I do," she said, forcing herself to speak calmly. "If it please your worship, I can explain what happened."

His eyebrows lifted slightly. "You speak like a person of some quality."

"Yes, sir, I am—"

"The more pity that you should have fallen so low," he said, shifting his gaze again. "Above five pounds, you say, watchman?"

"Aye, your worship."

"The law is clear. Your sentence, young woman, is that—"

"Wait!" Maggie cried. "You cannot treat me like this. Please, sir, there are people who will speak for me. You simply must let me tell you who I am and explain how it all came to—"

The magistrate glared. "I need do nothing of the sort, but I own, your manner intrigues me. Who will speak for you?"

She had meant to invoke the name of Lady Primrose, but even as the words leapt to her tongue, she realized that if her ladyship were suspected to be a Jacobite—as indeed, certain of her hosts had suggested might prove to be the case—naming her now might do no good, and might well do the cause they both served much harm. Without thinking more than that, Maggie blurted the only other name she knew in London. "The Earl of Rothwell, your worship! I am kin to the Earl of Rothwell!"

To her utter dismay, the magistrate began to laugh.

IV

Maggie stared at the magistrate in astonishment. The rest of the courtroom fell silent until he stopped laughing, but then, behind her, she heard the unmistakable sound of a chuckle. She kept her eyes riveted on the magistrate. Her head ached.

"Rothwell, eh?" His voice still rang with amusement, but he was looking past her now. "You are related to him, you say?"

Swallowing, she said, "Well, not precisely related, your worship, but—"

"I thought not. What, *precisely,* did you mean to say?"

She swallowed again, wishing he had done nearly anything else but laugh. It would be just her luck, she thought, to discover that the magistrate himself was in fact the Earl of Rothwell. But surely so highborn a personage would not spend his time meting out justice in so lowly a court as this one. She drew a steadying breath. "Lord Rothwell has a . . . a particular interest in my family, sir."

The magistrate, still peering over his spectacles past her, said lightly, "Come now, Mr. Carsley, how is it that you have not yet enlightened this court? Surely, if this young woman is kin to the Earl of Rothwell, you must have heard of her, sir."

A calm voice—surely the same one that had chuckled—said from behind Maggie, "Since we have not yet heard her name, I can hardly be expected to have recognized it. As to the young woman herself, I cannot recall ever having met her."

Maggie looked over her shoulder. It was the artist who had spoken, and he had done so in the unmistakable tones of a gentleman. A young man some three or four years older than herself, he was dressed casually, not at all like a man of fashion. His chestnut hair bore no trace of powder and was drawn back and tied with a plain black ribbon. His features were even, his eyes a sort of golden hazel color. When his gaze shifted to meet hers, she saw only curiosity in his expression.

She turned back to face the magistrate and said firmly, "I do not know that gentleman, your worship."

"Do you say, then, that even his name is unfamiliar to you?"

"Certainly it is. I am but newly come to London, sir. In attempting to find a particular address, my coachman took a wrong turning, and we were attacked. He and my maid were killed, my belongings were stolen, and I was left without money or protection, which is how I come now to be in this predicament."

Titters and chuckles of disbelief filled the courtroom, but the magistrate made no rebuke and in fact appeared to share the amusement. "A very good tale," he said approvingly, "but it will not serve you, I fear. You speak well, and I should not be at all surprised to learn that you had at one time or another served as a lady's maid or in some like position, and try to ape your betters, but since Mr. Carsley cannot speak for you, I fear—"

"Forgive my interruption, sir," the calm voice said, "but I see no reason that I cannot speak for the young woman. If it will help her, I am perfectly willing to do so."

Maggie turned to him, unsure whether he spoke sincerely or meant merely to mock her. His expression was serious, and she saw that his demeanor was that of a man accustomed to having his wishes attended to. Had he not been engaged in an occupation so distasteful as drawing scenes in a public courtroom, she might have thought him a member of her own class. He smiled at her.

The magistrate said severely, "Now, now, sir, take care lest you act too impulsively. Since it is patently clear that this woman does not even know the name Carsley, I find it impossible to believe that your brother can have anything to do with her."

"Your brother!" Maggie stared aghast at the young man.

"Don't blame me," he said with an engaging grin. "He don't recognize the connection unless he is forced to do so, and in point of fact, he is only my half-brother."

"But—" She broke off when he held up a restraining hand.

He said calmly to the magistrate, "She knew the title, your worship, and there must be cause for that. I daresay there are many who do not know the family name, and I see so little of him these days that I cannot claim to speak for him; however, I do recall his mentioning sometime or other in the not too distant past that he had undertaken a responsibility of some sort. Therefore it is entirely possible that this young woman is his ward, and I can assure you that I should not like him to discover after the fact that I had allowed her to be hanged if he is indeed responsible in any way whatsoever for her safety."

The magistrate grimaced, no longer in the least amused. "My dear sir, this young woman is no more than a common thief!"

Carsley sighed. "Not common, sir, if you will permit the contradiction. Only consider how politely she speaks. In any event, the purse was recovered, so I suggest you allow Rothwell to decide what should be done with her. She can always be clapped up again later if he does not wish to claim her."

"Will you engage to return her to custody if you discover that she has lied to this court, Mr. Carsley?"

"I will engage to present her to Rothwell, sir, and I can promise you that if she is lying, he will swiftly make her wish that she had chosen to allow you to hang her."

Maggie squared her shoulders and met Mr. Carsley's stern look, but inside she was quaking, and whether it was at the thought of being presented to Rothwell or being returned to Bridewell, she did not know. Why was it, she wondered dismally, that so frequently persons who presented themselves to her as rescuers proved rather quickly to be otherwise?

The next few moments passed in something of a daze, but it was all too soon that she found herself standing outside the stone archway beside Mr. Carsley, facing a canal that flowed down the middle of a wide road crowded with all manner of traffic. Despite the fact that most of the pedestrians looked like many she had seen in Alsatia, she drew a long breath of fresh air and looked around with interest, feeling her freedom as if it were her father's strongest whisky. At last, she turned to her companion and said, "Mr. Carsley, thank you for helping me."

"You know," he replied, looking shrewdly at her, "you do talk like an educated woman, but you look like something dragged out of a hedge. Who the devil are you and what were you thinking to fling Rothwell's name at that fool magistrate?"

"You said yourself that he had recently taken up a new responsibility. How do you know I did not speak the truth?"

"Ned is always taking up new responsibilities, so it was the first thing I thought to say, although, in my view, it is usually his money that's wanted, not his protection or advice. But that is all beside the point. I want to know who you are."

She paused. Once mentioned, Rothwell's name had worked like magic, and having made it through the dreadful court proceeding without giving her own name, she hesitated now to reveal it. "I ought to have known your brother's surname," she said, choosing momentary diversion instead. "It was foolish of me to mention him without knowing even that much about him, but you see—"

"Half-brother," he said, taking her arm. "I think we had better repair to my house so that you can at least wash your face and tidy your hair before I take you to him."

Maggie dug in her heels. "Oh, no! That is, although I am most grateful to you for intervening on my behalf, sir, I cannot face your brother. And there is no need to take me to him, since you must know by now that he is not even aware of my existence."

"I suspected as much," Carsley said. "Still, I promised the beak I'd take you along to Ned, so I must. What happens after that, he will decide. Can't say I blame you for wanting to turn tail and run, though, for it won't be a pleasant experience. Not looking forward to seeing him myself," he added, giving her a less than friendly look. "I prefer to keep my distance if you want to know the truth of the matter."

"But I do have friends in London," Maggie said, "so if you would just lend me enough money to take a hackney coach or a chair, I could go to Lady—"

"To Lady whom?" he asked when she broke off in confusion.

He seemed like a pleasant young man, but in view of the possible dangers involved, to reveal an acquaintance with her ladyship before speaking to her might not be wise. "Please, just believe that I do have friends," she said. "Surely, you could spare me a shilling or whatever it costs to hire a chair."

"But I can't," he said flatly. "I gave my word."

"Oh, for heaven's sake, what does that matter? You do not want to see your brother—and certainly I don't want to see him—so there is no need for you to take me there." She stared at him in dismay when a new thought struck her. "Look here, do you mean to drag me back to that horrid place afterward? The magistrate said you were to do so if I proved to be lying, and you know even now that I lied through my teeth."

"You have not been listening," he said, tightening his grip on her arm and urging her downhill. "We'll go this way, to the river. You will not want to walk all the way to my house, so I shall splurge and hire a barge for us at Blackfriars."

Maggie could see the Thames—wide, blue, and sparkling—at the bottom of the hill, and curious to see the river that had been called the lifeblood of London, she let him guide her toward it without more protest, but she did not intend to drop the subject altogether. Looking up a moment later, searching his face for answers, she said, "I heard everything that was said in that courtroom, sir, and that man said you were to return me if you were to discover that I had not spoken the truth."

"What you did not hear, however, was me saying I would. I said only that I would engage to present you to Rothwell and that I will do. I don't give my word lightly, but when I do, I feel honor bound to keep it." He grimaced again at her appearance. "I do wish you had something more presentable to wear."

"No more than I wish it," she retorted, "but all the baggage I brought was on my coach, and that entire vehicle—not to mention four horses—disappeared in Alsatia before I had regained my wits, so I cannot tell you what became of my other dresses."

"So that tale was true, was it? Were you really in Alsatia at the time?"

"I was. My coachman, being new to London, took a wrong turning and in a single moment drove from a perfectly civilized road into an altogether uncivilized one. My coach was mobbed and overturned. I am lucky to have escaped with my life."

"How did the coachman manage to go amiss?"

"I am sure I cannot tell you. His directions were quite clear, to take Fetter Lane from Holborn, turn into Fleet Street, and then take the sixth turning toward the river."

"He must have turned the wrong way into Fleet Street. I do not know which street is the sixth, but I can tell you that nearly any turning he might have taken from Fetter Lane east—until you were well past Bridewell, at all events—would take you into Alsatia. The fashionable areas are to the west. Look here," he added, albeit in the same matter-of-fact tone, "were you harmed in any other way?"

Her head was pounding now. She looked at him,

encountered a straight look, and blushed, saying quietly, "I bumped my head, and it aches a bit, but that is all."

"Then you were lucky indeed," he said. "Now, do you mean to tell me your name, or must I make one up? I shall need to call you something, you know, when I present you to Rothwell."

"I am Margaret MacDrumin, Mr. Carsley." Watching him carefully, she could see no sign that he recognized her name.

He nodded, saying, "I take it then, that you are now resigned to meeting Ned."

"I suppose I am." She sighed. "Will he be very angry?"

Carsley shrugged. "We must hope not, but if he is, you may believe that he will be more angry with me than with you."

That was hardly reassuring, but she could think of nothing to say in response, and he fell silent for a time. Despite her headache, she was drinking in the sights and sounds of the city. There were costermongers everywhere, crying their wares, and a man and woman danced for pennies on the footway.

As they neared the riverbank, the noise grew louder. Iron cartwheels and horseshoes clattered on the cobblestones. Carters shouted, and pedestrians looked to be in constant danger of being crushed against the walls of nearby buildings, for there was no protective raised pavement in this area, and it was next to impossible to tell where the footway ended and the street began.

Maggie stayed close to Mr. Carsley, and felt a vast sense of relief when they were seated at last in one of the long narrow barges that carried paying passengers from point to point along the river. They went with the current, so their passage seemed swift to one who was in no hurry, but she was too fascinated by the view to ponder her fears. Seen thus from the river, the city was clearly much bigger than Edinburgh, and more impressive.

Mr. Carsley pointed out landmarks he considered to be of interest, and although she was certain she would never remember Puddle Dock Laystall or the Steelyard, she was just as certain she would never forget the Dung Wharf with its huge pile of manure or St. Paul's Cathedral, looming above the whole city.

"There's London Bridge, straight ahead," Carsley said, "and the water tower. Most of our water comes from the river. Wooden pipes carry it all over the city."

"I suppose you've painted many pictures of London, sir. It's all so magnificently picturesque."

"I leave that sort of thing to Canaletto and Scott. My work is more anecdotal, but since I don't have Will Hogarth's amazing technical memory, I can't simply paint things I have seen, so I must make sketches first, which is why you saw me doing so in the courtroom. I've done a number of court paintings this year."

Having no wish to repay his kindness by criticizing his choice of subject matter, Maggie said nothing, and a few moments later the barge arrived at the Old Swan Stairs.

Carsley helped her to the landing, saying cheerfully, "We're nearly there. I've got any number of my pictures sitting about in my house, you know, if you'd care to see them."

Maggie returned a light reply, but it occurred to her as he guided her across Fishmongers' Hall terrace and behind the water tower that she ought not even to accompany him to his house, for it was not at all a proper thing to do. But she could not wait for him in a public street either. Not until he spoke again to explain that they had arrived at Fish Street Hill did she summon up the nerve to say, "Are you truly taking me to your house?"

His smile was understanding, and he said, "You need not trouble your head about your reputation. I've a housekeeper of sorts, and another chap lives with me. This way now."

"I thought the bridge was near here." She looked around, disoriented, for the river had disappeared altogether, and they were apparently back in the center of town.

Carsley laughed. "We are on the bridge," he said. "Look yonder, at that space between the houses. From there you can see the water. That point is nearly halfway across."

She did not believe him until she could lean over the parapet and see the barges plunging between the huge footings that supported the bridge. "That looks like fun," she said.

"It's dashed dangerous. The tide's on the rise now, so it is relatively safe, but as the river goes down, the current runs more swiftly and lots of accidents take place. Here's my house."

To her astonishment, his home was over one of the many shops that lined each side of the bridge. When he opened a narrow door between two of these, indicating that she should precede him up the narrow dark stairway, she began to feel ill at ease, but once they reached the top and he opened the door, she forgot her fears. The room she entered was charming, a drawing room with windows at each end overlooking river and bridge, and filling the room with light. There were no curtains, the furniture was comfortable-looking but not shabby, and the two windowless walls were covered with colorful paintings.

"How wonderful," she exclaimed.

"We like it. Dev, you here?"

At first a grunt and mumble from a sofa turned toward the river windows was the only reply, but a moment later a shaggy, dark head rose over the sofa back and a pale, doleful face appeared. "So you're back, are you, James? Who's the wench?"

"She is Miss MacDrumin. Get up and greet her properly, you ass. Though he don't look the part, may I present Lord Thomas Deverill, ma'am. I thought you were going out to drown yourself today, Dev. Did you forget?"

Maggie turned and stared at Carsley, certain she must have misheard him, but though his eyes held a lurking twinkle, Lord Thomas said morosely as he got to his feet, "Didn't forget. As you no doubt recall, when your dashed unfeeling brother forbade me ever again to speak to my darling Lydia, I resolved first to poison myself, but not knowing where to effect such a deed, I resolved instead upon drowning. So today I hired a coach and ordered the jarvey to drive to Tower Wharf, intending to throw myself into the water at Customs House Key. I left the coach, intending never to return to it, but upon coming to the key, I found not only that the water was too low but that a dashed porter was seated on some goods there as if on purpose to prevent my demise." He sighed. "The passage to the bottomless pit being thus shut against me, I returned to the coach and came home."

"Lord Thomas," Maggie exclaimed, appalled but fascinated, "you cannot truly wish to put a period to your existence!"

"Of course he doesn't," James said. "If he did, he would simply have cast himself off the bridge."

Lord Thomas cast him a darkling look before saying to Maggie, "James has no soul. I shall no doubt cast myself off the bridge tomorrow, and then how will he feel?"

Carsley said, "You are soft in the head, Dev."

"No, I ain't. What would you have me do? If I weren't a younger son, I'd be perfectly eligible to court your sister, wouldn't I? If I were my own brother, they'd roll out the red carpet, but as it is, Rothwell wants none of me."

"Where is Mrs. Honeywell?" Carsley asked abruptly.

"Gone out to fetch cutlets for supper."

"Well, stir your stumps then, and fetch Miss Mac-Drumin a basin and pitcher so she can wash her face. And if you can find a comb or brush, bring that along as well. I've got to take her to Ned, and I won't take her looking like she does now."

For the first time, Lord Thomas looked directly at Maggie, who shifted her feet, embarrassed to think how bedraggled she must look. But when he only nodded and went away, her embarrassment vanished, and she felt almost like laughing.

"Never mind Dev," Carsley said. "The poor fool can't think of anything but my sister."

"Does she care for him?" Maggie asked, moving to obtain a clear view of the river.

"She thinks she does," he answered, "but I daresay that is only because Ned says she must not. A contrary wench, is Lydia."

"Good gracious," Maggie exclaimed suddenly, "this building hangs right out over the water!"

"Don't fret. There are quite solid iron supports underneath the overhanging bits."

"I cannot think why you haven't painted this view a dozen times," she said, "but there is not one picture of it amongst those hanging on the wall."

"I won't ask what you think of those. Most ladies are oversensitive to such stuff."

She looked more closely at the paintings on the wall and grimaced when her gaze came to light on a portrait of a pair of female boxers in a ring, surrounded by cheering, leering men.

"Surely, you never actually saw anything like that, sir!"

"On the contrary, one sees it every Friday night at Figg's Boarding House in Wells Street. Those females are from Billingsgate, which is peculiarly noted for its rough women."

"Why is there gold showing between their fingers?"

"Women who box must hold gold coins so they don't begin pulling each other's hair out," he told her. "If one drops a coin, she forfeits the match. You were quick, Dev," he added when Lord Thomas returned, precariously carrying a basin and ewer. "Take care you don't drop those things."

"I won't. Do you require aught else, Miss MacDrumin? I ain't much of a lady's maid, but I'll do what I can."

"Thank you," Maggie said, adding with a sigh, "I do not suppose you know where I can procure a new gown."

Lord Thomas shook his head, but Carsley said suddenly, "Dev, I daresay if you were to nip down to the shops you might find a shawl or some such thing that she can cover her shoulders with."

"Good Lord!" Maggie had moved to peer at her

reflection in the mirror hanging over the little fireplace, and what she saw appalled her. She had known her skirt was filthy, but she saw now that her hair was tangled beyond belief, smudges covered her face, and the habit-shirt of her travel dress was not only as filthy as her skirt but her corset showed through several of its rents. Heat suffused her cheeks when she realized she had been carrying on a conversation with two gentlemen in such a state.

Speechless, she turned to pour water into the basin, and not until she had scrubbed everything that showed did she turn her attention to her hair. A few tentative tugs with the comb Lord Thomas had provided accomplished little, and she was about to give up when Carsley took it from her and began ruthlessly to drag it through her tangled curls.

"Ow! You're hurting me! Remember my headache, sir!"

"Stand still. If you think I'm taking you to meet Ned looking like you've spent the day boxing the Billingsgate women, you've another think coming. I'll get you something in a minute for your headache."

"How dare you! Ow!" By the time he had finished, Maggie had tears in her eyes and would cheerfully have murdered him, but when he turned her to look again at her reflection, she had to admit that with his artist's eye he had accomplished wonders with her hair. It would not really be tidy again until it had been washed and thoroughly brushed, but she had not thought anyone could make it look presentable, and he had done more than that. Fifteen minutes later, Lord Thomas returned with a soft moss-green woolen shawl, which she accepted gratefully. It would not cover the filthy gown, but it brought out the green flecks in her hazel eyes, and it felt warm and soft to the touch.

Carsley disappeared briefly and returned wearing a fresh shirt, a clean coat, and a tie-wig, and carrying a glass with cloudy liquid in it, and small parcel. He still looked very casually attired for a gentleman, and his wig was askew, but she supposed he believed he had dressed up for the occasion.

Giving Maggie the glass, he said, "Drink it. It will help your headache."

When she had obeyed him, they bade Lord Thomas farewell, and Mr. Carsley hurried her out the door and along the footway to the north end of the bridge. When he turned toward the Old Swan Stairs, Maggie said, "Should we not take a coach, sir? Surely, it will take a long time for us to be rowed back up the river."

"Not as long as it would take to negotiate the streets near it," he said. "The distance is only a bit more than two miles, and the current is not so fast while the tide is coming in."

He chose a barge with a pair of stout oarsmen, apparently unconcerned by the cost of the extra man, and Maggie sat back to enjoy yet another view of London. The sun was in front of them now, but it took less time than she had expected to retrace their route, and when they had passed Blackfriars Stairs, Carsley directed her attention to the Temple, then added, "Look yonder now. That tall archway leading into Essex Street is the only one of its kind on the river."

Longingly Maggie looked at Essex Street, then glanced back at her companion, now pointing out decrepit tenement buildings and explaining that they comprised the once magnificent Essex and Arundel House estates. She wished she could convince him simply to order the bargemen to let her out at once, but she had already learned enough about Carsley to know he would refuse.

The breeze on the river was chilly, and she was glad to snuggle into the warm shawl. Looking back as they passed Somerset House, she decided that, except for the massive shape of St. Paul's Cathedral looming above all else, the city looked like a vast harbor, its rooftops like ships with church-spire masts.

Carsley pointed out Cuper's Gardens and Salisbury House before he fell suddenly silent. Maggie realized then that the sun was now on their right, the great river had curved. She could see another bridge not far ahead, nothing like London Bridge, for it bore no buildings and its footings were wide apart. She started to ask a question, but just then the bargemen changed the pace of their strokes, angling the vessel toward the shore. Looking at Mr. Carsley and seeing his jaw tighten, she kept silent, knowing they had reached their destination.

Her heart began to pound. The houses they approached were enormous—clearly homes of the very wealthy. The trepidation she had felt before—when she had realized the enormity of invoking Rothwell's name in the courtroom—had eased considerably in the comfortable little house on London Bridge; but now, as the barge glided into place at the stone steps between the two largest houses, and she saw Carsley's gaze fix on the one on the right, she experienced twice the apprehension she had felt before. Everything she had heard about the earl told her he was a man to be reckoned with, one powerful enough to have been awarded vast estates in the Highlands after the uprising, and a very wealthy man besides. Certainly, rents from MacDrumin land had not paid for Rothwell

House. What on earth, she wondered yet again, had she got herself into?

Allowing Carsley to help her from the barge, she felt increasing nervousness when he opened the gate at the top of the steps and commanded one of the two footmen in the passage to pay the bargemen. Annoyed to think she was near panic, she strove to control her fears. The house was large, but it was only a house. The footman was only a footman. Breathing deeply, feeling calmer, realizing her headache had practically disappeared, she went with Carsley through the doorway on the right, up a flight of steps to a terrace overlooking the river.

The view was spectacular, and for a moment she forgot her nerves, but Carsley allowed her no time to savor the scenery. His hand tightening on her elbow, he propelled her through a door held open by another liveried footman."

"Fields," he demanded when a stately butler entered from another room, "Where's his lordship?"

"In the bookroom, Master James. May I—"

But Carsley did not wait to hear the rest. He sped Maggie through the high-ceilinged, elegantly appointed room, on through a stair hall with a soaring spiral staircase and a splendid domed ceiling, past another wooden-faced footman, into a room that was clearly the library. He came to a halt so quickly that she almost expected to hear his heels squeak on the polished floor, and she found herself staring at a large, elegantly dressed man seated behind a massive desk. When he looked up in mild surprise, she felt her apprehension melt away, for if this man was Rothwell, she need fear no more. He was nothing but a fop.

v

Rothwell concealed his astonishment with difficulty. He had not seen James for a fortnight, and he could not for the life of him think what the lad was doing dragging a disreputable female into Rothwell House library, but since he rarely gave way to ineffectual emotional outbursts, he said only, "Hello, James. Ought I to have been expecting you? My memory, you know, is so rarely to be depended upon that I suppose I must have forgotten."

"Your memory is excellent, Ned, as you know perfectly well. Not only were you not expecting me, but I had no intention of setting foot in this house for a good long time after my last visit. Well, not my last *visit,* precisely, but the last time we exchanged words. Blast me, that's not what I meant to say either, but I daresay you understand me well enough."

Rothwell allowed himself a slight pause, knowing that if he spoke too quickly he would reveal his amusement, then said, "I do comprehend your tangled periods, so I must suppose that your reason for bursting in upon me in this fashion is a singularly important one. Do you mean to present your companion?"

James flushed and said angrily, "If you are thinking

that I have come to you for money, let me tell you plainly that you have never been more mistaken in your life."

"But I have taken great pains neither to think nor to say any such thing. I asked only if you mean to present this female to me. You behave as if I'd asked you if you brought her here to illustrate how low you have sunk into squalor."

The young female's eyes flashed, and he saw with flickering interest that they were a singularly greenish shade of hazel. She had scrubbed her face and hands, and attempted to arrange her hair with some style, but beneath the cheap shawl, her gown was as filthy and bedraggled as that of any street wench. She looked as if she would dare to speak to him, but James forestalled her.

He sputtered, "I have not sunk anywhere, Ned. If you only made an effort to understand *my* feelings, we would not be at odds so often. You may be an all-round brilliant fellow where others are concerned, but you don't know a thing about me."

"Not so, dear boy. I know you believe you have cast off the trappings of wealth—except when you run short of funds, of course—and that you find meaning in numerous activities that do not generally interest a gentleman but lack the discipline to succeed at any of them. I have not yet attempted to bring you to heel, but only because you have done nothing yet to force my hand. I devoutly hope this young person's presence in my library does not indicate an unhappy change in that state of affairs."

"Lord Rothwell," the young woman said sharply, astonishing him, "I cannot allow you to continue to speak of me as if I were a drab off the street. I'll have you know I am no such thing."

"Dear me," Rothwell said, raising his eyeglass and peering at her through it in sudden suspicion that she was no ordinary street wench. She was not at all in awe of him, for one thing, and spoke as if to an equal. She was therefore either demented or of gentle birth. "I believe I have misjudged you, young woman. You speak rashly, but you speak in educated tones."

"I am very well educated, sir, though I cannot see what that fact has to do with the point at hand. I fell into a predicament from which your brother was moved to rescue me, and though he insisted upon presenting me to you, I see now that he erred in doing so. Therefore, if he will be so kind as to escort me to the door, I willna trouble you further." She turned as if assuming that James would comply, and Rothwell wondered if he had really detected the slight accent or if he had misheard her.

"No, you don't," James said, grasping her arm in what appeared from her grimace to be a very firm grip. "I know I keep telling you he is only my half-brother, but even so, you've no business to be talking to him in such a rude way, particularly when you were so quick to claim his guardianship earlier today."

"I did not!" Once again Rothwell thought he detected that unusual lilt in her voice, but the rebuke undoubtedly surprised her. Clearly she had not expected James to side with him on any point. He found himself studying her more carefully. Her face, animated by anger now, was an exceedingly pretty one, and though she was small of stature, her figure—which he could surmise easily enough despite her deplorable clothing—was slender and delicately curved. The greenish hazel eyes sparkled, her cheeks were bright with color, her chin tilted up defiantly, and her full lips parted, revealing even white teeth.

"What's this about guardianship, James?" he said, adding when she moved to speak, "No, madam, you will keep silent. I cannot deal with you properly until I know who and what you are."

James said, "Her name is—"

"My name is of no concern," she said quickly, "and you need not deal with me at all, Rothwell, for I've friends aplenty in London, and though I was wrong to speak out your name as I did—"

"Upon my soul," James exclaimed, "you know perfectly well you had no business to do so. Look here, Ned, I brought her to you because I promised the beak I would do so, but if you don't want her here, I'll take her away again now that I've kept my word. I knew you would be vexed, but there was no getting around it if I was to get her out of that awful place, which it was plain I had to do once I saw that she had no business there."

"What place?" Rothwell demanded, still looking at her and noting that though her face was bare of cosmetics, her complexion suggested strawberries floating in the richest cream. Her lips were not only full but well defined. When she opened her mouth to reply to his question, he said hastily, "James, tell me in plain words, where did you find her?"

"In the magistrate's court at Bridewell."

"Good God." He saw her flush deeply and bite her lower lip, and found himself imagining what it must taste like. Her lips fascinated him. The lower one was redder now than the upper, but both were dark enough without rouge to make a man think of kissing them. Struggling to recover his equilibrium, he could not even imagine what it was about the wench that stirred his fantasies so. There was something about her though, even standing there in ragged clothing, that intrigued him more than any woman of his vast prior acquaintance had ever done with fashionable clothes or elegant speech. He wondered how her tawny hair would look, falling free around her shoulders. She had not shifted her gaze, and the mossy green shawl she wore made her eyes look like enormous green jewels. Mentally chastising himself for a fool, he reined his errant thoughts in abruptly and said, "Tell me the whole, James, *without interruption.*"

Maggie knew from the look Rothwell gave her as he snapped out the last two words that they were intended not for James but for her, and the command stirred an impulse to defy him that was perfectly familiar to her, since it was her normal reaction to being given a direct order. But the hint of steel in Rothwell's voice had surprised her, for it was not at all in keeping with her first impression of the man, or even with her second; so, in order that she might study him more carefully, she held her tongue while James Carsley described the courtroom scene and listed the charges that had been laid against her.

Rothwell listened well, she saw, and without rapping out more questions or making unnecessary comments. He was a handsome man, though his eyes lacked a certain warmth and his lips seemed better acquainted with mockery than good humor. She detected a shrewd intelligence behind his generally lazy manner, and decided he was not the fool she had first thought him. The notion was not a reassuring one. When his gaze came to rest upon her at the point where James described her claim to be related to him, she found herself wishing he would smile. He did not.

When James finished, Rothwell was silent for a long

moment. Maggie was still standing, and she shifted her feet impatiently, fearing to hear what he would say but wanting whatever was going to happen to be over and done. She was strangely hesitant for once to speak her mind, and although she met his gaze directly when it shifted again to her, the effort required to do so was far greater than she had expected. His expression was no longer the least like that of an amiable fop. His eyes were as gray as flint and looked nearly as hard. She braced herself.

"You clearly have the regrettable habit of speaking before you think," he said, more calmly than she had thought he would. "Before we go on, I shall take the liberty to suggest that you learn to curb that habit before you are much older lest it land you in much worse difficulty than it has today. Who are you?"

"May I sit down?" she said, determined to prove to herself that he did not daunt her. "We set out very early this morning, and my day has been overfull. Moreover, I dinna care to be kept standing aboot like an errant school child." To her annoyance, she heard yet again that slight hint of Highland accent in her voice. Her tendency to speak so when she was distressed was one that her father frequently deplored, although he was more often guilty of the lapse than she was.

"Answer my question first, if you please."

Stiffly, taking care to enunciate clearly, she said, "I am Margaret MacDrumin."

"A pleasant name." His demeanor was still calm, and she could not tell if he recognized her surname. "And your friends," he added just as casually, "where are they to be found?"

"In Essex Street," she answered quickly, believing that information at least to be perfectly harmless, "and since I now know that the street is not far from here, I should prefer to seek their help at once and not discommode you further."

"You do not discommode me at all, and since you saw fit—however impulsively—to claim my protection, I must assume at least enough responsibility for your safety as to insist that you remain at Rothwell House until your friends can come for you—if indeed they prove willing to do so."

Dismayed, Maggie stared at him for one speechless moment before she exclaimed, "You willna dare to keep me here!"

"Oh, but I will, Miss MacDrumin, and do not think you have fooled me for a moment as to your true purpose in coming to London. Though you are the second of your sort to astonish me with your education, you have not entirely managed to overcome your barbarian antecedents, for they color your voice enough to be recognized. And if that were not enough, the mere mention of Essex Street would be, for I know as well as you do whose house is to be found there, and although the viscountess and her friends have thus far managed to keep out of prison, they have not managed entirely to conceal their loyalty to a lost cause."

"It is not lost yet," Maggie snapped without thinking.

James looked from one to the other and said, "Ned, what the devil are you saying?"

"Only that your friend is a damned little Jacobite. I would not be at all surprised to learn that she comes to London bearing messages from the Highland leaders to their supporters here, for it would be just like them to send a female to do such work."

Uncomfortably aware of the papers in her corset,

Maggie hardly dared to breathe, lest one of the two men hear them crackle. Then Rothwell got to his feet, and she received another shock, for he proved to be well over six feet tall and even broader across the shoulders than Kate's cousin Dugald.

"Ned," James said quickly, "I didn't know, but perhaps it would be better to send her to her friends. I did not realize—"

"No, James." Rothwell flicked an imagined bit of lint from his cuff. "Miss MacDrumin has claimed my protection, and while it would be remiss of me not to point out to her the error of her ways, or the errors of her so-called friends, she shall have my protection. You may sit down now, Miss MacDrumin, and we shall discuss what is best to be done with you."

"How dare you!" Maggie said furiously. "I've no doubt you recognized my name at once. You might as well admit it."

"Of course I recognized it," he said. "It is a most uncommon name, after all, and I see it quarterly. Moreover, even my worst enemy has never accused me of being a simpleton."

Maggie saw that James looked confused again, and said with a grimace, "I did not lie altogether, Mr. Carsley, as you see—only about being kin to you—for I am the daughter of the man whose estate your brother—forgive me, your *half*-brother—stole."

"You must be demented," James said, "Ned is no thief!"

Rothwell took a gilded white enamel snuffbox from his waistcoat pocket, flicked it open, and helped himself to a delicate pinch.

She sneered at him. "You do not deny the charge, I see."

He replaced the snuffbox. "On the contrary, Miss

MacDrumin. The estate had become no more than spoils of war, rewarded to me for services rendered to the victors of that war."

Maggie gave an unladylike snort. "The uprising was no war, Rothwell, and well you must know it, but you English are every dreadful thing I have heard you named and arrogant, selfish, and stupid besides. You know nothing whatsoever of the world outside your precious England. And you, sir, must be amongst the worst. What sort of man takes over a vast estate and years later still has not so much as set foot on the place? What gentleman allows others to run his estates for him without so much as occasionally looking into things to see if they are being run properly? And what sort of scoundrel allows minions to run roughshod over the very people who must trust him to see to their protection?"

"Yet again, I fear you let your tongue run away with your brain, Miss MacDrumin. Just precisely what people do you mean?" His words were unemotional, his voice apparently calm, but Maggie saw a muscle jump near one corner of his mouth and felt extreme satisfaction to think she had touched a nerve.

"Your tenants, Rothwell, and the very fact that I must describe to you things your factors and our horrid bailie do in your name is evidence enough of your deplorable neglect."

James said angrily, "Now see here, just who do you think—"

"Enough, James." Rothwell spoke quietly, but James obeyed without question. A silence fell, and Maggie watched the earl warily, knowing full well that she had overstepped the bounds of what any gentleman would accept, even from a guest in his house, and she was by no means certain she counted as such.

He looked as if he were about to speak again when the door behind her opened and the expression on his face changed to one of controlled annoyance. He said, "What is it, Lydia?"

Glancing over her shoulder, Maggie saw a beautiful girl with shining raven hair, wearing what she was certain must be a gown in the very latest fashion, with wide rustling skirts that were flatter and less bell-like than her own. The deep neckline of the gown showed off the girl's plump breasts and swanlike neck to perfection. Her dark eyes twinkled merrily, and she did not look the least bit abashed by her half-brother's tone.

"I beg your pardon, Ned," she said with a casual air that underscored her lack of contrition, "but Frederick told me that James was here, and I did so want to beg him to stay to dine with us. Mama is in one of her pets, you see, and he is the best one to smooth her over. It is about the painting, I'm afraid."

James looked startled and turned in protest to his sister. "Surely you did not show her—"

"Don't be absurd," Lydia said, grinning at him, "and you need not look so wildly at Ned either. He saw both portraits the day you put them in the gallery and laughed till I thought his sides would split, so he will not scold you for painting them. I refer to Mama's own portrait. You were very cruel, you know, to refuse to paint her yourself when she pleaded with you to do so."

"Lydia," Rothwell said in a long-suffering tone, "this is neither the time nor the place to discuss that. May I make known to you Miss MacDrumin, who will be our guest here for a time."

Maggie said instantly, "But I do not want to stay!

You must know you have no right to keep me here against my will."

He looked directly at her. "But I do have that right. According to what James has told me, you can remain here either as my guest or in my custody. If you require to have the matter made clearer, I believe we can find at least one magistrate quite willing to explain it to you. Do you care to put it to a test?"

She swallowed her fury. "No, sir. I believe you would get your own way anywhere in London."

"I am glad you understand that. Now, as to the next point, you are to have nothing to do with anyone living in Essex Street, particularly the dowager Viscountess Primrose. You see," he added gently when she grimaced, "I name names." He paused as if he meant her to digest this information, but when he spoke again his tone was more cordial. "While you are here, you will find a companion in my sister, and I suppose, since all your belongings were stolen, I will be obliged to provide you with some proper clothing. Lydia, have you a gown you can lend Miss MacDrumin so that she can join us for dinner this evening?"

Lydia looked Maggie over from tip to toe, her eyes bright with curiosity. "I think so. Will James stay to dine, too?"

"He will. No, no," he added when James sputtered a protest. "You got us into this, and you will do your best to divert your mother this evening so that Miss MacDrumin is not required to spend the whole of it explaining her antecedents. I think, Miss MacDrumin, that it would be as well if you were to neglect to provide my mother with your entire history. We will simply tell her that you found yourself stranded in London after your baggage and coach were stolen, and requested our assistance."

"As you please," Maggie said, wishing he were not still standing and looking right at her. There was something about the man that made it difficult to fling hard words at him—except when one was in an utter passion—even when one desired nothing so much as to do so.

"Much better," he said approvingly. "You run along with Lydia for the present and make yourself tidy. I will order dinner put back an hour for your convenience."

Lydia exclaimed, "Oh, Ned, Mama will be so put out! She declares that she is exhausted from sitting all afternoon for her portrait and must have her dinner as soon as possible, so that she can retire for the night to recuperate."

"Blast me," James said, "I have never heard such humdudgeon in all my life. How can she be exhausted from sitting? And why, pray tell, has she decided to have yet another portrait painted? When I refused to paint her, she said nothing about finding someone else. Indeed, the whole point of the exercise, she insisted, was that she wished to puff off to all her acquaintance that her dearest son, the artist, had painted her."

"The Court painter, don't you mean to say?" Rothwell said in a tone so dry that Maggie's thoughts were diverted from her own troubles at once. She looked curiously at James.

"As to that," he said, flushing, "I certainly never told her any such pretentious nonsense. She made it all up herself."

"She merely misunderstood our somewhat heated discussion of the matter, and you did not set her right," Rothwell pointed out.

"No, but see here, Lydia, I know she never meant to ask someone else to paint her portrait. Why, Father had a formal one done before he died, to match his own."

Chuckling, Lydia exchanged a look with Rothwell and said, "But that is just the problem, dear James. That portrait was done so many years ago that it is now quite out of date."

"But she wore a masquerade costume! It was all the rage to do so for such portraits then, just as it still is now. How can the thing be out of date?"

"Oh, James, don't be a ninnyhammer. Mama isn't having an entirely new portrait done. She is merely having her hair repainted so that the style will be *au courant.*"

James stared at her. "You cannot be serious."

"Oh, yes, I am. Just you go and look at it. Mr. Sayers has been painting it in Mama's sitting room, and she is not there now, for she has gone upstairs to dress for dinner."

"Which is what Miss MacDrumin must do," Rothwell said. "Take her up at once, Lydia. She can have the bedchamber overlooking the Privy Garden, next to yours. See that her needs are attended to, and tell your mama that though I sympathize with her exhaustion, the needs of our guest must come first."

"Well, I will tell her that," Lydia said doubtfully, "but I cannot pretend to think she will be pleased."

"Her wrath, as always," Rothwell said, "will be visited upon my head, not yours. Oh, go along, James," he added when that young man moved toward the only other door in the room and placed a tentative hand on the latch. "See the fool portrait. I can tell you would like nothing better, but when you have seen it, perhaps you will return and play a game of chess with me. There is so rarely anyone here who can give me a decent game."

Looking over his shoulder in evident gratification, James said, "Well, I will then, but I do want to see what Sayers is doing. He's a very good man, you know, for that sort of thing."

At a sign from Rothwell, Lydia touched Maggie's arm and said, "We must hurry, for I daresay you will want a bath."

Rothwell said firmly, "She will."

Flushing, Maggie looked at him and encountered a look of unexpected warmth that nearly undid her. She had been watching and listening to the others with no little amazement, but she had been singularly aware of the earl nonetheless. His tone of voice had reverted to the lazy drawl he had employed at the beginning of the interview, and she had actually begun to wonder if she had imagined certain other qualities he had seemed to possess. But his whole expression had changed, and the way he looked at her now, instead of disconcerting her, sent a glow through her whole body. She was still annoyed with him. She still did not know precisely what to make of him. But as she turned to go with Lydia, she felt as if she were walking away from a cheerful fire out into the cold and the unknown.

Alone again, Rothwell wondered what he had got himself into. That his guest was the damned little Jacobite he had named her was certain, and no doubt Lydia, whose penchant for rebellion had prompted her upon more than one occasion to endorse the ridiculous allegiance such persons maintained to the Pretender, was even now pressing Miss MacDrumin to relate details of her past, while expressing delight in her presence at Rothwell House.

Though it had been foolish of the young woman to

claim his protection, now that she had, he could not cast her adrift, for in fact, as one of his newest tenants, she was entitled to look to him to shield her from harm, a point she had not hesitated—albeit obliquely—to fling in his teeth. And he certainly could not abandon her if it meant insuring her further association with Lady Primrose and others of that sort. Far better that the chit should remain safely beneath his roof, where he could keep an eye on her and perhaps even exploit her acquaintance to learn more about the intended movements of Charles Stewart. She could have no idea that the Pretender's imminent visit was anticipated with such interest by certain members of the British government.

She would no doubt be angry to know that he looked upon her in such a way. He was as certain of that as if he had known her for years instead of less than an hour. She certainly was not what he had first thought her, and Jacobite or not, one had to admire her for her lack of feminine guile. She was reprehensibly careless and too quick to speak without thinking; but she was direct, impulsive, and uncomplicated, which, in a day when women were generally manipulative, fawning, flirtatious, and greedy, made her unique among her sisters. And if she held her temper on a shorter leash than most women of breeding, and had touched him on the raw with her damned accusations of neglect, she was nonetheless remarkably intriguing.

He looked forward to seeing the change his sister would contrive in Miss MacDrumin's appearance, for he had a notion the little Scottish lass could be made to look very well indeed. That thought stimulated others, and he allowed his imagination free rein until he was interrupted by James's return.

James was shaking his head. "It's dashed nonsense,

Ned. What maggot gets into females' brains to stir them to such absurd lengths? If Mama is having her hair repainted, surely she ought also to have her face redone as well, but it's been left alone."

Rothwell chuckled. "You must not expect me to condemn her for her vanity, my dear James. Have you not accused me of being the worst offender in the family in that regard?"

James eyed him warily. "I have accused you of that and worse, Ned, but you rarely find such comments amusing. I own, I had expected you to be uncomfortably grim about all this. I know you must be vexed, but Dev and I could scarcely keep her with us in the bridge house, you know."

"You did exactly right," Rothwell said, rising to fetch the chess board, then adding as he took his seat again, "You may take white if you like. I believe I had that honor the last time we played." When James had moved his king's pawn, Rothwell moved his own to meet it, saying with a smile, "Perhaps the time has come for me to learn more about my Scottish estate."

VI

Lydia did not allow Maggie much time for introspection, demanding the moment the library door shut behind them, "Where do you come from, Miss Mac-Drumin, that you speak of being held against your will, and why did my brother talk of magistrates?"

"Please, Lady Lydia, I wish you will call me Maggie. Never before have I been called Miss MacDrumin so frequently in so short a span of time, and indeed, I am not accustomed to it."

"Well, I will do so, but only if you call me Lydia, and only if you answer my questions."

Maggie smiled ruefully, realizing that her head was beginning to ache again. "They are not questions that I can answer briefly, I fear, but I will tell you as much as I can." She glanced around. "This is not the place for it, however."

"Secrets?" Lydia's delicately arched eyebrows soared upward. "Oh, I love secrets!" Tucking Maggie's hand in the crook of her arm, she added cheerfully, "Come upstairs now, and I will show you your room before I take you to mine. Formal dress is not required tonight, for no company will be here, so a simple gown will suffice if we can but find one to fit you. My maid will delight in dressing you, I know, but you are so small and I so much taller, that I think she may have trouble finding something of mine that you can wear."

She showed Maggie to a well-appointed bedchamber decorated in shades of peach and white, with a floral carpet on the highly polished floor and peach-colored hangings around the bed. Bed steps had been cunningly devised to serve as tables flanking it, and the coverlet was exquisitely embroidered. Accustomed to much more Spartan surroundings, it having never occurred to her to decorate a bedchamber, Maggie gazed around in pure delight.

" 'Tis a marvelous room," she said, "but faith, it must be meant for royalty."

Lydia laughed. "No such thing! Lud, even if the king did not have his own residence nearby, I doubt that Ned would invite him to stay here, although he has frequently invited him to visit Rothwell Park—in Derbyshire," she added with a sigh, "which is quite the most distant and dismal place imaginable. Fortunately, Ned has duties that keep him in town most of the year."

"What sort of duties?" Maggie asked. Rothwell was proving to be quite an enigma, and it occurred to her that the more she could find out about him, the better she might deal with him.

But Lydia only laughed and said they were not of the least interest to females. "James says they mostly have to do with lending money, and although James *would* say that, I think it must be true, for really I think Ned must spend most of his time with his tailor and his barber." Then, literally pulling Maggie out of the room, she said, "We must make haste, for before I make you tell me all about yourself, I daresay you will want a bath. I should if I were such a mess as you are."

Feeling the telltale warmth creep into her cheeks again, Maggie said, "I assure you, I do not customarily look like this, but I have had the most extraordinary day imaginable."

"You shall tell me all about it," Lydia said, "but first I will ring for Tilda and your bath water, and then I must run tell Mama that James will stay to dine and that Ned has ordered dinner put back. She will be displeased about that, but she will be glad about James and will no doubt celebrate his presence by treating us to a dish of her precious Bohea after dinner, so I must tell Fields to be sure someone puts sugar on the tray. Although it is quite awful to put stuff in one's tea, James utterly detests Bohea without it."

Her maid, a buxom, rosy-cheeked young woman, entered soon after she tugged the bell, whereupon Lydia gave swift orders and left the room. Tilda was gratifyingly unconcerned with Maggie's history, paid no heed whatsoever when she removed the papers from her corset, and not only produced upon request a pretty reticule for her to put them in but seemed delighted by the challenge of turning her out in prime style in less than an hour's time.

"Though I don't mind telling you, miss, it will be something to accomplish. How would you like me to do up your hair?"

Discussion of this and other such important topics occupied them until Lydia's return. She came in smiling, and said that her mama was just as displeased as she had feared she would be. "And she ought not to be, for James brought her some lovely lotion for her face. He is always bringing her things, because he is nearly as good at mixing up such stuff as he is as doctoring people. But, now, Maggie, tell me everything!"

Maggie obliged. The bath had eased her headache,

and there was quite enough to tell without actually disclosing her real reason for coming to London so that between revealing just what sort of court painting James did and deciding what to wear, what remained of the hour passed swiftly. Ready at last, she stood before Lydia's looking glass, gazing at herself with pleasure, still dazed by the thought that such a splendid outfit was considered to be informal. Lydia explained that the term meant only that one's gown covered all that lay beneath, except sometimes for a bit of petticoat if one's gown opened up the front. Maggie's white petticoat, speedily hemmed a good four inches shorter than it had been, did not show, for the front section of her pink damask gown was undivided and fastened around her waist beneath the loose, trailing back of the gown. Her bodice was laced over a snowy white handkerchief, and the dress was worn over a small hoop with a lacy white apron.

"The hoop will take up any extra length," Lydia had said, "for I never wear one with that gown. It must be a small hoop though, for otherwise you will be overturning chairs and stools in Mama's bedchamber."

"Her bedchamber?" Maggie said, tucking an errant strand of hair back into the elaborate twist of curls that Tilda had arranged, unpowdered, atop her head while the maid lightly powdered her face with a hare's foot. "What on earth would I be doing in your mother's bedchamber?"

"Eating your dinner," Lydia said, her eyes twinkling. "Oh, you need not try to conceal your astonishment. I promise you, it is not a common English custom. Mama is merely determined to get back at Ned after he put back dinner to accommodate you. She heard once that kings and queens dine and even hold audiences in their bedchambers, so she is quite determined to do so to-night. Just pretend it is the sort of thing everyone does and you will survive it perfectly well."

She too was ready, and Maggie thought she looked like a princess in her emerald green gown with its embroidered and ruffled yellow silk apron. Everyone wore aprons, Lydia told her. It was all the rage to do so, even at quite formal parties.

Maggie slipped the reticule over her wrist, took the fan Tilda handed her, and followed Lydia from the room. Her heart began to thump as they approached the dowager's bedchamber, which proved to be a much more elaborately appointed room even than Lydia's. The rich red velvet hangings, dark wood furniture, and Turkey carpet were magnificent, albeit a trifle overwhelming, but Maggie soon forgot them in her amazement at finding her hostess reclining languidly against a huge pile of pillows in the bed, wearing a low-cut robe of brocaded purple silk with a tiny white-lace, beribboned cap perched atop hair that was expertly powdered and arranged in artistic puffs and curls. A single, enticing sausage curl dangled free, casting a shadow on one plump bare shoulder. She was attended by her tirewoman, a despotic-looking female with an air of vast superiority, who hovered over her, alert for the least sign that her services might be required.

The gentlemen were already present, but before either of them could utter a greeting, the dowager said haughtily, "Present that young woman to me at once, Lydia. It is just like Rothwell to thrust a guest upon me when he can see for himself that I am utterly undone by my extremely arduous day."

Lydia obediently introduced Maggie, adding, "You need not have dined with us, ma'am, if you are not feeling quite the thing. You'd have done much better to have ordered a tray brought up and left us to our own devices in the dining room."

"As if I should so much neglect my duties as hostess," Lady Rothwell said with a sniff. "I am sure I know as well as does Rothwell the honor due to guests in this house. Although," she added, shooting a gimlet look at Maggie, "it is generally thought a trifle odd to entertain a guest of whom one has never heard."

Rothwell said evenly, "I thought I had explained that Miss MacDrumin is the daughter of a once-powerful Highland chief—the very man, in fact, whose estates were awarded to me after the late uprising. She no sooner entered London than her coach was attacked by ruffians, her servants foully murdered, and all her belongings stolen. Naturally, she appealed to me for assistance. You would not have desired me to be so unkind as to refuse."

Casting him a look of acute dislike, the dowager said, "You will do as you wish, Rothwell, just as you always do."

James said hastily, "Now, really, Mama, you mustn't abuse Ned in front of Miss MacDrumin. Only think how uncomfortable you will make her."

The dowager turned to him and smiled, the expression altering her countenance considerably. Maggie saw then that she had once been pretty, and wondered if her temperament had been more agreeable as well. "My dearest one," Lady Rothwell said dotingly to her son, "the stuff you brought me made my skin as soft as a baby's. I cannot think why you waited so long before honoring us again with your company, but you are quite right to scold me," she added, turning to Maggie. "Pray forgive me, Miss MacDrumin, and do sit down now, all of you, so that they can begin to serve. I protest, I am quite, quite famished."

A table had been laid with all the accoutrements of a formal dinner, and while they had been talking, a footman had lighted two branched candlesticks. He stood ready now to assist Lydia to her chair, and a second man pulled one out for Maggie, while the two gentlemen moved to take their own seats unaided. Lady Rothwell apparently intended to dine from a tray.

The meal was one of the oddest Maggie had ever experienced, and she found herself utterly fascinated. Conversation was desultory, and the dowager bore her part in it with as much grace as if she had been sitting at the table with them instead of propped up in her bed. Indeed, aside from the odd setting, it might have been any family meal anywhere, until Rothwell raised his wineglass to toast the king.

Maggie hesitated to join in until she remembered similar toasts made by many of her Jacobite hosts. Then, as she raised her wineglass over her water glass, she saw that Lydia, opposite her, was doing the same thing. Their gazes met briefly, and seeing the glint of mischief in Lydia's dark eyes, Maggie glanced involuntarily at Rothwell.

He returned her look placidly but with slightly raised brows, and she murmured quickly, "To the king."

"James," Lady Rothwell said abruptly, "have you seen my new portrait? I must tell you, dearest one, that I am still prodigiously vexed that you would not oblige me."

"And I have told you, Mama," James replied patiently, "that I do not paint such stuff. Sayers is doing an excellent job."

"Stuff?" Lady Rothwell was indignant. "How can

you, the Court painter, refuse to paint a portrait of your own mother?"

Exchanging a look with Rothwell, James drew a deep breath and said, "I am no such thing, ma'am, and I am sorry if anything I might have said gave you such an impression. I do portraits, of course, but I promise you, they are not what you would like."

Lydia giggled, and James shot her a quelling look before he added, "I have been painting anecdotal court pictures, ma'am. It is quite a different thing, I assure you."

"But truly a most fortunate thing," Maggie murmured.

"What's that you say?" the dowager demanded. "I tell you, I do not know what modern manners have come to. In any event, what can you possibly know of my son and his business? I do not understand you, any of you. Court is Court, is it not?"

Lydia and James both began to speak at once, but Rothwell's voice carried easily over theirs and silenced them. "James paints common scenes, ma'am, street scenes and the goings-on in the law courts, much like the ones that fellow William Hogarth paints. Surely, you have seen *his* work."

Lady Rothwell sniffed and directed a stern look at her son. "I certainly have, and it will not do, James. I have indulged your every wish since the day you were born, but you cannot expect to make a good match if you sully your name by associating with riffraff. I have spoken to Lady Portland about her niece, the heiress one. Coming into more than eight thousand a year, she tells me. 'Tis not all I had hoped for you, of course," she added, glaring at Rothwell, "but it will do well enough, so there must be no more associations with common rabble."

"Please, Mama—"

"Now, don't fuss. I know what is best for you, just as I know what will suit Lydia. Children simply must trust their parents in these matters, for they lack the experience necessary to make such important choices for themselves. Maria, move that branch of candles a little, if you please." When this was done to her satisfaction, she turned archly back to her son and said, "You have neglected us for so long, James dear, that I daresay you have not heard that your sister has made quite a marvelous impression on young Evan Cavendish. Just think if she can bring him round her thumb, what a triumph that would be!"

Lydia wrinkled her nose distastefully. "Mr. Cavendish is the sort of man who thinks the sun rises and sets by his actions merely because he is some sort of distant relation to the Duke of Devonshire. He simply oozes condescension."

"You should feel honored that he took notice of you," Lady Rothwell said. "Every young woman in town will set her cap for him next Season, and having met him before, you might well walk off with the prize by showing only a scrap of resolution."

Lydia opened her mouth to reply, but once again Rothwell forestalled her, deftly turning the subject to a more general one. Maggie was grateful to him. She had seen a contentious look on James's face similar to the one on Lydia's, and she had not the least doubt that had Rothwell not intervened, an ugly scene might have ensued.

When they finished eating, the dowager did offer them tea, and a large, locked tea chest was produced. She unlocked it with a small key she wore around her neck, and Maggie watched the subsequent ritual with fascination. She did not much care for the taste of

Bohea, and would have been willing to put a bit of sugar in hers had her hostess not made it plain by her reaction to James's liberal additions that she did not approve. They did not linger afterward, for Lady Rothwell announced her intention of retiring immediately.

Rothwell bore his half-brother off to play another game of chess, and Lydia took Maggie back to her bedchamber, clearly ripe for confidences. Shutting the door, she leaned against it and said dramatically, "If Mama forces me to marry Mr. Cavendish, I vow and declare I shall throw myself off the new Westminster Bridge into the Thames."

"Faith, you would not really do such a dreadful thing, would you?" Maggie said, making herself comfortable in one of the room's several well-cushioned chairs and thinking Lydia sounded quite as ridiculous as Lord Thomas had sounded that afternoon but wanting nothing to spoil this budding and, for her, unusual friendship. If she was to stay in this house for even a few days, she would welcome kindness, and she liked the younger girl for her warmth and her open manner. "Please, Lydia," she said earnestly, "you must not say such things, even in jest."

Lydia's pretty mouth pouted, but then her eyes began to dance and she said with a chuckle, "Well, I am much more likely to elope, and how Mama would hate that, for she sets such store by the family name, you know, and the vast importance of the Earls of Rothwell. Not that she thinks so much of Ned, for to be sure he is descended from only one of King Edward I's queens, whilst James and I can boast descent from two."

"Faith, can you indeed?"

Lydia chuckled again. " 'Tis prodigious absurd, is it not, but that is why Mama sides with Ned against me in this instance. She does not hold with adding younger sons to the pineapple plant that represents our family tree. But she will soon discover that nothing can prevent what is already predestined."

Though Maggie's headache had all but disappeared during dinner, it was beginning to return, and what with talk of watery graves, loathsome young men, and pineapple plants, she felt nearly as dizzy as she had when she had come to her senses in Alsatia. In self-defense, she fastened her attention on Lydia's final word. "Predestined? Whatever do you mean?"

"Lud, 'tis the most wondrous thing," Lydia said ardently, moving away from the door and drawing the dressing chair up next to Maggie's. Seated, she explained, "Little more than two months ago, at a fair, a gypsy fortune teller read my palm and told me I would meet my heart's desire dressed all in blue, walking along the Mall, which is precisely how I chanced to encounter Lord Thomas Deverill. He was strolling with James at the time, and it was love at first sight for both of us. 'Twas prodigious romantic, but Ned, thinking his power so great that he can even shackle Providence, has most cruelly forbidden poor Thomas the house, and takes every care that I shall not meet him in company.

"I have met Lord Thomas," Maggie said, adding tactfully, "He seems to be rather a passionate young man."

"Lud, yes," Lydia agreed, "and I am excessively glad to know you have met him, for I collect that he must have been in James's company when you did, and when I tell you that after Ned forbade him the house, he actually threatened to poison himself, you will understand my relief. And before you accuse *him* of jesting, let me tell you that once before when Ned was cruel, Thomas actually tried to hang himself with one of my hair ribbons. So you see, I have good cause for my relief. That is . . . you do not suppose he might have poisoned himself *after* you met him!"

"No, indeed," Maggie said, overcome by her sense of the absurd. "He had altogether given up the notion of poison in favor of drowning himself."

"What?"

"Oh, don't be a goose," Maggie said, chuckling. "He had already looked at the water and decided not to do it after all. Really, Lydia, don't you find him just a little silly?"

"No, I do not! And it is unkind of you to suggest such a thing when, if it were not for Tilda's being cousin to James's Mrs. Honeywell, I should have no way even to hear about him, for Ned keeps me so close these days that it is well-nigh impossible to do anything of which he does not approve."

Having learned enough to realize that Rothwell had excellent cause to watch over his half-sister, Maggie was nonetheless sincere when she said, "I am sorry to hear that, for he has said he does not want me to leave the house and I simply must contrive to evade his protection at least once, and rather soon, too."

"Where must you go?" Lydia asked, instantly diverted from her own difficulties.

Maggie hesitated. The last thing she wanted to do was imperil Charles Stewart or his cause, and she was by no means sure Lydia could be trusted with even the smallest of secrets, but she was rapidly becoming convinced that if she was going to evade Rothwell's protection, she would need help from someone, and she did not think she could look to James to provide it.

Lydia had been watching her and now her eyes widened and she said in a voice of dawning excitement,

"You wish to meet with your friends! That is why Ned looked so forbidding when he said you were not to set foot in that particular street. I do not recall which it was, but I did wonder about his order, because it seemed such an odd thing, and I know nothing about Lady Primrose. Is she a Jacobite? Are you? I saw how you toasted the king. Oh, you can tell me, Maggie. You must know that you can! Did you not see that I, too, toasted the king over the water?"

Making up her mind, Maggie said, "I did see you, Lydia, but anyone might overhear us now, so I cannot give you a full explanation. Suffice it to say that I must at least contrive to get a message to Essex Street, for not only will her ladyship be wondering what became of me but I am expected to attend a masquerade ball at her house tomorrow week."

"A masquerade! How exciting, for you must know that because the stupid king, though he was used to be quite fond of such entertainments, has taken them in dislike, all due to Elizabeth Chudleigh's attending one, two summers ago at Ranelagh Gardens, dressed—or undressed, one should say—as Iphigenia. She is maid of honor to the Princess of Wales, and his majesty was quite shocked, though he said it was no more than might be expected from that household, for he holds them all in the greatest dislike. At all events, then the earthquakes came, you see, which so many felt to be a judgment—"

"Earthquakes?"

"Lud, yes, did you not feel them in Scotland? The first was in February, the second a month to the day later, and so naturally a third was expected in April. Many families evacuated to the country. We did not, for Ned said it was all foolishness, but Mama and I did have warm earthquake gowns made, so that if we had to sit up all night outside we should not catch our deaths.''

"And was there a third?''

"No, but masquerades fell sadly out of fashion, and even at Ranelagh, they are now called ridottos instead, and loo masks are held up on sticks like quizzing glasses instead of being properly tied round one's head with strings to conceal one's identity. Indeed, there has been only one so far this year, at Ranelagh, for most balls are now in the Venetian style. But I should adore to go to a proper old-fashioned masquerade!''

"Well, I must go,'' Maggie said, a little disturbed at having aroused such enthusiasm, "but first I must somehow get a message to Essex Street.''

"But that part is quite easy,'' Lydia assured her. "Tilda frequently carries messages for me, and she can just as easily arrange to take one for you. Getting oneself out of the house is the difficult part, particularly since Ned said he would punish me most severely if I did any such thing again after the last time,'' she added with a mischievous twinkle.

Maggie grimaced. "I daresay I ought not to allow you to help me at all,'' she said.

" 'Pon rep, of course I will help you, but only if you promise to take me to the masquerade.''

"Don't be foolish,'' Maggie said, truly alarmed. "I certainly will do no such thing.''

"You must,'' Lydia said complacently. "You cannot manage to get there yourself without my help.''

Maggie stared at her in consternation, trying to think of an argument that might sway her. Finally she said rather weakly, "You said even you cannot evade your brother's all-seeing eyes.''

"Piffle. To meet real supporters of the true king, I would sell my soul. It is only necessary for us to scheme a little, and the first thing is to get a message to your friends."

Hoping that once she had engaged Lady Primrose's assistance, Lydia's would be unnecessary, Maggie agreed, and sending the message proved to be as easy as Lydia had promised; however, the reply, instead of promising the necessary assistance, begged her to stay away from Essex Street at all cost, since she had so unfortunately drawn the notice of the Earl of Rothwell. The message was couched in such terms as must have bewildered anyone intercepting it, but to Maggie it was perfectly clear, and quite unacceptable. She had set out to meet the prince, carrying messages assuring him of the support of his Highlanders, but it was not only to deliver these that she felt obliged to meet him. She wanted to make certain he understood the dire straits in which his Highland followers now found themselves.

That her plans might involve Lydia she could not like. Not only did she wish to keep the girl away from Essex Street for her own sake, but Maggie was afraid of Rothwell's reaction if he were to discover that she had taken his sister to a masquerade. She had seen a good deal of the earl in the few days since her arrival, and though he seemed disinclined to speak to her, she was very much aware of his presence. More than once she had caught his gaze upon her, and when it was warmly approving, she was grateful, but when she saw him looking bored or a stern, she found herself instantly hoping he would not discover her intent.

He had said nothing as yet about her future, and she was glad, for the last thing she wanted to hear was that he had arranged to send her home. That first night he had commanded his stepmama to escort her and Lydia the following day to the silk warehouses in Bedford

Street, where they had selected fabrics to be taken to Lady Rothwell's mantua maker. Lady Rothwell's woman accompanied them, so there had been no opportunity to slip away, although, in truth, Maggie had no wish to do so. The fashions had changed considerably since her last visit to Edinburgh, and while she remained under the elegantly attired Rothwell's roof, she had no wish to look like a country dowdy, and thus had been extremely grateful when the first gowns were delivered on Monday.

Throughout the course of these busy days her mind was fully engaged in seeking a way by which she might attend the ball herself without Lydia's company. Knowing she could not simply wait until Saturday and hope that whatever plan she made might succeed, she decided to make a practice attempt as soon as possible, but the first real opportunity did not present itself until Wednesday afternoon.

The earl had gone out shortly after breakfast, intending to spend the day in Westminster, and when the dowager ordered her carriage to take herself and Lydia into Mayfair to pay calls, Maggie enlisted Tilda's help. Donning one of Lydia's capes and a pair of new kid gloves, and with the maid at her side, she strode determinedly to the Privy Garden entrance and informed the footman on duty there that she and Tilda were going to a nearby shop to purchase ribbons for one of her new gowns.

The young man looked a trifle disconcerted, but in the face of her confident air, he moved to open the door.

"One moment, Miss MacDrumin."

Starting and barely stifling a sigh of exasperation, Maggie turned. "I thought you had gone out, Rothwell. Tilda and I were just going to purchase a few ribbons. Lydia said we might find some at one of the shops in Whitehall Yard."

He nodded as if in agreement but gestured languidly toward the open door of his library. "Step in here a moment, if you will. I daresay I can direct you to a better shop than Lydia's."

His demeanor was that of an amiable fop offering assistance on a matter of dress, and though Maggie was not deceived for a moment, with a glance at the footman, she capitulated. "Go back upstairs, Tilda. I shan't want you after all."

"Yes, miss," Tilda said, turning quickly away.

Striding to the center of the library and waiting only until she heard the door shut behind her, Maggie said without turning, "I suppose you think—"

"Never mind what I think," Rothwell said, sounding much closer than she had expected. "You do not want to hear it."

Turning, she found that he was quite near—so near, in fact that she had to look up to see his face—and thus she became aware of a delicate spicy scent before she saw that he was looking stern. The flintlike look that she had seen only once before was in his eyes again, and his voice was hard when he said, "I believed I had made my orders plain, but in the event that you somehow managed to misunderstand them, you are not to leave this house without a proper escort, which does not include my sister's doltish maidservant."

Maggie stiffened at his tone but could not help taking a step backward. To cover her confusion, she took a deep breath, glared at him, and stripped off her kid gloves. Then, turning away toward the cheerfully crackling fire in the hooded white marble fireplace, and holding out her hands in the hope that he would believe she sought only the fire's warmth, and not an escape from his disturbing closeness, she said over her shoulder, "You presume too much, sir. I am grateful for your protection, but I do not require your guidance. I am quite capable of deciding where I shall go and with whom."

"One hesitates to contradict a lady, of course," he said smoothly, "but the difficulties that brought you here prove quite conclusively that you are mistaken in that belief. I should dislike having to command my servants to prevent your leaving the house without my permission, but if you force me to it, that is precisely what I will do. London is a dangerous place, and since you refuse to promise that you will not associate with the many Jacobites in residence here, you leave me little choice."

Turning sharply, she snapped, "How dare you treat me like a prisoner, Rothwell!"

Seeing his lips twitch with amusement did nothing to quell her rising temper, but when he spoke, his tone was controlled. "I assure you, you are no prisoner. You may come and go as you choose, so long as you are with my stepmother or with Lydia and at least one stalwart footman. That is no more or less than the protection I provide to every female residing in this house. Even maidservants are expected to go in pairs or to request male escort before venturing into the public streets, for as you have discovered, the streets are not safe for unescorted females."

"Tilda was to go with me," Maggie said, gritting her teeth.

"Yes, but you are not a maidservant. Ladies of the house do not stir from its bounds without the escort of at least one or even two footmen. If you tell my stepmother that you wish to shop for ribbons, she will no doubt order her coach out for you, and perhaps Lydia will also wish to go."

In the face of this eminently reasonable and altogether maddening speech, Maggie was left with no recourse other than to submit with as much grace as she could muster. Blocked at every other gate, feeling she had no choice but to enlist Lydia's help, Maggie fully expected that young woman to be indignant when she learned that she had attempted to proceed without her.

But Lydia, hearing her tale of woe, only chuckled and said, "I told you to leave it to me, you know, but no doubt I am to blame for your lack of success. Oh, don't poker up like that. I said nothing to Ned, but he has had so much experience putting obstacles in my path when I wish to do things of which he does not approve that for him to deal with you is no doubt child's play by comparison. Look here, do you think perhaps your friends might come to fetch us by barge?"

Maggie turned to look out the window. They were in Lydia's bedchamber, overlooking the Privy Garden courtyard. "They dare not come here," she said. "I did not tell you before, but they fear being brought to your brother's notice."

"They have cause," Lydia said. "He is determined to help German George keep the Stewarts from recovering the throne of England. But we shan't let him stop us. Let me think."

Maggie was amused to see that Lydia had apparently fallen into a brown study, but she still felt uncomfortable allowing the girl to lend assistance. Had the confrontation with Rothwell not convinced her she would be a fool to make any other attempt to leave the house without help from someone experienced in defying him, she would not do it. It was wrong to encourage Lydia to go against Rothwell's wishes, and no doubt just as wrong to allow her to mix with Jacobites when her family opposed their cause.

That thought brought another, even more unpalatable, on its heels. Could Lydia's presence at the ball endanger the prince? A moment's thought was enough to dismiss the notion. What purpose was there in holding a masquerade, especially when such diversions were out of fashion and favor, if not to provide concealment for all who attended? Prince Charles Edward Stewart need reveal himself to no one outside the inner circle. No doubt there would be others among the guests as unsuspecting of his presence as Lydia would be. And as for any danger to Lydia herself, the chit would be as safe at a Jacobite ball as she was anywhere else in London. None would dare to harm Rothwell's sister. Her mind made up at last, Maggie said quietly, "Is there really a way we can elude your brother's protection, Lydia?"

"Oh, to be sure," she replied airily, "when I truly wish to get out, Ned never knows a thing about it. I allow him to catch me often enough that he thinks he has me utterly under his thumb, but when I wish to escape him, I can certainly do so."

"And you never get caught unless you want him to catch you?"

"Oh, no," Lydia said. Then, encountering Maggie's skeptical gaze, she blushed and said, "Well, not usually. I confess, there has been an occasion or two that I would as lief not discuss, but if it means a chance for me to meet real London Jacobites, I promise you we shall not be caught."

Maggie was still doubtful. She had learned enough about Rothwell's beautiful half-sister to know she was capable of saying, even believing, whatever would serve her interest best, but if the information she had received before coming to London held true, his highness was already in the city—and there were only three days left before Lady Primrose's masquerade ball.

As if Lydia had somehow intercepted her thoughts, she said abruptly, "It was foolish of you to arouse Ned's suspicions by attempting to slip out today, for now he will be doubly watchful, and if he should catch us, he will be most unpleasant about it."

Maggie said, "You really ought not to go with me, you know. It is quite unnecessary for both of us to risk his wrath."

"Piffle. Of course, I shall go with you. Now," she said, cutting off Maggie's next protest, "getting out on a Saturday evening is not so difficult even at this time of year, for there is always a party of some sort somewhere, but I believe this week Mama intends to take us to an insipid soiree at Lady Portland's. We cannot allow that, since the party will be a small one and we shall be entirely too noticeable to slip away. Moreover, Mama expects James to go with us, on account of Lady Portland's niece being such an heiress."

"Goodness, Lydia, I could not be party to allowing you to slip away from your mama at the Countess of Portland's house."

"No, did I not just say that would never answer? Now, hush, and let me give this more thought. 'Tis the greatest of pities that you stirred Ned's mistrust."

"I'm excessively sorry," Maggie said, meaning every word.

"Lud, do not repine," Lydia said. "You could not have known how fatal your actions might be."

"Hardly fatal," Maggie said dryly.

"Yes, fatal, for it utterly killed most of the opportunities we might have created for ourselves. 'Pon rep, I believe our only chance now rests upon the sacrifice of another."

"Sacrifice? Lydia, what on earth are you talking about? I won't allow you to sacrifice anyone."

"See here, Maggie, you cannot continually be putting up obstructions if I am to get us to that masquerade. You do absolutely wish to go, do you not?"

"Yes," Maggie said contritely. "I beg your pardon."

"Very well, then I fear we must use Oliver—Ned's bargeman, you know—and the reason I call that a sacrifice is that Ned said that if I managed to twist Oliver round my thumb just once more, he would turn him off without a character."

"But then—"

"We shan't get caught, Maggie, and even if we do, Oliver won't be cast off. I daresay Ned meant it at the time, but he is very fair about things, usually, and I do not think he will really turn the poor man off if he should chance to discover that he helped us. He will know it was all my doing, not Oliver's."

Maggie felt strongly that she had mixed a brew that was rapidly boiling out of control, but her determination to attend the masquerade was too great for her to quibble even over such details as sacrificing Oliver, and she realized that if she had to have Lydia's company, they would both be a great deal safer with Rothwell's brawny young bargeman than in one of the public barges or a hackney coach. If worse came to worst, she could always plead the man's case with Rothwell herself and say that, between them, she and Lydia had overcome Oliver's better judgment.

VII

Saturday, September 19, 1750

Constantly, even at times uncomfortably, aware of Miss MacDrumin, Rothwell realized that she had settled more quickly than he had expected into the routine of his household, and hoped she had given up her intention of stealing out in search of her Jacobite friends. But he was also aware that for the past few days Lydia had been behaving with uncharacteristic rectitude, and he had become increasingly suspicious of them both, so much so that he was presently having trouble attending to his conversation with Sir Dudley Ryder.

The two men sat in Rothwell's library, enjoying a late-afternoon glass of wine, but Sir Dudley's mind, as usual these days, was on business, specifically on the young Pretender's activities. He said sharply, "Are you listening, Ned? The city is alive with rumors that he is here."

Rothwell poured more wine from the decanter into Ryder's glass, settled back comfortably in his chair, and dragged his attention back to their conversation. With a guilty awareness in the back of his mind that he had said nothing to Ryder about his unusual guest, he said, "Do any of your rumors suggest that Charles is actually raising an army?"

"What other reason can you suggest for his presence?"

"If he really is in London," Rothwell said dampingly. "Calm yourself, my friend. We know for a fact that there is no army approaching the city, for you may be certain we should have heard by now if there were. At most, he is trying to arouse support amongst his precious Jacobites, and that may be entirely to our benefit. Let him learn how little support he actually has here."

"Are you so certain of that? My people seem to believe that both the city and the surrounding countryside are infested with those damned Jacobites."

Rothwell chuckled. "Your people justify their positions by keeping that particular pot boiling, my friend, and you ought to know better than to believe every single thing they tell you. Has anyone mentioned even the existence of an army?"

"No, but—"

"Has anyone suggested that the greater part of the English populace is so disenchanted with the *status quo* that they will leap to join the Stewart upstart if he beckons to them?"

"Well, no, not yet, but what of the damned Scots? They've never hesitated to attack us, given the least reason to do so, and they do not love King George."

"Nor do I love him if it comes to that," Rothwell said bluntly. "It is difficult for anyone save his own wife to love a man whose sympathies are entirely Hanoverian, and whose parsimony is carried to such lengths as to make George One look generous." He sighed. "So far has the British monarchy fallen."

Ryder smiled. "Is this treason I hear?"

"No, George Two is the lawful king, whatever the Jacobites would have us believe, and peace is better than war for all of us. We've had too much war for any sensible man to want more."

"I won't argue with that sentiment, but Charles Stewart means no good, Ned. You know that as well as I do."

"But I don't condemn the man for his stupid wishes, which is the primary difference between us, Ryder. Young Charles concocts ambition out of spun-sugar dreams, nothing more, and he has already shot his bolt, as he will soon discover for himself."

"But you know as well as I do that many people hate having a German king, and yearn for a return of the Stewarts."

Rothwell shrugged. "More spun-sugar, my friend. Only think of the ones you know personally who pretend to harbor such dreams. How many are capable of acting on them, and how many will simply disappear when action is demanded? I think most of your wicked Jacobites are like my silly sister, Lydia, who delights in toasting the king over her water glass, pretending that she supports the Stewart cause. Do you suppose for a minute that Lydia wants war, Ryder?"

"No, of course not, but most Jacobites are not like Lady Lydia," Ryder said, taking up his wineglass as if in response to Rothwell's mention of toasting, then pausing to add, "Why, she is a mere child and female at that."

Again Rothwell chuckled, his thoughts returning instantly to his guest. "Is it her sex or her youth that makes you believe she is no danger to the Crown? Think carefully before you answer, and remember, I pray you, that Joan of Arc and Lucretia Borgia were both young females when they wreaked their worst havoc amongst their enemies."

Ryder choked on his wine. "Of all the unnatural things to say about your own kith and kin, that is the worst! Good lack, Ned, next you will be suggesting that that sweet, innocent child is a traitor to the Crown!"

"No such thing," Rothwell said, regarding his friend with amusement. "I merely point out to you that you see threats where most likely none exist and yet have a tendency to see serenity where there might well be mayhem a-brewing."

"You've got maggots in your brain."

"I devoutly trust not. I have spent many years creating a peaceful existence for myself. I should very much dislike having it turned upside down through mere want of foresight." He was not thinking of his half-sister, though he could see that Ryder thought he was. Before his friend could retort, he added glibly, "Do you care to accompany me to Cupid's Gardens this evening? I had thought to see how the rabble are disporting themselves these days. We might pick up a rumor or two, as well."

"We might indeed, but since you give rumors no credence, I would prefer to have a pleasant dinner at the Cider Cellar, as I had planned to do. Indeed, I'd hoped you would dine with me and then take a look in at Drury Lane afterward, but—"

"Say no more. You had only to ask." Rothwell got to his feet, adding, "I will just tell them to inform my bargeman that I shan't require him this evening after all, and then I shall be entirely at your disposal."

He stepped into the hall to find Lydia on the point of entering from the central hall. She hesitated, clearly surprised to see him, but she said quickly and in a perfectly friendly way, "Good afternoon, Ned. Do you mean to dine with us this evening?"

"No, my dear. Won't you be dining with Lady Portland?"

"Oh, no, for it is not that sort of party, merely an evening of interminable poetry and music. I am persuaded that it will be unconscionably boring, and feel rather guilty at subjecting poor Maggie to it at all, particularly when Mama is so distressed at James's refusing to escort us. I fear she is quite determined to match him with Lady Portland's wealthy niece."

Dryly, he said, "Shall I gratify her by offering to replace James tonight, puss?"

He thought she looked appalled but her recovery was so swift that he told himself he was mistaken, becoming certain of it when she smiled sunnily, saying, "I know you are jesting, Ned, but it is not at all funny. Mama would make us all most uncomfortable if you even suggested such a thing. Oh, hello, Sir Dudley," she added, making him a curtsy. "I did not know you were here."

"We are on the point of departing to dine at the Cider Cellar, my lady," Ryder said. "That is, I thought we were. Did you not come out here to dismiss your bargeman, Ned?"

"I did," Rothwell said, noting with amusement that his sister seemed delighted by Sir Dudley's presence, and wondering if she were rather more interested in his friend than he had previously thought she was. By the time he had arranged for word to be sent to his bargeman, and for his cloak, gloves, stick, and hat to be fetched for him, Lydia had disappeared and he was able to dismiss even that brief notion as a foolish one.

* * *

Maggie was seated in the window embrasure in her bedchamber, idly watching a pair of gulls fight over some morsel or other in the courtyard below, when Lydia burst into the room, fairly crowing in triumphant delight.

"Our worries are over, Maggie! I did not even have to try to cozen Oliver into leaving Ned at Cupid's Gardens long enough to row us to Essex Stairs. 'Tis a good thing, too, because I think that it might well have proved to be beyond even my powers of persuasion. Moreover, how could we know Oliver would be able to get away to fetch us, and how could he have known when to do so? Truly, the whole venture was fraught with peril, but now 'twill be as easy as winking."

"What has happened?" Maggie, having little faith in her new friend's powers of persuasion, had been ready to give up altogether once they had discovered that Rothwell intended to avail himself of his barge that evening. It was no more, she had told herself, than they ought to have expected, for Fate was notoriously perverse in such matters. But Lydia's beaming face gave her hope again. "Has Oliver agreed to take us, then?"

"Of course, he has. I told you he would two days ago. I went down to the hall, looking for one of the maids to send out with a message, and most fortunately, before I found one, Ned came to say he means to dine with Sir Dudley, and since they go to St. James's Square, they'll take chairs or a coach, which leaves us Oliver all to ourselves. He can await our return at Essex Stairs, which will be much the best thing, I promise you."

Maggie believed it. She thought they ought also to arrange for Oliver to accompany them from the river to Lady Primrose's house, for she had no notion how far up Essex Street it was to be found, and as she had discovered during her short time in London, anything might happen. She was not so much concerned for herself as for Lydia. Just the thought now that she would be taking Rothwell's sister to a Jacobite ball made her wince, for she had been imagining these three days past what the earl's reaction would be if he should find out. There being no way to get out of taking Lydia, however, she pushed her fears aside and demanded to know precisely what the minx had done.

"Well, I had racked my brain for an answer to our problem, for I am not one to give up easily, you know, and I had pretty nearly decided that the best thing would be to send for Thomas to meet us in the Privy Gardens with a carriage, and then to sneak out across the Richmond House terrace, but that would have meant bribing one of her grace's footmen to leave the gate unlocked, and not being certain which one would be on duty there today—"

"Lydia, stop," Maggie begged, not even attempting to conceal her dismay. "Richmond House! How could you think of trespassing there? Even if we had done so abominable a thing, we could not have enlisted Lord Thomas's aid in such a cause as this."

"Oh, piffle, of course we could, only as it happens we need not do so, so I merely told him to meet us at the ball instead."

"You what?" Feeling faint, Maggie sat straighter on her chair and stared at Lydia, dumbfounded. "You didn't."

"But I did. It is a perfectly splendid opportunity for us to meet, since there is not the least chance of Ned's turning up. I have told you and told you how difficult he makes it for us to see each other, and even if one or another of his friends is present, which is most unlikely, no one will recognize us because it is to be a masquerade. Thomas will be masked, and so will everyone else, and of course we will leave before the unmasking. And do not say that he was not invited, for that would be the merest quibble, since I was not invited either!"

"No, you were not," Maggie said tartly, "and, in faith, I ought not to let you go. There is no reason that I cannot entrust myself alone to Oliver. Surely, he would see me safely to Essex Stairs. There is no need for you to go at all."

"Oliver would tell Ned," Lydia said, glaring at her.

"I suppose you mean by that, that you would tell him to do so," Maggie retorted. "What an abominable girl you are."

"I'm not, and I wouldn't! Well, perhaps I would, but it would be only because you would be mean not to take me. This may be the only opportunity I have in my whole life to take part in a great cause, and I simply must do so. But I would not have to make Oliver tell, Maggie. You are nothing to him, you know, and Ned is his employer. Oliver would feel obliged to tell him."

"Then why—"

"Because Oliver never does tell on me, that's why," Lydia interjected with a decided note of triumph in her voice. When Maggie frowned, however, the younger girl abandoned her attitude for one of pure entreaty. "Oh, Maggie, pray don't be angry with me. Please, please, take me with you!"

"Lydia, it simply is not right. Though it is terribly important that I get to that ball, I really ought not to take you, and in any case, it would be utterly wicked to allow poor Oliver to lose his position on my account or yours."

"He won't," Lydia said stubbornly. "Ned won't turn him off, I tell you. He never blames anyone else for my misdeeds. If he does find out, he will scold me and I daresay he will have a few harsh words for you as well, but it will be worth it. Well, won't it?" she demanded. "Only think if one day they should succeed in placing Bonnie Prince Charlie on the throne. I vow, I long to see him there. Everyone says he is dreadfully handsome!"

"He is pretty enough, I suppose," Maggie said with a sigh.

"You have seen him! Oh, tell me, what is he like?"

"He is very grand," Maggie said. "He was sitting in his tent when I visited his encampment with some girls from my school. We had slipped away just to see him, and there were other ladies there from the town as well. Everyone made a circle around his tent, and after a time, he came out. He saluted us, then mounted his horse and rode off to view his men. Soon all the ladies of Edinburgh were wearing white cockades, whatever their political persuasion. They ordered tartan dresses, stitched Jacobite mottos on pincushions and garters, and many even sent him presents of plate, linen, and other such things."

"Oh, I wish I had seen him," Lydia said, sighing deeply. "I have only seen his likeness etched on a Jacobite wineglass."

Maggie smiled. "It was exciting, to be sure, but life in Edinburgh was not so pleasant then, and even though the ladies thought him wonderful, their menfolk did not like him so well."

"But so many followed him!"

"Highlanders followed him," Maggie said quietly. "Too many lowlanders prefer peace to making war, even in a rightful cause; and indeed, Lydia, I do not know that he will be more succe—" She broke off, aghast at what she had nearly given away, then quickly covered her slight hesitation by saying, "We do not know that he can ever succeed."

"Perhaps the people we meet tonight will encourage him to do so," Lydia said, adding cheerfully, "and at all events, there will now be no difficulty getting away, because as soon as I told Mama that I had the headache a little, she agreed that you and I ought to remain quietly at home for the evening, and I am quite sure she has said nothing about that to Ned. Indeed, I think she means to press Lady Portland to assist her in making a match between poor James and that niece of hers, and thinks our presence would impede her efforts. It is of no account, however, for James will never agree to marry her."

"I thought younger sons were generally made to do what their elders thought best for them," Maggie said.

Lydia, moving to take a pink silk domino from her wardrobe, chuckled and said, "Mama never knows whether to be angrier with Ned when he tells James what to do or when he refuses to do so. It is sometimes most amusing. But James is very recalcitrant, and I daresay even Ned could not force him to wed where he does not choose to do so. I think," she added with a more thoughtful air, "that James—like certain other younger sons—intends to marry only where he can discover a mutual affection. He will not wed merely to fill his pockets with silver or even gold."

Ignoring the oblique reference to other younger sons, Maggie said, "But surely James would not marry to disoblige his mama."

"N-no." Lydia sounded uncertain, but then she added with more assurance, "But he would not marry just to oblige her, either." When Maggie did not reply,

Lydia rang for Tilda and said, "We had better begin to dress now, for we must be ready to slip out as soon as it is dark enough for us not to be seen."

Maggie agreed, and although she was nervous about deceiving Rothwell, Lydia's confidence had convinced her that slipping out of the house would present no real difficulty. Not until the two of them were tiptoeing down the service stairs to the ground floor did she remember the footmen in the water-stairs passage. But when she expressed her fear, hissing the words close to Lydia's ear, her companion chuckled openly, saying, "Never fear, Tilda will have called our man away to help her with some odd thing or other, I promise you."

"But what of the other? Surely, he will mention seeing us. You said before that you don't even know which it will be."

"There will not be anyone by now," Lydia said confidently. "Her grace, being in mourning, does not entertain, and although she keeps a man there during the day, she does not at night. Anyone who visits her after dark knows to enter from the Privy Gardens, and our man is well able to guard her terrace gate."

As she had promised, the way was clear, and they hurried through the passage gate to the water stairs. Oliver awaited them with a large grin on his face, and held the barge steady with one oar while they boarded and made themselves comfortable. The air was chilly, and they wrapped themselves gratefully in the furs and blankets stored beneath the seats.

The moon had not yet risen, and the dark sky was full of stars. The river glimmered with the reflected torchlight and lamplight of the many windows over-looking it. Westminster Bridge cast a dark shadow, its arches outlined by the gleaming water beyond. As they passed beneath the bridge, Maggie heard the lively sounds of an organ and violin, punctuated by shrieks of laughter, coming from up ahead.

Beside her, Lydia gave one of her low chuckles. "Those lanterns you see yonder are hanging in the trees of Cuper's Gardens," she said. "Most folk call them Cupid's Gardens, and nice girls don't go there. Sometimes," she added when another burst of feminine laughter sounded across the water, "I think nice girls don't have nearly as much fun as not-nice girls do."

Maggie, aware that Oliver could hear every word they said, thought she ought to say something either wise or blighting, or at least attempt to change the subject; however, she could think of no wiser course than to ask about sights they were passing, and she had heard enough about them from James, so she held her tongue, hoping Lydia would take the hint and do likewise.

The hope was a futile one, but although Lydia kept up a stream of artless chatter, Oliver was rowing with the current and it was not long before they reached the stairs with the tall narrow archway at the top. Embarking, Lydia gave Oliver strict orders to stay right where he was, and Maggie, realizing now that he would be loath to leave his vessel, did not argue. In any case, once they passed beneath the high stone arch, she saw that they would have no difficulty finding their way.

Lady Primrose's house was near the river, and a steady stream of persons wearing rich dominos, fancy cloaks, and character costumes were descending from chairs and coaches in the street. Adjusting their dominos and masks, she and Lydia joined the throng and entered a high-ceilinged, narrow entryway, lighted by the myriad candles of an enormous crystal chandelier and dominated by a stairway that circled and swooped in a polished mahogany spiral up and up toward the domed and painted ceiling.

Their hostess awaited them at the first landing, unmasked and richly dressed. She was flanked by a couple Maggie did not know, but who were dressed as Henry VIII and Jane Seymour. All three extended gloved hands to each guest, murmuring welcome but making no effort to identify anyone. Maggie, squeezing Lady Primrose's hand significantly, let the person in front of her move beyond earshot before she leaned nearer and whispered, " 'Tis Maggie MacDrumin, my lady."

Her ladyship's brown eyes widened in dismay, but she kept herself otherwise well in hand, saying faintly, "Welcome, my dear. Just go with the others. The orchestra is tuning up and will begin playing a grand march in a few minutes. We hope you enjoy your evening."

But Maggie was not to be put off so easily. She had not expected to find his highness receiving guests with his hostess, for it would be much too dangerous, but she realized now that it was entirely possible he would be in the same house with her and never make himself known. How on earth was she to meet with him?

"Please, my lady, you must arrange for me to—"

"The ladies' withdrawing room," Lady Primrose said firmly, "is off the next landing." Pointedly, she turned to greet Lydia, who curtsied, murmured politely, and hurried after Maggie.

When they entered the ballroom, the orchestra could scarcely be heard above the rumble of conversation, and some moments later, when Maggie discerned the first notes of the grand march, she realized that few others in the room had heard them.

"Aren't we going to dance?" Lydia asked a few moments later. "Everyone seems to want only to talk."

Maggie was gazing around the crowded room, searching for some sign of the prince's presence, though she had not the least notion what that sign might be until she detected a flurry of activity across the room, centered on one figure. Seated amidst a bevy of ladies, who buzzed around him like hungry bees, he wore pink and silver Turkish dress, with a large bunch of diamonds pinned to the silver-gray turban perched atop his elegantly curled and powdered tie-wig. He looked, Maggie thought, like Osman III in the midst of his seraglio.

Lydia, flicking her fan impatiently back and forth, was still looking around, clearly fascinated by the splendid costumes and no doubt fascinated as well by the fact that she stood in the midst of a veritable army of Jacobites.

Nearby a female voice carried above the general babble. " 'Pon rep, Amanthus, have you beheld our beloved hero? You must confess, he is a genius—more, a gift from heaven!"

"To be sure, my dear," her companion agreed heartily as they passed Maggie and Lydia, "he has such vivacity, such piercing wit, such clear judgment. In short, he is the top of perfection and truly heaven's darling."

Lydia's mouth dropped open, and she stopped in her tracks, but she was not watching the two women. Maggie saw at once that her gaze was riveted on the Grand Turk, and wondered what demon had possessed Charles to make such a spectacle of himself.

"It's him," Lydia squeaked. "Oh, I know it is! I've got a wineglass with his likeness etched on it. Oh, Maggie, present me!"

"Don't be absurd. No one is being presented, and I doubt that is who you believe it is, in any case," she added hastily.

"Piffle, I heard those women. That man is—"

"Hush, Lydia, you must not say the name."

Lydia's eyes grew round and her expression changed instantly to a conspiratorial one. "Oh, I won't breathe a syllable," she said. "You can trust me. You know you can."

"I know," Maggie said mendaciously. "Now, do hush. They are trying to begin the dancing.

Before long, with the help of numerous servants and several guests, the grand march was organized and the ball began in earnest. By then Maggie realized she need not have hushed Lydia so quickly, for little was being done to conceal Prince Charles from his admirers. Of slender build and medium height, he sat as one enthroned, the black loo mask he held up casually with one hand doing little to conceal his long oval face, large dark brown eyes, neat aquiline nose, and generous mouth as he sipped his wine and received his subjects' devotion. More and more did he appear to be the Turkish potentate he had chosen to represent that evening. Ladies continued to flutter about him, but Maggie noted unhappily that the gentlemen were paying him little heed.

Determined to present her messages, and deciding that there was no great need in such company to be particularly secretive about it, she waited only until she was certain that Lydia was engaged to dance the minuet before dismissing her own would-be partner and making her way determinedly to the prince. His female audience, apparently hanging on his every word, made way for her with such reluctance that had she not been resolved upon her course, they might well have prevented her. As it was, she was a little out of breath when she made her curtsy.

"I am Margaret MacDrumin, your highness," she said, rising in obedience to a languid signal from the hand holding the wineglass. "I bring messages from my father, Andrew MacDrumin of MacDrumin and other loyal supporters of the true Crown."

"And where is this father of yours, Miss Margaret, that he does not present his messages in person and sees fit to send only a female to our presence." Charles Stewart did not even look at her. His gaze drifted beyond her, aimlessly, as though he really did not expect it to encounter anything he much wanted to see.

"My father is too carefully watched by English soldiers and their Scots toadies, sir," she said calmly, fighting a sudden, quite unexpected, sense of irritation. "He couldna come without endangering you, but he wants you to know that he and the others remain loyal to the cause and will take up arms again the moment you march into Scotland with your armies."

A fleeting look of bitterness crossed the prince's pale face, and for a moment before he took the messages from her and lifted his mask again he looked directly at her, but his tone was still one of boredom when he said, "They await my armies, do they? Does it not occur to the MacDrumin and his friends that if everyone waits for someone else to produce these armies, there will be none forthcoming at all?"

Before Maggie could remind him that Highlanders took their lives in their hands if they so much as held arms in their possession, a female wearing a diaphanous gown of silver-trimmed pale blue silk insinuated herself between Maggie and the prince and said dotingly to him, "Armies will rise up out of the very ground to follow you, dear sir, when you decide the time has come to march. We are your devoted slaves, I promise you."

He murmured something, but his attention had wandered again, and when he lifted his glass to sip, Maggie felt a sudden urge to shove the foolish woman aside, grab him by his royal shoulders, and shake him till his teeth rattled. From all she could see, he was content to sit amongst his admirers, stewing himself in wine and complaining of lack of support, which would help no one. Why on earth, she wondered, was he not moving about the room, talking to the men, stirring them to action? Fighting to control her frustration long enough to find a place where she could vent it safely, she turned sharply away, only to come face to face with James Carsley, easily recognizable despite his mask.

He grabbed her arm and pulled her out of the circle of the prince's admirers, muttering, "Where the devil is my sister?"

"Dancing with someone, of course," Maggie replied curtly.

"How could you bring her to a place like this? You know perfectly well that this nest of Jacobites is no place for the Earl of Rothwell's sister. Ned will flay you both for this."

"He will know nothing about it unless you are so mean-spirited as to tell him. For that matter, I daresay he will not be pleased to learn that you were here yourself."

"He has long since given up trying to pipe the tunes for my dancing. In any case, I am here only because Dev told me Lydia meant to come, and don't pretend that you truly think she ought to be here, though 'tis certainly a pretty way for you to be revenged upon my half-brother. I know you have little enough liking for his dictatorial ways."

"I would never take revenge in such a way, no matter what Rothwell did, and certainly not against his innocent sister. Lydia insisted upon coming, and indeed, sir, I did not know how to get away without her, and I had to come."

James looked past her, his mouth tightening. "I've seen portraits of that fellow," he said grimly, "and that's where you were when I found you. He had his mask up then, so I didn't recognize him, but I do now. Have you gone quite mad?"

Her gaze followed his and she saw that the prince had indeed lowered his mask to talk to Lady Primrose, who appeared to be expostulating with him. Turning back to James, she said with a sigh, "I am not mad, sir, I promise, though I daresay I must be a little muddled at least not to deny all knowledge of his identity or beg you not to tell anyone. But he does seem rather to be advertising his presence to all and sundry."

"By old Harry," James muttered, "is that what you admire?"

"He is not as I remember him," she admitted. "I believe he is drunk already, for one thing, though the ball has scarce begun." Two men had joined the group they were watching, and they too seemed to be speaking urgently to the prince.

"He is certainly cast away," James said, observing him with a no doubt experienced eye. "He's not what I expected, although, according to Ned, he is no more than a cipher these days anyway."

Her temper flared, but honesty forbade her to argue the point. She could no more imagine the man in the pink and silver Turkish costume leading a host of her fellow Highlanders into battle than she could imagine him flying on a magic carpet. Her hopes seemed to crumble to ashes as she stood watching him ignore what were no doubt entreaties to be sensible from those who had joined him, and hold out his glass to be refilled yet again.

"Let's get out of here," James said. "Where's Lydia?"

"Dancing," Maggie told him again, "wearing a pink domino."

They searched the teeming crowd, and finally Maggie, with relief, saw Lydia approaching arm in arm with a man in a black domino. Not till they were nearer did she recognize Lord Thomas.

Grinning at James, Lord Thomas said, "Told you I'd find her in a trice, and she's perfectly ready to depart, too, for I've told her I arranged a splendid surprise for her that she's very nearly spoilt by leaving Rothwell House tonight. Can't think why you made such a fuss though, James. We must know dozens of folks here. Saw Lady Carolyn Petersham, for one. Can't think why she wants to go dressing herself up like a Turkish slave girl to fawn at the feet of that sultan fellow yonder. Stap me, he's gone now. That's devilish odd. Made quite a tableau, they did."

Involuntarily Maggie's gaze followed his, and she felt vast relief to see that the prince had apparently accepted the advice of others and made himself less conspicuous.

James said abruptly, "We must go at once. Come, Lydia."

She began to protest, but Lord Thomas tucked her hand in the crook of his arm and said with a teasing look, "You'll soon be glad, my sweet—if we are not

too late, that is. It is half past eleven already, so do as
James bids you and make haste."

James took the lead to make a path for the others
through the crowd, and Maggie, following close behind, bumped right into him when he suddenly
stopped. Something in the way he stood warned her,
but she was nonetheless dismayed when he shifted so
that she could see the tall masked figure who blocked
his way. It was Rothwell, and the fury in his eyes
stirred feelings that James's anger only moments
before had not touched. Her knees threatened to give
way beneath her. Her heart began to pound.

Behind her, Lydia said, "What's toward there? I
thought we were in a great hur—Oh." Not another
word did she say.

VIII

Outside on the flagway, before anyone else could speak, James said hastily, "What brought you here, Ned?"

"Information received," Rothwell snapped. "I have no wish to discuss it here in the street, but if you know what's good for you, you will present yourself at Rothwell House first thing tomorrow to explain to me, if you can, how the *devil* you dared to escort Lydia and Miss MacDrumin to such a house as this one."

"Boot's on the other foot," James said, glancing apologetically at Lydia.

Lord Thomas said naively, "Stap me, Rothwell, what sort of information did you receive? Seemed an innocent enough party to me, but then James and I only just arrived, you know."

"I see."

The look Rothwell cast his sister and Maggie boded no good for their future, and when Lydia visibly wilted, Maggie gathered her courage to say as calmly as she was able, "It was not Lydia's doing, sir. It was mine."

"I am quite well aware of that," he replied, his flickering glance sending a flood of ice water through her veins. "We will not discuss that in the street either, however. My carriage awaits us yonder."

Lydia looked at Maggie, then muttered unhappily, "We came with Oliver, Ned. He is waiting at Essex Stairs, and I daresay if we don't tell him you have come for us, he will soon begin to believe we have been abducted, or worse, and raise an alarm."

"No doubt," he agreed. "I believe we'll make use of him then, for not only will the journey be quicker by water but I have something to say to young Oliver as well as to you."

Lord Thomas said, "By Jove, Rothwell, if you ain't going to use your carriage, perhaps you won't mind if—"

"By all means, take it if you want it."

James said, "Thank you, Ned, we will. Do you still want to see me tomorrow?"

Rothwell's grim expression relaxed slightly and he said, "Since I must suppose now that you came here only to take them away, no. I owe you my thanks, James."

"Rubbish, but we will take the carriage. Save us walking or paying good coin for a public barge."

As the two younger men walked away, Lydia, reaching up to untie the strings of her mask, said, "I doubt that you are the great surprise Thomas promised me, Ned. I wonder what it was."

"Don't take that mask off," Rothwell ordered harshly. "How many people inside already know you were there?"

"N-no one," she stammered. "At least, I did not identify myself to anyone, but someone might have guessed, I suppose."

"We will hope no one did," he said grimly.

They had walked some steps toward the tall archway before Maggie, remembering what Lydia had told her earlier, said, "I hope you will not blame your bargeman for any of this, Rothwell."

"I certainly do blame him," was the uncompromising reply.

Lydia said urgently, "But you mustn't, Ned. I utterly coerced him, and so it would be wickedly unfair to blame him. Punish me if you must, but please don't punish Oliver."

"He was warned to take his orders only from me."

Maggie said quietly, "I must tell you that I was determined to come here tonight, sir, and had Oliver not agreed to lend us his escort, we should most likely have hired a public conveyance instead. Faith, but we were safer with him, I think."

Rothwell was silent, and though Maggie was sure her defense of the bargeman had only plunged her deeper into trouble with the earl, she was not sorry she had spoken. She did not want Oliver to suffer unfairly for helping her.

Although it was not a great distance from Essex Stairs to Rothwell House, the current was running swiftly, so Rothwell hired a second man from one of the many who made themselves available along the river for such duty, to help Oliver row them. They all removed their masks at last, but in the second oarsman's presence nothing was said about the incident, and Maggie was grateful for Rothwell's silence. She hoped the crisp night air and restful sounds of the water against the wooden barge would calm his exacerbated temper before she was forced to confront it. They might well have exerted a soothing effect, but it was lost the moment they rounded the curve in the river to hear a chorus of masculine voices upraised in song ahead, vigorously if discordantly accompanied by stringed instruments.

"What the devil?" Rothwell demanded.

"Lud, it must be Thomas's surprise," Lydia said, exchanging a look of dismay with Maggie. "He must have hired them to serenade me. No doubt it vexes you, Ned, but 'tis prodigiously romantic of him, you must agree!"

Maggie could have sworn that she heard Rothwell growl, but he said nothing more about the serenaders, who were floating in a barge of their own off the Rothwell-Richmond Stairs. At Rothwell House, the earl waited only until he had paid the extra bargeman and seen him off in a public vessel before saying to Oliver, "I will have something to say to you about this tomorrow, but for now you may take yourself off to bed."

The young man accepted his dismissal with wary gratitude and turned away to cover the barge for the night. Silently, Rothwell led the way to the gate, opened it, and gestured for Maggie and Lydia to precede him. When Lydia hesitated, casting a last, wistful glance at the serenaders, Maggie took her arm and urged her quickly up the stairs.

Inside the house, when Lydia began to thank Rothwell for his leniency toward Oliver, he cut her off with a gesture and a warning look at Fields and Frederick, who had entered the grand saloon to take their wraps. Giving his gloves, mask, hat and cane into the butler's keeping, he said, "You may go up to bed at once, Lydia. I will speak with you tomorrow."

"But—"

"Now, Lydia."

"Oh, very well," she said, moving obediently ahead of him into the stair hall. At the foot of the stairs she looked over her shoulder at Maggie, grimaced expressively, and said, "We'll go to my bedchamber. We have a great deal to talk over."

Maggie would have been perfectly willing to accompany her, but she was not in the least surprised to feel a strong hand grasp her elbow or to hear his stern voice say, "Miss MacDrumin is not going upstairs just yet, so you may go straight to bed, Lydia. Step into my library, Miss MacDrumin."

For a minute, Lydia hesitated, looking mutinous, but she held her tongue, and as Maggie was propelled toward the library, she heard the younger girl's footsteps clicking upward on the uncarpeted stairs.

Rothwell said nothing more until he had released her arm and shut the library door, but then, without so much as asking her to sit down, he spoke with chilling fluency for several uncomfortable minutes without pause. Her experience with her quick-tempered father having long since shown Maggie the futility of attempting to interrupt a gentleman's tirade in full spate, she braced herself to withstand the verbal flood in dignified silence, but she quickly learned that Rothwell's anger was altogether different from MacDrumin's. Where her father tended to explode into fury, to shout, and to say whatever he took it into his head to say—albeit with admirable, even formidable, fluency—Rothwell's anger was coldly controlled, his manner cutting, his points not only unanswerable but driven home with painful accuracy. By the time he paused for breath Maggie's dignity was in shreds and she was fighting tears. She did not want to meet his icy gaze, and thus felt a certain pardonable pride when she was able to force herself to do so.

With barely a quaver in her voice, she said, "I am sorry to have vexed you. May I go now?" And with these simple words, she speedily discovered yet another difference between Rothwell and the fiery Mac-Drumin, since the latter, once he had exploded, would impatiently have dismissed her.

Rothwell said, "Do you have nothing to say for yourself?"

The steel in his voice sent another tremor up her spine, but valiantly, her throat aching with suppressed tears, she said, "I have apologized, sir. I do not know what more I can say."

"That was no apology, Miss MacDrumin." His voice was gentle now, but still without warmth. In fact, its very gentleness made it all the more frightening. "Having lived a good portion of my life with a woman whose notion of plain-speaking is just that sort of verbal nonstatement—not to mention having listened to speeches in Parliament the sole purpose of which seem to be to make a listener think he is hearing one thing when he is hearing quite another—I am a veritable expert on such methods."

She stared at him. "I do not understand you, Rothwell. I most certainly apologized."

"Not properly, you didn't. You said only that you are sorry to have vexed me, nothing more. While perfectly understandable, that has nothing to do with the matter at hand." When she remained silent, thinking over his words, he said in that same soft tone, "Perhaps you might explain just what sort of idiocy prompted you to take my sister to a Jacobite ball. Are you sorry about that, or is no tactic beneath your contempt as long as you can accomplish your purpose, whatever that might be?"

The accusation shocked her. Turning away, fighting for calm, she said, "I certainly meant no harm to

Lydia, sir. She is my friend, and had it not been for the necessity of—"

A powerful hand seized her shoulder and spun her back to face him. A second hand gripped her other shoulder, and no longer at all calm, he gave her a shake. "How dare you pretend your interests are more important than hers! What kind of woman are you that you think nothing of compromising an innocent young girl's reputation merely to serve your own self-ish and quite ridiculous ends? Was getting to that ball truly worth ruining Lydia, who has shown only kind-ness and generosity toward you?"

"We . . . we remained m-masked the whole time," she said, fighting the aching constriction in her throat and wishing he would let her go. "I would never have allowed—"

"I don't want to hear what you think you might or might not have allowed," he retorted, his grip tighten-ing. "Shall I next discover that it was not by chance that James encountered you in that court room, that his bringing you here was in fact part of some complex Jacobite plot? Fiend seize you, madam!" He shook her again. "What manner of villain are you?"

Tears welled into her eyes. She was aware that his fingers would leave bruises on her shoulders, but she made no attempt to free herself, putting all her energy into finding words that would calm his terrible anger. "I . . . I am no villain, sir, truly. I did not wish to take Lydia with me, but you had made it impossible for me to get away on my own, and she said she would help. After that, there may have been a way to prevent her from going, but I did not know of one." She had been gazing at his elaborately embroidered waistcoat as she spoke, but he was silent for so long that at last she forced herself to look up. His gaze was too penetrating. She looked quickly away again.

He released her, and the frightening gentleness turned his words to a spine-tingling drawl when he said, "In point of fact, you are still telling me that you believe my sister's reputation to be of less importance than meeting your Jacobite friends."

"I don't believe that at all," she cried impulsively. "Had I not thought it so imperative that I meet—"

"Just so," he said when she broke off in dismay at what she had nearly said. "If you want to deceive me, you had much better learn to think before you speak, for I am more than seven, you know. You say you could think of no way to keep Lydia from going with you, but the fact is that had you thought before acting, you could have prevented her going in any number of ways, not least of which was by staying here yourself until a more felicitous opportunity occurred to meet with your friends. So suppose you tell me the whole truth. I have already taken note of the fact that you did not deny taking part in some damned Jacobite plot."

Maggie's tears were forgotten, and her quaking knees threatened to buckle altogether when she realized where the conversation was leading. Rothwell was too shrewd. Having ascertained at once that he was unaware of Charles Stewart's presence at the masquerade, she had not thought she would have to defend herself against anything more felonious than attending a masked ball in a suspected Jacobite's home, but it was clear now that he suspected more, and for that she had no one to blame but herself and her own hasty tongue.

Hoping to divert his thoughts, even if it meant subjecting herself to another tirade, she said, "I cannot tell you the whole truth, sir, and if that causes you to wash your hands of me, I shall understand. Indeed, and I do not know why you brought me back here to Rothwell House at all, when you might just as easily have left me with my friends."

"Your friends," he said, and his tone was arctic now, "would most likely have refused to keep you. I can assure you that, mask or no mask, I was recognized by more than one person I passed in that house, and if you can look me in the eye and tell me that your so-called friends would welcome you back knowing I have any interest in you whatever, you are either a greater fool or a greater liar than I believe you to be; which," he added grimly, "would put you well beyond the realm of most fools and liars. You are self-serving, reckless, and stupid, Miss MacDrumin. Your friends would have to be even more dim-witted to keep you in their midst, for you have far too great a tendency to speak and act without thinking to be of use to any self-respecting conspiracy. Now, go to bed before I lose my temper altogether. You badly want thrashing, my girl."

Turning away quickly so that he would not know he had succeeded at last in making her cry, Maggie had her hand on the door handle when the icy drawl she was rapidly learning both to fear and to detest came again. "Before you take it into your head to try to run away, you had better know that I will give orders at once for my servants to prevent your stepping a foot outside this house without my express permission."

Maggie fled blindly, tears streaming down her cheeks, no longer caring if anyone saw her. When she reached her own room, she gave way at last to all the pent-up anxiety and tension of the past week and flung herself onto the bed to cry her eyes out. Though she did not once think of Lydia's suggestion to visit her bedchamber, or even of her small triumph in deflecting Rothwell's thoughts from such details of the masquerade as were guaranteed to infuriate him even more, it was long before her tears stopped flowing and even longer before she slept.

IX

Rothwell did not sleep well that night either. Not only did his mind's eye persist in presenting him with a picture of Miss MacDrumin's chalk-white fact as it had looked while he spoke his mind to her, but he wondered what she was attempting to hide from him and devoutly hoped he had not made a grave mistake.

His conscience was pricking him badly, because for once in his life he had put personal, rather inexplicable motives ahead of duty when he had failed to tell Ryder that he knew (or, to be more exact, *suspected* he knew) where a certain masquerade was most likely being held. And while he could congratulate himself for not having caused the descent of government agents upon a party at which his own sister happened to be a guest, he was unable to console his conscience with that fact for the simple reason that he had not for a moment suspected that she would be.

He had, however, suspected that Miss MacDrumin might somehow contrive to be there. That was why, when Ryder had received an urgent message at Drury Lane Theater, informing him that a Jacobite meeting was taking place that very night at some unnamed location under cover of a masquerade, Rothwell had not instantly told the Attorney General that he had for some days been harboring beneath his very roof a suspected Jacobite with friends in Essex Street to whom she seemed anxious to present herself.

Instead, taking base advantage of Ryder's departure for his office to launch a city-wide search for a ball bearing the presently unfashionable look of a masquerade, and knowing he had little time before they found it, Rothwell had gone straight to Ryder's own flat, conveniently nearby in Wych Street, to secure a domino and loo mask. Since Ryder had been particularly fond of masquerades before the demise of their popularity, Rothwell had succeeded in this effort by the simple expedient of demanding that his friend's servant instantly produce the required items.

Well aware that Ryder would soon learn of his impudence, he decided it would be beneficial for him to obtain any information he could before then, and it occurred to him that no matter how much Miss Mac-Drumin had deserved castigation, he might have done better to have treated her more gently. But though she would be even more guarded with him now than before, he still hoped he could exploit her impulsive tongue to gain the information he sought. Even then, the best he could hope for was to lessen Ryder's anger, since no information would be enough to keep him from demanding to know why Rothwell had not apprised him of Miss MacDrumin's Jacobite connections the instant he learned of them.

Rothwell was not certain himself why he had not, and he wondered why it had not so much as crossed his mind to leave her in Essex Street when he had found her there. The plain fact, despite what he had told her, was that the thought had not even entered his head. As the long night passed and he still could not sleep, he tried to convince himself that he had instantly realized that she would be an excellent source of information.

He did sleep at last, but it was still early when he arose the next morning. He attended morning prayer service in the chapel at the north end of the Privy Garden, had a solitary breakfast, and then retired to his library to deal with matters of business. His half-sister was not an early riser, and he knew she would linger in bed until Lady Rothwell rousted her out to attend chapel at eleven o'clock, but he was in no hurry to confront Lydia. That scene would be an unpleasant one, and he had not yet decided how he intended to punish her.

Hearing all three ladies leave the house shortly before eleven, he realized his servants had assumed that his order did not include preventing his guest from attending church, and hoped she would not give his stepmother the slip. Deciding to deal with Lydia as soon as they returned, he tried to fix his attention on his work. Fifteen minutes later Fields announced Sir Dudley Ryder, who strode into the library, looking grim.

Warily, Rothwell stood to shake his hand, then waved him to a chair near the fire and sat down again at his desk. Ryder refused refreshment and waited only until Fields had gone before saying tersely, "He's here, Ned, in London."

"Charles?"

"Aye. The blasted scoundrel inspected the Tower of London defenses yesterday and is said to have remarked that the main gate could be blown in by a petard! And this morning he had the temerity to attend church in order to be formally received into the Church of England. And him with a Catholic cardinal for a brother! The whole business would be laughable if it weren't so damned maddening."

"Straighten your wig," Rothwell said, thinking quickly. "I cannot talk to a man who looks demented. Where is he now?"

"Good lack, if I knew that, don't you think I'd have had him in irons by now?" But Ryder obediently straightened his wig, and his tone was calmer when he added, "He's committed treason, Ned, but for all the fear he shows, he must think us no more dangerous than a gaggle of geese. He's taunting us, and there's little I can do about it. Do you recall the message that took me from the play last night? He is said to have *danced* at that damned masquerade, as indifferent to his peril as any man could be."

A cold chill struck Rothwell as a number of things suddenly became blindingly clear to him, and even as he decided to have one damned little Jacobite's head on a platter, he realized that Charles Stewart's presence at the masquerade rendered Lydia's attendance there more dangerous to her than ever. He had cause, yet again, to be grateful for his skill at masking his feelings, for he was able to keep his tone matter-of-fact, even slightly amused, when he said, "I'd not have thought Charlie the type to enjoy disporting himself dressed as a harlequin or some such thing. Are you quite certain he was present?"

Ryder nodded glumly, stretching his legs out and crossing his ankles. He smothered a yawn and said, "Our best fellow—the one I told you about—tumbled to it late in the day. Got wind of a Jacobite masquerade but evidently did not know the location or that the Pretender would be there. When he discovered the ball was at Lady Primrose's house, he went to have a look first, knowing it would be such a crush that he could do so without causing much ado amongst his own set. As soon as he saw Charles, he sent word to us of course, but even so, we were too late. My lads found only her ladyship and a few lingering guests, all feigning innocence, but Lady Primrose was so nervous that one of my lads said he expected her to expire. Guilty as they come, of course, but not a man present would speak against her."

"Not even your own?" Rothwell was thinking furiously.

Ryder grimaced. "As I said before, I haven't a notion who he is. He may well have been one of those who lingered at the scene, but I wouldn't know him if we met. As to whether he'd agree to stand up in a court of law and speak against a member of the *beau monde* is more than I can say. After all, he's got to be one of them himself, don't you think?"

"Judging by the information you receive, yes. A servant could not know such details."

"My thinking, precisely. At all events, he is out of the inner circle at the moment and professes to have no idea where the Pretender is staying. We know he is not in Essex Street, for I've had the entire street watched since midnight."

Rothwell was watching Ryder narrowly to see if there was the least hint in his expression of knowledge he did not want to share. He clearly had not heard yet that Rothwell had been in Essex Street, but he might have learned about Lydia's presence. Though not certain his friend would shield her from his displeasure, he knew Ryder harbored at least a tenderness for Lydia and thought it might be enough to stir him to protect her. He would certainly expect Rothwell's temper to ignite at the slightest whisper of her presence at a Jacobite ball. But he could discern no uneasiness in

Ryder's demeanor. Though the Attorney General looked tired and frustrated, he did not look as if he harbored guilty knowledge.

"Have you had any sleep at all?" Rothwell asked.

"Three hours on a dashed uncomfortable sofa in my office. I've got my lads out sweeping the streets, but I doubt they'll turn Charles up under a cobblestone. That man's got more bolt holes than a philandering hedgehog." He yawned again. "Came to see if you'd come out and dine with me. I don't want to go home. It is not my nature to sit and stew, but I know I shan't get anything of worth accomplished there, and although I'm well nigh dead on my feet, I doubt I'll sleep for hours yet."

"I cannot go out, but you are welcome to stay and dine with us," Rothwell said, deciding it would be better to keep Ryder under his eye and away from Wych Street until he had had more time to think. "My stepmother likes to dine early on Sundays, so dinner will be served at two. Will that suit you?" When Ryder nodded, he got up to fetch a pack of cards and added, "We can play a few hands of piquet in the meantime."

Ryder seemed able to keep his mind on the game, but Rothwell's thoughts kept drifting and he played badly. Certain now that he had misjudged the incident of the previous evening, and had blamed Miss Mac-Drumin for one thing when she had actually been guilty of something much more serious, he wanted very much to find that young woman at once and shake her until her pretty teeth rattled. He remembered his resolution, however, as well as his obligation to Ryder and knew it would do no good to berate her if berating only made her button her lips.

He began to doubt now that she would tell him anything of value anyway, for he realized that if she had known all along that Charles Stewart meant to attend the masquerade, she had betrayed none of that knowledge; and, despite her apparent habit of allowing her thoughts to spill freely and without check from her brain to her tongue, she had not said a word to arouse his suspicion, or Lydia's either. He could not for a moment imagine his garrulous sister keeping such news to herself. Nor could he imagine her keeping silent for long about having been present at a ball graced by the notorious Bonnie Prince Charlie. Whatever else he might forgive Miss MacDrumin, he would not forgive her for taking Lydia there. That thought, however, triggered an instant mental vision of what her difficulties with Lydia had been, and he could almost sympathize with her—almost, but not quite, for his imagination next presented him with a vision of the likely scenes he faced when he informed Lydia and his stepmother that he had decided to send them home.

So preoccupied did he become with these thoughts and the necessity to keep at least a portion of his mind on the game that when the door to the library opened and Lydia peeped in, looking contrite and most alluring in a sack dress of flower-striped silk over a moderate, fan-shaped hoop, it took him a moment even to recall that he had told her he wanted to speak with her.

"Oh," she said, quickly assuming a more formal demeanor and making a swift but graceful curtsy to Ryder, "I expected to find you alone, Ned. How do you do, Sir Dudley?"

As Ryder leapt to his feet to make his bow, Rothwell said, "We can talk later, my dear. Ryder is staying to dine with us."

"Oh, lovely," she said, flirting with Ryder over her fan. "I daresay that since we are to enjoy your company, sir, I must run upstairs and tidy myself." And with that, she was gone.

Rothwell tried to return his attention to his cards but again failed to concentrate, allowing Ryder to win not only that hand but the two that followed. Thus, although he had not yet decided how to handle his half-sister, let alone his guest or the confession he still owed to his friend, he greeted his butler's announcement that dinner was served with profound relief.

Both Miss MacDrumin and Lydia were waiting in the hall with his stepmother when he emerged with Ryder from the library, and he gave thanks for the latter's excellent manners when he introduced him to his guest, for although Ryder shot him a look that said he recognized her surname at once, he expressed no vulgar curiosity and said only that he was happy to make her acquaintance. If Miss MacDrumin looked a little pale at learning he was the attorney general, Rothwell hoped Ryder would put it down to simple shyness. Nevertheless, he knew that Ryder's awareness of who she was, meant that little time remained before he would be ordered to explain himself.

Conversation at the table was desultory for the most part, although Rothwell noted that Miss MacDrumin was unusually silent, replying politely but succinctly and only when she was directly addressed. She wore a deceptively simple, light-blue silk gown, the snug bodice of which seemed to caress her gently curved breasts and tiny waist, but he thought the color was not as becoming to her as the mossy green she had worn the first time he saw her. The blue failed to bring out the green flecks in her eyes, making them look yellow, almost like a cat's. She still looked pale, but her cheeks reddened when he caught her gaze and she looked swiftly down at her plate, making him wonder if she knew he would have more to say to her. She barely spoke to Ryder, but since that gentleman's attention was mostly engaged by Lydia, Rothwell did not think he noticed any lack.

Lydia seemed determined to flirt with Ryder, and Lady Rothwell, in an excellent mood for once, interjected only one or two references to her oft-mentioned belief that James had as much right to at least one of the late earl's titles as Rothwell did. Ryder, accustomed to such observations from her, paid them no heed, diverting her to other topics with long-practiced skill, and all in all, Rothwell thought the meal passed off more pleasantly than he had any right to hope it would.

When Lydia archly suggested that Sir Dudley might enjoy a stroll through the Privy Gardens with her and Miss MacDrumin after dinner, Rothwell said, "I have matters of importance to discuss with Miss MacDrumin, my dear, but no doubt Ryder will be delighted to stroll with you."

He saw alertness replace anticipation in Ryder's eyes and was almost grateful when Lady Rothwell said sharply, "Surely, you cannot want your sister to be so particular in her attention to a single gentleman as to stroll alone in a public garden with him!"

He replied calmly, "Ryder is entirely to be trusted, ma'am, I assure you, but should you have concern for Lydia's reputation, I daresay he will be pleased to have your company as well, or she can take her maid." Realizing that though Ryder was trustworthy, Lydia could not be trusted not to say something unwise, and hoping at least to prevent her from saying anything about her activities of the previous night before he had talked with Ryder himself, Rothwell said abruptly to the nearest footman, "Fetch Lady Lydia's maid and a warm wrap for her." Then he turned to Miss MacDrumin and added in much the same tone, "If you have finished your dinner, I will speak with you now in the library."

"Certainly, my lord." She rose gracefully to her feet.

Seeing that Lydia was watching him with visible alarm, as if she were debating the wisdom of yet again leaving Miss MacDrumin to his less than tender mercies, he managed a smile and said, "I trust, puss, that you will keep Tilda near enough to assure your mama that Ryder will not attempt to speak improperly to you."

"As if he would!" But the worried look faded, and she grinned saucily at him.

Glancing at Ryder, who looked unamused, Rothwell smiled at him rather more mockingly, and said, "After you, Miss MacDrumin."

She went peacefully, her head held high, and if her wariness returned when she found herself alone with him in the library, she nevertheless retained her dignity. Remembering how easily she had stirred his temper the night before, he was determined to control this discussion, and to remain calm if only because he knew he would learn nothing of importance if he did not. The cold anger he had felt when Ryder told him Charles Stewart had been at the ball had dissipated somewhat over dinner, but he was well aware that it lay just beneath the surface of his calm, ready to stir at the least provocation. It did not help that he had decided that for Lydia's own protection he would have to send her home at least until the latest anti-Jacobite fever had subsided. He knew too that the time had come to send Miss MacDrumin home as well. He had not really had time to deal with the arrangements before—or told himself that he had not—but he would have to do so now, at once, and that thought pleased him no more than the others.

He was still collecting his thoughts when she said quietly, "I ought to have known you would count the attorney general amongst your friends, Rothwell. May I assume from his cordial manner that you have not yet told him about me?"

"I have not, though he recognized your surname, I believe."

"What else will you tell him?"

"I have not decided." He had not expected her to ask direct questions but thought she would remain silent as she had the night before, and let him lead the discussion. Her questions added to his guilt about not having spoken to Ryder and made him feel unusually defensive. It was not a feeling he enjoyed.

She drew a deep breath, turned away, and said with an odd little sigh, "What will happen when Sir Dudley discovers that Lydia attended a Jacobite masquerade?"

The provocative words proved more than he could stomach. Despite his resolution, something snapped, and without a second thought he grabbed her shoulders just as he had done the night before and spun her back to face him.

"How dare you attempt to blackmail me!" He snarled the words, furious with her in a way he could not recall feeling toward anyone in a decade or more. "Is it not enough that your actions force me to send Lydia home for her own safety? Now you dare to taunt me with the very danger into which you have carried her, even to threaten to betray her yourself to the authorities! By God, I never thought you could sink so low!"

"Faith, I did not!" Her face had gone white with

shock, and he felt her shoulders tense beneath his hands. Tears filled her eyes, and her voice caught when she added, "I . . . I would not!"

"Do not think you can move me with tears," he said harshly, but he released her at once and stepped away, angry with himself for so quickly losing the control he had been determined to keep. What power did this woman have, he wondered, that she could so easily infuriate him?

Choking back her tears, she said, "You must think me utterly despicable to accuse me of such a dreadful thing."

He regarded her closely, his fury oddly suspended, and was quickly convinced that her distress was genuine. "I do not despise you," he said, calmer now. "If I misjudged you, I will apologize. In my own defense I can only say that your question was easily misunderstood."

"I suppose it was," she admitted, "but I promise you, sir, I asked only because I assumed that Sir Dudley must eventually discover that Lydia was there. I would never betray her to secure my own advantage."

"But you have already done that," he said, in control again and determined to make her understand what she had done. "Your betrayal was in leading her into grave personal danger, and you certainly acted to gain advantage for yourself." His voice was gentle, and he hoped it would encourage her to confide in him.

Clearly, however, she—like so many others before her—had already learned to mistrust that tone, for her eyes opened wide and the wariness flooded back into them. "Wh-what do you mean?"

Looking directly at her again, he said without equivocation, "For what purpose did you go to Essex Street last night?"

"I . . . I told you already. It was imperative that I see Lady Primrose."

"To reassure her of your safety, no doubt."

She bit her lower lip.

Reaching out, he put his hand under her chin, tilting her head up, making it impossible for her to look away, then said sternly, "You went to see someone else, did you not, Miss MacDrumin, someone far more dangerous than Lady Primrose?"

Was there a flicker of fear in her eyes? She certainly grew pale again, but she did not try to look away, and though her lips must have been dry, for she licked them, her voice was steady when she said, "I do not know whom you mean."

"Liar."

The color flooded back into her cheeks, and her eyes flashed, but even as she opened her mouth to deny the charge, she shut it again and squeezed her eyes tightly shut as well. Then, to his surprise, she looked at him again, clearly struggling with herself to do so, and said in a firmer voice, "I beg your pardon, sir. You are right to name me so, but I am bound by my sworn word to others to say no more."

He found his respect for her increasing, and releasing her chin, he said, "I will make this easier for you. I know—as does Sir Dudley—that Charles Stewart was at that masquerade, seeking support for his lost cause." He laid careful emphasis on the last two words, and waited for her to dispute them.

She did not. Her creamy brow furrowed for a moment before she said, "Will they all be arrested?"

He considered the question for a moment before replying, "I have no wish to misjudge your words again. Are you asking me if arrests were made or if you yourself stand in danger of arrest?"

She looked surprised. "My dear sir, I must suppose that the greatest threat to me lies with you. I should think, too, that your power is sufficient to protect Lydia and James, should accusations be laid against them. My concern is for the others who were present, of course, for Lady Primrose and her guests."

"There have been no arrests at all," he said, "but rid yourself of the notion that my political power is so great that it would override a charge of treason against anyone in my household. On the contrary, by advocating the release of certain once-powerful Scottish leaders, I have already annoyed certain persons in power, who would be only too happy to charge me with harboring Jacobites."

"Were any leaders actually released?"

"MacKinnon of MacKinnon, for one," he answered promptly.

"But that is wonderful," she said. "Papa will be pleased, for he has been concerned for the MacKinnon's health."

"MacKinnon said he did not know your father."

"You asked him?" When he nodded, she said quickly, "Why did you advocate his release?"

"Because I believe we can more quickly mend matters and strengthen the union between our two countries if we do not create more martyrs," he said bluntly.

"Oh." She digested his words for a moment, then with a wry smile she said, "I hoped you might have had a certain sympathy for our cause, sir."

"I don't. I have no sympathy for traitors."

She flushed, but her eyes flashed, and he knew he had made her angry. She said, "Not all of us are traitors, Rothwell, though German George and your precious English government have seen fit to treat us all as such. They care naught for the horrors wrought by Cumberland's armies after Culloden, or for the innocent Scottish men, women, and children who were turned out of their homes to starve, or murdered in cold blood. I know well that you English hate all Scots, but we are a proud lot, sir. You will never crush us."

"Scottish pride is proverbial," he said, "but it becomes ridiculous to more civilized persons when it is accompanied by abject poverty and plain jealousy. When you add to that the habit so many Scots have of resorting to base chicanery—"

"How dare you!" Her cheeks flamed, her eyes spat fire, and her bosom heaved with indignation, but he felt no compassion now. Once again, she had spoken out without thinking, and she needed a sharp lesson in civility.

"I speak no more than plain truth," he said bluntly. "Your fellow Scots are best known for rash behavior, a savage taste for fighting, and a reckless disregard for law and order. And pray do not try to tell me you hail from different stock, for although your father was never *proven* guilty of his part in that devilish uprising, I have no doubt that he was as guilty as MacKinnon. The only difference is that he seems not to have taken part in the gathering of chiefs the day after Culloden, but that might well be because he is a coward as well as a scoundrel."

She slapped him hard—and clearly without thought that he might retaliate—and snapped, "You know nothing about Scotsmen, Rothwell. You sit here safe and smug in London with your vast wealth and your powerful friends, never having had to fight for anything! You never so much as lifted a finger to acquire your fortune either, I'll wager, but just inherited it from your father. No doubt you inherited your power as well. But my father has had the full responsibility of our clan to shoulder. He deals with every clan member's problems, not just his own, but he has managed to support them all and protect them all despite every obstacle the English have thrown in his path. You English," she went on, her words dripping contempt, "have broken every promise you ever made and have even defied your own Treaty of Unification in order to take property that is not rightfully yours and to justify murder, torture, and rape."

"That's enough," Rothwell said sharply, the sting in his cheek exacerbating his temper even more than her words. He would not give her the satisfaction of acknowledging the pain, however, and kept his hands rigidly at his sides as he said, "Not only have you just proven my point about the violent nature of Scotsmen by your own action, my girl, but your argument carries no weight. There is no crime in inheriting position and wealth, or in enjoying the advantages of one's birthright. Your father no doubt became a clan chief by that very same road, and if you try to pretend you have lived a life equal to that of other members of your clan, I won't believe you for a minute. You are too well educated, for one thing, and too damned sure of yourself for another. But we are not going to stand here flinging insults at each other. We don't have the time for it, and we have already strayed too far from the only point that matters."

"The only one that matters to you, perhaps," she retorted, but he read chagrin in her expression and was glad to know she was sorry now for striking him, if for nothing else.

"You are entitled to think what you like of me," he said, "but before I finish with you, I intend to make you understand just how badly your actions have endangered Lydia."

"Since you know now why I was determined to go last night, you must also realize I had no choice but to take her with me."

He did understand, particularly now that he realized she held blackmail in contempt, for Lydia was not nearly so nice in her notions. Nonetheless he said grimly, "The only fact that matters now is that you did go, both of you. Though it is true that neither your attendance nor Lydia's is presently known to the authorities, if it should become known, I cannot be certain of protecting either of you. I do have influence—and I will thank you to remember that before you fling my power in my teeth again—but as I said earlier, I also have enemies who would delight in seeing anyone under my protection prosecuted to the full extent of the law, which includes, in case you were not aware of it, seeing them hanged for treason. I do not say it would go that far," he added quickly, seeing her dismay, "only that there are people who would try. As to those with whom I still do exert some influence, I might as well tell you that, having concealed not only your identity and connections from them but also my suspicions last night as to where the masquerade was being held, any request of mine for favorable treatment will undoubtedly fall on deaf, even hostile, ears."

"But how would they know?" she asked, her manner much more subdued now.

"They would know," he said, grimacing at the memory of his impudent gesture in borrowing Ryder's own gear to disguise himself for the masquerade. At the time he had thought it amusing. Now he wondered at his own stupidity.

She was watching him. "Will you really send Lydia away?

"I must. She will leave for Derbyshire in the morning, just as soon as she and her mother can gather what they need for the journey. I'd send them at once if I thought I could induce my stepmother to travel on a Sunday, for Lydia cannot be trusted to keep a still tongue in her head. Even though I daresay I shall be able to prevent her from being hanged, or even arrested, I won't succeed in protecting her from a great deal of embarrassment if it becomes known that she was at that damned ball."

"But we were masked!"

"Can you assure me that no one there recognized Lydia? What about young Deverill? Are you sure you can trust that rattle not to tell someone? I certainly have no such faith in him."

Suddenly, to his horror, her eyes filled, and the tears spilled over and streamed down her cheeks.

"Good God, don't cry!" Dismayed, and without giving the possible consequences a single thought, he caught her shoulders again and pulled her close, putting his arms around her and letting her weep against his chest.

x

Telling herself that her tears were no more than a natural result of the emotional upheavals of the past half hour, Maggie allowed herself the unfamiliar luxury of being held and comforted for several minutes before she clapped a firm control over her emotions and attempted to free herself from Rothwell's embrace. His arms tightened briefly, as if he were reluctant to let her go, but then he released her. Pulling her handkerchief from her sleeve, she blew her nose and tried to collect her thoughts, noting that his lordship still looked shaken and most concerned.

Having spent a good portion of the previous night reviewing alternatives, she had already concluded that in Rothwell himself lay her sole remaining hope for improving the situation in Glen Drumin. The problem, as she knew from the dealings she had had with him, was how to convince him of that fact. Seeing the way he looked at her now, remembering other warm looks she had encountered, and being well aware of the way the new blue silk gown clung to her admittedly shapely person, she wondered if she might exploit his feelings to her own, and Glen Drumin's, advantage. But although such weapons were among the very few effective ones in a female's limited arsenal, and though her tears had clearly moved him, she felt an unfamiliar aversion to manipulating Rothwell, even if it really could be done.

Still with that look of compassion, he said quietly, "I am sorry to have distressed you so, but truly there is nothing else to be done to insure Lydia's safety. In the event that you fear she will blame you, let me assure you that she will not. She will believe, as I do now, that you had no real understanding of the danger into which you led her."

It was tempting, for she realized as she met his gaze that in acquitting her of acting out of spite he had also managed to acquit her of all ill intent. She wanted him to think well of her, and knew he would think better of a female who innocently admitted that knowing no better, she had tripped blindly into danger at the urging of others, than he would of one who had been willing to use any means she had at her disposal to get her own way. But although she would lie in an instant to protect her cause, or even to protect another, truly innocent person, she was loath to lie to him on her own behalf, or even to use feminine wiles, and that was what he was opening the door for her to do.

Unexpectedly her tears began to flow again, trickling down her cheeks and the back of her throat, but the thought that he could so easily affect her merely by being kind strengthened her resolve. Gathering herself, holding back her tears by the simple expedient of avoiding that compassionate gaze, she said gruffly, "You were right to be angry with me, sir, and you are wrong now to think I did not recognize Lydia's danger. I should have to be a fool not to have known she had no business to be there. Even had I not known who would attend Lady Primrose's masquerade, I certainly knew you would not approve of your sister's keeping company with Jacobites, and in that alone I must have endangered her. Though it is true that I did not know how to keep her from accompanying me once she had made up her mind to do so, I realize now that in the face of such difficulty I ought to have given up my plan altogether. I apologize to you, and I shall apologize to her as well, for although you say she will understand, I know she will be furious with us both if you truly force her to leave town. Lady Rothwell will be quite furious, too."

He took a step toward her, but she quickly held up a hand, saying, "Please, let me finish before my resolution fails. I know you mean only to make this easier for me, though I cannot imagine why you should, but you are making it harder instead, and I daresay you will not feel so sympathetic when I tell you that I would do it again, in an instant." She dared a glance at him, and felt a frisson of fear when she saw how his lips tightened and his eyes narrowed. No longer could she believe she still had his sympathy, but she felt better, having made her confession. She wanted very much to persuade him to do as she wished; she did not want to feel as if she had tricked him into doing it.

Grimly, he said, "Neither your feelings nor Lydia's can be considered. She must go to Derbyshire for her own protection. As to my stepmother's feelings in the matter, they need not concern you. She will do as I bid her. As to yourself, the sooner you leave London, the safer you too will be. In any event, you cannot stay here once my stepmother leaves.

"I have done what I can this past week to discover what exactly happened to your coach and servants, and though I am certain your people were killed and their bodies disposed of by their killers, since you cannot identify anyone, the matter will have to be laid to rest. It will no doubt be best, therefore, if you accompany Lydia and her mother into Derbyshire, from whence your transportation back to Scotland can be easily arranged."

"Will you take me home yourself, sir?" There, it was out. So much for seduction and trickery. She held her breath.

"I will certainly accompany you all to Derbyshire," he said. "Not only will my stepmother demand as much of me, but I should feel uneasy sending you all off alone. From Derbyshire, I will arrange a proper escort for you to Scotland."

"That will not do, I'm afraid."

He stared at her. "I beg your pardon?"

"I am sorry to vex you further, but if you simply pack me back to the Highlands, my friends and family—your tenants—will continue to suffer. It was primarily with the hope of relieving that suffering that I came to London. My true cause must not be abandoned, sir. Right must never be abandoned, but I now believe the best man to help us is you. The land is yours, the people your tenants; therefore, the responsibility lies with you."

"I am not going to assist your barbaric Highlanders to rise against their lawful king," he said.

"Nor do I ask such a thing," she said, keeping her temper easily since he had not refused outright to go. "I merely point out that people on your land are starving, that many are abused by your factors and by a local bailie, who, despite his Highland heritage, is paid by the English to side against his own."

"He is there to uphold the law."

"English law! Do you know what has been done, sir? Do you know that my father's people are forced to make payments to you they can neither afford nor earn, arbitrary payments of rent to a landlord to whom they feel no allegiance, who cannot be bothered to see for himself if the land will support them! That in itself is a rape of the Highlands. As to certain other things that are done in your name, sir, if they are legal in England, they certainly never were or will be in Scotland."

"You exaggerate. I would never condone such things."

"How would you know? Do you know that your factors and your bailie have been known to beat men who cannot pay the rents they order them to pay? Do your men tell you when they accost young females to demand sexual favors? Or is that the way you desire business to be done on your estates? Perhaps I am merely naive as to how you manage things in Derbyshire!"

"Again you exaggerate the case, my girl, and it will do you no good," he replied calmly. "I not only receive quarterly reports from my Scottish agents, which thus far have contained no mention of difficulty, but I am told there has been no need even to approach most of my tenants, since your father regularly pays what is owed by all. If the land will not support such payments, then how do they continue to be made, if you please?"

Feeling warmth in her cheeks, and knowing it derived from the knowledge that she had stepped dangerously close to a topic she had no wish to discuss, Maggie hoped he would credit her increased color to her temper and said quickly, "If my father pays, it is to spare our people more rough treatment. Surely you are not so foolish as to assume that your agents, when you are not at hand to direct them, behave with all

propriety. If you do, sir, then you are even more innocent in the ways of the world than I am." She was not
surprised to see anger leap to his countenance again,
but still he held himself under what she had come to
think of as unnaturally rigid control.

"You overstep, yet again, the bounds of what I will
tolerate," he said flatly. "I am not going to Scotland,
certainly not at this time of year. No," he added when
she began to protest, "do not argue with me. In fact,
you may go now. I will speak to Lydia myself, so pray
do not say anything about this to her. You can better
spend your time preparing for your own departure."
With that, he moved to open the library door.

Sounds of arrival in the hall stopped the next words
on Maggie's tongue, for she saw that Lydia and Sir
Dudley had returned from their stroll. Exchanging a
speaking look with Lydia, she heard Sir Dudley say,
"Ah, Ned, before I leave, there is a small matter I
should like to discuss with you—privately, old fellow,
if you have a minute to spare me just now."

"Certainly," Rothwell said, adding, "Lydia, you
may wait here in the hall until Sir Dudley leaves. Miss
MacDrumin, you will oblige me by going upstairs at
once."

Having no difficulty interpreting the stern command
to mean that he did not want her to speak to Lydia at
all before he did himself, and perfectly willing to let the
first flood of that damsel's fury wash over his head,
Maggie obeyed him, not even tempted to tiptoe back
when she saw the library door close behind him and
heard Lydia hiss at her to "come back and talk to me!"

In the library, Rothwell watched his friend with no
small misgiving, for it was clear he was searching for

words to express himself, and that was no natural state for the attorney general. At last Ryder said, hesitantly, "I dislike bringing such a matter to your attention, and . . . and naturally I am quite well aware that I may have misunderstood, but in all fairness . . ."

"Fiend seize you, Ryder, cut line."

"In point of fact, dear fellow, something that minx Lydia said—though, to be sure, she covered the slip quickly and most adroitly! If I were not experienced in such matters, I might not have noticed at—"

"Ryder." Rothwell's tone was ominous.

"That damned masquerade last night," Ryder said quickly. "I don't say she was there, but I recall what you said once about the child's fancying herself something of a Jacobite, and—"

"Lydia's a damned fool," Rothwell said, not mincing words. "Look here, Ryder, I'm not going to say she was there—I am *not* a fool—but I do have a confession to make and you won't like it."

"Perhaps I had better sit down." He suited action to words.

Rothwell said, "When you go home, your man is going to tell you that I visited your flat last night and demanded a loo mask and domino, which he provided me." He was watching the play of emotions on Ryder's face and added with a sigh, "You see, though I said nothing to you, I was able to guess where the masquerade was being held."

Ryder's lips tightened as if he were attempting to restrain himself, and his voice was carefully controlled when he said, "In view of Lydia's slip today, I think I understand your decision, but you will owe me for this, Ned. You are treading on thin ice in more respects than one, for if I am not mistaken, there is something more you should have told me. I once observed that the name MacDrumin is an unusual one, yet your guest was introduced to me today without a single reference to her antecedents."

Rothwell sighed and said, "If you are going to accuse the young woman of being a Jacobite, let me remind you that there has never been a word of evidence against her father."

"I would not go far to plead his innocence, however, and you must know the girl's very presence in this household could prove dangerous to you."

"She will not be here long enough to constitute a danger," Rothwell said, seeing daylight at last. "She came only to beg me to do something to ease the lot—a strained one, she insists—of my tenants in Scotland. She had the curst nerve to accuse me of taking no interest in their welfare. I daresay they do not like paying rents to an outsider, but as I told her, they have no one other than themselves to blame for their predicament. I am sending her home tomorrow, and my stepmother and Lydia will accompany her as far as Derbyshire. I think," he added with an oblique glance at Ryder, "that it is an excellent time for Lydia to renew her acquaintance with Rothwell Park."

"That may be true," Ryder agreed, but he was observing Rothwell with an expression that made him feel unnaturally wary. "Do you know, Ned," he said mildly, "I believe I agree with Miss MacDrumin. It is more than time that you visited that new estate of yours. In light of recent occurrences, I need information, specific and detailed information, from someone I can trust—pray note my extreme generosity in including you in that category, old friend—regarding the exact state of the current personalities and politics of that barbaric region. I can think of no one more worthy of the charge, or presently more vulnerable to a little very polite blackmail."

"Damn you," Rothwell said, but he was already resigned to his fate, and not dreading it nearly so much as he might have expected. "Get out now, Ryder. I still have to break the news of her impending exile to Lydia."

"It is no less than you deserve," Ryder murmured as he got to his feet. "Can I take this to mean you will go?"

"Yes, I'll go." He sighed. "Send Lydia in, will you?"

Maggie had finished what little packing there was for her to do by the time the door to her bedchamber was flung back on its hinges and Lydia stormed in. Dashing tears from her eyes, she grabbed the swinging door, slammed it shut behind her, and shrieked, "I *hate* him!" Striding across the room, she flung herself into a chair near the window embrasure and added fiercely, "He is a devil. I hate him, I hate him, I hate him!"

"You must be angry with me as well," Maggie said. "You have every reason. Don't spare me, Lydia."

"Lud, it was not your fault. I daresay Ned scolded you as dreadfully as he did me, and no doubt blamed you for taking me along, on account of your being a few years older than I am, though how he thinks you could have stopped me, or have kept me from writing to Thomas—Oh, yes, he knows about that now, too, for it slipped out when I was shouting at him about something else altogether. In any event, you could not have stopped me, so it is most unfair if he did blame you."

"I am not so certain of that," Maggie said dryly.

"If only he had not found us there," Lydia said with a sigh. "I'd give a quarter's allowance to know how he manages to know just what one is doing when one least wants him to, but so it is more often than not. Lud, but it was a shock to see him loom up before us like some avenging god." Her lips twisted. "Not that one would ever mistake Ned for a god. I daresay gods are never put out of temper by a bit of lint on a sleeve or a cuff turned improperly, but Ned flies into the boughs over such things until one quite pities poor Fletcher—his man, you know—and really—"

"Lydia," Maggie interjected, "Rothwell is not merely being devilish. If he is more angry with me than with you, it is because you would never have gone there had I not taken you."

"But he was mostly angry on account of my arranging to meet Thomas," Lydia said, adding thoughtfully, "Of course, Thomas was also vexed, but at the time I thought it was because I had not been invited, and later, of course, I realized it was because he had gone to such trouble to arrange his little surprise for me."

"Lydia, did you tell Lord Thomas that the prince was there?"

" 'Pon rep, no! Goodness, Maggie, how could you think I would betray him, even to dearest Thomas? And in case you were wondering," she added stiffly, "I did not confide a word about last night to Sir Dudley either."

"I never thought you would do that," Maggie said. "I only asked about Lord Thomas because you are especially fond of him."

"Well, I never came near telling Thomas, but in fact, I very nearly did slip with Sir Dudley," Lydia confessed. "It was only a tiny slip and, and I covered it so quickly that I am certain he did not suspect a thing.

Well, it stands to reason, because he would have pelted me with questions, and he did nothing of the sort. Really, I ought to be put out with you. I know it is a great secret and Prince Charles visits London only at his extreme peril. I did not even tell Ned. Lud, to think he was actually in the same room with Charles and does not even know!"

Knowing that if Rothwell had not mentioned Charles to Lydia he must assume she did not know the prince had been present, Maggie remembered that he had not seen the glaring display the prince had made of himself and realized now that he had not learned of it from Ryder either. The thought flew through her head in a twinkling, but even so, she could see that her slight hesitation had stirred Lydia's curiosity, and said quickly, "The prince is not the only one imperiled, my dear. You do understand that most people there last night were Jacobites, do you not?"

"Well, of course, I do. I am one myself. Ned says that is absurd, but then he is a Whig. I don't know what James is, but I daresay he is also a Whig, for I have never heard him utter so much as a word in favor of the Stewart claim, and most Tories are thought to be sympathetic to Jacobites, you know."

"Oh, my dear," Maggie said, shaking her head, "being a Jacobite is not at all the same thing as being a Whig or a Tory."

"Lud, I know that. People get very upset if one so much as mentions James Stewart. They call him the Old Pretender, which is dreadfully disrespectful, I think, but even though Ned says that being a Jacobite is just like committing treason, that must be nonsense, because I know lots of perfectly respectable people who toast the king over the water, and none of them gets arrested, but now nothing will do but that Ned must pack me off to Derbyshire and you off to Scotland, and I daresay we shall not stop him, for he means to escort us both himself."

"Only to Derbyshire," Maggie told her. "Though he has promised to provide an escort for me, he won't go to Scotland."

Lydia shook her head. "That cannot be right, Maggie, because I distinctly heard him tell Mama that it would be a pity, since he had to go so far just to take us home, not to go. And when she said he would be crazy to go at this time of year, he said he had heard the shooting and hunting were excellent now."

Hardly daring to believe her, and wondering what on earth could have changed his mind, Maggie said faintly, "Did he tell your mother the whole tale then?"

"Not the whole, just enough so that she flew into the boughs and raked me down just as if Ned had not already done so and as if it were all my fault, which it is not! She is prodigiously shocked, as I suppose I need not tell you; nevertheless, she agreed with me that it was not necessary to drag me out of town. Of course that was only because she still harbors hopes of making a match for me with Evan Cavendish, who even Ned said is not a good match for me. It is Evan's money, of course, that entices Mama. It is always the money. She thinks that since James was so unfortunate as to have been born after Ned, and since I am but a mere female, we can make our marks only by marrying wealthy and titled persons. I do not care a fig about such stuff, of course, nor does James, but that is precisely what has put Mama into such a passion now. I cannot bear to think how uncomfortable she will make us, all the way to Derbyshire."

Privately Maggie thought the dowager very vain and rather stupid. The only person she seemed to care

a whit for, other than herself and her legion of splendid ancestors, was James, whom she doted on. When
he was at hand, that did not keep her from condemning his artistic endeavors and what she called his medical dabbling, but Maggie had noticed that she took
every opportunity to praise him to others, declaring
him to be a fine artist—much better than Canaletto or
that dreadful Hogarth—and commending his potions
and remedies to all her friends. Now, in an attempt to
stir Lydia to a better humor, Maggie said lightly, "We
shall have to cheer your mama by suggesting to her
that since James will remain in London, he might well
succeed in bringing Lady Portland's niece round his
thumb whilst you are gone."

That drew a laugh, but Lydia shook her head. "You
may suggest that if you like, but I promise it will not
improve her humor, for she will know as well as I do
that without her here to harass him, James will not
make the least push to engage that girl's interest. In
point of fact," she added with a musing look, "I mean
to entreat him to accompany us. Mama is never as
unpleasant when he is around as she can be when he
is not, for he is quite her favorite, despite the fact that
he rarely exerts himself to please her except by bringing her an occasional lotion or potion. It is the oddest
thing, for I tried and tried when I was younger to be
the sort of daughter I thought she wanted me to be,
and she never paid the least heed. It was always James.
But one cannot dislike him, you know. It is not his
fault that she dotes on him. I don't think he even cares
about such things."

"Nor will he care to journey into Derbyshire," Maggie said dryly. "Your brother loves the city too much
to leave it."

"Oh, you do not know James," Lydia said. "He has

any number of odd tastes and is forever finding new ways to amuse himself. It is not all painting and such. Why, he spent months following Dr. Brockelby about, not because he ever thought he might wish to become a doctor, of course—persons of our station never do— but merely because he likes to know things. And he knows lots of other things, too. Even Ned says James spent his time at Eton and Oxford more wisely than he did, and Ned is not stupid by any means. He does become irritated with James, however, because he says he never applies himself to anything of importance, which is why they disagree so frequently. James does not think much of the things Ned thinks are terribly important, either."

"But none of that," Maggie pointed out with a sigh, "is any reason for your brother to leave town now to go to Derbyshire,"

Lydia smiled mischievously. "Nonetheless, I shall persuade him to go. Indeed," she added with an arch look, "I daresay it will not be nearly so difficult as you think it will, for unless I miss my guess, dearest James has developed a fondness for you."

"Nonsense." Maggie was astonished by the suggestion.

"No such thing. Why else would he have come for us with Thomas last night? Moreover, he has always had a preference for fair women—which is why I think he will never look twice at Lady Portland's niece, who is quite dark—and he has said more than once that he admires your spirit and thinks you are different from any female he has met. If that is not what a gentleman says when he is intrigued by a lady, I do not know the signs."

Maggie knew better than to suggest that Lydia's limited experience hardly made her an expert in such matters, and she was glad later that she had held her tongue, for to her great surprise, the imperious letter Lydia sent off by footman to her brother resulted in his appearing at Rothwell House early the following morning, prepared to set off at once for Derbyshire.

If Maggie was surprised, she saw that Rothwell was amazed. He had been attempting to explain his decision to visit Scotland after all, an attempt both hampered and punctuated by Lady Rothwell's continued complaints. When James entered the breakfast parlor, both fell silent, but Rothwell recovered first, demanding, "Good God, James, what brings you out so early?"

James grinned at Lydia, bent and kissed his mother's cheek, and said, "Good morning, Mama. Are you still vexed about all this? Lydia sent to tell me that Ned had come over the tyrant again, so you behold in me your personal and most sympathetic courier. Good morning, Miss MacDrumin. I trust that my family has not dismayed you with all their distempered freaks."

Maggie could not resist his cheerful smile, but she saw the moment she returned it that his surprising behavior might well cause more problems than his presence would alleviate, for the dowager, having responded with delight to his unexpected entrance, was now regarding Maggie with profound disapproval.

"James," Lady Rothwell said sharply, "perhaps you will be better able than I was to convince your brother that it is quite impossible for us to leave town on such short notice."

James put a hand on her shoulder and gave it a gentle squeeze, saying, "Come now, Mama, surely you know it is beyond my poor powers of persuasion to influence Ned in any way whatsoever. Indeed, I shall feel that I have exerted myself a good deal merely to convince him to let me accompany you."

"But do you *wish* to go to Rothwell Park?" Lady Rothwell demanded, clearly thinking the notion a ludicrous one.

James shrugged. "As to that, I daresay it will be nearly as dismal there as Lydia says it will, but that is precisely why I cannot refuse to lend my cheerful countenance to your expedition. Someone must do something to protect you all from falling into flat despair along the way. Besides," he added, grinning, "if I practice a few small economies now, I shall not find myself short of funds again before January, and will be spared the indignity of a lecture on my personal finances from my unfeeling brother."

Rothwell had been watching him narrowly, but at this sally he smiled, saying, "I take it then that your notion of economy is to hang on my sleeve for the duration of the journey."

"Certainly. You will scarcely believe that I truly mean to act as your courier. I know perfectly well that your excellent Fletcher sees to all arrangements when you travel. I could never do so well. Indeed, I know you could not get on without him."

"So little do I enjoy this sort of expedition, however, that had I known you'd agree to visit the country at this time of year, I'd have willingly entrusted the whole business to you."

James raised his eyebrows. "Would you, indeed? I thank you for the vote of confidence—I think."

Lady Rothwell made an unladylike sound. "If that is how you feel, Rothwell, believe me, I would not object to having my son's escort in place of yours. You *can* leave everything to him."

With a gleam of mockery in his eyes, Rothwell

shook his head and said, "I am sorry to disoblige you, ma'am. Though I have no doubt of James's ability to see you safely to Rothwell Park, I do doubt his ability to transport you there against your will, and since it is by my wish that you are going at all, it is also my responsibility to see that you make the journey safely."

If he expected gratitude, he did not get it, and when Lady Rothwell turned away, clearly displeased, Maggie knew without question that their journey was unlikely to prove a pleasant one.

Nor did it. Although hostilities stopped short of outright war, neither Lydia nor her mother pretended to feel anything other than resentment at being transported from town to country, and the dismal weather did nothing to soothe their tempers. When the four carriages required to carry them, their servants, and baggage left London, the air was chilly and damp, and rain began to fall before they reached Stevenage. On the second day, having left the Great North Road at Stamford, as they neared the village of Oakham, the rain began to fall harder.

Huddled in furs beside Lydia in the gently rocking second carriage, Maggie was grateful that they were not in the lead coach with her ladyship and Maria Chelton, the rather taciturn woman who had served as her maid for many years. Lady Rothwell, having felt a headache coming on, had moaned and groaned so much that at the first break in the weather Lydia had asked if she would not rest better if she and Maggie were to ride for a time with Rothwell and James.

The two men had been passing the time playing piquet, but when the change was made they had welcomed the young women with evident pleasure. James, moving to the rear-facing seat to make room for them, said, "I did not expect to be kept confined like this. Generally, it is possible to ride nearly every day until mid-October, but this is too much. We'll have snow before long!"

Rothwell had descended to help Lydia and Maggie into the coach, and when he took Maggie's hand, she had smiled at him. Now, as he sat opposite her, she remembered the warmth of his responding smile and kept her gaze lowered, reluctant to seem as if she were encouraging his attentions.

Lydia sighed. "The road is a mass of puddles. We can never make Rothwell Hall tonight."

James laughed. "Or in any weather, you goose. Bless me, it is more than fifty miles yet!"

"Is that so far? It is no more than half past one, and I know Ned frequently makes the journey in two days. I thought since we were traveling with him, we would do so too."

"When Ned travels, he goes by post chaise with no more impediments than Fletcher and a portmanteau or two," James said, still chuckling, "which means he can travel more than ten miles an hour on some roads. Even on the Great North Road, which is one of the best-kept in England, I daresay we went no more than eight in any hour. And I can tell you, too, Ned never stops at Stevenage his first night out of London. But then," he added with a teasing look at his sister, "he never lingers until nearly eleven o'clock before *beginning* a journey, either."

There was nothing Lydia could say in answer to that, for the delay had been as much her fault as anyone's. No sooner had the dowager ordered her servants to repack her trunk for the third time, having made certain that some object or other that would be quite indispensable in Derbyshire had truly been packed, than Lydia had suddenly remembered some item of her own that might well have been overlooked and had to turn out another box or bundle to be certain it had not.

Rothwell had shown more patience than Maggie had thought he possessed through all the minor crises, and James, too, had been completely resigned to the delays, making no complaint even when his mother, having climbed into her coach and settled herself, suddenly demanded to know if her hartshorn and distillation of nightshade had been packed. Since everyone was quite sure they had been, it was even more annoying to be informed that she had not wanted them packed away but required them to be near at hand throughout the journey, so that Maria Chelton had to unearth them from the bottommost container in the baggage coach. Even now, both men showed merely amused forbearance at Lydia's annoyance.

She glared at them. "I trust we will get there tomorrow and that you are not telling me we have another two days of this to endure. Mama does not think it right for Maggie and me to ride with the two of you, even if you are my brothers, and I daresay she will only allow it for a short while. I just hope her affliction is not the onset of something dreadful, or she will give it to us both before we reach Rothwell Hall. If she lets us stay in this coach another hour, I will be surprised."

Rothwell said placidly, "We will reach the Park tomorrow."

When Lady Rothwell insisted they stop at the George Inn in Melton Mowbray, he said he thought she would be more comfortable at the Flying Horse in Nottingham. She resisted, but Rothwell's will prevailed, and Maggie saw that he exerted himself to be patient. The dowager felt better the next morning, relieving Lydia of the concern that they would all take her illness, so it was a shock to everyone when, upon their arrival at Rothwell Park, Fletcher, who had scarcely been near the dowager, descended from the servants' coach only to faint dead away on the ground at his master's feet.

XI

Lady Rothwell, descending from her coach as a number of persons hurried to assist the fallen valet, said tartly, "It is a wonder that we have not all succumbed to this ague, what with being rattled and bounced all the way from London with such uncivilized haste. Good gracious, do not bring him near me, you fools! Take him into the house through the buttery porch. Come, Maria, let the servants deal with all this. I must rest."

Maggie, waiting while Lydia gave her orders to the servants, who were attempting to deal with poor Fletcher and the baggage, noted that Rothwell Park House, situated on a bold eminence on the east side of the River Wye, looked exactly as she had expected the ancient noble residence to look. The coaches had approached over a triple-arched stone bridge and up a short slope, through a high gateway, into a paved courtyard. Until then, the high crenellated walls and towers, which had provided her first view of Rothwell Park, made the place look like a medieval castle. Now, looking at the beautifully weathered gray stone house that formed the central block, she could see that it was an ancient baronial residence to which numerous additions had been made over the centuries.

James reached into the coach to fetch a fur muff and shawl that Maggie had left inside, and when he smiled as he handed them to her, she was glad his mother had gone into the house. Lady Rothwell's attitude had grown more brittle and steadily more protective the longer they were on the road together, and Maggie realized the dowager was concerned lest her plan to marry her son to a wealthy Englishwoman might be imperiled. Then, as she returned James's smile and let him tuck her hand into the crook of his arm, she caught Rothwell's gaze on them and realized the dowager was not the only one to misinterpret James's kindness.

Mistaking her slight frown for anxiety, James said gently, "Fletcher is in no danger, I promise you. He has merely taken Mama's cold. He always finds it impossible to sleep well whilst he is traveling, and attempting to please Mama—an impossible task—has undoubtedly added strain to what is always a difficult job. With a good rest, he will soon be as good as new."

Turning her back on the now scowling earl, she replied, "I hope you are right, Mr. Carsley, but Fletcher's illness will mean a delay in my departure, will it not? His lordship will not want to travel without him."

He agreed, then clearly thinking the point a trivial one, he shouted at Lydia to let the servants do their work, and come inside.

Maggie saw that Rothwell had brought order to the chaos in the yard with a few well-chosen words, and he soon joined them. They entered the house through the great hall, which exemplified the typical medieval arrangement, even in Scotland, and where Maggie could easily imagine medieval de Carsleys dining on the dais at the upper end, separated from their retainers by a great salt dish. There were two huge fireplaces. The walls were paneled and hung with loose arras tapestries looped back on iron hooks at the doorways, and a gallery providing access between upper floors ran the full length of the vaulted chamber.

From the hall, they passed through what was plainly the dining room, the ceiling of which had been painted with red and white panels containing heraldic emblems, then went up a short flight of stone steps, through a pair of dog-gates, past more tapestries, and came at last to what Lydia announced was the long gallery. She added, pulling her cloak tighter around her, "Now, Maggie, will you confess that I was right and Rothwell Park House is no more than a great, cold medieval pile of stones?"

"It is very large," Maggie said.

Lydia nodded. "Large, freezing, and full of drafts. 'Tis monstrous cruel of Ned to imprison us here. His rooms are here, at the north end of the gallery, but mine is up one more flight of stairs, and you will be near me. I will help you settle in."

"Don't get her too settled," Rothwell said behind them. "She leaves for Scotland in the morning."

Lydia stared at him. "I thought you were going with her."

"I am."

"But you cannot mean to travel without Fletcher!"

"It will be a grave inconvenience to do so," he said with a sardonic look, "but cruel though you have named me, I am not so cruel as to drag him along when he is ill, and I do not propose to wait until he recovers. Come, puss, do you think me unable to dress myself?"

"Lud, can you?"

James and Maggie, and even Rothwell himself, laughed at her wide-eyed amazement, but they all learned, just as soon as they gathered for dinner, that Lady Rothwell took a dim view of the notion that the Earl of Rothwell might travel without his valet and general factotum at his side.

"You cannot do that," she said flatly when his intention was made known to her at dinner. "The fact that you choose to visit a barbaric land is no excuse to behave like a barbarian yourself, Rothwell. You must take Chelton."

"I am sorry to disoblige you, ma'am, but though I recall that Maria Chelton's husband briefly served my father, I scarcely know the man and have no intention of taking him with me."

"And just who do you think will maid this young woman?" the dowager asked, shifting ground so swiftly that Maggie suddenly found herself the focus of every eye in the room.

Rothwell said patiently, "One of the maidservants can go along to look after her."

"What can you be thinking? You will compromise her reputation beyond mending if you force her to travel alone with you, protected only by a dim-witted chambermaid, and one of your own, at that, accustomed to following *your* orders!"

His annoyance showed, but he said evenly, "If you can suggest an alternative, ma'am, I am willing to hear it."

"Certainly, I can. Maria must go with her."

A heavy silence fell, and it was Lydia who recovered first, exclaiming, "Mama, you could not get along without her!"

"I am quite willing to make the sacrifice," Lady

Rothwell said grandly. "I will not have it said that I allowed Rothwell to take advantage of any young woman. Moreover, Maria has spent so little time with Matthew this year that he has dared to complain of her neglect. Now that she is here, he would be most displeased to see her sent off to Scotland with Rothwell."

Rothwell said dryly, "There is no need to displease anyone. I will leave Maria here with her husband and take some other dragon to look after Miss MacDrumin's reputation."

Lady Rothwell said calmly, "A married couple will lend a greater degree of respectability to your journey than can be gained by any other means short of my accompanying you myself—and I do not intend to set foot in such an outlandish place—but whether you like it or not, Rothwell, Miss MacDrumin must have a proper companion, or her father, if he is any sort of gentleman at all, will be outraged by the slight to her position."

Maggie, bristling at the dowager's casual defamation of Scotland, was surprised when Rothwell conceded to the plan at once. He said, "No doubt you are right, ma'am, and your solution will certainly get Fletcher's vote, at least. He is as convinced as Lydia is that I shall be poorly turned out if I am forced to do without him, and although Chelton will not measure up to his London standard, Fletcher must agree that the man will do well enough in the less civilized environs of Scotland."

When the dowager nodded serenely, Maggie snapped, "I'll have you know, sir, that Scotland is perfectly civilized, more so in many ways than England is!"

James laughed. "You will not convince Ned or

Mama of that. I daresay they both believe all Scotland is full of aborigines who gibber at visitors in some sort of foreign tongue."

"Not *all* Scotland," the earl said with a smile, "merely the Highlands. No, no," he added with a sudden, unexpectedly warm look at Maggie, "sheathe your claws, Miss MacDrumin. I promise you, I am jesting. I admit I know little about your Highlanders other than that they can be formidable on the battle-field, but I've already learned that many of them are better educated than I thought, and although I intend to remain in Scotland only long enough to see you safely home and look over the estate, I am certain I shall learn much more about them before I return."

"You know, Ned," James said thoughtfully, "I believe I'd like to have a look at the Highlands myself. I've never so much as set foot in Scotland, you know." He grinned at Maggie. "My education is sadly lacking, too, but I am certain I can find any number of subjects to paint, and no doubt you will be delighted to set me straight about the numerous misconceptions I must have developed over the course of my misspent life."

"Certainly I will, sir," she replied, grinning back at him.

Lady Rothwell stiffened. "I do not think that at all wise, James dearest. Surely, you will prefer to remain here and look after us. I cannot feel entirely safe at Rothwell Park, you know, when neither you nor Rothwell is in residence."

James grimaced, thought better of it, and said coaxingly, "Mama, really, if you have been thinking I would stay with you and Lydia, you ought to have known better. I came along only to lend my cheerful countenance to what otherwise promised to be an uncomfortable journey for you all, and now, since you have expressed concern for Miss MacDrumin's safety, you must agree my next duty is clear. Two gentlemen must be thought safer company than one, particularly since you would not expect Rothwell and Miss Mac-Drumin to travel in the same coach as their servants."

"There is nothing amiss in Maria's riding with them."

"Ah, but if Matthew longs for his wife's companionship, he will be most annoyed to be relegated to ride with the baggage whilst Maria plays gooseberry. Moreover, Ned and Miss MacDrumin will much prefer to have me. You do not object, do you, Ned?"

"No, indeed, I will be glad to have your company."

"Then that's settled," James said, shooting a look of glowing satisfaction at Maggie.

She was suddenly aware of hostility in the very air around her, and though she could not be certain of its origin, she rather thought she knew. Rothwell had returned his attention to his plate, and Lady Rothwell too appeared concerned only with her dinner. She made no further effort to dissuade James, but Maggie was nearly sure that it was she who was upset, for Lydia wore one of her mischievous looks. The servants, ignored throughout by everyone, continued with their duties.

The rest of the evening passed slowly, and by the time Maggie went up to the bedchamber allotted to her—a chilly, stone-walled room much more like ones she was accustomed to in Glen Drumin albeit nearly as prettily decorated as the rooms in Rothwell London House—she was convinced that the dowager viewed her as a threat to James's future well-being, but she did not know whether Lady Rothwell was more distressed by that fear or by James's refusal to submit to her will. Nor did she know whether the dowager actively disliked her or was simply having second thoughts about sending her highly skilled tirewoman to the wilds of Scotland with such a low creature. Lady Rothwell was civil to her but no more than that.

The following morning—a sunny one at last—they were ready to depart at the early hour ordained by Rothwell the night before. Lady Rothwell had not yet risen from her bed, of course, but Lydia arose early on purpose to see them off, and although she suggested wistfully that she would like to accompany them, she took Rothwell's flat refusal in good part, hugged Maggie, and bade them all a fond farewell.

Matthew and Maria Chelton likewise presented themselves in good order, but if either one was particularly pleased by their new duties, Maggie could see no sign of it. Matthew Chelton was a dour man, lean of body and stern of face—a lowland Puritan to the life, Maggie thought. And Maria, who in London had seemed a haughty dame, even higher in the instep than her mistress, seemed somehow diminished when she stood next to her austere husband. She looked as if she had been crying, and Maggie, aware from her brief sojourn in London that servants enjoyed their own strict hierarchy, in which a dowager countess's dresser was a woman of high estate, had no doubt that Maria believed she had sunk to the very depths in being commanded to wait upon a mere miss.

The gentlemen having decided to take advantage of the improved weather and ride the first few stages, Rothwell ordered Maria to sit in the lead coach with Maggie, leaving dour Matthew to solitary splendor in the baggage coach. Though the lead coach was Rothwell's best, and better sprung than most, Maria did not seem happy to be separated from her husband, nor he from her. The tirewoman was sulky and disinclined to talk. So much, Maggie thought as she let down the glass window to wave a last farewell to Lydia, for looking after her and bearing her company.

Several times during that first hour, she attempted to engage Maria in conversation, but although the woman replied politely whenever she was addressed, her replies were monosyllabic and unencouraging. Like her mistress, she was civil but uncommunicative.

Watching the passing countryside and catching only occasional glimpses of the two horsemen, Maggie soon found herself thinking about the earl again. Despite his calm assumption of always being right and knowing what was best for everyone around him, his temper clearly had its limits. Perhaps that was why she sensed such a crackling vitality whenever she was in his presence. On the journey into Derbyshire, she had seen him exert more patience with his stepmother than anyone might have expected of him, and she had seen enough of the always stylish, generally cool-tempered gentleman to know that although he was different from any Highland or Lowland man she had met, he attracted loyal and dedicated admirers. If she could judge by his stepmother, even his enemies accorded him respect.

She glanced at Maria, who still sat with her hands in her lap, looking out the opposite coach window. They were moving faster than they had with the dowager along, but if the swaying of the coach discomfited her, she gave no sign. Maggie found the constant lurching and rocking over the poor road tiresome at best. It was not long before she developed a headache and began to wish that she too might ride with the men.

Rothwell had said that he meant to enter Scotland by way of Carlisle, and since she had come to England through Berwick-on-Tweed, the countryside was new to her. Having left his second coachman with his own horses at the end of the second stage, Rothwell hired another whenever he changed teams, in order, he had said, always to have a man traveling with them who knew the best route. By this means, and by keeping to post roads and frequently changing teams, they were able to maintain the fast pace, and by the time they reached Carlisle on the evening of the second day, Maggie was exhausted and sick of her own company.

A drizzling rain had begun to fall shortly before they came within view of the city walls, but the town felt friendly to her nonetheless, for she knew that Carlisle was one English city where Bonnie Prince Charlie had been welcomed. She knew, too, that for their loyalty the people here had suffered nearly as much in the aftermath of Culloden as the Highlanders had. She did not attempt to explore the city, however, for not only was she exhausted but she knew the earl would forbid it.

She slept soundly, as indeed, she nearly always did, and it was still raining the following morning when Maria, having shared a room with her husband, woke her and helped her to dress. When they joined the men in the coffee room for breakfast, Maggie saw that although Rothwell was as elegantly dressed as ever, he wore his dark hair uncurled and without powder for once, simply tied back with a plain black ribbon. She liked the change, but when he said casually that he hoped to make Edinburgh in less than two more days, she forgot about matters of costume and fashion and objected at once, strenuously.

He said, "I am told that royal mail carriers generally travel from London to Edinburgh in only four days."

"But on horseback, sir, not as passengers in a coach that careens like a ship in a storm. If you insist on maintaining this wicked pace, I wish you would hire a horse for me to ride, for I shall be as ill as Fletcher was if you do not. Indeed, I do not know how it is that you and James are not as exhausted from riding as Maria and I are from traveling in the coach."

"The pace does not seem fast," he said, "but perhaps we are more accustomed to riding for long hours than you are to being shut up in a carriage. For you to ride with us would not be seemly, however, and in any case no one will be riding this morning. We would be soaked to the skin in minutes."

"Well, if you sit in the coach with me, I shall not complain," she said with a sigh. "I daresay you will slow the horses soon enough if you are made to endure the awful rocking."

Rothwell said, "Perhaps, but we will sit with Matthew in the second coach. My stepmother had second thoughts about the propriety of your traveling with two of us in a closed carriage." He glanced at Maria, who seemed more cheerful now than at the start of their journey. "Did she not, Maria?"

"She did, my lord, and she was quite right."

James chuckled. "What nonsense! Tell me, if you can, just what Mama thinks we can do to Miss Mac-Drumin with four of us squeezed into the family coach? I do not care a fig for what you choose to do, Ned, but I mean to ride with her in the more comfortable coach. I daresay she is bored to distraction with Maria's company and will be delighted to have mine."

Maggie's spirits lifted considerably. "Oh, thank you, sir. you can have no idea how grateful we will be to have someone else to talk to." She glanced guiltily at Maria. "I fear I have annoyed Mrs. Chelton with my frequent attempts to chatter."

"Not at all, miss," the woman said stiffly, glancing

at her husband, who was offering Rothwell more toast. Maggie had noted from the beginning of their journey that the earl preferred to be attended by his own servants, even at public inns.

James laughed. "You may be certain that I will talk to you, Miss MacDrumin. I say," he added, "would you mind awfully if I were to call you Maggie? Traveling all together like this does make us all seem like one family, so if you *don't* mind—"

Rothwell said firmly, "Sit where you like, James, but you will address her properly. He will undoubtedly soon make you wish for solitude again, Miss MacDrumin, but perhaps, if you do not dislike it, I will also ride with you, just to see that he toes the mark. This coach is indeed much better sprung than the other and boasts glass windows, too, which keep out the elements much more efficiently than leather curtains."

Maria sniffed. "But this one is not so large, my lord, that it will not be prodigiously overcrowded with four of us."

Matthew, overhearing her, said expressionlessly, "It is not for you to question his lordship, Maria."

When she flushed deeply, Rothwell said, "She is quite right, however, and I recall now that my stepmother said you had been looking forward to spending time with each other. You may sit with Matthew for a time, Maria. I promise you, Miss MacDrumin's reputation will be quite safe so long as two of us are with her."

Maria looked as if she might so forget her position as to argue, but with a look at Rothwell's placid countenance and another at her husband's stern one, she capitulated. Thus, when they took to the road again, although the gentlemen still rode when it was possible to do so, Maggie frequently found herself with more congenial company than Maria's. James knew a number of games that could be played while traveling, and even Rothwell relaxed. The miles flew by, and to her astonishment, they reached Edinburgh by eight o'-clock the following evening.

A quick meal, another deep sleep, and she was ready to depart when the sun rose. Rothwell's hair had gone unpowdered only that one rainy morning, and his extreme elegance and air of command assured them of excellent service wherever they stopped; however, once in Scotland, it seemed to Maggie that a good many more persons than necessary found duties to attend in their vicinity, just to catch a glimpse of such sartorial splendor.

James was his usual, casually dressed self, and if he occasionally seemed amused by the attention his brother drew, he expressed that amusement with no more than a twinkling look flashed at Maggie. The natives, however, regarded the earl not with amusement but with awe, and although Matthew continued to serve their meals, local servants jumped to obey Rothwell's slightest gesture or most casually expressed desire, and when he indicated that a dish did not please his English taste or sit well in his English stomach, they rushed to produce new dishes or local remedies to ease his slightest discomfort.

That morning, although he said he had not slept well, he wore elegant riding dress, complete with jeweled smallsword, and after a brief discussion with the chief ostler in the innyard, he announced that they would take the post road to Stirling. "The chap says the road is used daily by post boys from Edinburgh," he told the others, "so it should be adequate for the coaches."

Maggie said quickly, "It is faster to take the ferry

across the Firth of Forth, sir, and go to Perth from there."

"But we are not going to Perth. I have it on excellent advice that the best route to the Great Glen lies through Stirling, Callander, and Fort William."

"If you are taking me home, however, the best route lies through Perth to Dunkeld, not through the Great Glen. Do you not know the location of your own estate?" Her voice was tart.

He looked taken aback, and fell silent for a moment before he said quietly, "I was told the estate lies near Inverness."

"So it does if one is trying to describe its location to an Englishman," she said. "The nearest large town—indeed, the only one large enough for an Englishman to have heard of it—*is* Inverness. But one need not travel up the Great Glen to reach Glen Drumin. That would be a most lengthy journey, sir."

"But surely a better way for coaches, Miss MacDrumin."

"By taking the post road out of Perth, we can take coaches as far as Dalwhinnie, Rothwell, or even Laggan if the weather is not too bad. We will have to ride over the Corriearrack, of course, for the road over the pass will take carts but not carriages. My father keeps horses at inns in several villages, however, for just that purpose."

"I see." He fell silent again, and Maggie wondered if he would question her knowledge. Having made the journey from Edinburgh to the Highlands and back numerous times during her school years, she knew she was right, but she knew, too, that men rarely took it kindly when their decisions were disputed. The silence lengthened, but when James shot his brother a quizzical look, Rothwell said at last, "I will bow to your superior knowledge of the roads, ma'am. We go by way of Perth.''

With the ferry ride only an hour away, he and James decided to ride in the coach with her, and when they neared the Firth, James said in a doubtful tone, "Should one look forward to the experience of being ferried in a carriage? I confess, it is something with which I have little familiarity despite our excellent service on the Thames. As I recall from my geography lessons, the Firth of Forth is rather wider than the river.''

"Perhaps it is, a bit," Maggie said, smiling at him. "But I have made the journey a number of times, you know, and found it most enjoyable. One stays in one's carriage, and my father has been known to sleep the entire way and not remember the crossing. The horses must be unharnessed, of course, so as not to drown if there should be some sort of accident.''

"May we be as lucky," James said with a comical look. He continued to express his mistrust of the ferry, but when they reached it, Maggie saw that he already had his sketchbook in hand and his concentration during the crossing was profound.

She looked at Rothwell and saw that he was watching his brother, looking amused. He glanced her way just then and smiled unexpectedly. Warmth leapt to her cheeks, and she felt suddenly as if they were alone in the carriage. The sound of James's moving pencil became part of the background noise, like the gentle lapping of the water against the sturdy ferry barge or the rhythmic knocking of the bargemen's poles against the sides as they exerted themselves against the strong, lateral current.

"What do you expect of me, Miss MacDrumin?" Rothwell asked, his voice low in his throat, almost as if the words came from within him, without prior thought on his part, impulsively.

The question caught her off her guard, but she rallied quickly, replying, "We want you to help us, sir. Papa's people are as much yours now as his, and they are not pawns on a chessboard, you know, but human beings. Once you see for yourself that our old ways are best, you will help us to recover them."

"But the whole world is changing," he said gently. "I fear that if the Highlanders are to survive, they too must be willing to change. Life has become urban, with towns as the centers of thought and art as well as commerce, and Britain is the center of everything. We are fighting wars and pushing frontiers of trade, and the outside world has begun to enter the most remote corners of the land. One can no longer sit content in a village, Miss MacDrumin, chewing over local gossip and such fantastic bits of news as manage to reach it from the cities. One must keep well-informed both to prosper and to learn to cope with modern life"

"Fine words, sir, but what precisely do you mean to say?"

"That perhaps the old ways are not the best ones," he said, "that there are other choices that might prove better ones."

"Faith, sir, do you think it is so easy as that—one merely makes a choice? You do not know what you are talking about!"

"Don't snap my head off. I merely suggested that there are no doubt choices that have not been considered yet. I am not fool enough to insist upon one way over another from the outset."

He sounded eminently reasonable, but although she could not think why his words made her so angry, they did. She wanted to snatch him bald-headed, even to shake him. But the thought of shaking him suddenly stirred other thoughts, and she began to think she had spent too much time in close proximity to him that day. She had no time to dwell upon her thoughts, however, for the coach lurched onto the road again, and James snapped his sketchbook shut, demanding to know where they would stop to eat. "My stomach will be gnawing at my backbone long before Perth."

"A medical description you no doubt learned from the admired Dr. Brockelby," Rothwell said, grinning. But he knocked against the ceiling, and when they drew up, leaned out to discover what the driver of the second coach could tell them.

Two hours later the carriages drew up in the yard of a neat little tavern in Kinross. It boasted a coffee room with but a single table, but when the landlord learned that Matthew Chelton meant to serve them, he cheerfully agreed to lay covers for the Cheltons and the two coachmen in his kitchen, and the meal that was set before them proved to be a tasty one. Maggie took an opportunity afterward to beg a towel and cloth from the innkeeper's wife and wash her face and hands.

Clouds had gathered again, and in the distance thunder rumbled, so neither gentleman was inclined to ride. Maria, moving toward the second coach with Matthew, looked as if the thunder made her nervous, but Maggie welcomed it, since it meant she would enjoy better company. Thus, she was a little annoyed when Rothwell seemed inclined to doze, and James opened his sketchbook the moment the coach began to move, leaving her once again to her own thoughts. Still, she felt a certain elation, knowing they were nearing the Highlands, and with each passing mile the feeling grew stronger.

James closed his sketchbook a half hour later, saying, "You look like a cat with a dish of cream." But the next moment his smile vanished and he leaned forward to look closely at Rothwell. "Ned, what is it? Here, answer me!"

Rothwell stirred uncomfortably. He looked pale, and his voice lacked strength when he said, "I fear the food at that inn has made me ill. I feel sick, and it's hard to stay awake."

"Good Lord. Here, driver!" James pounded on the ceiling. "Stop the coach!" Before the coach had rolled to a stop, he had opened the door and was hanging onto the roof, unstrapping one of the bundles. He dropped it to the ground, jumped down and ripped it open, taking a flat case from the articles within. "You've complained of the food since we left England, Ned, but this is the worst yet. Let me help you out of the coach."

Maggie helped too, becoming more anxious as she watched how carefully Rothwell moved. He seemed to be very ill indeed, and she had a terrifying fear that he might expire on the spot. Pushing such thoughts ruthlessly aside, she called to Chelton, peering out of the second coach, to come and aid his master.

James, ignoring everyone but Rothwell, took a bottle from his case and removed the stopper. "Swallow a good jolt of this stuff, Ned. It will fix you right up."

Rothwell obeyed, screwing up his face in distaste. "What the devil are you dosing me with? It tastes like poison."

"A concoction of dried rhizomes and roots of ipecac," James told him. "It will cure what ails you, I promise."

Rothwell's face grew ashen, but the look on his face became one of pure dismay. "James, you wretch! Help me to that ditch. Miss MacDrumin, have the goodness to go away. Far away."

For a moment, Maggie did not understand his meaning, but then she realized his predicament, and managed to turn her back before he relieved himself of everything he had eaten. His retching made her feel ill herself, but once James and Chelton had helped him make himself presentable again, and helped back into the coach to rest, she felt fine. With their coachman's help, James replaced the bundle on the roof, but Maggie noticed that he brought the flat black case inside with him.

"Is he going to be all right?" she asked as he put the case beneath his seat alongside the two smallswords.

"Oh, I think so. I'll keep the ipecac at hand, but I've rarely known anyone to need a second dose. Ned may continue to feel uneasy for a time, but he will most likely sleep now."

"What else do you keep in that box?"

"That's my remedy box. I gathered the things in it with the help of Dr. Brockelby, who also showed me how to use most of them. I've got any number of useful remedies, and never travel without them. One never knows when they will be useful."

Impressed, she asked him to tell her more, and once he assured himself that Rothwell was comfortable, he described his experiences with the London doctor in such a way as to make her wish one moment that she could learn such things herself and the next to be grateful she had no need to do so.

Rothwell recovered quickly and took particular care after that to eat only simple dishes prepared as they were in England. Thus, except for the Cheltons, whose time together did not seem to Maggie to be pleasing either of them much, the next few days proceeded pleasantly if uneventfully. The clouds disappeared, they made better time than even Rothwell had hoped, and Maggie began to believe the coaches would make it all the way to Laggan, the tiny village at the foot of the Corriearrack.

The roads were bad, but the scenery became increasingly magnificent, and she happily identified flora and fauna for her companions and pointed out leaves already turning color for winter and drifting to the ground. A stronger chill touched the air, for it was now October, and the wind increased, warning of storms to come, but the day they left Blair Atholl and made their way up Glen Garry's steep incline was a fine one. They seemed to have it all to themselves, too, for they had not passed another vehicle or a horseman for hours.

The road followed the sparkling waters of the river Garry. Hills rose on either side of them, the upper slopes thick with evergreens, the lower with willow and aspen, the leaves twinkling with sunlight as they rustled on silvery branches. The air was redolent with the scent of pine. The lead coach had been rocking more than usual and when it suddenly stopped altogether, Maggie, who thought they had been luckier than anyone deserved, to have got so far without an accident, was certain their luck had run out at last. Rothwell was unperturbed, but James, letting down the coach window to look out, said in dismay, "There's a child lying in the road ahead, apparently injured. I must help him."

He grabbed his remedy kit from under his seat and stepped down from the coach just as a number of armed men burst from the nearby shrubbery and a deep voice cried, "Hold where ye stand, English, and hand o'er yer baubles or forfeit yer lives!"

XII

Seeing the boy leap to his feet and vanish into the thick shrubbery, Rothwell said in an undertone, "Say nothing, Miss MacDrumin. I doubt they will harm us." He kept his eye on James, unsure of how he would respond, for despite all his wanderings through lower-class neighborhoods of London, Rothwell doubted that he had much experience with criminals.

Putting his right hand in his coat pocket and gripping the small pistol he carried there, Rothwell moved to step from the coach. When the same deep voice commanded him to remain where he was, he said plaintively, "My good fellow, you must realize we have been cooped up in this deuced uncomfortable coach for hours, rattling over your wretched roads. I vow, I shan't even complain about being robbed of my last penny if you will only allow us to stretch our legs. The lady will no doubt succumb to the vapors if she is not allowed to breathe a bit of fresh air, for she is very much shocked by this outrage."

"Ye've a wooman wi' ye? Coom out then, lass. We'll nay harm ye."

Rothwell had not so much as paused in his descent from the coach and stood now, looking around with an air of languor, his hand still in his pocket, his fingers curled around the pistol grip. His coachman, he noted swiftly, kept his attention on his horses, and the second fellow seemed willing to follow his wise example. Rothwell cursed his own stupidity, knowing that once again he had underestimated the Scots. Aware of the ban against Highland weapons, he had thought there would be little to fear, and so although his drivers carried blunderbusses, the weapons—like his sword and James's—lay useless beneath their seats.

There were four bandits, all wearing masks and thick knitted caps, and it looked as if the smallest one, standing silently some distance from the others, must be the leader, for only that one carried a firearm. Rothwell's experienced eye told him the flintlock pistol was ancient, but the steadiness with which it was held spoke of proficiency in its use. The others wielded wicked-looking cudgels, and one man, much larger and more burly-looking than the others, seemed particularly menacing.

"Yer purses, gents." The large one was doing the talking. "Hand 'em over, if ye please."

Rothwell, hearing a small gasp behind him, glanced into the coach and saw that Miss MacDrumin was sitting on the edge of her seat, looking wide-eyed. He gave her a reassuring smile, but in her fear, she seemed to have eyes only for the slender bandit with the pistol, the one he realized now must be the leader of the group. James, too, was watching that one. To his credit, James had done nothing rash and looked at Rothwell now as if he awaited instructions, making no move to hand over his valuables. Nor did Rothwell intend for him to do so.

The burly fellow, losing patience, stepped toward James, whereupon the leader, apparently dismissing

Rothwell as being of no consequence, turned to keep the pistol aimed at James, and in turning, presented his profile to Rothwell, the large flintlock held steadily out in front of him, away from his own slim body.

Rothwell's shot echoed from the nearby hills, and as the flintlock went flying, the leader shrieked with pain. The burly man halted instantly in his approach toward James and spun around on his heel. The boy who had lain in the road ran from his place of concealment toward the leader, but the two other men hurled themselves furiously at Rothwell, their cudgels held high.

"Hold!" James's bellow and the sudden appearance of a pistol in his right hand stopped one of them, and Rothwell was able to deal with the second, avoiding the cudgel with a twist of his body and throwing the fellow neatly over his hip. When he straightened, he saw James watching the leader, who still stood, rubbing a bloody hand against already filthy breeches. James held out his pistol, saying abruptly, "Take this, Ned. You are a better shot than I am, and I want to look at that hand."

The unfired pistol was thrust into Rothwell's hand, as Miss MacDrumin descended from the coach to stand beside him. The other men had put down their cudgels, and they also watched James. The boy, tugging at the leader's sleeve, trying to look at the injured hand, was gently set aside, and the leader watched warily but silently as James approached.

To Rothwell's astonishment, instead of looking at the hand as he had said he would, James reached out and snatched away the mask and cap. Fine, very long flaxen hair spilled forth. The leader was female, a young and rather pretty female, at that.

She glared at James and jerked away from him.

"Keep your distance, ye filthy Sassenach, or I'll spit ye where ye stand."

"With what?" James asked curiously, his voice carrying easily over the murmur of the river and the restless movement of horses. "Your pistol lies yonder, and your fingernails are bitten to the quick. Let me see your injured hand."

"I'll not!" She whisked the hand behind her and, stepping back from him, bent swiftly and reached with her left hand for her right boot. When James moved toward her, she straightened with a vicious-looking dagger in hand; and when he stopped in astonishment, she spat full in his face. "Come touch me now, ye villainous wretch!"

To Rothwell's amusement, James reacted with even greater speed, grabbing the girl's arm with one hand, the dagger with the other. Flinging the weapon far across the river, he forced her to bend forward, clapped his left arm around her waist, and with visible force applied his right hand to her backside. She shrieked again, this time with fury, and Rothwell watched her men carefully, lest they try to intervene. Not one moved. Every one stared at James, mouth agape, apparently frozen in place.

Maggie clutched Rothwell's arm. "Stop him, sir! Oh, stop him! He mustn't. Kate will murder him!"

Rothwell realized at once that she knew the girl but said nothing, keeping his eyes on the bandits and making no effort to stop the man he had thrown from getting to his feet again. Like the others, the fellow watched James, who was clearly relieving pent-up feelings in a thorough way. His victim continued to scream her fury, calling him names and assuring him he would rot in hell for what he was doing to her, right up to the moment that James dumped her into the chilly waters of the river Garry.

"That ought to cool you," he said, placing his hands on his hips and looking sternly down at her when she came up sputtering, "You're a hot-tempered wench and no mistake, but before you spit or shriek insults at a man, be certain he cannot punish you. Only a fool stirs the temper of someone stronger than herself." Turning away then as if to emphasize the fact that he had no fear of her, he said to Rothwell, "What shall we do with this lot?"

"We should hail them before the nearest magistrate," Rothwell said, shifting his gaze to Miss MacDrumin.

As he expected, she stiffened and said, "You must not do that. You have just proved they are no threat to anyone." He noted that she did not look at the bandits when she said this. The drenched figure in the brook was watching her, but she said nothing, and Rothwell thought her expression was a bit rueful.

He said, "Their aptitude, or lack of it, is scarcely the point just now, Miss MacDrumin. They are criminals and no doubt ought to be hanged." To his satisfaction he saw that the vixen in the brook seemed unnerved at last, but she got to her feet without a word, and though she slipped on the rocks, she refused to accept James's hand when he reached out to help her.

A note of desperation entered Maggie's voice. "Please, let them go. They did not know it was your coach they attacked. Moreover, the nearest magistrate is back at Blair Atholl. Do you intend to make them walk behind the second coach, tied together all in a string?"

He pretended to consider the point. He had already decided no good would come of trying to take the sorry group anywhere, let alone back the way they had come. They would be more trouble than they were worth, but he wanted to see how strongly she felt about them. If she was in league with them, it would behoove him to know it before he traveled farther in her company.

His hesitation encouraged her to say, "Please, she is soaked to the skin and there are clouds boiling up to rain again. She will catch her death plodding behind these coaches."

Glancing up, he saw that she was right about the weather. New dark clouds had formed in the south. He said, "James, take their weapons. Be certain to get them all. Matthew, help him. And check their boots," he added. When the young woman beside him gave an audible sigh of relief, he shifted his attention to her, adding sternly, "You have some explaining to do, my girl. Get back in that coach."

Obeying him, Maggie swallowed hard, wondering what she would say, and remembering that in her shock at what James was doing she had spoken Kate's name. She could not hope a man as astute as Rothwell had missed that. When he had got down from the coach, affecting that languid air of his, she had been surprised, but she realized that he had done it only to fool Kate's men into mistaking him for a harmless English fop. She had been fooled by the affectation herself in the beginning, so she had not been amazed when Kate and the others dismissed him and focused their attention on the more dangerous-looking James. She had not known that Rothwell was armed, however, or she would have tried to warn them. She trembled now to think he might have killed Kate.

She doubted she would have the strength to deny Rothwell the explanation he demanded. He could stir her emotions in ways no man ever had before and just trying to return his steady look when he turned to be certain she had obeyed him made her wish she could make him forget that he was angry.

James, with the cudgels, came toward the coach. Shouting over his shoulder at Matthew to search for the dagger and pistol, he added in a normal tone, "Dash it, Ned, if I'd known you'd want the devilish things, I'd not have flung that dagger so far. More to the left, Matthew," he shouted, watching the man paw through shrubbery on the opposite bank. "He'll not thank me for making him wade that icy river. Good thing it's not deeper."

"Better that he find it than that this lot does."

Maggie glanced at Kate, but Kate did not look at her. She and her men, and young Ian, were standing under a large willow, watching the search. Both weapons were found at last, and when Chelton moved to join his wife in the second coach, Rothwell and James climbed into the first with her. They were soon on their way again, leaving the bandits behind. She waited.

James said, "I've never seen the like. Imagine a female leading a gang of cutthroats! Who'd ever believe such a thing?"

"Well, Miss MacDrumin?" Rothwell's tone was hard, and she could feel his gaze upon her. When she did not look up, he added gently, "Miss MacDrumin must tell us if highway robbery is yet another quaint custom of this so civilized country of hers."

Her skin felt too tight for her body, and though she did not look up from her lap, she knew that James was also watching her now. She was not afraid of either man, but anticipation of their displeasure—Rothwell's, especially—made her uneasy, and she could think of nothing to say. In the thickening silence her mind snatched at and rejected one possibility after another until at last, looking at Rothwell, she said, "If Highlanders do things that are considered outrageous elsewhere, it is because they have been reduced to such straits by English oppression."

"Nonsense, they are criminals."

"They are not! They are desperate to put food on their tables." She saw that he did not believe her, and knew she was on treacherous ground, for her own father disapproved of Kate's activities and said she had no good cause for them. But then he smuggled whisky for much the same reasons, so Maggie had never been certain which of them, if either, to believe. Their methods terrified her equally, not because they were inept, for MacDrumin never failed and—despite the recent incident—Kate rarely did, but because the activities themselves were so dangerous.

Kate laughed at the danger. With no man of her own, and no brother still living who was old enough to look after her family, she had done her best to provide for herself, her mother, her old Granny MacDrumin, and young Ian. When MacDrumin had shouted at her and tried to convince her to let him provide for them, Kate told him fiercely that, having condemned her mother for marrying a MacCain, he need not try to control them now, and he had not forced her to obey him.

"That young woman ought to be married," James said grimly. "A husband would soon tame her."

Relaxing a little, Maggie choked back a laugh. "There's not a man in the Highlands brave enough to *try* to tame her. They all know her temper, you see, and keep a safe distance. Even her cousins dare not command her, and I warn you, you had best hope she never lays eyes on you again after what you did to her."

When James snorted, Rothwell said quietly, "So you admit you know the wench, do you? I hope you do not condone robbery."

"Kate looks upon her activities as acts of war, not mere robbery," Maggie said, trying to match his quiet tone. "She attacks only Englishmen, never Scots, and she has never harmed anyone. I do know her, sir, and have for ten years."

James said musingly, "She must have been a fierce child."

Maggie nodded. "Her mother brought them all back to Glen Drumin to live with her parents after her husband died. The MacCains were no more pleased by the marriage than the MacDrumins, you see, so Kate grew up hating both clans equally and determined to look out for herself. Papa has done what he could for them from the first, more since most of the men in Kate's family died. It was he who pushed us to be friends, and we have remained so, though I was away at school part of the time."

Rothwell said, "I will believe your friend's life has been difficult, but if she continues on her course, she will be hanged. Robbery is robbery, plain and simple."

"As she views the matter," Maggie said stubbornly, "the English, having stolen from us, should be made to return some of the ill-gotten gains. When people are hungry, sir, they do things they would not do if their bellies were full. I believe it is the same way in London."

To her surprise, James agreed with her. "She's right about that, Ned. Even the folks in Alsatia might not be quite so vicious if their bellies were full."

"They are full," Rothwell said grimly, "of cheap gin."

"Which just shows," Maggie retorted, "that all you said before about town life being better for people is simply not so."

"I never pretended to believe that town life is perfect," he said, "but there are certainly more ways to make one's living in town than in the country."

"Next," Maggie said scornfully, "you will try to tell me that everyone in London has an excellent job."

As the discussion continued, Maggie realized she was enjoying a discussion she had not expected to enjoy at all. Rothwell did not dismiss her arguments, but encouraged her to express her opinions. Although James contributed his mite from time to time, she thought he seemed unusually distracted by his own thoughts, but before she realized so much time had passed, they were fording the river Truim near the village of Dalwhinnie. It was still daylight when they arrived in the village, and Maggie said, pointing, "You can see the Corriearrack from here."

James whistled. Rothwell was silent. And Maggie was not at all surprised by their reactions. The south side of the pass was extremely steep, and seen from a distance, it looked perpendicular, like a sheer rock wall.

"So that is your civilized homeland," Rothwell said with a slight smile. "Will you forgive me, I wonder, if I declare here and now that it seems much more like a natural habitation for wild men than for civilized ladies or gentlemen?"

James, still squinting into the distance, said, "Are those man-made walls?"

Chuckling, Maggie said, "That is one of the famous roads built by your General Wade after the first Scot-

tish Uprising, nearly forty years ago. It boasts seven-
teen traverses on this side alone—those walls you
see—and rises to a height of two thousand five hundred feet. The other side declines more steadily, passing through numerous glens and valleys all the way to
Fort Augustus."

Rothwell said, "And how far is Fort Augustus?"

"A long day's ride from the top," she replied, "but
we don't go nearly so far, as I told you before. We
must spend the night here, however, for we can never
make Laggan before dark, but Papa has friends
nearby who will be happy to accommodate us."

The earl's eyes narrowed suspiciously, and he said,
"One encounter with friends of your family is quite
sufficient for one day. We will put up at the alehouse
here tonight."

Maggie perfectly understood his feelings, but their
accommodations at the alehouse were the least comfortable they had suffered so far, and having to share
a room with Maria while Matthew slept on a pallet in
the chamber shared by Rothwell and James did not
make the experience more acceptable.

Dalwhinnie was one of the places her father kept
horses, but when she suggested the next day that they
might do better to ride in order to reach Laggan
sooner, Rothwell cast a glance skyward and said, "We
will take the coaches. The innkeeper assures me that
the road to Laggan is passable, and not only will that
mean having less distance to arrange transport for the
baggage but we will stay dry if those clouds yonder
mean rain."

"But if the coaches break down we could well be
stranded midway," she protested.

James said, "If MacDrumin keeps horses here, it
would be foolish not to make use of them, Ned. We

can ride, and if one of the coaches should break down, the women will have less difficulty mounting a saddle-trained horse than a coach-horse."

Thus, to Maggie's undisguised annoyance, she was left to sit in the coach by herself, for although Matthew asked if she would like Maria's company, his attitude was forbidding enough so that she quickly said she would prefer to be alone. She had less than an hour of solitude to endure, however, before the clouds began to spit rain and the men tied their reins to the second coach and scrambled inside with her.

The going was even slower than she had expected, and she felt sorry for the coachmen. James, apparently oblivious to the frequent rocking of the coach, and to the dim light as well, amused himself with his sketchbook. Maggie could not imagine how he could draw at all in a moving carriage, but his pencil sped over the page as it had on numerous other occasions. The one sketch she had recognized looked as if he had tried to capture the robbery on paper, but she could not tell what he was drawing now. It looked like he had outlined some sort of portrait. He glanced up, caught her gaze upon him, and changed his page.

Rothwell hid a smile at James's evasive action. Remembering his stepmother's visible displeasure toward Miss MacDrumin, he wondered what she would think to know his artist's interest, at least, had been captured by a female highwayman, and a Scottish female at that.

The sky was darker, he noted, more like night than midday. He hoped the coaches would not fail, and was grateful yet again for the surprisingly sturdy windows that at least let in what light there was. They had stopped again, at the top of a hill, so the coachmen could affix the skidpans to slow their descent. When they lurched forward again, the lumbering pace reminded him of certain Channel crossings he had made, and the rain dashing against the coach added to the illusion of a ship beating against a heavy sea, straining her timbers, creaking in protest as she fought her way over the waves. A ridiculous fancy, of course. Ships did not have glass windows that rattled in their frames, threatening to shatter over the occupants at any moment.

Miss MacDrumin, he noted with a flickering glance, did not seem much affected by the wild weather or the wretched journey, but no doubt, having spent her life in this disorderly but rather fascinating country, she was accustomed to it. He glanced at James and saw that his brother had given up any attempt to draw and was dozing. Storm and roadbed making conversation difficult, Rothwell leaned back against the squabs and contemplated the possibilities that might present themselves for his dinner. So far, he had not been much impressed by Scottish food. Though he had not been sick again, the fare at such alehouses and inns as had enjoyed their custom had been uninspired, and he doubted he could hope for better in an out-of-the-way place like Laggan.

Miss MacDrumin was smiling again and for no apparent reason. She seemed quite ridiculously pleased to be back in her homeland, though how anyone, let alone a female who was plainly gently-bred, could be happier in such a barbaric environment than she had been in one of the most comfortable homes in London was beyond his comprehension.

The alehouse in Laggan, when they reached it several hours later, did not alter his perception of the

Highlands. The house was much larger than the one in Dalwhinnie, its great size due to its location at the foot of the Corriearrack and the fact that few were brave enough to make the journey, up or down, in darkness. Thus the alehouse—in warmer months at least—was assured of numerous overnight guests. But although there were clearly others staying there, it was by no means full, and the best Rothwell could say in its favor was that neither he nor James, nor even Miss MacDrumin, would have to share a room.

Matthew would be pleased to have Maria's company, Rothwell thought, although he noted that Maria wore a sulky expression, as usual. She had certainly changed from the haughty woman he knew in London, but he had no patience with her airs or her megrims. It was annoying enough to have to put up with her wooden-faced husband in place of the capable Fletcher.

Inside, the house was drafty despite a huge fire crackling on the hearth, and their bull-like host was taciturn at best. Although he greeted Miss MacDrumin with obvious respect, his demeanor when he spoke to Rothwell was nearly as wooden as Chelton's. If he cheered up at all when Rothwell ordered four rooms, a hearty meal, and mugs of ale for himself and James, the earl could not discern the change.

The Cheltons went upstairs with a maidservant to see to the bedchambers, and Rothwell, sipping tepid ale, said, "We'll stay here a while and warm ourselves."

Miss MacDrumin seemed content to sit by the fire, and he believed that even his stepmother could not disapprove of her remaining there, even in the presence of a few strangers. Somehow it did not seem as improper as it would have been in an English inn.

When the coachmen came in, having seen to their horses, both greeted the host warmly and demanded whisky.

Watching them drain their mugs with apparent satisfaction, Rothwell held out his own and said, "I have not tried your famous Highland whisky yet. It is a good time to do so, I believe."

Obligingly, the publican took his mug, emptied the dregs of ale, and refilled it from a dusty-looking jug. The aroma of strong whisky assaulted Rothwell's nostrils. Suppressing an urge to choke, he sipped with extreme care. The fiery liquid turned to silk upon his tongue, and he exchanged a look with James. Suddenly, Scotland seemed a far more fascinating place.

James, watching him, said, "I'll have some too, by Jove."

By the time dinner was served, both men had enjoyed a second cup of the strong brew and Rothwell was feeling very mellow. The fire was warm and cozy, its glow adding much to Miss MacDrumin's beauty; James was the best of companions, and the inn was a most tolerable place after all. The whisky made even the food acceptable, though the mutton chops were tough and the baked turnips blackened. No sweet was offered, so Rothwell accepted a third mug of the excellent whisky in its stead.

When Maggie announced that she and Maria were going to retire, he began to get to his feet, having a notion that he ought at least to see them safely to her door, but she only smiled at him and said with an impudent but understanding note in her voice that they would manage safely on their own. Since it was her country, he accepted her word and returned to sit by the fire to finish his drink, telling the sleepy-looking Matthew that he might join his wife as soon as she had finished maiding Miss MacDrumin, without waiting up for himself or James.

"Heady stuff," James said when the women and Matthew had gone. "The best I've tasted, I think."

He seemed less affected by the brew than Rothwell was, but after a close evaluation, Rothwell decided that he probably looked completely normal and in control himself. None of the others in the room paid them any attention, and when the strangers—all men—spoke to each other, they spoke in the guttural language that was their native tongue.

Rothwell sipped slowly, enjoying the whisky and the crackling fire. He refused a fourth cup from their rather more congenial host, and finally, concentrating on maintaining his dignity, he accompanied James upstairs, dragged off his clothes, left them in a heap on the floor of his tiny room, and fell gratefully into bed. Thanks to Chelton's earlier attentions, he found little to complain about other than that the sheets had cooled and felt a bit damp against his naked skin.

He fell asleep the moment his head touched the pillow, only to be rudely awakened less than two hours later. The room was totally dark, and for a moment he was disoriented before he remembered where he was. Recognizing the onset of a headache, he cursed the whisky he had drunk and turned over, deciding he had imagined the noise, but he had no sooner closed his eyes when a sound like a muffled scream shocked him wide awake and sent ripples of fear racing through him. It had sounded like Maggie.

Leaping out of bed, he snatched up the quilt to cover himself, and rushed for the door, barking his shin on a chair before he remembered where it was. Cursing fluently but moving more carefully, he found and opened it. No one was in the narrow corridor, but a second scream drew him swiftly to a nearby room. He threw open the door and rushed into the darkness, only to trip over something in his path.

The quilt was snatched away as he fell headlong onto a bed, on top of a slender, soft body that suddenly hardened and began to twist and writhe beneath him. Small hands clutched at his shoulders, pushing him, scratching him, and a woman's voice cried out in terror. The room was suddenly filled with light, and Rothwell looked over his shoulder to see the huge landlord loom in the doorway, holding a branch of candles aloft in one beefy hand, and looking like the wrath of God in human form.

"God-a-mercy, ye fecksome prick-me-dainty," the man growled, "ye'll no attack innocent lassies in my hoose! I've a good mind tae take ye straight ootside and string ye tae the nearest tree!"

Several men crowded into the doorway behind him, and before Rothwell could gather his wits to explain what had happened, a deep, disturbingly familiar but unknown voice said, "Dinna do sae daft a thing as that, Conach. Nae doot, the mon be lawfully married tae the wench. Are ye not, me lord?"

XIII

Rudely awakened from her usual deep sleep, Maggie was aware only of the heavy body atop her own and an instinct to get it off her. When the room suddenly lit up and seemed to fill with strangers, she became more disoriented, but she recognized Rothwell's face close to hers at the same moment that the landlord threatened to take him out and hang him. When the second voice sounded, she had just realized the earl was completely naked, and quite failed to hear what was said.

Rothwell stiffened and tried to sit up, tugging at her quilts in what was clearly a futile attempt to cover himself. Trying to help him, she too grabbed the quilt, but it was caught tight beneath him, and when she tried to yank it loose, her hand slipped and inadvertently she touched his naked flesh. She snatched her hand away.

The landlord was watching her. He said, "That dinna look to me as if the lad can be her husband."

Rothwell was not looking at her, which was just as well, for in view of his lack of attire and Conach MacLeod's understandable confusion, she did not think she could look either one of them in the face.

Conach was glaring at the earl, daring him to respond, but so far he had said nothing, and since she had not the least idea what he was doing in her bed, she too kept silent.

She was glad to hear James's voice above others in the corridor, and a moment later, he pushed his way into the room. "What the devil is happening here?" he demanded, but to Maggie's surprise, he looked only at Conach and the others crowded near the door. He did not so much as glance at Rothwell.

Conach stood his ground. "We'd expect ye tae tak' his side, but lord or no lord, he'll no tak' advantage of an innocent wee lass in my hoose. I've no fear of any damned Englishman, and I'll be mortal glad tae hang one."

"Och now, Conach," said a second, deeper voice, "I've told ye, the man must be married tae the wench. 'Tis mortal sad, I agree, but ye canna hang him fer consorting with his ain wife."

Maggie went still. She could not see the man who had spoken, but she recognized his voice now as easily as she would have recognized her father's. It was Kate's big cousin, Dugald. She hoped neither Rothwell nor James would catch a glimpse of him, since both would surely recognize him from the hold-up.

James's voice was chilly, and for once he sounded like a highly bred English gentleman when he said, "I fail to see how my brother's affairs are any concern of yours, landlord, but I shall give you the benefit of the doubt and accept that you meant only to protect a female guest in your house. His lordship will also forgive you, no doubt, since she is indeed his wife."

Maggie felt Rothwell stiffen again and saw him open his mouth to speak, only to shut it again when James shot him a fierce warning look. The earl had managed to cover his lower half, and Maggie had all she could do now to conceal her increasing amusement. She did not know what Kate and the others intended exactly, but she would do nothing to spoil their fun, for when James had overstepped the bounds of what was acceptable by spanking Kate, Rothwell had done nothing to stop him, and this was no doubt Kate's way of getting even with both men. But although Maggie was not stirred to intervene, she was conscious of a strong hope that neither Rothwell nor James would soon discover the perpetrators of the harmless little prank.

Conach was glaring at Rothwell. "Faith, my lord, what say you? Be the lass truly your lawful wife?"

Maggie waited for him to deny it, but he did not. Instead he looked again at James, but Conach also looked that way, and James remained rigidly still, his lips pressed tightly together. At last, grimly, Rothwell said, "You seem to leave me little choice but to say she is my wife."

The landlord relaxed. "That's all right then, and we'll be wishing you a good night. Forgive the intrusion, my lord." James relieved Conach of the branch of candles before he went, and a moment later the corridor was empty, the three of them alone. Maggie wriggled to put more distance between herself and Rothwell, and he looked at her ruefully.

"I hope you do not think I came here to ravish you. You must have heard the scream that awakened me. I thought it was you, that you were in danger."

"I heard nothing," Maggie said truthfully. "I sleep soundly, sir. I did not waken until you fell on me."

He paused, frowning. "Where the devil did that scream come from if it didn't come from here, and what the devil," he added, glaring at his brother, "did you mean by telling those fools I was married to her?"

James said hastily, "It is a dashed good thing you did not contradict me, Ned, and it's no use looking as if you'd like to murder me either, for I had no choice. Awoke to a clamor and when I stepped into the corridor, the lot outside this door was shouting for your blood. Two fellows told me the innkeeper would hang you if you weren't married to her, so I dashed well wasn't going to tell them you were no such thing. I'd wondered as much as anyone what you were doing in her bedchamber, so you can hardly blame *them* for misunderstanding, and what difference can pretending you're married make in any event? Once we cut free of this place, we'll have no cause to see any of them again."

"True," Rothwell said with a sigh.

"Where the devil are your clothes?" James demanded. "Surely, you didn't run naked down the corridor."

Rothwell's face reddened but he said, "I told you, I thought Miss MacDrumin was in danger. I snatched up a quilt." Pointing, he added, "That one on the floor behind you. It must have caught on something when I rushed in, tripping me up, but if you will give it to me, we can leave Miss MacDrumin to go back to sleep."

Struggling to conceal her amusement as she watched James retrieve the quilt and hand it to the earl, Maggie said, "Th-there is j-just one small thing you ought to know, Rothwell."

Attempting to wrap himself up in the quilt, he clearly was listening with only half an ear, for his tone was distracted when he said, "And what is that?"

Keeping a mildly interested eye on his expression, she said, "In Scotland, marriage by declaration is perfectly legal."

An arrested look leapt to his face, but before he could respond, James said abruptly, "Just what the devil is marriage by declaration?"

Still watching Rothwell, she said, "I am not altogether certain of the exact points of the law, but I believe that by declaring himself my husband before witnesses, your brother has become just that, by law."

"By old Harry," James said, staring at Rothwell, "that can't be right. Tell her she's mistaken, Ned."

Rothwell was standing now, and he looked down at Maggie with such a grim look in his eyes that she no longer had trouble suppressing her amusement. He said, "I see you realize this may be a more serious matter than you thought, Miss MacDrumin, but you need not concern yourself. Whatever Scottish law is, I can assure you the laws of England do not include any such nonsense, and I certainly will not hold myself accountable to Scotland."

Sobered, she said, "I do not expect you to, sir. Moreover, whatever the circumstance may be, I am certain the whole matter can be put right just as soon as we reach Glen Drumin and explain things to my father."

"There is nothing to explain," he said coldly, looking more dignified than she had thought it possible for any man to look wrapped up in a quilt.

He and James departed, and she wondered why she should feel disappointment that the problem Kate and her cohorts had created should be so easily resolved. For it would be resolved, of course, though there might be a bit more to it than Rothwell thought, since many of the people at the inn this night would be only too delighted to spread word of her so-called marriage. The thought of being married to him ought by rights to be dismaying, and was certainly not a thought over which to linger, but in her mind's eye she could still see his smooth skin, pulled tight over muscular shoulders that proved, had she had any doubt, that his elegant coats required no padding.

She had caught more than a glimpse of shoulder, however, and she felt warmth flood her cheeks at the wish that she might have taken more leisure to look, to see what the front of him was like. She had not seen many naked men, and most of those were related to her and were much older than she, with hairy chests and backs, even hairy backsides. But Rothwell's back had been smooth to her touch—tight, smooth, and hard with muscles. His weight on top of her had not been at all frightening after that first violent moment of waking. She would sport a few bruises from his fall though. She thought one of his elbows might have grazed a rib.

Marriage. It was not the first time the thought of it had drifted through her mind. She had assumed that one day she would marry, that her father would suggest someone or that some young man from another clan, or even her own, would come courting her. But that had been when she was younger, before the troubles. She had not thought much about marriage since the uprising, for there had been too much worry at the time, and too many difficulties afterward, including MacDrumin's devilish whisky.

She wondered what Rothwell would think should he discover the laird's primary source of income, especially since he liked the whisky. She had seen that much herself tonight, for Conach MacLeod, like most hosts in the area, sold only whisky purchased at prices uninflated by the wicked English duty, and to her certain knowledge, he purchased his from Andrew MacDrumin.

Despite increasing anxiety to convince Rothwell that reasons existed for actions even as unconscionable as Kate's, she had managed to avoid any mention of whisky. Illegal production was much more prevalent in the Highlands than activities like Kate's, and Maggie had a notion that Rothwell would be even less tolerant of smuggling than of robbery. He would no doubt threaten to hang the smugglers, too. In England criminals were no doubt hanged in vast numbers. Indeed, she knew they were, for not only had she been threatened with hanging herself but she had seen with her own eyes felons hanging in chains along the road to London.

England was a dismal place. She could not imagine living there for any length of time. She was not like Lydia or Lady Rothwell, glorying in social activities like masquerades, routs, and musical evenings, reveling in such mundane daily decisions as what to wear and how to arrange one's hair. Not that there had not been pleasant moments. The bedchamber she had occupied had been the prettiest of its ilk that she had ever seen. For that matter, Rothwell London House was more magnificent than any house she had ever seen, even in Edinburgh. And the gowns—she regretted the fact that she had not stayed at least long enough to collect the last several being fashioned for her by Lady Rothwell's mantua maker. Not, she thought with a sigh, that Glen Drumin was any place to wear such things. It was a pity one could not take the best of both worlds and somehow mix them into a pleasant whole. One could not, however, and lying there in bed, smelling the damp, familiar aromas of the Highlands—the pine trees, the peat, the herbal tang of plants and shrubs, even the rain hushing through foliage and pattering on the window—knowing she was nearly home again, she made up her mind that once she reached Glen Drumin, she would never leave it again.

She slept at last, and the next morning when Maria came to help her dress, she realized the woman was unaware of the events of the previous night, and was glad of it. At breakfast when Rothwell asked Conach about horses, she kept her eyes riveted to her bowl of porridge, loath to interrupt, but hoping that Conach, who seemed much more cheerful than he had the day before, would not attempt to cheat the earl, since she had told the latter at least twice that MacDrumin kept horses at the inn for the use of anyone who required one to get to Glen Drumin.

To her profound relief, Conach said civilly, "The laird keeps three here, yer lordship, and for my sins of the nicht, I'm bound tae offer ye three more. And, gin ye wish it, I'll ha' the rest o' yer bags carried on tae Glen Drumin. That be fair enough, I trow, for an honest mistake. I didna ken ye was wed tae the laird's daughter."

Deciding the marriage business had gone far enough, and certain that Conach would be reasonable now that his temper had cooled, Maggie said, "I think perhaps you ought to know—"

"Maggie, hush," James said with unwonted sternness, and at nearly the same moment, Rothwell held out his hand to Conach and said, "I will accept your generous offer, landlord, and I thank you for it. Chelton, collect at least a change of clothing for Mr. James and myself; and Maria, do the same for Miss . . . that is to say, for your mistress. We'll use the sixth horse as a baggage pony, but we'll not be able to carry a great deal with us, so use some judgment and work quickly. We leave as soon as the horses can be made ready."

Obedient to the wishes of both gentlemen, Maggie

held her tongue, and was not surprised when the Cheltons, to whom news of her marriage must have come as quite a shock, did likewise. Not until they were actually on the road did Maria, riding stiffly beside her with Rothwell, James, and Chelton behind, demand in much the same tone she might have used in London to know what the landlord had meant by saying Rothwell had married her.

Quietly Maggie said, "It is a simple misunderstanding, Maria. Pay it no mind."

"But that man addressed you as his ladyship," Maria said. "I should like to know by what cause—"

"Enough, Maria," Rothwell said. "As Miss MacDrumin said, there has been a misunderstanding, which in view of our position as foreigners in these parts, we thought it best to leave alone."

Maria sniffed. "No doubt a wise decision, my lord, for it is a barbarous land peopled with barbarous folk and not fit for persons of consequence."

Chelton said, "His lordship did not request your opinion, Maria. He'll be better pleased if you hold your tongue."

Seeing Maria's painful flush, Maggie snapped her mouth shut on the rebuke she had been about to utter herself, and even felt a stab of pity for the woman.

A moment later Rothwell said in his customary, placid tone, "Fall back and ride with Chelton, Maria, and see what you can do to soothe his temper. I want to ride with Miss MacDrumin."

Maria did not look at all pleased by the request, but she did as she was bid, and as Rothwell brought his bay horse alongside Maggie's gray, he said, "You may instruct me, Miss MacDrumin. I am rapidly learning that you were quite right to take me to task for my ignorance about my Scottish estate. Is this dreadful specimen truly one of Wade's roads?"

"It is," she said, grateful for his matter-of-fact tone, "and it will get a good deal worse before it gets better." The river Spey, swollen from the recent rains, flowed swiftly past on their left, and the area around them was lushly green, but the mountain pass ahead rose all the more starkly because of that. "The road took six months to build," she told him. "It was built when I was three, so I cannot tell you much about that, but Papa remembers it vividly. They used it to transport troops and artillery from Stirling to Fort Augustus."

"Surely that cannot be right," Rothwell said, frowning. "To transport artillery means using wheeled vehicles."

"But they did," she assured him. "General Wade himself drove over it with his officers in a carriage drawn by six horses, all the way to the summit and down the other side. It is still possible to take two-wheeled carts over the road, but most folks prefer to walk rather than chance a runaway carriage."

"Why has it not been better cared for?"

With a wry grin, she said, "Do you think we wanted it, sir? Not only was it an unwarranted intrusion into our midst but an inconvenience as well. Our horses are not generally shod, you see, and the gravel whetted away their hooves, rendering them unserviceable. For that matter, many of our people do not wear shoes. Clambering over river stones is nothing to them, but gravel is intolerable to their naked feet. And this track has been used by cattle drovers for over a hundred years. The gravel wore down the beasts' feet, and they too had to be shod. Which all goes to show," she added bitterly, "that we ought to have a Scottish king who would understand such things about us."

"Neither your bonnie prince nor his father fit that qualification," he said, but his tone was matter-of-fact, not argumentative. "Not only can they know little about your troubles, despite the young Pretender's sojourn in these mountains, but they are Catholic. Perhaps you do not understand the importance of that fact, but—"

"Don't patronize me, Rothwell," she snapped. "I know about your Act of Settlement. It was passed by the English Parliament, never by the Scottish."

"Here, you two," James said, urging his horse up on Maggie's other side, though the road was scarcely wide enough to accommodate three abreast, "no wars today. Look at this splendid scenery instead. By old Harry, it's enough to turn me into a landscape painter. And at least, ahead, with loose scree above us and a sheer wall of solid granite below, we need not fear being attacked by wild men and thieves, leaping at us from the shrubbery. Isn't that right, Ned?"

Maggie opened her mouth to tell him what she thought of such nonsense but shut it again when she saw the amused twinkle in his eyes. "I suppose you think that observation a humorous one," she said, "and I suppose you believe, too, that women ought not to discuss politics. You will soon learn, sir, that Scottish women discuss many things that properly bred Englishwomen do not. We have no good opinion of English government for one thing, and reason is on our side. Your Act of Union was no more than a political move to abolish the Scottish Parliament and our Privy Council, and the result, as anyone of sense would have known, has been total rule from London, which no one in Scotland wants."

"Perfectly understandable, too," James said. The road had begun to rise sharply, and he let his mount fall a little behind theirs. But still apparently determined to keep the conversation on harmless topics, he demanded identification of every bird, plant, and animal he spied, exclaiming in delight when a huge osprey plunged to the river to catch its dinner.

His efforts were admirable, but it was not long before a chance remark of Rothwell's stirred Maggie's temper and she accused him of refusing even to try to understand the Scots.

Exasperated, James said tartly, "As I recall the matter from my history lessons, ma'am, nearly as many persons in Scotland as in England advocated passage of the Act of Union."

"True," Rothwell said, but Maggie saw that he was watching her expectantly, his look one that might have been respect.

"Because we were supposed to gain by it," she snapped. "Instead we have endured oppressive taxes and a government over which we have no control."

"And so," Rothwell said, "the Highlanders make their own rules and conduct their own affairs without regard for the laws that govern the rest of the country."

"But that has always been our way," Maggie said. "We were isolated from everyone else for so long that we learned to build on our personal loyalties and traditions, and that has been our way since long before England even had a government, sir. Our civilization was already old when the Romans invaded Britain."

"That does not mean your way is the only way," he replied, and his calm incensed her all the more, since it seemed to her that he was now dismissing her arguments as he would those of a child. He said, "As I pointed out in a previous discussion, it is not we English who are forcing all the changes here."

"You are quite impossible, Rothwell. You are so all-knowing, so superior in your English sense of rectitude. It is a pity that I am too much of a lady to slap some sense into you."

"You are welcome to try if you like, but I must warn you that although I allowed it once, I am not likely to let such behavior become a habit with you."

She stared at him, caught the glitter in his eyes, and a shivery chill swept through her body. The desire to slap him vanished like smoke in the wind.

James chuckled. "I don't advise violent action, ma'am. Ned may look like a fop, but he is quite able to defend himself."

Dragging her gaze from Rothwell, she managed to smile at James and said, "Fine words from you, sir, or do you believe violence should be solely reserved for men to use against women?"

"I?" James looked surprised. "Why are you attacking me? I am not a violent man."

"Are you not? What about what you did to poor Kate?"

"Poor Kate, is it? That was not violence, ma'am, that was well-merited punishment. Your precious Kate was scarcely an innocent victim. The little vixen aimed a pistol at me and spat in my face. If she had been a man, I'd have done worse than put her over my knee, so she ought to count her blessings."

Since Maggie did not feel that she could defend Kate's actions, she was glad when Rothwell suggested just then that they dismount and walk the horses for a time. The mountains around them looked blue in the shrouding mist, but they could see Ben Nevis, rising above the rest.

Though they soon remounted, their pace remained slow because of the very steep incline, and became slower when Maria's mount cast a shoe and she was forced either to walk or to ride pillion with Chelton. Maggie had noted by then that the increasing height of the road and the frequent sheer drops were making Maria excessively nervous, so she made no effort to urge her to move more quickly.

Clouds began to gather again before noon, and within an hour a light steady rain began to fall. They took what cover they could in a natural cave formed by huge boulders, and waited for the shower to pass. As a result of such delays, darkness was falling by the time they reached the summit.

The north side of the Corriearrack, being the watershed for the river Tarff as it flowed from its source high in the Monadhliath mountains to Loch Ness, was vastly different from the south side. Though nearly as steep, the hills, valleys, and glens were lushly green and thickly forested, with water rushing through every declivity. Though the clouds overhead had begun to scatter, full darkness came swiftly, and with the increasing canopy of foliage, few stars could be seen. Chelton lighted torches, however, and they soon found the track leading off the main route to Glen Drumin.

For the next hour there was little conversation, because every rider had to concentrate on following the track and not losing sight of the horseman ahead. The road into the glen was only a narrow path, and traveling in darkness was not wise, Maggie knew, for more reasons than one. She kept listening for telltale sounds ahead that might warn of enemies about, or even friends, since her father had surely received word of their coming by now, but the shout when she heard it came from behind.

Looking quickly over her shoulder, she saw a cavalcade hurrying them. At first she could not tell how many there were, or who they were, but she heard Rothwell mutter, "Bandits again? By God, this time I'll—"

"No," Maggie said quickly. "Bandits don't shout first, sir, and they rarely travel with horse carts."

"Carts? On this sorry excuse for a road? Good God, yes, I can hear the wheels now."

"Aye, sir, and from the sound they are traveling at a wicked pace. 'Tis amazing the carts don't fall apart. We'd best move aside and let them pass."

He agreed, and they drew their mounts off the track, and waited for the carters to pass. As the men approached, however, they slowed their pace, and one shouted, "Who goes there?"

The carters carried no lights, and in the darkness beyond the circle of their own torchlight Maggie could see no faces, but she had suspected their identities the moment she had heard the carts, and the shouting voice was more familiar to her than her own. She cried, "Papa, oh, Papa, it's Maggie!"

A moment later, she found herself being lifted down and hugged so hard she thought her ribs would snap, and MacDrumin said gleefully, "So, you've come back to us, have you, lass? But let the lads pass us by whilst you tell me how you liked London."

"It was very large, Papa, and very noisy, worse than Edinburgh. Oh," she added, remembering her companions, "I must present the Earl of Rothwell, Papa, and Mr. James Carsley. They were kind enough to escort me home."

"What became of Fiona and Mungo?" MacDrumin demanded, making no response than a curt nod to the earl and James.

Tears sprang to her eyes when she said, "Dead, Papa, both of them. Mungo took a wrong turning

when we were looking for . . . that is, when we first got
to London," she amended swiftly, adding, "Horrid
men attacked the coach and pulled me and Fiona into
the street. I hit my head on something and fell unconscious but I was not otherwise hurt. When I came to
my senses again, Fiona and Mungo were gone and I
was told they were dead. The coach was gone, too,
which is how I came to seek his lordship's protection,"
she added glibly.

"By what I hear, you got more than protection,"
MacDrumin said, turning to Rothwell at last and extending a hand. "You ought to have had the banns
called like a proper Christian, lad, but I'll overlook
that and bid you welcome to the family."

Out of the darkness came a mischievous feminine
chuckle, and Maggie recognized the voice as Kate
MacCain's.

XIV

Grimly Rothwell returned MacDrumin's handshake, but he too had heard Kate's laughter and knew he had been the victim of a trick. He wondered if Maggie had been party to it, and tried to tell himself it did not matter. In any event, he hoped James had not heard the vixen's laughter, for they would learn more about MacDrumin of MacDrumin and his followers by keeping their tempers than they would if they alienated him from the outset.

Keeping his voice under rigid control, he said, "The marriage is a matter for further discussion, MacDrumin, but this is neither the time nor place."

"There is naught to discuss, but under every stone lies a politician," MacDrumin said with a sigh. "You must know she will have no dowry, lad, and although I'd have driven a hard bargain arranging the settlements, the time for that has fled, thanks to your own impetuousness."

"Papa," Maggie said hastily, "it is not so simple as—"

"Whisst," MacDrumin snapped, cupping a hand to his ear, "I hear hoofbeats!"

When the group fell silent, Rothwell heard them

too, coming swiftly from behind, leading him to think that, like MacDrumin, the riders must know the track well, or be singularly foolish.

"These woods are infested tonight," MacDrumin muttered. "Get those carts moving, lads. I'll deal with them."

Rothwell had not considered what might be the contents of the four carts, but he did so as they rattled past him, and when two riders emerged from the darkness a few moments later and declared themselves in solid English tones to be officers of his majesty's Customs, he was not very much surprised to hear it.

MacDrumin chose to take an indignant tone. "What the devil are a pair of excisemen doing in Glen Drumin, if you please?"

"We are on the king's business, Lord MacDrumin," the spokesman replied, "and we mean to examine those carts of yours and the packs on that pony, and any other gear you may have. It will do you no good to protest, I assure you."

Even in the dim light Rothwell was able to discern the gleam of unholy glee that leapt to MacDrumin's eyes, but his demeanor was otherwise that of a man wholly unconcerned, even slightly amused, when he said, "The king's business, is it? Well, lads, you'd do well to make haste with your duty then, for if you are meaning to detain the Earl of Rothwell after his long day's journey, then you'd best have excellent cause for your impudence, for he won't thank you for interfering in his honest business."

"From what I'm told, you would not recognize honest business if you tripped over it, MacDrumin," the spokesman said with what Rothwell suspected was complete accuracy. "Earls now! What new lies will you dare to spout next? Get down, Foster, and have a look at the goods on that pack horse first."

Before Rothwell could object, MacDrumin said swiftly, "You've forgotten the law, my lads. 'Tis a Scottish one, which would account for it, but still you're bound to it by your own Parliament. You can confiscate the carts, but you cannot search them except in the presence of a proper magistrate. Not, that is, unless you've been granted a commission beyond your ordinary one by the Lord High Constable in Edinburgh."

The spokesman said quickly, "We'll take them then, and you along with them, MacDrumin. Go ahead, Foster."

"Just one moment," Rothwell said coldly enough to stop Foster with a foot halfway to the ground. "I do not know by what right you have the infernal impertinence to question my identity without so much as asking me to verify it, but I am certainly Rothwell. You will touch nothing belonging to me or my party."

"That's telling them, lad," MacDrumin said approvingly when the two law men glanced at each other. "He's Rothwell, right enough, and a powerful man in London, not to mention being my son-in-law, so you'd do well not to annoy him. Here he's come all this way expecting to celebrate his nuptials, only to learn he's a funeral to attend instead, and now he has to put up with your nonsense as well. Take yourselves off, and leave us be."

"Begging your pardon, I'm sure, my lord," the spokesman said, speaking directly to Rothwell and attempting to ignore MacDrumin, "but we've had word of an illegal shipment of whisky being moved this very night, and our men have been scouring the hills from Fort Augustus to the Corriearrack in search of it. I've no wish to offend you, but my orders are clear—to search every bundle, person, or vehicle I encounter. I am sure I've no need to point out that whilst your high estate must be respected, your rank does not preclude my asking permission to search."

"Very reasonable," Rothwell said, amused to see MacDrumin grimace and Maggie catch her lower lip between her pretty teeth. He added in the same tone, "If you will just show me this special commission of yours, authorizing you to make such searches . . ."

"Well, as to that, my lord," the spokesman said, "we were rousted out rather hastily, you see, so I've not got the papers on my person at the present moment. You will understand, I am sure, and give us your permission to—"

"He'll do no such thing," MacDrumin said, clearly delighted but affecting outrage. "If that don't beat all. No papers, you say? Surely, you have your ordinary commissions—Not them, either? Why these fellows are naught but a pair of thieves, Rothwell, for if they were what they claim, they would know the law requires them to carry their commissions at all times to prove their authority. Highway robbers is what they are, and if they don't take themselves off at once, I'll set my own lads on them to teach them manners, and not a magistrate in all Scotland will say aught but that they deserved it!"

The excisemen did not linger to see if he would carry out his threat, for one look at Rothwell's grim countenance told them whose side he would favor. When they had gone, MacDrumin shook his head and said, "Slipshod, that's what they are these days. There's no excuse for it."

Maggie said instantly, "Papa, who died?"

"Och, and isn't that just what I've been wondering

myself," MacDrumin said, "but if we don't make all haste to the house now, it won't matter a whit, for if those two fools don't go straight to Fergus Campbell, I'll own myself amazed, and once they do, he'll be down upon us in a twink. Up with you now, lass," he added, tossing her back into her saddle.

Looking down at him, Maggie said anxiously, "Papa, you won't take the . . . the carts to the house!"

Rothwell, himself interested in the reply to that question, noted that MacDrumin avoided his daughter's eyes when he said hastily, "Whisst now, we won't stand nattering if you please. Due to delays caused by this feckless weather, certain items were left too long in the kirk, with the result that we were forced to move them with undignified haste. But it will all be for naught if we don't get to the house well ahead of that rascal Fergus Campbell, so we'll have none of your prating, lass, nor anyone else's either," he added with a darkling look at the others.

Quite unimpressed by the excisemen, but considerably amused by the peppery MacDrumin, Rothwell held his peace until they reached Glen Drumin House. Not until the heavy front door was swung wide, revealing a cavernous hall lighted only by candles and a roaring fire in a fireplace big enough for six men to stand upright and shoulder to shoulder inside, did it occur to him that he was being welcomed—and with singular grace, considering the need for haste—to what was in fact his own house.

With apparently no sense of irony, MacDrumin said, "Make yourself at home, lad. Take him to the fire, Maggie, and these others too, so they can dry out a bit and warm themselves before our little playlet begins. You others," he shouted, "I want every man, woman, and child you can gather here in the hall before Campbell and his louts arrive. And bring in the oat cakes and whisky you carry with you. A funeral requires food!"

"Papa, please," Maggie said, trying to catch his arm.

When he shooed her away, his mind clearly on more important matters, she turned to Rothwell and said ruefully, "I do beg your pardon for the uproar, sir, but it will soon be done, I think, and then we can make him understand the situation."

Having a fair notion that MacDrumin already understood the situation perfectly well and had little wish to face the fact that his scheme was doomed to fail, Rothwell drew her out of the way of a man carrying a keg, and said, "I collect this Fergus Campbell is a more worthy adversary than the pair we met in the woods. It is possible, is it not, that your father will be in no position to discuss anything later."

"Fergus Campbell is the bailie I told you about," she said, her distaste for the man clear in every syllable. "He is descended from a clan that murdered a hundred innocent folk in their sleep sixty years ago at Glencoe, but although he inherited much of their wickedness, he is a stupid man. I suppose it is possible he can outwit Papa, but he has never done so yet."

Rothwell said nothing more, remaining near the fire to warm himself and watching the bustling activity with amusement. A tall clock near the stairs was striking eight when James came to tell him the Cheltons would bring in the boxes from the pack horse, since MacDrumin's men seemed all to be otherwise occupied.

A number of them were arranging small kegs in a rectangle some six feet by three, and MacDrumin, who had been shouting orders to all and sundry, paused to look at the arrangement and nodded approvingly. "That's the way, lads, but only two levels, mind, no higher. Now then, someone fetch out the good white linen tablecloth."

"Papa, no," Maggie protested. "That was Mama's, and must be kept only for special occasions."

"And what, may I ask, could be more special than a funeral? Rory, put those oat cakes and some whisky on the table yonder, lad. Dugald, you can put that lid in place now."

Rothwell recognized the big man who approached MacDrumin, carrying what appeared to be a coffin lid, as the huge one from the hold-up, and hearing a gasp from James as the man put the lid atop the arrangement of kegs, he knew his brother had also recognized him. James shifted his gaze to search the gathering crowd, and when he suddenly lunged forward, making a path for himself by pushing people aside, Rothwell did not need the feminine shriek of fury that quickly followed to know that he had seen Kate, drawn his own conclusions from her presence, and no doubt meant to wreak his vengeance then and there.

When a number of people stepped hastily back, Rothwell saw that James had grabbed Kate and that she was struggling angrily, attempting to free herself. She froze, however, when a man ran into the hall and shut the big front door with a bang, shouting, "Horsemen, laird! 'Tis Fergus Campbell himself!"

Seeing that Chelton and Maria had come into the house, Rothwell moved to intercept them, and noting the look of profound disapproval on Maria's face, said sternly to her, "Not one word if you value your position with my family. This is no business of ours. Do you hear what I am saying, Chelton?"

"Oh, aye, my lord. Be silent, Maria," he added

when Maria turned away with a disapproving grimace. "It is no business of ours to be interfering with the Scots."

MacDrumin saw the pair just then and swept down upon them, saying, "Here's a pair of psalm books for you two, and one for you, Rothwell. Take your places with the others, quickly."

The Cheltons both looked affronted by the abrupt order, but at a look from Rothwell, they obeyed. More than thirty people, including sleepy-looking maidservants and a fat woman Rothwell thought must be MacDrumin's cook, gathered around the whisky kegs, which with their covering of white linen over the coffin lid, looked exactly like a funeral bier.

MacDrumin was kneeling at the head with a large, well-worn Bible open in his hand, and all the others held psalm books. When the big front door was thrust open again and a big man strode into the hall, followed by the two excise officers, the people around the bier set up a wail for the dead. MacDrumin made a sign to the officers to stop where they were and began, in sonorous tones, to read the service for the dead.

Astonished, the three men halted in their steps, but the big one paused only briefly before demanding harshly, "What new devilry is this, MacDrumin?"

" 'Tis not devilry at all, Fergus Campbell, but the Lord's own business, and I'll thank you not to interfere with such."

"And why would ye be having a funeral at eight o'clock in the nicht, ye auld scoundrel? Ye've run yer limit this time. I'll just be having a look at yon corpse."

MacDrumin drew himself up and said in measured accents, as if he were explaining a simplicity to a backward child, "We are having the service now because the chief mourner was delayed by yon wicked weather and could not get here before now. These proceedings—as you would know had you half the familiarity with these parts that you boast of to your English friends, were planned two days ago for this very afternoon, and the corpse has been lying here before yon great fire for some eight hours now, and ought to be making its dissatisfaction with that state of affairs known to all and sundry at any moment." He wrinkled his nose, and Rothwell was so fascinated that he imagined he could smell the rotting flesh.

Frowning, MacDrumin added, "You may certainly look if you insist upon it, Fergus. No doubt you will take no infection. At all events, Granny MacDrumin cannot have been right to say the poor fellow died of the smallpox." He paused significantly.

"There's been no smallpox here in years," Campbell snapped, but Rothwell noted that he stopped midstride and seemed hesitant to go nearer.

"Very true," MacDrumin agreed, "and doesn't that just show how dangerous it is to our people to be letting all manner of strangers infest our mountains? They wander in from other parts where such dreaded diseases are much more common. Och, but 'we are all fleet of life, Fergus Campbell, like tree leaves, weak creatures of clay, unsubstantial as shadows, wingless—' "

"Ye're raving," Campbell said. "I've heard naught of anyone dying, ye auld fraud, and heard naught of strangers neither."

"Och, but you're a 'savage-creating, stubborn fellow,' and why should you have heard that my daughter and her new husband, the Earl of Rothwell, were on their way to Glen Drumin? For it is"—MacDrumin looked straight at Rothwell—"his lordship's own servant who lies in this casket, the very same one who brought word of their coming. And though I tell you it was the lad's own weak English constitution that failed him in our wild Highland country, it comes to my mind that Granny is frequently right, so if you've a mind to stare this corpse in his rotting face, Fergus Campbell, do it quick.''

There was a pregnant silence, and Rothwell was careful not to let his gaze encounter James's for fear that his rigid gravity would desert him. In truth, the old reprobate possessed a remarkably fertile imagination.

One of the excisemen said suddenly, ''Never mind the coffin, Campbell. '' 'Tis the baggage they brought which must be confiscated. There were four carts and a pack horse!''

MacDrumin chuckled and shook his head. ''You won't take them, because his lordship's servants have already stowed his lordship's gear away. If you will but look at him, my friends, you will see that he presents—despite the hard day he has endured—an elegant and fashionable appearance. Can you doubt he requires four cartloads of baggage?''

Finding himself suddenly the focus of every eye, Rothwell decided he had suffered enough. Looking down his nose at the pompous Campbell, he said with calm if somewhat querulous authority, ''I quite fail to comprehend this interest in my baggage, or by what right you people have interrupted this proceeding. I collect that you two''—he flicked a glance at the excisemen—''are English, but you have already admitted you carry no authority to annoy us. As for you, my good man,'' he added, shifting his gaze with contempt to Campbell, ''I do not know what business you have to be in this house at all.''

Campbell straightened to his full height and

growled, "I've authority enough, my lord. I am the rightfully appointed bailie for these parts."

"Dear me." Rothwell paused, letting his gaze harden. Then, abandoning all affectation, he added in a chillingly quiet voice, "But you have no authority over me, Campbell."

"Perhaps not, my lord, but my present duty has naught to do with you, because I mean to—"

"You are in my house, not MacDrumin's, which is a fact of which, in your position, you ought to be well aware. You have, in fact, trespassed onto my land and broken into my house, for you were certainly not admitted with my permission. You have no business here, Campbell. Go away and take your men with you. Your presence is an affront to what ought to be a most solemn occasion, and your blustering has begun to bore me."

Campbell's face suffused with angry color, but he recognized defeat, and with an abrupt sign to his men to follow, left the house. A breathless silence filled the air until MacDrumin murmured, " 'For then, in wrath, the Olympian Pericles thundered and lightened, and confounded Hellas.' Well done, lad."

Recognizing the source of the laird's quotations, Rothwell looked straight at him and replied, "Since the rest of that won't serve you, sir, I suggest that you quickly 'bring me a beaker of wine so that I may wet my mind and say something clever.' "

With dawning delight, MacDrumin slapped his knee and exclaimed, "You've read Aristophanes, have you? MacKinnon said you were a good man, and I knew he was right the minute I laid eyes on you, for all you dress like a popinjay." He turned to Dugald and said, "Have some of the lads stow those kegs in a safe place and take others to be certain Fergus and his lot get clear of the glen." Turning back to Rothwell, he said, "I can do better for you than mere wine, lad, for though I've some splendid claret in my cellar, this occasion calls for more than claret. A pair of chopins, someone!" Taking two large mugs from a servant who had anticipated the order, he handed one to Rothwell with a grin and said, "There are two things a Highlander likes naked, lad, and one of them is malt whisky. Many thanks to you."

Accepting the mug, and noting absently that James had cornered Kate MacCain again near the fire and seemed to be arguing with her, Rothwell glanced at the silent, weary-looking Maggie, then looked at Mac-Drumin again and said, "I might as easily have betrayed you, you know."

"Not likely though, now you're one of the family."

"I am no such thing, which you must know as well as I do," Rothwell said, feeling his temper stir again. "After watching your recent performance, I don't doubt you were party to the damnable trick that was played on me, sir, but no matter what may have been said then, your daughter and I are not married."

MacDrumin tilted his head a little and with his eyes atwinkle beneath their bushy brows, he said, "Did you not declare yourself wedded to the lass?"

"In a way, I suppose I did, but—"

"And were there not witnesses to hear that declaration?"

"There were, certainly, but—"

"Then you are wedded to her, lad, and I wish you well. She's a wee bit of a handful, I know, but you look like a man who can tame her well enough if you put your mind to it."

"Now see here, MacDrumin," Rothwell said, "that

declaration business may mean something under Scottish law, but it certainly is not the law of England."

"Och, lad, it pains me to contradict you, but you're very much mistaken. By ancient Scot law yon declaration constituted a witnessed verbal contract, even though you did no more than agree that you were married to her in order to save your hide when you were caught in a compromising position. Not only is such a contract binding for life under ecclesiastical law but it carries with it full property rights in civil law; and, since neither you nor Maggie, bless her heart, denied the declaration at the time, you are well and truly married by the laws of both England and Scotland. The English have failed to keep most of the promises they made before the Act of Union was signed, but one they have kept is that an Englishman is just as much bound by our ancient laws as a Scotsman is. Faith," he added with a comical look, "when Fergus Campbell recalls that fact, he'll be plaguing us again. But there's naught you can do about your marriage, lad."

"Oh, yes, by God, there is," Rothwell snapped. "Property rights, you said! That's what this is all about, isn't it? You contrived the whole business amongst the lot of you, thinking to regain property you believe to be rightfully yours, but I'll tell you what can be done about it, you villain. I am *not* married to your daughter. I've not touched her, nor will I do so."

"Just as well you hadn't before the declaration," MacDrumin said, in no way discomposed. "Prenuptially conceived children cannot inherit either in Scotland or in England."

"Papa!"

Maggie's cry was one of outrage, but Rothwell said furiously, "Be silent! There will be no children, Mac-

Take advantage of this offer to enjoy Zebra's newest line of historical romance novels....Splendor Romances (formerly Lovegrams Historical Romances)- Take our introductory shipment of 4 romance novels -Absolutely Free! (a $19.96 value)

Now you'll be able to savor today's best romance novels without even leaving your home with our convenient and inexpensive home subscription service. Here's what you get for joining:

- 4 BRAND NEW bestselling Splendor Romances delivered to your doorstep every month
- 20% off every title (or almost $4.00 off) with your home subscription
- FREE home delivery
- A FREE monthly newsletter, *Zebra/Pinnacle Romance News* filled with author interviews, member benefits, book previews and more!
- No risks or obligations...you're free to cancel whenever you wish...no questions asked

To get started with your own home subscription, simply complete and return the card provided. You'll receive your FREE introductory shipment of 4 Splendor Romances and then you'll begin to receive monthly shipments of new Zebra Splendor titles. Each shipment will be yours to examine for 10 days and then if you decide to keep the books, you'll pay the preferred home subscriber's price of just $4.00 per title. That's $16 for all 4 books with FREE home delivery! And if you want us to stop sending books, just say the word...it's that simple.

Drumin. I shall have this . . . this nonsense annulled, and if I cannot do that, I will, by God, petition Parliament for a divorce. And I'll get one if I have to manufacture evidence for it myself!"

"Whisst now, lad—"

"Don't 'whisst now' me, you misbegotten old reprobate! You may think yourself a devilish crafty fellow, but you'll not get the better of me. Not by a—"

The pistol shot startled everyone in the room, silencing all but James, who snarled, "You damned little vixen! By heaven, I'll serve you as I did before for that. How dare you—"

Rothwell snapped, "James, what the devil is going on there?"

"I'll tell you what the devil, my lord," Kate MacCain said furiously, waving a smoking pistol to punctuate her words. "This . . . this overbearing brother of yours dared to lay hands on me again, and I don't take such treatment from any man. If he moves another step toward me, I'll shoot his—"

"Put that damned pistol away, Kate MacCain," MacDrumin roared. "You've gone and put a hole in my ceiling, that's what you've done, and you've no business even to have the thing. Are you daft, wench? If Fergus Campbell heard that shot, he'll come back and clap us all in jail. I've told you before, no weapons!"

"Aye, you've told me, right enough, but I'll not take being mauled about by this English lout, any more than I'd allow one of your lads or my own to do such a thing."

"I wasn't mauling her," James said defensively. "I was just talking to her when she drew the pistol, and when I tried to take it away, the damned thing went off. I'll admit I was angry to see her again, particularly when I found she was responsible for what happened to Ned. Oh, yes," he said when Rothwell stiffened. "She admitted it was all her own notion—to get even with me, if you please, for giving her a thrashing that was even more well-deserved than I thought. She thought I'd get to Maggie first, because my room was nearer, but now she's entrapped you, Ned, and she is not the least bit sorry. The innkeeper was in on it from the first, and it was Kate herself who screamed, and who no doubt tripped you and ripped your quilt away."

"I did not trip him," Kate muttered, glowering. "He was in such a haste to fling himself into Maggie's bed, he tripped over his own big clumsy feet."

MacDrumin said hastily, "Enough, now. Rory, for the love of God, take Kate home. Her granny will be fretting for her. And if you find young Ian about, take him, too. He ought to be in bed. Go on now, Kate, not another word do I want to hear from you. As for you, Rothwell," he went on with a wary note in his voice, "I ken that you're angry, lad, but 'twill do no good to rant about it now. If you've no desire to share your wife's bedchamber, I'll show you to one of your own, which, knowing English habits, I've already ordered made ready. Though I cannot deny I'd like you for my son-in-law, since it would solve any number of problems, what you do with your future is yours to decide. I'll not interfere."

Rothwell nodded, watching the young man called Rory, unsure that he could succeed in removing the angry Kate, or that James would let her go. James looked at Rothwell, however, and obedient to a nod, he relaxed his hold with a frustrated grimace, whereupon Kate tossed her head and turned to Rory.

"Aye, Rory we'll leave now," she said. "Good night

to you, Maggie. If you're unco cross with me, I'll not blame you."

Maggie said quietly, "I am angry, Kate, but I suppose I'll get over it. Go home to bed."

Rothwell shifted his gaze sharply, wondering what Maggie was thinking. He had known the instant MacDrumin congratulated him on his marriage that someone had told him about the incident at Laggan; and he had been certain from Kate's mischievous laughter that she had been not only the one who had told MacDrumin but most likely was the one who had tricked him in the first place.

He had been flinging accusations rather indiscriminately since then, and had even wondered if Maggie might have been party to the prank, but he was certain now that she was not. He had seen his own dismay reflected in her face when MacDrumin had said the whole business carried the full weight of law. MacDrumin's part was more difficult to decide, but in view of the distances traveled, he could imagine no way by which Kate could have received her orders from the laird beforehand or have reached him afterward before Rothwell's own party had. At best, she and her men could have been but a few hours ahead of them that day.

Now, despite her cryptic comment to Kate, Maggie looked only tired. He seemed to be the only one who was angry, for even James looked more frustrated than upset. Rothwell had no difficulty understanding that his brother felt chagrin at being bested by one small but most irritating female. He felt that same frustration. There did not seem to be any way to avoid having the whole business come out when he returned to London. His enemies—nay, even his friends— would delight in the news that he had been entrapped, no matter how briefly, into a marriage that was not of his own choosing.

The hall was emptying rapidly of everyone without duties there. The Cheltons had already gone upstairs, so when MacDrumin picked up a branch of candles and repeated his offer to see Rothwell to his room, he nodded and called to James to accompany them. Until he had time to sort out his feelings, to know he was in control of his temper again, he did not want to be alone with the unpredictable MacDrumin. If matters were indeed as the man described them, he would do himself no good by protesting, and there was still the comparatively minor problem of his promise to Ryder. It was clear now that getting help from anyone at Fort Augustus or Fort William would be difficult if not impossible, so if he was to learn what exactly was going on in the central Highlands, he would have to do it himself.

He bade Maggie good-night, and was surprised when she only nodded vaguely in reply to MacDrumin's order that she, too, seek her bed, for her bearing was stiff and her attitude such that Rothwell was certain she had no intention of obeying. An English daughter would not think of ignoring an order given by her father or brother. Even Lydia, rebellious as she could be, dared not defy him to his face. She might seek ways and means of getting her own way, but she always at least tried to make her actions appear impulsive or hasty rather than defiant.

MacDrumin gestured with a branch of candles he had picked up toward the angled stairs at the end of the hall, and paid no attention to his daughter's vague reply but led Rothwell and James to a bedchamber on the second floor, where he said good-night. The room was plain, boasting little more than a large bed, a wooden chair, and a huge wardrobe. It contained nothing of a decorative nature other than the cheerful fire now crackling in the small, hooded fireplace.

Chelton looked up from the small portmanteau he was unpacking and said, "I've sent for hot water, my lord, and I set Maria to unpacking the few items Miss MacDrumin—or, should I say—the new Lady Rothwell . . ." He paused expectantly.

James began, "By old Harry, Ned—"

Rothwell cut him off with a gesture. "It is her right for the present, James. Let her enjoy it while she can. Go on to bed now. We can talk about it all in the morning."

James hesitated, and Chelton said, "You have the bedchamber next to this one, Master James. I took the liberty to command one of the serving men to attend you there."

"Thank you," James said, adding bluntly, "Ned, just how long do you mean to stay here?"

"I don't know yet," Rothwell told him honestly. "I was certain MacDrumin would resent my presence, but he seems to welcome it. God alone knows why."

"Seems a practical fellow," James said. "Perhaps he hopes his daughter will somehow retain some control over the family property if he don't antagonize you too thoroughly."

"He can't really think he has not done that already," Rothwell said thoughtfully, "or were you too taken up with Kate MacCain to pay heed to what I said to him earlier?"

"Do you know they call her Mad Kate? One of the servants told me. Seems she's got such a reputation for temper in these parts that most men are terrified of her."

"You ought to be one of them," Rothwell said with

a wry twist of his lips. "Her pistol might well have unmanned you, considering where she had the damned thing pointed."

James chuckled. "Give me ten minutes alone with the wench, and I'll teach her never to do such a mad thing again. I'll tell you the truth, Ned. I'd like to see her with a clean face and a decent gown. She may be a vixen, but she's a dashed pretty one."

Shaking his head, Rothwell said, "Even with a clean face that woman would be too dangerous to play with, James."

"No more dangerous than our Maggie," James retorted, "I know you hold her innocent in all that has transpired, but think about this. Had she not cozened you into coming to the Highlands, you would not be in the fix you're in now."

The door opened, heralding the arrival of Rothwell's hot water, and sparing him the need to reply. James took himself off soon afterward, and when Rothwell was ready for bed, he dismissed Chelton, pinched out his candle, and climbed into bed, surprised to find it comfortable. The coverlet was a thick, cotton-covered eiderdown, the pillows were also down-filled, and the sheets were dry and well-warmed with a warming pan. He could still smell rain in the air, and pine boughs, and another scent as well that he had been aware of for several days that Maggie had said was the tang of good Highland peat. He rather liked it.

Lying there, he heard a distant murmur of men talking in the yard below—MacDrumin's guards—and he thought about the bailie, Fergus Campbell. The man had looked like a ruffian. No wonder the women did not like him. MacDrumin did not seem to fear him, however, which must mean Campbell was utterly ineffective in his position. Even had his host not been impudently candid about the contents of the barrels carried so swiftly into the house, Rothwell would have realized they contained whisky. The fact that they had been so determinedly concealed from the bailie, he knew, meant no duty had been paid on their contents.

But, whatever he owed Ryder, he was not here to help the likes of Campbell, and while he certainly could not condone the illegal production of whisky on his own property, he would go slowly until he knew that whisky smuggling was the only illicit business being conducted in the glen. MacDrumin was clearly a force to be reckoned with, so the more one learned about his activities, the easier it would be for Ryder's men to ferret out other such enterprises throughout the Highlands.

Then, and not the least of his problems, there was Maggie. James chose to blame her for enticing them to the Highlands, but he knew that was only because James did not know Rothwell had put himself in a position that allowed Ryder to blackmail him into coming. And in truth, he knew, too, that he had no one to blame but himself, for the simple fact was, he had done little against his own inclination since leaving Eton at the age of fifteen to go to Oxford, and nothing at all since the day he left Oxford.

That he had landed himself in a pretty predicament was undeniable, but he would get himself out of it, and there was nothing to be lost in the meantime if he took a week or two before returning to London to look things over in Glen Drumin. An annulment would be simple enough to obtain at any time, since Maggie would not be able to claim consummation of her marriage. In the meantime he had only to avoid touching her.

That he had been thinking of her as Maggie for

some time now was not good, he told himself, and regardless of what he had told James and Chelton, he must not think of her, even for a moment, as his lady, only as Miss MacDrumin. Keeping a guard over his actions would be easy. He had only once or twice been tempted to touch her, although there had been a time or two when, catching her eye and smiling, he had felt a certain glow when she smiled back, but the woman had a temper nearly as bad as Mad Kate's when it was stirred, and she was far too stubborn a wench to tempt him. She talked without thinking, and her political notions were nonsensical, just the sort to be expected from a woman.

Honesty brought him up short. What did one expect from a woman? He could not recall having ever discussed politics with one before his conversations with Maggie. Certainly he had never done so with Lydia or his stepmother. Neither had ever shown an interest, and if they had, he would have discouraged them. But although he disagreed with ninety-nine percent of what Maggie said, he enjoyed their conversations. She stimulated him, his thoughts. A mental vision of her flitted through his mind, and he knew he was not thinking of her political views anymore. He was thinking of her golden hair, her hazel eyes, and her silky soft skin, the way her lips pouted when she was thinking, the way her eyes flashed when she disagreed with him; and, suddenly, it was as if he were touching her, stroking that silken skin. She had seen him naked, and he wanted to see her so. He knew then that, far from being certain he would never lay a finger on her, he wanted to do just that, to touch her, to stroke her silken skin, to make her laugh and moan and shriek with ecstasy. His body responded to the thoughts, and he groaned. He was a fool.

XV

Maggie waited in the hall for MacDrumin to return, hoping he would not attempt to delay a confrontation. She was certain he would not simply go off to bed after seeing Rothwell to his chamber, for he was likely to have more orders to give his men once the Englishmen were not right at hand. He might not want to take time before that to speak with her, but she intended to see to it that he did.

She could not believe she was legally married to Rothwell. The whole notion was ludicrous. Not that marriage by declaration was new to her, for she had often heard of couples resorting to that means when there was no priest or parson at hand to perform a proper wedding, which was frequently the case in isolated areas during the wintertime, when what roads and tracks there were lay under a dozen or more feet of snow; but she had never heard of any couple being married by such a means against their will.

Her father must have been joking, punishing Rothwell for his impudence in coming to claim his estate. She would confront him, and he would admit it, and she would tell him precisely what she thought of such pranks, and the whole business would be over. The marriage would be disavowed, and there would be no need to suffer the indignity of annulment or divorce. Otherwise, she had seen enough of Rothwell to know he did not make idle promises, and could not doubt that he would seek one or the other. And from what she knew of him in London, she was certain that whatever he demanded would be granted to him.

The thought of divorce chilled her, but at least annulment was possible, and she thanked God that the earl had not decided to use the excuse of his so-called marriage to ravish her. Other men given such an opportunity would certainly have done so, but whether from principle or out of sheer temper, he would not take advantage of her even now, and for that she must be grateful.

Hearing rapid, familiar footsteps echoing on the stairway, she moved quickly to intercept MacDrumin as he came down the steps, but he made no attempt to avoid her. He was grinning from ear to ear, and before she said a word, he caught her up off the floor and whirled her around in a near-crushing embrace.

"Och, lassie," he said, chortling as he set her down again, "what a thing it is to win a hand again! Thanks to you, we MacDrumins will hold Glen Drumin for yet another generation."

"How can you say so, Papa? Even if this so-called marriage somehow continues one day past Rothwell's appeal to Parliament, his heirs will not be MacDrumins. They will be Carsleys."

"Bah, 'tis all the same. His sons will be my grandsons, with MacDrumin blood running through their veins, and they'll not be Englishman, whatever his lordship tries to make of them. Indeed, and it would be all the better for you to keep your own name and give both to your sons. It is often done here, after all, particularly when a powerful man like myself has no sons and his daughter marries well, which, bless you, you have done."

"Papa, this absurd marriage cannot be valid, and even if it is, his lordship will make short work of ending it."

"I don't doubt he has that power, lass, which is why I did not argue the point with him," MacDrumin said with sternness in his voice, "but you must see to it that he does not. Faith, you must see how important it is to us. You will be proper mistress here again, a thing you owe to our people. If you can but manage to stay married to the man, you'll be able to influence the way he spends his money, and more of it will find its way to the glen, to the good of us all. If he leaves, if he obtains his blasted annulment, then Glen Drumin will surely remain at the mercy of Fergus Campbell and his ilk."

Maggie regarded him with sudden suspicion. "Papa, was entrapping him your idea then? Did you send Kate to trick him?"

He chuckled. "Not I, lass, I give you my word. Och, but I would have done it in a trice had I but thought of it. That Kate! Who would have believed she could be so clever?"

"Not clever, sir, vindictive. She dreamed it up merely as a way to get even with Mr. James Carsley. No doubt she would have been happier had he been the one to burst into my room."

"Then she's not as clever as I thought, for that would have served no good purpose at all. I'd be seeking the annulment myself, for I'll not allow you to marry a younger son. I doubt the lad has a penny beyond what Rothwell gives him."

"You are right about that, I think. James is an

artist, a capricious one, who takes an interest in any new thing that crosses his path. His sister told me he goes to Rothwell whenever he needs money." The thought that it might have been James instead of Rothwell who rushed to her rescue was singularly unsettling. It would not have mattered, since Rothwell would be as anxious as MacDrumin to end an alliance between herself and James—indeed, as anxious as he was to end his own involvement. Nonetheless, the notion was disturbing. She had no interest in James Carsley, nor could she imagine staying married to the earl. When she said as much to MacDrumin, he was obdurate.

"Now, look here, my lass," he said sharply, "for once in your life you must do as you're bid, because this business is far too important to allow foolish sensibility to impede it. You must do whatever is necessary to keep Rothwell here in the glen, and whilst he remains, you must do all you can to encourage his attentions, even if that includes enticing him to your bed."

"I'll not! I'll do no such wicked thing!"

" 'Tis not wicked at all. Haven't I just been telling you you're rightfully married to the man? 'Tis no more than your bounden duty, lass, that's what it is."

"It is not, and I won't!"

" 'There is nothing worse in the world than a shameless woman, save some *other* woman.' You will!"

"Good God, Papa," she demanded, employing Rothwell's favorite epithet, "would you have me behave like a strumpet?"

"Don't take that tone to me, lassie mine, or you'll soon find I haven't forgotten how to put you right across my knee!"

"Aye, and isn't that just the first thing a man thinks

to do when he cannot command a woman?" she demanded icily. "I'll have you know, 'tis just what put us in the fix we're in today!"

"And what the devil do you mean by that?"

"Didn't Kate tell you the whole then?" Maggie snapped. "When she spat in Mr. Carsley's eye, he smacked her until she screeched so loud you ought to have heard her from here. Then he dropped her into the river, to cool her off, he said."

MacDrumin's angry look vanished, replaced by amusement. He chuckled, then laughed until his cheeks were red. When he caught his breath, he said, "That daft lad dared to thrash our Kate?"

"He did," Maggie said with a sigh. She could understand his impulse to laugh, but the results were anything but funny.

"The poor English lad knew no better, I vow, but no wonder she tried to shoot him. She cannot think marrying Rothwell off to you was satisfactory retribution."

"Very likely not, but the damage is done, sir, and as you can see, there was no cleverness involved. So, unless you do expect me to behave like a strumpet, I fail to understand how you mean for me to entice Rothwell to my bed."

"You must think of a way, that's all."

She would have argued longer, but he silenced her, saying he had to speak to his men since there was every likelihood Fergus Campbell was plotting more mischief. "We've those barrels to move to a safe place, and more to get out within the sennight. 'Tis our busy time of year, lass, so I've no time to dawdle about talking. 'Tis action now, for the pair of us."

His dismissal angered her, and so did his casual assumption that she would now try to entice her so-called husband to her bed. She was determined to do no such thing, but she could not deny MacDrumin was right in that it would do them no good for Rothwell to return at once to London. It would not be in the best interest of the people of Glen Drumin to let him go back before he had seen their troubles for himself.

She was afraid her father had made one bad mistake, letting Rothwell and James know about the whisky. Rothwell was hand in glove, after all, with England's Attorney General, and would no doubt delight in carrying information about the illegal activity straight to him. Then what would become of them? Before the earl returned she would have to show him plainly the desperate shifts to which his tenants had been reduced in order to survive. But no matter what happened, she would not entice him to her bed.

So perverse was her imagination, however, that no sooner did her head touch her pillow that night than she began to wonder what it would be like to share a bed with him. No matter what else she tried to think about, her mind kept shifting back to the thought of his hands on her body, and hers on his. She could almost feel the flesh of his shoulders as she had at Laggan when Conach MacLeod entered her room, holding his branch of candles. She remembered the way the candlelight had flickered and danced, creating golden lights and mysterious shadows. Turning over, she buried her face in her pillow and forced herself to think about Kate and what she had done, and James, and the pistol shot—one more thing the earl could report to the authorities. Kate could be arrested for such an act. The woman was daft.

The clock in the great hall had struck three before Maggie fell asleep, and the last thought she had then and the first she had when she awoke to find sunlight streaming into her room, was Rothwell. Was he up yet? Had he already ordered his baggage packed, intending to depart? Or, worst of all, had he gone?

Getting up at once, she snatched clothing from her wardrobe, dressed hurriedly, as much by guess as by habit, without bothering to shout for a maid or Maria. There were no bells to tug at MacDrumin House, but there were servants aplenty, though she had never felt the need to have one all to herself.

Twisting her hair into a knot, she pulled a mobcap on over it and glanced at the result in the small glass, deciding the soft creamy lace edging was becoming and that the narrow red ribbon threaded through the inner edge of the lace was a cheerful addition. She had not thought much about such things before her visit to London, not even at school in Edinburgh, but now as she smoothed her bodice and shook out her skirt—one of her own old gowns but of a pleasing shade of chestnut—she was glad she had some pretty things to wear. Hastening down to the hall, she found the earl and James already enjoying a large breakfast at a table set before the cheerful fire.

Besides hot porridge and fresh cream, there were mutton collops, fresh-caught grilled trout, bannocks, and manchet loaves. When she entered, James, dressed casually as usual, was liberally spreading butter and quince marmalade on a chunk of wheat bread torn from the manchet. She noted at once and with some relief that Rothwell, attired with his customary elegance—though the rest of their baggage could not have arrived yet—was not wearing riding dress. Both men got to their feet, and when a servant moved to hold her chair, she sat down, bidding them good-morning and waving them back to their seats.

"Papa has not come down yet, I see," she said,

striving to sound calm, which under the circumstances was no easy task.

"On the contrary," Rothwell said, smiling with more warmth than she had expected to see. "I'm told he was up hours ago and has gone to call upon someone or other. No doubt, that is merely the explanation he ordered given to me, however, and he has actually gone out to dispose of last night's cargo."

"Faith, ma'am," James said with a chuckle, "were all those little kegs full of illicit whisky?"

Determined that they would get no information out of her to use against her father, she said with feigned innocence, "I know little about such things, sir. You will have to ask Papa." Signing to a hovering servant to serve her from the dish of collops, and helping herself to a chunk of the manchet loaf as he did, she avoided looking at either Rothwell or James, and hoped they would leave that subject for a new one. When the silence lengthened, she dared to look at them again, and saw that Rothwell was peering through his eyeglass at a dish of conserved myrtle. James was thoughtfully chewing bread and marmalade.

With a sigh of relief she turned her attention to her own breakfast, whereupon James said, "I own, Miss MacDrumin—Egad, I need not call you that any longer! You're my sister now, same as Lydia, so I'll call you Maggie."

Involuntarily she looked at Rothwell, but what he was thinking she could not tell. Quietly, she said, "You may certainly call me Maggie, sir, but your puzzlement reminds me that difficulties may arise as to how others should address me."

She had not heard the front door open, but she heard it bang shut and, turning, saw that her father had returned. Evidently he had heard the exchange, for he said briskly, "There's no question at all, lass. You are the Countess of Rothwell and must properly be addressed as 'Lady Rothwell' or 'my lady.' Is that not so, lad?" His look challenged Rothwell to argue.

The earl signed to a servant to clear away his dishes, and said smoothly, "Certainly, MacDrumin, for the present. I have already instructed my servants to do so."

MacDrumin strode nearer the table and peered into the mug by Rothwell's right hand. "That's ale," he said accusingly.

"It is perfectly customary to take ale with one's breakfast," Rothwell said.

"Not in Scotland," MacDrumin retorted. "Were you not offered good whisky?"

James laughed and said, "Forsooth, sir, 'tis rather strong stuff with which to break one's fast."

"Bah, infants drink it from birth here in the Highlands."

Maggie choked on her porridge and sputtered, "Papa, really!"

"They do!"

"Only a teaspoon as part of the christening ceremony," she told Rothwell and James. "It is said to test their strength."

"No doubt it kills off the weak ones," Rothwell replied. He seemed relaxed, and she was glad but a bit wary.

James said, "Egad, I'll have some of that whisky. 'Tis the best I've tasted anywhere. I'd like to know how it's made."

His attitude was so ingenuous that Maggie acquitted him of all evil intent, and MacDrumin, pouring him a chopin of the potent stuff with his own hands, said with a smile, "Thinking to make some up yourself back home in England, lad?"

"Why, I believe I could, you know, once I see how it's done. I like learning new things."

MacDrumin snorted. "You'll never match ours. You need pure mountain water for distilling, peat for your fires, and the best malted barley. Only then could you try to match the excellence of Glen Drumin whisky."

"Excellent stuff," James said, sipping appreciatively.

"Aye, 'tis said that with Glen Drumin whisky, a man could make sea-water into a passable toddy," MacDrumin said. He paused thoughtfully, then added, "If you've really a wish to see how we make it, I could take you to see a working bothy."

"Papa!"

"Whisst now, lassie, where's the harm? 'Tis perfectly legal for a man to distill whisky for his own use, which is all we do, after all," he added with a look of bland innocence.

"If a bothy is a still, I'd very much like to see one," James said earnestly.

"I, too," Rothwell agreed, not much to Maggie's surprise.

She looked warningly at her father, but MacDrumin nodded and said, "You want to see the whole estate, lad. I'll be right glad to take you round myself, and I believe Maggie will want to ride with us, too, won't you, lass?"

She agreed reluctantly, and James said, "Will we be riding near the MacCains?" When the others looked at him in surprise, he added, "We'd do well to carry arms if there's a chance we might encounter that wench today. Someone ought to take her in hand. Where are her parents, that they let her behave so?"

"Kate's father died ten years ago, and two of her brothers fell at Culloden," Maggie said evenly. "Her mother does naught but sit in her rocking chair and rock all day, and though her granny tries to help, she is getting on in years, so the burden falls on Kate to look after the others."

"What about her large cousin, Dugald?" Rothwell asked.

"He does what Kate asks him to do, but although he is her cousin, he is first a MacDrumin, and Kate has never really forgiven the MacDrumins for condemning Rose MacCain's marriage to a man from a rival clan. Kate hates to be beholden to anyone. After her brothers fell at Culloden, she declared she would never depend upon any man again, and would look after her own by herself. And so she has done ever since, for the most part."

"That's right," MacDrumin said with a sigh. "The lass acknowledges no master, not even myself, though as the MacDrumin, I have every right to command her obedience. From time to time she does obey me, but only when it suits her."

Just then the big front door swung wide, and a boy appeared in the opening, the sunlight outlining him from behind, creating a halo effect where it touched his golden hair. He stepped into the hall and said urgently, "Laird, the Abershiel worm be failing, and Dugald said—" Stopping short, he let the door swing to behind him and looked warily at Rothwell and James, who still sat at the table. Maggie knew the blue-eyed, freckle-faced towhead recognized them from the hold-up, for he was Ian MacCain, the same lad who had stopped the coach by lying as one dead in the roadway. She saw, too, that the men recognized Ian.

"What worm was that, laddie?" MacDrumin asked casually.

Ian looked from him to the others and back again, then said glibly, "Why, 'tis the worms ye gi'e me fer fishing, Laird. They be right faulty, them last ones. The ones ye gi'e me afore when I weren't having any luck, they worked like ye'd cast a spell on 'em." He grinned at Rothwell and James. "Niver seen the like. His lairdship soaked them worms in whusky, and not ten seconds after me first cast, me reel began tae screech like a banshee."

"You'd caught one that quick?" James exclaimed.

"Not me, the worm," Ian said with a flashing grin. "He'd got a salmon right by the throat and wouldna let it go!"

The men roared with laughter, and MacDrumin rumpled the boy's hair, saying, "You're a right one, Ian, my lad."

"He is that," Rothwell said, his eyes still alight with laughter, "and he thinks quickly on his feet, too, but suppose you explain what he really meant, for I don't believe that his first reference was to a fishing worm. He would not call such a thing the 'Abershiel' worm, now, would he?"

Maggie grimaced, and young Ian's expression changed from triumph to dismay, but the unflappable MacDrumin said only, " 'Even if I persuade you, I won't persuade you.' You're right quick yourself, lad."

With almost an apologetic air, Rothwell said, "I live with a stepmother who frequently exploits double meanings, MacDrumin. A man exercises the art he knows. But do explain the boy's urgency and understand that I mean to discover precisely what sort of business is being run on my estates."

"Aye, you've the right," MacDrumin said, avoiding Maggie's gaze. "You've said you want to see a bothy, and like as not, Abershiel will do as well as any. We'll ride part way, so you'll be wanting to change your clothes. And, Maggie lass, you change too, and you're married now, lass. You must wear a kertch."

Flushing, not trusting herself to reply civilly, Maggie arose and walked quickly toward the stairway, but Rothwell caught up with her before she reached it. "What is a kertch?" he asked.

"Only a three-cornered kerchief," she said. "Married ladies in Scotland wear them to show their status, whilst maidens wear caps or let their hair hang down their backs."

"I see." He was silent for a moment, then said ruefully, "I tend to forget you are as much a victim of Kate's prank as I am."

"I feared you would believe I was a party to it."

"The thought did cross my mind, but you are too quick of speech and too open of countenance to be sly. Why are you concerned that your father means to show us his still?"

"That should be obvious," she said tartly, moving again. "I believe you will betray its whereabouts."

He stopped her with a hand on her arm and gently turned her to face him. They were on the stairway now, and she was aware of servants' activity in the hall below, but only for a moment. When her gaze met his and he smiled, she forgot the others.

"I must be candid with you, I think," he said. "I will not condone illegal activities on my land, and although your father seems to remember the fact only when it suits him to do so, this is my land. But I promise I'll do nothing to harm him or to increase whatever risk exists for my tenants. What problems they have must be resolved, but I intend to punish no one, and I will betray no one in Glen Drumin to the authorities."

She searched his eyes, trying to decide if he meant what he said. Finally, softly, she said, "Can you make things better?"

"I don't know," he said frankly. "I cannot know until I see how matters stand here. But understand me. I will not tolerate smuggling. If whisky is produced, it must be done legally."

She smiled sadly. "They will not agree to that."

"They will have no choice. But your father awaits us. Go and change your dress, and I'll meet you below. And, Maggie—"

She had begun to move when he told her to go, but she turned back, surprised by how much she liked the sound of her name on his tongue. "Aye, sir?"

His gaze held hers. "Wear that kertch of yours."

His eyes gleamed in a way she had not seen before, and she licked suddenly dry lips before she said, "Aye, sir," and ran away up to her bedchamber without so much as pausing to wonder why her resolution had so quickly failed her.

Her wool dress was well-suited to riding but she smoothed her hair, pinned on a lace-edged kerchief in place of her cap, and found a light shawl to drape over her head and shoulders. The once-plaid shawl had been dyed the color of chestnuts and was not so cheerful as it had been before the English outlawed Highland tartans, but it would serve the purpose well enough and was more comfortable to wear than a heavy cloak.

In the yard, she saw that Rothwell and James had

both donned smallswords as well as their riding dress and were waiting with MacDrumin. Taking young Ian and a pair of MacDrumin's men with them, they rode to the top of the ridge, watching for white coverings on peat stacks outside the small cottages they passed, or white flags fluttering from trees, the telltale warnings that an exciseman or the bailie had been seen in the glen. All was safe, but Maggie soon realized that her father was not heading directly for Abershiel. He was taking a somewhat circuitous route. At least he was showing some sense, she thought, though she doubted that he would fool Rothwell.

When they could ride two abreast, the earl urged his mount alongside MacDrumin's, and Maggie heard him say, "I've been telling your daughter, sir, that I mean to do what I can to help the people here."

"Then perhaps you will convince your friends in Cloud-Cuckoo-Land, which is to say your English Parliament, to end the wicked excise tax on good Scotch whisky."

"I doubt that my power is so great as that," Rothwell said, "but perhaps a way can be found to pay it, or get it reduced—"

"Och, lad, 'twould be a wickedness to pay it, high or low. We've a government telling us we're all one country while it's got its thieving hand in our pockets, calling whisky a foreign product if it goes into England, and demanding payment of duty for production if we sell it only in Scotland. 'Tis a wicked disgrace. We'll not give satisfaction to yon fool excisemen."

Ian, riding behind pillion behind James, said suddenly, "Me granny kilt an exciseman once."

Maggie bit her lip, but James said with a grin, "Did she, lad? And just how might she have done that?"

"We dinna know. She tellt us the wee skinny man coom into her kitchen one day and skeert 'er clean oot of her wits 'cause she'd still got her pots oot from the night's work. 'I've clean caught you this morning,' he says. 'Oh, aye,' says me granny, spearing him wi' a look, 'and did anyone see ye coom in, laddie?' 'Nay,' he says. So rolling up her sleeves, me granny says, 'and by the Lord Harry, naebody will ever see ye gang oot!' "

The men laughed and MacDrumin said, chuckling, "A good tale, the bairn tells, but you need not be thinking his granny's a murderess. 'Tis true the fellow disappeared, but there was no evidence to show he'd ever gone near the MacCain place, and no one doubted he just got tired of being an exciseman and went home again to England. Any number of them have done just that."

They had been riding downhill for a time and came now to a river with a log bridge laid from rock to rock across a narrow part over a roaring fall of water. On the opposite bank scattered farm buildings could be seen at the base of a hill that sloped gently toward the ridge top. Dismounting, they left the horses with a man to watch them, and Maggie watched Rothwell and James, knowing that such makeshift bridges could terrify men who were unaccustomed to them. Neither of the two hesitated to follow MacDrumin and the boy, however, although Rothwell did pause to let the others go ahead and waited for Maggie.

"Would you like a hand across?" he asked.

"I've done it since I was a child," she replied, smiling so he would not think her ungrateful.

He nodded but kept close behind her while they crossed, apparently undisturbed by the gaps between the logs or the tumultuous water beneath them. When they reached the opposite bank, he moved up beside her, and she thought it rather pleasant to have a man watch out for her safety, until he said abruptly, "Surely you do not go out and about all alone here."

She looked at him, surprised. "But I do. Why would I not?"

"You must know it is dangerous for a female to roam these mountains alone. You yourself have mentioned certain dangers."

"There is no danger to me, Rothwell, for I am well known to be the MacDrumin's daughter. No one would dare to harm me."

"You must not do it again," he said harshly, "not so long as you continue to be my wife, at all events."

The others had reached Abershiel farm, and MacDrumin shouted to them to make haste, so Maggie held her tongue, but she would tell Rothwell soon enough that he could not dictate to her. Even if the marriage was held to be legal, she had not accorded him that right.

MacDrumin led the way when they rejoined him, until Dugald emerged from between two large boulders to meet them. Shortly afterward, they came to the bothy, a primitive affair consisting of a hole dug into the side of a hill, its roof formed by strong branches covered with turf. From a distance, no outward sign of it could be seen. Inside, the copper still stood on a furnace made of loose stones that had fallen from the granite wall.

"That wee copper coil," MacDrumin said, pointing out the worm to his guests, "condenses the spirit as it passes through from the wash-still and drips to the spirit-still on the lower level." He indicated an earthen jar two feet high with a wooden lid below the tub with the coil, then turned back to Dugald and said, "What's amiss with the worm, lad?"

"Just got old, Laird," Dugald said. "It's begun tae leak. Like tae snap soon, so we've need of a new one right quick."

"Dismantle it then. Take what bits you cannot spare and leave the rest with the worm for Rory." MacDrumin grinned at Rothwell. "We'll let German George provide us with a new worm."

James, fascinated by the working of the still, paid no heed, but Rothwell frowned and said, "You must be jesting, MacDrumin."

"I am not. Your government offers a reward of five pounds to anyone who reports the whereabouts of an illicit still. The worm's our most expensive bit, so when it wears out, we leave the worn one and a few other bits to prove a still was there. Rory goes to the gaugers, reports he's discovered a bothy, and when he shows them, he gets the reward—enough to buy new copper piping. We'll move the stills to a new bothy."

"We thought tae move this 'un over the ridge to Arlnack burn, Laird," Dugald said.

"Nay, lad," MacDrumin replied. "In spate, the Arlnack runs black as soot, and we must not sacrifice quality to quantity. We'll keep the bothy in Glen Drumin, even if it means biding a wee bit till we find a safe place."

Maggie, encountering Rothwell's thoughtful gaze, smiled at him. He did not smile back.

XVI

The more Rothwell saw of MacDrumin's operation, the more he began to regret his promise to Maggie. In the days following the visit to the Abershiel bothy, he learned the whisky's hold on Glen Drumin was formidable. Nearly every member of the clan was involved, and it was clear to the meanest intelligence that his rents were paid exactly as Ryder had suspected they were, with profits from the whisky. In return, clan members contributed other services. The man who for years had provided shoes for the chief's family still did so. Likewise did men who had looked after the livestock or tended the barley, and women who had woven the cloth or baked the bread, continue to supply those services. And in return their rents were paid. It was done, MacDrumin told him, in quite the most practical way, the very traditional manner that the English seemed determined to destroy.

As tactfully as possible, Rothwell said, "The government's reason for changing the clan system has nothing to do with peacetime practices, sir. The plan is to diminish the ease and speed with which a clan chief can raise a large army."

MacDrumin snorted. "Your people were grateful

enough when Campbells and MacKenzies raised armies to fight for the English."

"All that is over and done," Rothwell said reasonably. "What we must do now is learn to live together in peace."

"Faith, it will not happen. Even those who supported the Hanoverians do not believe we've been well treated by them. German George is no more popular in Edinburgh than in Inverness."

Nor was he popular in London, Rothwell thought, but he did not say so. His point remained valid, if only he could get MacDrumin to agree to it. With that goal in mind, he willingly accepted all invitations to ride out and about the glen, even taking his own oat cakes and whisky to stave off hunger when MacDrumin chose to ride the ridgetops, rather than visit tenants.

James rode with them several times but preferred to take his sketchbook and ramble about on his own, or to visit ailing tenants with his remedy kit in hand. Rothwell, seeing him more than once in the company of young Ian MacCain, suspected that James had developed quite a liking for the boy, whose ability to tell an amusing tale delighted him. It was possible, too, that James still harbored an interest in young Ian's sister, for he had certainly encountered her once or twice, and had even said he liked her spirit and found her amusing.

Rothwell enjoyed the rides with MacDrumin. He liked the old man's wicked sense of humor, and when they were not arguing, thought he told a story even better than Ian. He particularly enjoyed tales the older man told of outwitting excisemen or the bailie, for MacDrumin had no qualms about revealing his triumphs. Rothwell delighted in hearing of the otherwise virtuous parson who hid kegs in his pulpit, and laughed till tears ran down his cheeks when MacDrumin described frightening off a new exciseman, who spent a night at Glen Drumin House, by hanging a stuffed dummy from a tree outside the man's window and telling him it was the body of the last excise officer who slept there.

The excursions with MacDrumin also gave him an excellent excuse to avoid spending too much time with Maggie. Not only did he not trust his own desires but she had made it clear that she still did not trust him to keep their secrets, and did not approve of her father's willingness to show him over the entire estate. She kept busy, apparently with duties of her own at the house, though he was not certain what they were. He had noted the appearance of a few bright cushions here and there, and she had taken to wearing to dinner one of the simpler gowns made for her in London, but she seemed resolved to keep him at a distance and had scarcely spoken to him since the visit to the bothy.

She was not speaking much to James either, and had refused to visit Kate when Ian had said his sister wished she would do so. Rothwell was certain the refusal was due to the fact that James now seemed to find as much food for humor in their so-called marriage as Kate did. Rothwell was a little put out with James himself, since he had spoken more than once, with relish, of Mad Kate's cleverness in contriving the trick at Laggan.

Riding with MacDrumin at the end of the week, the earl tried yet again to suggest alternative methods of providing for the people of the glen. "What will they do if you are arrested for failing to pay the duty on your whisky?" he asked bluntly.

MacDrumin chuckled. "Since I'm not likely to be caught, the worry is small. The duty is unfair, lad; it's as simple as that. None is demanded from makers of English gin, and God knows cheap gin creates more ills than ever a dram of Scotch caused anyone."

Rothwell, unable to resist the grin, smiled back, but his tone was dry when he said, "I suppose you are going to tell me that Scotch doesn't make a man drunk."

"And why would I be telling you any such daft thing? 'Tis not the Scotch makes a man drunk, 'tis the man drinks too much Scotch. And if you see as many drunkards in a square mile of the Highlands as in that same London mile, I'll own myself amazed."

There was no answer to be made to that. He had not seen anyone drunk in the glen, though he had seen vast quantities of Scotch served over the past few days. Nowhere did they go that they were not welcomed with a dram, for everyone had a jug handy to refresh a visitor, and no sooner did one enter a yard or cross a threshold than jug and chopins were got out. And Rothwell willingly admitted that given a choice between old French brandy and Glen Drumin Scotch, he would take the Scotch every time.

The silence between them that day was a companionable one, but MacDrumin was not the man to allow any silence to go unfilled for long. He said abruptly, "You're going the wrong way to work with that lass of mine."

Rothwell had been trying to think of a way to bring up ideas he had that might help the men of the glen find real jobs to support their families, so it was a moment before he realized what MacDrumin had said. Then he replied warily, "I was not aware that I had gone to work with her at all."

"Aye, and isn't that just why I thought I'd draw the error to your attention," MacDrumin said. "You ought not to have told the lass she wasn't to go out on her own, not when our folk depend on her to be telling me of misfortunes that do not customarily fall within my realm. Not only is she bound to defy your order but the responsibility is one she takes seriously. It's no different from what you will expect your wife to see to on your own estates, I'm thinking."

Rothwell said flatly, "See here, MacDrumin, I have not changed my mind about having this fool union annulled at the earliest possible moment, but in the meantime, you cannot pretend it's safe for any young woman to roam these mountains without an armed man or two to attend her. During the past week, I've heard one tale after another of men and women accosted by Campbells or others of their ilk who take unfair advantage of their government favor. Does it not concern you, man, that your daughter is as likely as anyone else to suffer such an indignity?"

"She'll be warned of any outsider in the glen," MacDrumin said calmly, "and there's not a man here who would not seek to avenge any wrong done to her, so it would take a brave one, or a fool, to accost her."

"Nonetheless, I don't like it. She must do as she's bid."

"Tell me, lad," MacDrumin said shrewdly, "do your women in England always do what they are told?"

"If they know what's good for them, they do," Rothwell said, suppressing memories of Lydia's worst escapades.

"I see. I suppose you will tell me next that they always agree with their husband's or father's opinions in such matters."

Rothwell started to nod, realized MacDrumin was laughing at him, and said with a responsive chuckle,

"You do know how to put a man in the wrong, don't you, sir? I should have to be a fool to tell you any such thing. One day you must meet my young half-sister." When MacDrumin did not reply but only waited expectantly, he sighed and said, "Very well, I shall attempt to couch recommendations I make to your daughter only in the most diplomatic terms, for the short time we remain married."

Grinning in apparent satisfaction, MacDrumin directed his attention to a fork in the path and told him to keep left and mind he didn't hit his head on a low-hanging limb.

Rothwell did not resent MacDrumin's enjoyment of the situation. He knew the man was no fool, and that it must be obvious to him that his reluctant son-in-law was growing daily less recalcitrant. Rothwell himself was certainly aware of it. No sooner had he resolved to think of Maggie only as Miss MacDrumin than he had ceased to think of her as anyone but Maggie. And if that was not bad enough, since he had resolved not to lay a finger on her, all he could think about was touching her, holding her in his arms again, and kissing her until she moaned with pleasure and begged for more. In short, he wanted to take his lovely wife to bed, thought he was a damned fool not to do so, and was afraid his wily father-in-law could read his mind.

It was as well, Maggie thought as she cleared a creeping bramble from her path, that Rothwell had not asked what she meant to do that day. He had ridden off with her father soon after breakfast, and James had gone out directly afterward with young Ian, presumably to make more sketches. He had set up an easel in the north parlor, a small but comfortable chamber off the end of the great hall, where he said the light was best for his work, and had already begun to paint. When she had asked to see his picture he had refused, grinning and saying he meant it to be a surprise. Only Ian had seen it, and he was as close as an oyster when it came to discussing James. James had developed quite a liking for the boy, who in turn utterly worshipped him, following him about like a friendly puppy.

There had been none of the difficulty she had expected in keeping the Carsley men in Glen Drumin. They seemed willing to stay, interested to learn all they could about the glen and its people. She still did not doubt they meant to pass along a good portion of what they learned to the authorities in London, and could not understand why her father seemed determined to help Rothwell discover all they would need to condemn him.

When she had taxed MacDrumin with her worries, he snapped, "Will you whisst now, lass? I'll tell the man what I think he ought to know, for 'tis my belief the more he knows about the glen and our people, the more reason he'll have to do what's right. Faith, I've no wish to be hearing what you believe your own husband means or does not mean to do when you've not so much as discussed it with him, and go out of your way to avoid him."

"Don't call him my husband," Maggie had retorted. "He may be so in name, but that's all. It will never be more, for all he believes he has the right to tell me what I may or may not do."

To her surprise, MacDrumin had only smiled and shaken his head, but she had meant what she told him, which was precisely why she was walking through the woods at the upper end of the glen on this bright sunny afternoon. She was going to pay her respects to Rose MacCain and Kate's granny, having decided she had avoided the MacCain place long enough, and had been wrong to do so. Kate's granny liked her, and Rose became almost animated when she paid a call, so even if she was still angry with Kate, it was unfair to make the others pay the penalty. She would tell Kate what she thought of the fix she had put her in, and then it would be done and they could be friends again. Maggie missed having another female to talk with, and Kate had been her friend too long to let even the incident at Laggan come between them.

Before going to the MacCains', she had visited one of the outlying cottages near the ridgetop above Abershiel. Passing the site of the old bothy on her way, and seeing that its remains had been fixed up to look like a working still, she knew Rory had done his work and the old worm would be replaced with a new one before another sennight was gone.

To get to the MacCain place, she had followed the ridgetop for a short distance, enjoying the panoramic vista spread out before her. She could see the rugged northeastern slopes and the vast, fertile fields below, where barley would be growing in the spring. The October colors were bright, the air clear and crisp, and she loved the solitude of the woods. A golden-brown pine marten slipped gracefully from one log to another, as unconcerned as if he roamed the forest alone. He was early, Maggie thought, for martens were generally nocturnal of habit, and it was not yet three in the afternoon. Wondering idly what had disturbed him, she continued her ramble, watching for the oddly crooked pine tree that served as her landmark for the path to MacCains'.

She saw the small white warning flag fluttering from

a sprawling oak near the well-tramped path at the same moment she heard the men's voices, but feeling secure both in her location and her innocent purpose, she walked on. Voices carried easily in the clear mountain air, and it was a few moments before she encountered the men themselves. When she did, and saw that it was Fergus Campbell and one of his minions, Sawny MacKenzie, strolling idly along the path, she held her head high and kept walking, intending to pass them with no more than a civil nod.

"Well, Sawny," Campbell said in an overloud voice, "look what we've got here. 'Tis a wee, winsome lassie."

"Aye, she is that," the other replied, his grin revealing a gap where his two front teeth ought to have been. He was smaller than Campbell, wiry of build and sly of countenance.

"Why, I believe it is Maggie MacDrumin," Campbell exclaimed as if he had just discovered the fact. He tipped his hat to her. "Give ye good den, sweetheart. Whither be ye bound?"

Wishing now that she had kept hidden until they passed, Maggie kept her chin high and walked determinedly on. When Campbell replaced his hat and stepped into her path, eyes agleam with intent, she said stonily, "Let me pass, Fergus Campbell."

"Mayhap I will, mayhap I won't," he said, taunting her. "What will ye gi'e me an I do?"

" 'Tis what you'll be getting an you don't that ought to concern you," she retorted.

"Now, now, lassie," he said, gripping her arm and forcing her to face him, "ye canna talk so uncivilly tae a representative of his majesty's government. 'Twill be better for all, an ye treat me wi' proper respect."

"Take your hand from my arm."

"The lassie's got spirit, Sawny. Just look how her eyes flash when she snaps her wee tongue. Coom, lassie. Gi'e us a kiss and we'll say no more aboot yer uncivil conduct."

Trying to jerk her arm free, Maggie said crossly, "Do you forget who I am?"

"Nay, lass, but yer father willna muck aboot wi' Fergus Campbell. I ha' found no man outside the glen who will say yon precious earl had more than two servants and a single coachman, who's alive and well in Laggan and spends his days polishing two fine coaches, so I've a fine notion in me head that all the praying and the psalming was fer naught more than tae hoodwink me own self. If the MacDrumin canna show us a proper dead body, we'll be taking him off tae Inverness tae stand his trial, and this time the magistrate willna be taking his side of the matter. Not when I tell him we've found a MacDrumin still, and all."

"Have you, indeed?" she said tightly.

"Aye, we be going for it now. We've our methods, ye ken. Now we know of the one, we'll soon find the others, and when we do, MacDrumin will pay the price. Presently, however, we ask only the rightful toll fer the use of this path. So gi'e us a kiss, Maggie MacDrumin, and mind ye make it a good one."

She glared at him. "You know full well that I am no longer plain Maggie MacDrumin but the lawful Countess of Rothwell. Do you dare to lay a hand on Rothwell's wife?"

He laughed. "Your marriage makes nae bother, lass, since I've seen yer princely Rothwell. Fancy clothes and a pretty face, but naught for a real man tae fear. I'll deal wi' Rothwell, and gladly, but ye'll pay yer toll the noo."

"She'll pay me, too, Fergus," Sawny MacKenzie said. "Don't be keeping her all to yerself. 'Tis right selfish, that is."

"Aye, lad, I'll share, never fear." Catching Maggie's chin in one strong hand, he forced it up, then paused as if to savor the moment before slowly bringing his face closer and closer till their lips touched and she thought she would be sick.

She kicked him, hard.

With a roar of pain he released her to grab the ankle she had kicked, and she rushed past him, snatching up her skirts and running, hoping Sawny MacKenzie would not dare follow her. But it was not Sawny, it Campbell himself who caught her, and when he did, he shook her till she thought her neck must snap.

"Aye, yer a brave lassie, are ye not," he growled, his grip on her shoulders bruising her, his rancid breath making her feel ill again. His eyes glittered with evil purpose, and again he seemed to savor the moment, but this time she knew she would not be able to break free. His grip was too strong.

Desperate, she pushed him, hoping to take him by surprise, but he did not even sway where he stood. Her fury amused him. He smiled, and behind her she heard Sawny's responsive chuckle.

Sawny cried, "Ye've got her, Fergus! Show her what a naughty wee lassie she's been. Punish her, Fergus!"

"Aye, I'll punish her, right enough," Campbell said, jerking her against him and trying to capture her lips with his.

"Let me go, Fergus Campbell," Maggie snapped, struggling furiously. Then suddenly she went still, again hoping to take him off guard, and when he took her stillness for acquiescence and moved to claim his kiss, she brought a knee up sharply between his legs.

But this time he anticipated her, twisting so that she kneed only his inner thigh.

He slapped her hard across the face. "Ye'll pay for that, lass. By God, ye need a lesson in manners."

"Teach her, Fergus," Sawny said, dancing up and down now in his increasing excitement. "Oh, teach her, teach her!"

Anger and fear turned swiftly to terror, and when Fergus grabbed her hair in a fist to hold her, to claim the kiss he demanded, she wrenched her mouth free of the awful, seeking lips and screamed, "To me! Anyone, to me! A MacDrumin!"

He slapped her again, and her ears rang, but she fought like someone possessed, kicking, biting, trying to scratch him with her fingernails. He knocked her to the ground, and she lay stunned, aware of his mammoth figure looming over her, hearing Sawny's frenzied cries of excitement, but she was too shaken and numb to do any more to deter Fergus. He reached to grab her.

His hat blew off his head a split second before the pistol shot rang out, startling him so that he froze with his hand still held out toward Maggie.

"If you move one more muscle, Fergus Campbell," declared a familiar feminine voice from the shrubbery, "I'll blow so much of your daft head away, there'll not be enough left to hang your great fat lugs upon. Leave her be." Kate stepped out of the bushes, holding a flintlock pistol in each hand, and when Sawny stepped angrily toward her, she snapped, "You stand where you are, too, you wee louse. I'd take as much pleasure in ridding the world of a MacKenzie as a Campbell, believe me."

* * *

Rothwell and MacDrumin were on their way back toward Glen Drumin House when they heard the shot. MacDrumin, having announced with impudent candor that it would behoove them to stay away from Abershiel that day, had taken Rothwell on foot along the river to the upper end of the glen. On the way back they encountered James and Ian, fishing from the bank with whisky-soaked worms.

"As you see, young Ian's method works well," James said, raising his voice to be heard above the roar of the water, and indicating a string of trout dangling in a pool protected from the force of the river's current. "Do you care to join us?"

Both men refused, but they lingered a few moments to admire the catch and to enjoy the late afternoon sunlight sparkling on the water, before MacDrumin led Rothwell up away from the river to a forest path. It was just as the shrubbery hid James and Ian from view that they heard the shot.

Stopping in their tracks, they looked at each other and listened for a second shot. When none came, Mac-Drumin began to hurry up the path, but Rothwell paused to shout for James.

Despite the noise of the river, James heard him, shoved his rod into Ian's hands, leapt to his feet, and ran up the slope. Throwing both rods to the ground, the boy followed, but James reached Rothwell well ahead of him. "What is it?" he demanded.

"Shots," Rothwell said tersely, gesturing. "Mac-Drumin's gone on, but he's unarmed." Taking his pistol from his pocket, he thrust it at James. "Take this. I've got my sword."

Together they broke into a ground-eating lope, oblivious to rocks, roots, and dead branches in their path, and soon overtook MacDrumin. As they came up to him, he paused near a huge boulder at a curve in the path, holding up a hand for silence.

"What is it?" Rothwell muttered when he got near. He could not see along the path, for the boulder, close-growing trees, and dense shrubbery hid what lay beyond the curve from their view.

"Someone ahead," MacDrumin replied in a gruff undertone. "Not sure who. Thought I heard Maggie's voice." As he inched forward, Rothwell saw the murderous-looking dagger in his hand. He had not seen any sign before that MacDrumin was armed.

"Where the devil did that come from?" he murmured.

MacDrumin shot him a grin. "The air, lad, from God's pure Highland air. Now, whisst, will ye? 'Tis Maggie for certain."

But the voice Rothwell heard first was not Maggie's but Kate's, and from her tone, she was angry. "Daft louts," she snarled. "I ought to have killed them both."

To Rothwell's astonishment, Maggie laughed, but her voice sounded strained when she said, "Kate, what were you thinking? Fergus will have your heart sent to him on a platter for this."

"He may want it," Kate said, "but he'll not get it."

Rothwell, sensing James at his elbow, exchanged a glance with him and saw that he was looking uncharacteristically grim.

Behind James, young Ian had also heard Kate's voice. "Kate," the boy cried, "I'm here, Kate!" He ran out as Rothwell and MacDrumin stepped from behind the boulder, and both young women looked surprised and none too pleased to see them. Kate, despite the two pistols she held, caught Ian in her arms and hugged him. "Were you running to the rescue then, wee laddie?"

"Ye didna require rescuing," he said, grinning at her and returning her hug with interest. "I saw James run up the slope, and heard his lordship calling for him, and so I came to see what was happening. Who did you shoot, Kate?"

"No one. Just frighted off a pair of carrion crows. I did not mean to frighten anyone but them, though."

"I wasna skeert," he said indignantly, "but I left me rod behind when I ran tae see what was happening."

"And your trout, too?" she asked.

"Aye. I caught six, Kate."

" 'Tis a braw laddie, you are, Ian. We'll feast on trout the night, and your granny will be well pleased."

Casting a shy glance at James, Ian said, "James caught four, Kate, and he said we could have them as well."

Without looking at James, Kate said gently, "You must address the gentleman as Mr. Carsley, Ian."

"Nay, for he said I shouldna, that I may call him James, because we're friends the noo."

"He's right, I did say that," James said, looking at her as if he dared her to argue.

She still would not meet his gaze. She said to Ian, "Run fetch your trout, and we'll take them to Granny."

When the boy had gone, Rothwell, looking at Maggie, said abruptly, "What the devil happened here?"

Her chin came up with a jerk, and she said, "Do not take that tone with me, Rothwell. If you've a question to ask, ask it in a civil manner."

Rothwell saw MacDrumin's lips twitch, and managed to keep his temper, albeit with difficulty. He had been startled to hear the gunshot, then frightened to realize that Maggie was somehow involved, and even now, knowing it was Kate who had fired the shot, he could not seem to regain his poise. His tone was still curt when he said, "I want to know why Miss Mac-Cain fired that pistol."

Maggie folded her lips tightly together, and Kate, still ignoring James, looked at Rothwell and back at Maggie before she said cheerfully, "I can tell you, my lord. That great lout Fergus Campbell and his wee shadow, Sawny MacKenzie, were trying to force their attentions on Maggie, so I explained to them that they must not behave in so ill-mannered a fashion and sent them about their business."

MacDrumin snapped, "Where did they go?"

"Aye," James said in much the same tone. "Where?"

Kate pointed toward the path. "Yonder," she said.

"By God," MacDrumin said, "I will—"

"Wait," Rothwell said. "What do you propose to do?"

"Teach that spawn of Satan to keep his filthy hands off my daughter. Did he harm you, lass?"

"No," Maggie said quickly. "He just made me angry. But if Kate had not come along when she did—" She broke off abruptly when her gaze encountered Rothwell's.

He knew she sensed his mounting fury, for she looked wary, as well she should. He said grimly, "So you admit you were really in danger, do you? It may surprise you to learn that you are not yet out of it. MacDrumin," he added, turning to him, "I want to speak with your daughter, but I hope you will reconsider going after Campbell."

"Why should I?" MacDrumin asked testily. " 'Tis the best excuse I've had in a decade to raid the Campbells, and my lads will be sorely disappointed if I do not take it."

"I have come to believe you have sense, MacDrumin, and that all Highlanders are not savages. A raid on the Campbells over this incident would prove me wrong. I know you have little respect for the law, but I would ask you to let me handle this."

Much of Rothwell's diplomatic skill was required, and as much of his self-control, to convince the fiery chieftain and Kate, and even James, but he succeeded. He could not pretend, however, that he enjoyed similar success with Maggie.

Though the others left him in privacy to make his point with her, and though she listened with civility, when he finished lecturing her, she said, "You do not have the right to command me, Rothwell. I agree that when such persons as Fergus appear in the glen—persons, I remind you, that your English government foisted on us—a lady can no longer feel safe in her own woods; however, had I not strayed from the paths, I'd have seen the warnings and been quite safe. I will take more care, not because you command it but because it is sensible to do so."

He clenched his fists, experiencing a nearly overwhelming urge to bellow at her, even to shake her, or at least to take her in his arms and hold her tight, for he could now see bruises forming on her cheek where Campbell must have struck her. The sight infuriated him, and he felt as angry with her and with himself as he did with Campbell. Wishing he knew how to manage her, to keep her safe, at least, he knew the exchange had done nothing to smooth their relationship, and he soon realized that his refusal to support a raid on the Campbells and MacKenzies had not endeared him to MacDrumin, either.

Even James seemed put out with him, but he knew he was right. To begin a clan war over an incident where Maggie was as much at fault for walking out alone as Campbell was for behaving like a scurvy knave would be wrong. The fact that he would have liked nothing better than to murder Campbell with his own two hands did not alter that fact one whit.

The following day was Sunday, and although Rothwell had been grateful to learn the MacDrumins were not Catholic, as they might have been, since many Highlanders still followed the ancient faith, it had been almost as bad to learn that they bore no allegiance to the Church of England. He went with them to their kirk because he was curious and there was nowhere else to go, but he decided that he would arrange for a chaplain to accompany him when he next visited the Highlands.

The family had returned to Glen Drumin House, and gathered in the great hall for dinner, when the door banged back on its hinges and Kate appeared in the opening, carrying Ian's unmoving body in her arms. Tears were streaming down her face. She stumbled forward, gasping, "Help us, Laird, oh please, help us!"

XVII

Maggie was the first to reach Kate, but the men were right behind her. She saw at once that Ian was unconscious. A gash near his right temple was bleeding sluggishly.

"What happened?" she demanded, trying to take the boy from Kate, or at least help her carry him.

Before Kate could control her sobs enough to answer, Maggie was moved firmly aside and James reached to take Ian. To Maggie's astonishment, Kate relinquished him at once, saying, "Mind his left arm, sir. I think it is broken."

Maggie called sharply to one of the staring servants, "Send for the herb woman, quickly!"

"There is no need," Rothwell said, drawing her gently out of the way, while MacDrumin swept everything from the table to the floor so that James could lay the child down. "James knows what he's about," Rothwell added. "How does he look, James?"

"Not good," James said, leaning down to put his ear against Ian's small, thin chest. "He's breathing at least, and I can hear his heart beating. Maggie, have someone fetch clean cloths and warm water, and my kit from my bedchamber."

She turned to give the order and heard Rothwell, behind her, ask Kate again to tell them what had happened. Kate was watching James but said in a grim tone, without turning, "They were looking for me, the Campbells, on account of the pistols. My granny told me." Her voice broke, but she regained control and went on, " 'Twas like Glencoe, she said, only not the middle of the night. She said they rode into the yard—ten, at least—shouting for me, and when she shouted back that I wasn't there, they tore the place apart, she said. Granny snatched up her broom to bash one over the head, screaming at them to get out, but another knocked her to the ground. Ian heard her screams, because he ran in, waving one of my pistols, she said, and he went for Fergus Campbell himself, the brave wee lad, but missed his shot. Fergus picked him up then, Granny said, and . . . and . . ." She cleared her throat and wiped away tears, then went on in a firmer tone, "Fergus threw him across the room like a bundle of soiled laundry, and Ian's head hit the wall a terrible crack." Her voice broke in another sob, and tears flooded her cheeks.

Maggie wanted to cry, too. She put her arm around Kate's shoulders, and said gently, "What of Granny? Was she hurt?"

"Aye, but I don't know how bad," Kate said wretchedly. "Once I saw Ian, I didna think of anything else. I snatched the wee laddie up and brought him here to be safe." Another sob escaped. "I was afraid the men would come back. Granny told me to go, and I couldna bring her along, or my mother either, so they are both there, and . . . and Fergus might—"

She broke down, overcome by exhaustion and horror, and James said harshly, "Ned, I can't leave the boy, but they will need—"

"I'm going," Rothwell said. Maggie heard a bitterness in his voice, and another note as well, one that she had never heard before, a note that sent shivers up her spine.

Knowing it had cost Kate much to admit her fear, Maggie was not surprised to hear her say tautly, "I'll go with you."

"I'll go, too," Maggie said, giving her hand a squeeze.

Rothwell began to object, but MacDrumin interrupted, saying flatly, "Let them come. If Granny has been hurt, or Rose, the lasses will be more use to them than we will, and nobody will harm them whilst they're with us."

Rothwell agreed, and they left less than ten minutes later, escorted by a number of MacDrumin's men, but when they reached the MacCain cottage, they discovered there was little to be done for Granny or for Kate's mother. Both women were dead.

In the small front room, which looked as if someone had turned it upside down and shaken it, Rose MacCain slumped in her rocking chair, her eyes open, her face still. It was as if, Maggie thought, her life had just seeped away. Moving to close Rose's eyes, Maggie wondered if she had been like that when Kate first came home, and knew she might well have been. Rose MacCain had scarcely moved an eyelash even on her good days. Sensing someone beside her, Maggie looked up to see Rothwell, and said, "She is at peace now, I suppose, but how did they kill her?"

"I doubt that they meant to," he said quietly. "She probably died of the shock."

"Granny's where I left her," Kate said. "She must have been hurt worse than she admitted when she told

me to take Ian, not to mind about her. Why did I
listen? I ought to have stayed!"

Maggie moved quickly to comfort her, but Kate
stiffened at her touch. Waiting only until Maggie took
her hand away, she turned to glare at Rothwell. "This
is your fault." She spat the words at him. "Had you
taken them after what they did to Maggie, they'd
never have done this today. Only look at that great
bruise where Fergus hit her! But, you gutless English,
you see nothing wrong with making war on women—
aye, or beating them. You're no better than the
damned bloody Campbells yourselves!"

MacDrumin snapped, "That will do, lass. Hold
your tongue!"

"I won't!" Kate turned her fiery gaze on him. "Since
you won't deal with Fergus Campbell, I'll deal with
him myself—aye, and his whole nest of filthy vipers, if
I must. Rory and Dugald will help me, for all they be
MacDrumins; I've nae more use for the rest of ye!"

Maggie, seeing the rush of color to MacDrumin's
face, opened her mouth to intercede for Kate, but
Rothwell forestalled her, saying in the same quiet tone
he had used before, "Do not chastise her, sir. She has
the right to say all that and more."

The two men were looking right at each other now,
and three of MacDrumin's men who came into the
cottage stopped just inside the door and kept perfectly
still.

Rothwell went on, "I've been blaming myself from
the moment Kate brought the boy into the hall. I don't
say you were right in what you meant to do yesterday,
MacDrumin, but I was wrong not to listen. I do not
yet understand Highland traditions well enough to
issue commands or to refuse to hear you out when you
believe you know what is best to be done. I did not

want a clan war to begin over an incident in which I believed my own wife's actions were at fault, despite her bruises. I do not want a clan war now. But it never once occurred to me that Fergus Campbell could believe himself so wronged by Kate's action that he and his louts would wreak vengeance on innocent women and a child."

"MacDrumin said with grim approval, "Aye then, we'll go for them, lad."

"We'll go for him," Rothwell said, and his tone was as grim as MacDrumin, "but understand me, sir," he added when Kate's expression lightened hopefully, "I won't be party to a massacre. The men who did this committed a loathsome crime and must be punished, but they will all stand their trial in a court of law."

"And how will you get them to court?" Kate demanded, hands on her hips. "Do you think to arrest the whole Campbell clan?"

"When your brother recovers from his injuries, he will be able to identify Campbell and the others. When he does, we will take them to justice."

"Justice?" Kate snapped her fingers under his nose. " 'Tis that I give for your justice! When has there been justice in the Highlands since your soldiers came here? Men once knew how to deal with villains who made war on women and children. Some, I hope, still know," she added, looking toward the three still standing in the doorway. "Rory, are you with me?"

"Aye, Kate, I'm with ye."

Maggie saw her father exchange another look with Rothwell before the latter said, "We are all with you, Kate, but you will not go after Campbell yourself, or with your henchmen."

Kate began to argue, but MacDrumin cut her off, saying flatly, "No one is going after anyone until we have made a proper plan, Kate MacCain, and if you think yon Rory or any other MacDrumin will dare to defy me, you'd best think again."

When Kate still looked mutinous, Rothwell said, "You'll want to see your little brother, so it will be best, I think, if we all return to Glen Drumin House and make our plans there."

He looked at Maggie, and obedient to his unspoken command, she moved to Kate's side, and this time Kate did not object when she put an arm around her shoulders.

Kate remained quiet when MacDrumin ordered two of his men to guard the bodies and arrange for women of the glen to prepare them for burial. Maggie knew Rothwell was surprised that Kate would leave such a task to others, but she knew Kate had little love left for her mother. Rose had given up living to wallow in grief when her oldest sons had been killed in battle, and as far as Kate was concerned, Rose had died then. Granny was different, and had been well loved, but the old woman's death was presently a matter for vengeance. Kate would grieve later.

Maggie hoped they would find Ian's condition improved when they returned, but James looked grave and said there had been little change, although the boy had regained consciousness briefly, giving James cause to think his present condition might be just a deep sleep, and not an unnatural one.

"He ought to be dosed with herbs," Kate said anxiously, looking down at Ian, whose pale, thin face was barely visible beneath the white bandage James had wrapped around his head. "He should have all-heal at least, and roasted rhubarb to prevent fever. What have you done for him, Mr. Carsley?"

"I cleaned his wound," James said, "and with the

help of MacDrumin's farrier, who has experience in such matters, I straightened and bandaged his broken arm. I covered him, ordered the fire built up to keep him warm, and I ordered a room prepared so he can rest more peacefully, but I'll not dose him with anything stronger than broth or herb tea, and that only when he can swallow easily. To give him anything now would choke him."

"Will he live?" Kate asked abruptly.

James hesitated, and Maggie felt a frisson of fear.

Rothwell said, "Won't he, James? Surely his condition is not desperate."

With visible reluctance, James said, "I cannot be certain of that, Ned. Though he did regain consciousness, he did not speak, and when he tried to move, the exertion put him right out again. I don't like the way he looks, and I have seen others die from lesser injuries. No, you don't!" he exclaimed, catching Kate's hands when she rushed at him. Holding her, he said curtly, "Attacking me will change nothing. I am trying to be truthful. I know you are frightened—"

"I fear nothing!" she cried, trying to break free. "Curse you, you English bastard, let me go!"

Still holding her with no apparent effort, James said to Rothwell, "Call me if there is a change in the boy. I mean to deal with this at once." Giving the struggling, cursing Kate a shake, he put his face right in front of hers and snapped, "Be silent, now! You do Ian no good by shrieking at me like this, nor yourself either, so unless you want to be well-slapped, you will come with me, and we'll talk like sensible adults."

She stared at him in shock but made no protest when, still keeping a tight grip on one arm, he took her from the room.

MacDrumin shook his head. "Och, but that lad is

daft," he said. "He'd best take care to cover his head with a steel helmet at night, lest the wildcat takes a club to it. 'Tis a pity he cannot recognize danger when he encounters it."

"He'll manage her," Rothwell said, moving nearer the table. He glanced at Maggie, and she thought he looked as worried as she felt, but all he said to her was, "Will you see if the boy's room has been made ready for him? And perhaps you can arrange for Maria or one of the maids to sit with him once James is willing to let someone else do so. We have matters to discuss."

She knew he meant the men had matters to discuss and that she was being dismissed, but she went without protest, because she had matters of her own to attend to, not least of which was arranging for the servants to serve the dinner they had been about to eat when Kate's arrival had put all thought of food out of their heads. Though she had no appetite, they needed to eat.

Remembering that James had already given orders about Ian's room, and certain they had been carried out, she nonetheless went to check as soon as she had spoken to the cook. All was in readiness, although a window had been left open, so she shut it, stirred up the fire, and went to find Maria, deciding the woman ought to make herself useful.

Both Cheltons had had a hard time adjusting to life in the Highlands, for now that Rothwell seemed to be spending less time and effort over his appearance, he required less of Chelton's help, and although at first Maria had been willing to help with household chores, the MacDrumin servants had made it plain that they neither wanted nor needed help offered with such a superior air. Maria did what Maggie asked, but Maggie was not accustomed to being closely waited upon and found it disturbing to be constantly referred to as *your ladyship*. She had attempted to divert Maria without offending her by asking for help adding a few decorative touches to Glen Drumin House, but although Maria expressed willingness to embroider cushions and even to assist the housekeeper with such items as bed hangings and window curtains, she had done very little, and Maggie had not insisted. She thought both Cheltons were cold, unfeeling people whose sense of self-worth was much exaggerated, and she found it hard to understand why the dowager valued Maria, at least, so highly.

The tirewoman was found in Maggie's bedchamber, shaking a green stuff gown she had taken from the wardrobe. "I was sure you would want to change your dress, your ladyship," she said in her stiff way, with no more than an oblique glance. "It was not wise to leave the house so hastily without changing from what you wore to church. I am afraid that gown is quite ruined."

The reproach brought words of rebuke to Maggie's tongue, but when Maria moved toward her, she checked them at the sight of a bruise on her cheek as livid as the one on her own. She had begun to suspect from Maria's behavior when she was with Chelton that he was a brutal man as well as a dour one. Now she was sure of it. She had not given a thought to her clothes, but looking quickly down at herself, she said, "Faith, I do look a fright. Very well, I'll change, but make haste, Maria. Your services may soon be required elsewhere."

When she had explained about Ian, the woman looked at her in surprise. "You expect *me* to look after that common child?"

"I do."

"But he is no more than a street urchin," Maria

retorted, "or so he would be if this God-forsaken place *had* any streets."

It was on the tip of Maggie's tongue to tell her that any woman in the glen would be glad to sit with the boy, but she wanted Maria safely out of the way, because she was afraid if the woman got wind of her plan, she would go straight to Rothwell. Therefore Maggie said coldly, "Are you refusing to obey me?"

"No, your ladyship." The woman flushed deeply, making the bruise on her cheek look worse than ever. "I just thought—"

"I don't want to hear what you thought. You will be called if you are needed. Until then, I don't want to see you."

When Maria had gone, Maggie sat down and began to brush her hair. She felt nearly as guilty as Rothwell did over what had happened, for like him, she had not even imagined that Fergus Campbell might retaliate in such a dreadful way. She had feared he might make trouble for Kate for firing a pistol, and that had been frightening enough, but it was practically unheard of in the Highlands for men willfully to injure women or children. But much as she wanted to lay the blame for all that had happened at Fergus's door, she could not rid herself of the knowledge that if she had behaved sensibly (or had obeyed Rothwell), Kate's mother and granny would still be alive, and Ian would be telling one of his funny stories to James instead of lying at death's door.

If Ian died, there would be no witness to accuse Fergus or any of the others, and no point in attempting to hail them before a magistrate. And if Ian recovered, what then? She tried to imagine Rothwell and her father's men riding over the ridgetop to Fergus Campbell's house and asking him politely to accompany them to Inverness. Her imagination boggled. They could all be killed. No doubt Fergus thought he had killed anyone who might tell what had happened, so he would be home, but a surprise attack was the only way to take him. And if her father and Rothwell would not lead it, she knew someone who would.

Dugald had not been at MacCains' with them. He had no doubt been out searching for a place to put the new bothy, and thus had not heard her father tell Kate, and Rory, that he would not allow anyone to help her. Where Dugald led, Rory and others would follow, so it was merely a matter of getting a message to Dugald before MacDrumin or Rothwell talked to him.

Accordingly, Maggie twisted her hair into a knot, replaced her kertch, and went in search of a servant she could trust to take a message to Dugald. The servant left at once, and she went to the hall to see if their meal was ready yet. Two servants were putting food on the table. Kate stood alone by the fire.

"They've taken Ian up then," Maggie said.

"Aye," Kate said, "I sent that Maria away and was sitting with him, but James"—her cheeks reddened as she said his name—"said I must keep up my strength and sent me down to eat. He will sit with Ian till I'm done."

Her manner was subdued, and though Maggie knew she was desperately worried about Ian, it was unlike her not to be shouting her anger and stirring storms wherever she walked. This quiet, moody Kate was someone she scarcely knew. Drawing her a little away so the servants would not hear, Maggie said, "Whatever did James say to you when he took you from the room?"

"Leave it, Mag. I don't want to talk about it."

Rothwell and MacDrumin came in from the yard just then, and seeing that their meal was ready, Maggie ordered a plate sent up to James and moved with Kate to join them at the table. During the meal she tried to get the two men to tell her how they planned to arrest Fergus, but they evaded her questions deftly, and Kate said nothing to help her and soon begged to be excused.

"I must get back to Ian," she said.

Maggie got up quickly and followed her to the stairs, saying softly, "Wait, Kate. I cannot bear to see you like this. James only said Ian might die because the chance exists, not because he means to let him go."

"I know," Kate said, "but he says the body must heal itself, that herbs will not help. Does he really know anything, Mag?"

"What do you think?"

Kate hesitated, but new color rose to her cheeks and there was a softer look about her when she said, "I don't know if I believe in him because I want to or just because I do, that's all. I hope he does know." Looking a little shaken by her own words, she did not wait for Maggie's reply but hurried away.

The big hall was chilly, and candles were being lit against the increasing darkness, so Maggie returned to the fire, and when James joined the men a few minutes later, she tried to hear what they said, but they kept their voices too low. Thinking of what she would tell Dugald and what he would respond, she watched the crackling flames, lost in her own thoughts.

Rothwell's hand on her elbow sometime later startled her, and when she looked up into his eyes, she saw concern in them. He said, "I saw Kate go up. Is she all right?"

"She is afraid he will die," Maggie said, hoping he would tell her everything was going to be fine.

He said, "James is afraid, too, because Ian ought to have become more responsive by now. He hopes the fact that the child breathes as if he were sleeping is a sign that the body is mending. He has been able to give him water, but that is all."

"I thought Ian could not swallow," Maggie said.

"James told Kate to use a wet cloth to force a few drops at a time between the boy's lips. I thought at first he was merely giving her something to do so she would not feel so helpless, but he says the boy could die just from lack of water." He looked closely at her and added in a lower, more gentle tone, "How are you? You have been wearing much the same expression as Kate."

"How do you expect me to look? I have known Ian almost since the day he was born, and his grandmother since the day *I* was born, and this is all my fault!"

"Just a moment," he said, putting a hand to her chin, making her look at him. "What makes you think the fault is yours?"

"Because it is," she snapped, jerking her head away. "I thought you would be the first to agree with me."

"Why should I?"

"Didn't you tell me yourself not to walk out alone?"

"I did, but your being alone does not excuse those villains for what they did, Maggie. Your action had nothing to do with theirs. Nor did Kate's, and if she's going about looking like she does because she blames herself for going to your rescue, she is being foolish beyond permission."

"Kate might be doing that," she said, considering the notion for the first time. "Had we not both infuriated Fergus and Sawny, they would never have gone looking for her."

"The decisions to hurt and to kill were their own," he said, "and they leapt at the least excuse to do both. A man like Campbell has no business acting for the government and ought to be clapped up into jail for what he did."

"They all ought to be hanged," she retorted.

"I agree, but that will be up to a court to decide once they have been laid by the heels." When she did not answer, not trusting her temper, he added, "You will manage better tomorrow if you have a good night's sleep. Why don't you go up to bed?"

Telling her what to do again, she thought, but if she said anything, she would tell him what she thought of his absurd notion that justice prevailed in the Highlands. To the mighty went the right, as anyone ought to know, and the only way Fergus Campbell would learn a lesson was if someone stronger taught it to him. Instead of saying these things, any one of which was likely to stir not only Rothwell's wrath but MacDrumin's, she said she would offer to sit with Ian and give Kate a rest.

But when she got upstairs, she found James with Kate and Ian, and he was looking grim. He shook his head when she asked if she could help, and she saw by the way he looked that he was more worried about the boy than ever.

Deciding that Rothwell was right about one thing, that she would handle things better the next day if she got some sleep, and certain that since Dugald had not made an attempt to speak to her before dark, he would not show his face until morning, she went to bed, hoping he was already attending to Fergus Campbell.

It seemed as if she had no sooner put her head to the

pillow than she slept, only to come awake again during the wee hours, certain that something was amiss. There was no sound, nothing to indicate what had wakened her from her deep sleep, but her sense of something being wrong would not go away, so she got up, wrapped her shawl around her shoulders, and slipped out of her room. The torches lighting the gallery had been put out, but at the end, she saw light spilling from the room where Ian was sleeping, and her breath caught in her throat. She could hear sobs and knew at once that they were Kate's.

Running barefoot, heedless of the icy stone floor, she flew down the gallery to the open door. "Oh, my dear Kate, I'm so sorry" she cried, the words tumbling from her lips as she burst into the room to find Kate in James's arms, sobbing her eyes out against his shoulder. They stood beside the bed, blocking any view of its small occupant.

Over Kate's shoulder, James's gaze met hers, and to her astonishment he began to smile.

Rothwell said from behind her, "Ian's going to be well, Maggie. I've just sent someone to wake your father and tell him." His hands were warm on her shoulders.

"Really?" She turned to judge the truth of his words by his expression, but tears filled her eyes. "Ian will live?"

"See for yourself." He pointed to the bed, and since James and Kate had moved a bit, she could see the small figure there.

Ian's eyes were open. He was watching Kate, but he shifted his gaze to Maggie and murmured in a cracking voice, "Why is Kate crying? Did James make her cry?"

"Oh, my love," Kate said, pulling away from James

and kneeling beside the bed, "Oh, Ian love, you'll be well."

"Where am I? Kate, Fergus Campbell and a lot of others came tae the hoose! They said they . . ."

"Whisst now, love. Haven't I got you safe away, and hasn't James made you well again?"

James knelt beside her and grasped Ian's thin wrist.

Rothwell drew Maggie away. "We're not needed now," he said, "and you should get back to bed before you catch your death. Whatever possessed you to come running out here without so much as a pair of slippers on your feet? Have you no sense, woman?"

"Stop telling me what I should or should not do," she cried, her temper suddenly and most inexplicably flying out of control. "If I want my slippers, I'll get my slippers, but it can be no concern of yours, so keep your opinions to yourself!"

He shut Ian's bedchamber door and stood looking down at her until she could think of nothing but how near he was and how cold the stones were to her feet. Shifting stealthily from one foot to the other, she refused to meet his gaze.

He said, "The fact that I am your lawful husband entitles me to a number of rights that I have not chosen to assert." He paused as if to be sure she took in his full meaning, and she shifted her feet again. "Are you cold, little wife?"

She gritted her teeth, but even they would not cooperate, and when they began to chatter, Rothwell scooped her up in his arms and carried her back down the gallery to her bedchamber. "Put me down," she said crossly. "You take too much liberty."

"You should be glad I don't take more," he retorted, dumping her on her bed. "Get under those covers right now."

"I won't," she snapped, springing back to her feet, her hand raised to slap him. He did not speak, and in the dim light from the pale moon outside her window, he was only a gray shadow, but the crackling vitality of the man was undiminished and, sensing it and something more, she stopped her hand before it touched him. A moment passed before she realized she was holding her breath, and with a sigh she put her hand down.

"A wise decision, little wife. I am not a violent man, but I have already warned you that I won't take kindly to being struck. I'd no doubt feel a strong urge to retaliate in kind. Now, you may do as you choose, but I am going to bed. I've a good deal to do tomorrow."

"Aye, you behave like a husband only when it suits you," she snapped, and then, shocked by the words that had shot without a moment's reflection straight from her mind to her tongue, she tried to cover the slip by adding swiftly, "You'll never take Fergus to justice your way, Rothwell, but it does not matter, for I've sent for Dugald. He'll show you justice, *Highland* justice."

"I have already spoken to Dugald," he said. "In fact, I spent the evening talking to a number of our tenants, and sent messages to others. Tomorrow we band together to take Campbell and MacKenzie to Inverness to be held until the next assizes."

"Raising the clan shows some sense at least," Maggie said, reluctantly pleased that he had taken command of the situation, "but Fergus will refuse to go with you, so there will be battle done. Kate and I will—"

"You and Kate will stay here to look after Ian," he said harshly. "You will obey me this time, Maggie, or rue the day, and don't be looking daggers at me either.

Your father would tell you the same. This is men's business."

"It is MacDrumin business," she said stubbornly, "and if you think Kate will agree to stay behind while you avenge what was done to her family, you don't know her at all."

"I'll leave Kate to James," he said, gripping her by the shoulders, "and you will do as you are bid. I'll have your word on that before I go, Maggie. Defy me, and you will find out just how it suits your husband to behave."

She was still, wanting to tell him again what she thought of men who assumed they could order women around when they had no real right to do so, but his words triggered a memory of the words she had shot at him before, words she knew now he had heard perfectly well. The aching chill in her feet was forgotten. She was aware only of his warm hands on her shoulders, his grim sense of purpose, his tantalizing nearness.

He was still, too, suddenly. His grip did not slacken, but his breathing grew ragged and deeper. And though, except for the tight grip on her shoulders, he did not touch her anywhere else, her whole body sensed a crackling electricity between them. The silence lengthened, and she dared not look up into his face. She licked dry lips, and tried to breathe evenly, but her breath seemed to be as ragged as his. Then his grip on her shoulders tightened more, and he whispered, "Look at me, little wife."

She looked at his chest, and even in the dim light she could see it, broad and strong, rising and falling with his breathing, and she suddenly remembered what he had looked like without clothing, with no more than the cover from her bed wrapped around him. Her palms grew damp, her body tingled.

"I said, look at me, little wife. Do you disobey?"

Swallowing, telling herself she was not in the least afraid of this man, and was certainly not afraid of the way he made her feel, she looked up. Moonlight touched his right cheek, giving his eyes a dark and silvery glitter, revealing an intensity that sent shock waves through her. Her breathing was shallow and quick, and she could feel a sort of prickling sensation, as if her skin anticipated his touch. She could not look away. She felt as if she were caught in a spell, a magical webbing that entwined her and would not let her move.

She was being nonsensical. Licking her lips again, she murmured, "I am looking at you, sir. What now?"

"This," he said, and he kissed her.

His lips were hot against hers, and the spell deepened, for her own lips moved as if they were bewitched, as if they would take more even than he was willing to give. She moaned deep in her throat, and as his hands moved from her shoulders to her back, holding her close, stroking her, caressing her, her own hands responded, doing the same to him.

Heat coursed through her body, awakening it, stirring feelings and sensations she had never known before. She wanted him to continue, to waken any other feelings that lay sleeping within her, and when his tongue sought entrance to her mouth, she welcomed it, letting him have his will with her, feeling no inclination to stop him. The second time she moaned, he set her back on her heels and looked ruefully at her.

"I ought not to have done that. You bewitch me, wife, and there are matters I would explore with you at a more appropriate time. But I don't want you to think that because you can stir primitive feelings in me you can also compel me to change my mind about what I said. You and Kate will stay here tomorrow. Now, climb into bed, and I will leave you to sleep."

Still overcome by her body's response to his kiss, Maggie obeyed silently, and when he was gone, she lay thinking far into the night. It occurred to her at one point that he had left without repeating his demand that she promise to remain in Glen Drumin, and so when the sun's first rays entered her bedchamber, she got up, dressed quickly, and went in search of Kate.

They went carefully, cautiously, each carrying one of Kate's pistols, and Kate had her trusty dagger tucked into her boot as well. Knowing the men had followed the main track through the glen to the ridge-top, they took a shortcut Kate knew and topped the pine-forested rise above Campbell's house in time to see a host of men ahead, stealthily making their way downhill through a thicket of willow and aspen bordering a tumbling stream.

Kate looked grimly at Maggie. "Campbells, or I miss my guess," she murmured.

"Aye," Maggie agreed.

"They've not seen us yet. We must take cover before they do. Follow me and hope that if one of the horses makes a noise, they think it's one they've left behind themselves."

They turned into the thick woods that bordered the stream, the sounds of their horses' hooves muffled by a thick carpet of pine needles. Out of sight of the men, they quickly dismounted, tied their reins to tree branches, and with Kate taking the lead, moved as swiftly as they dared through the forest.

Suddenly Kate dropped to her haunches, motioned to Maggie to do likewise, and they crept forward until they could see the house in a clearing ahead. Maggie heard Rothwell's voice, then Campbell, and then she saw Campbell on his front step. Just then Kate grabbed her arm and nodded toward the stream, where willows and aspen were moving despite the lack of wind.

Before Maggie could open her mouth to scream, Kate drew her pistol and fired it in the air, and pandemonium erupted as the MacDrumin men dove for cover.

XVIII

Rothwell had believed MacDrumin's warning that Campbell would not be easily taken, but when they rode into the very clearing where the house was, without so much as a rustle from nearby bushes to suggest reinforcements at hand, he began to relax. They did not ride directly up to the house but took cover in nearby woods until, seeing no guards, he decided Campbell was confident his power as bailie would keep him safe, and motioned to MacDrumin and his men to move closer to the house.

"Show yourself, Fergus Campbell," MacDrumin shouted, "or are you too much of a coward to answer for your crimes?"

The front door of the house opened, and Campbell stepped outside, looking around casually as if he were merely answering the call of a friend. "That you, MacDrumin? What would ye?"

"We want you, you pestilential scoundrel, and I've my pistol aimed straight at your black heart, so put your murdering hands over your head and come out away from that doorway!"

"Faith, hold yer fire," Campbell said, obeying at once. "I've no wish for trouble. I dinna ken what ye're up in the air aboot, MacDrumin, but if 'tis talk ye want, I'll talk wi' ye."

Rothwell exchanged another glance with James, raising his eyebrows at this unexpected meekness on the part of a man they had been warned was a treacherous killer. When MacDrumin stepped out into the yard, Rothwell followed him, noting absently that Campbell seemed surprised to see the pistols in their hands.

"Do all yer men come armed, MacDrumin?" the big man said snidely, his tone louder than before. " 'Twill be a pleasure tae inform the magistrate that ye sae openly defy the law."

Rothwell said calmly, "These are no longer MacDrumin's men but mine, Campbell. I am Rothwell of England, and thus am not subject to acts applying specifically to Highlanders."

"To none of them, my lord?" Again the tone was snide, surely not that of a man expecting to be taken to justice.

A prickle of forboding stirred, and Rothwell saw that James too had drawn his pistol. Both men also wore smallswords, and Rothwell knew that MacDrumin was armed with a broadsword as well as his pistol. MacDrumin's men, many looking like the wild men Rothwell had once thought them with their shaggy beards, long hair, and voluminous, dyed-over plaids, carried clubs and the round leather shields they called targes, but if any of them carried other weapons, they did not show them.

They had all followed MacDrumin into the clearing, and some peered watchfully into the dense woodland that bordered three sides of the clearing while others kept their eyes on Campbell.

Rothwell realized that except for the noises made by

the men around him, the woods were unnaturally silent. Before, he had assumed the silence was due to their passage along the narrow track, but by now the usual forest sounds ought to have begun again. As the thought crossed his mind, a shot rang out, and as he dove for cover behind the nearest boulder, he saw the men around him throw their plaids aside, revealing that they were armed with more than simple clubs and targes.

After that single shot, which had seemed to come from behind them, more shots rang out from a willow thicket to the west. As Rothwell discharged his own pistol, men broke from the thicket and ran toward Campbell.

MacDrumin had foreseen such a move and with the help of two of his own men, pushed Campbell to the ground and stood over him, broadsword in his hand.

Motioning to James to follow, Rothwell dropped his pistol, hefted his leather targe, and drew his sword, making his way closer to the fiery chieftain as more shots rang out and battle erupted all around them. As he slipped past a pair of swordsmen slashing wildly at each other with the two-handed swords they carried, he saw one of MacDrumin's men raise a pistol and fire. The man instantly threw the spent pistol at the head of another ambusher who leapt at him, drew his dirk from his belt with his free hand, and dispatched the attacker forthwith. Grimacing, Rothwell hurried on, reaching MacDrumin as two men jumped him.

Campbell leapt to his feet, catching a broadsword flung by one of his rescuers. "Now, MacDrumin," he cried when he saw the chief fighting two men at once, "ye'll soon be baking in Hell!"

"Not likely," Rothwell snapped, and Campbell

turned in fury to meet his attack, grinning when he saw Rothwell's smallsword.

Blade met blade in a flurry of ringing, metallic cracks, and Rothwell quickly realized that Campbell's style, like that of most Highlanders, was fierce, savage, and murderously intense. But despite the difference in weapons, Rothwell soon saw that his own skill was superior, and had the fight remained a fair one, he might quickly have disarmed his opponent and ended it without serious injury to either of them.

The first warning of impending disaster was a dawning smirk on his opponent's face and a flickering glance to a point beyond Rothwell's left shoulder. Either would have been enough, without the feminine cry from the woods. Rothwell leapt agilely aside, using his targe to deflect a murderous sword slash from behind with but a hair's breadth to spare.

He scarcely heard the cry, for although his attention remained riveted on Campbell, he was already shifting position to defend against the second man, and with two of them to face, both wild and unpredictable in their methods, both using the heavier swords, and both willing to forget all rules of fair swordplay, he now had no choice but to dispatch one as quickly as possible in order to concentrate on the other, and Campbell was clearly the more highly skilled of the two.

No man could continue serious swordplay for longer than ten or fifteen minutes without pause before crying quits, and Rothwell knew he was tiring rapidly. The effort such fighting took, particularly in the heat of battle, was too great. He knew Campbell had to be tired, for his sword looked heavier and the man was not as light on his feet. Furthermore, he had had time to mark Campbell's habits and knew the man parried thrusts with the fort of his blade, returned edge blows from the wrist, and his favorite blows were delivered with the outside of his sword. Making up his mind in the split second as he turned to engage his second quarry, he parried Campbell's next blow and returned with a thrust to his face. When Campbell's blade flashed up to parry with the fort, Rothwell's blade slipped under with a thrust in prime to the man's belly, and Campbell was down.

The second man was quickly disarmed, and the battle was soon over, for the would-be rescuers, seeing Campbell fall, scattered and ran. MacDrumin and his men rounded up a number of them, and as Rothwell and James moved to help them, a familiar voice cried from the woods, "James, come quickly, Maggie's been hurt!"

Rothwell, hearing the urgency in Kate's voice, felt the blood freeze in his veins. Whipping around on his heel, he ran after James, knowing then that it had been Maggie who screamed the warning when the second man had tried to take him unaware.

When they found them, Kate had an arm around Maggie, and there was blood high on Maggie's left sleeve. She was pale and gritted her teeth against the pain. James knelt quickly at her side, using his sword blade to cut her blood-soaked jacket and habit shirt to bare the wound.

"How bad?" Rothwell demanded tersely.

"A shot grazed her," James replied. "It's a moderate cut and a bad abrasion, but if we can avoid infection, it won't prove serious. I'll make her an anodyne bread poultice when we return, to soothe the pain. That frequently prevents infection, too."

"It's a wonder they both weren't killed," Rothwell snapped, adding furiously to Maggie, "What the devil are you doing here? I told you to stay in Glen Drumin."

"So you did," Kate said, still holding Maggie protectively, "and had we done as you ordered, you'd all be dead by now."

"Nonsense," Rothwell said.

"It is not nonsense," Maggie said, wincing as James tended her wound. "Had Kate's shot not sent all you to cover, Fergus's men would have killed a good many of you with their first attack. You should be grateful, Rothwell."

"Grateful?" He wanted to snatch her up and shake her until her bones rattled, and it took every ounce of the control he had developed over the years to keep from doing just that. He did not look at Kate, nor could he watch James, who, having probed the wound for bits of metal, now called for his kit and went to wet cloths in the stream. Rothwell kept his attention on Maggie, demanding, "Just what did you think you would accomplish by disobeying me? Had the battle not gone as it did, you would have found yourselves at the mercy of Campbell's men. You might have been killed. Did you think of that? By God, if you ever deserved thrashing, Maggie, you deserve it now, and if you ever dare do such a thing again, that's just what I *will* do!"

His gaze locked with hers. Silence had fallen all around them, but he was beyond caring what others thought. He could not remember ever in his life being so angry with anyone. Knowing she had been wounded had frightened him witless, but oddly, it was learning that the wound was not serious that had released his pent-up emotions, and in a way he had never expected, enraging him so that he wanted to teach her a lesson, to punish her for the foolish disobedience that had put her life at such a risk.

She did not look away. He thought savagely that it was almost as if she dared him to touch her, and he had all he could do to keep his hands clenched at his sides. When James brushed past him, kneeling to clean her wound, he was grateful for the excuse to look away.

But she gasped at the first touch of James's cold wet cloth, and Rothwell looked quickly back. At the sight of tears springing to her eyes, he moved at once, meaning to take Kate's place, but Maggie said between gritted teeth, "Go away, Rothwell. You're an ungrateful wretch, and still no real husband to me, so I won't listen to anything you say!"

"If you can't say anything worth hearing, hold your tongue," he snapped, losing his temper at once. "You're naught but a foolish, hot-headed wench who's never been taught to obey, and it is more than time someone took you in hand. You might as easily have endangered us as helped us, or caused one of us to injure you in mistake for one of the enemy. Your actions were foolhardy and stupid, and you deserve—" He would have gone on, for his tongue had assumed a life of its own, but when she cried out in pain, he said abruptly, "Move aside, James. You're hurting her!"

If James was surprised to be given such an order, he did not show it. Instead, he handed the cold wet cloth to Rothwell and said quietly, "Be certain no powder remains in the wound, no matter how much you may have to hurt her, then bind it with the cloth strips from my kit."

"How is the lass?" MacDrumin demanded, coming up to them and looking down at his daughter's injury with a shake of his head. "You'll be needing a bit of whisky there, I'm thinking."

James nodded, but Rothwell, kneeling to take his place, said over his shoulder, "What the devil for?"

"Keeps infection off," MacDrumin said. "Cures well nigh anything I've ever heard tell of, even cholera and typhus. I've used the end of my own flask on Fergus, but since no one else was hurt badly, mayhap one of the lads will still have a bit left." He shouted, and a moment later, someone handed a leather flask to Rothwell. Following orders from MacDrumin, he poured the contents liberally over Maggie's wound, wincing when she shrieked with pain but saying grimly, "Serves you right." Then before she could reply in kind, he looked up at MacDrumin and said, "You gave yours to Campbell, you say. How is he?"

"Dead," MacDrumin said cheerfully. "Administered the last rites myself. No wine or bread, of course, but we always carry whisky and oatcakes, and they do just as well." He looked around at the villains being guarded by his men and added, "I'd like to hang the lot, but I expect you'd object."

"I would," Rothwell said. "We'll take them to the nearest assize town to stand their trials."

"That'll be Inverness," MacDrumin said. "I'll see to it. How's the lass now?"

"She'll do," Rothwell said, tying the last knot to fix the bandage in place. "Can you stand?" he asked her.

"I think so."

"I'll help her," Kate said, getting up.

"No, you won't," James said, taking her by an arm. "I want a word with you, my girl."

"Well, I don't want to speak to you," Kate said. "You men behave as if you were the only ones on God's earth with brains. I suppose you mean to tell me

I ought to have stayed in bed and not come to do what I could to help lay these scoundrels by the heels, and after they murdered my own kin."

"What I have to say to you," James said quietly, "will be said privately. I have no wish to make all these men party to our conversation. Will you come?"

"Oh, aye, I suppose," Kate said, grimacing.

As they moved off toward the horses, Rothwell helped Maggie to her feet. "Can you stand alone?"

"Of course I can."

He saw her sway and, without further discussion, scooped her into his arms, forcing himself to turn a deaf ear to her cry of pain. There was no way to get her home without hurting her, and she would bear it better, he knew, if he pretended to have no sympathy for her. Over his shoulder he said to MacDrumin, "I'm taking her back to the house to put her to bed."

"Oh, aye, lad, do what you like with her," MacDrumin said. "Take the few of our wounded along with you, and the rest can help me see this lot safe to Inverness."

Rothwell started to follow James and Kate, then stopped when he thought of something else. "Remember," he said to MacDrumin, "if anyone gives you trouble over those damned weapons of yours, remind them you serve me, and tell them I armed you all myself to protect my property against the criminal Campbell and his ilk."

MacDrumin's eyes twinkled. "As to *serving* you, that's as may be, but you've a keen, intelligent mind, and no mistake."

Rothwell watched them go, then looked down at Maggie, lying quietly in his arms. "Did you and Kate bring horses?" he asked.

"Aye," she muttered.

He felt a stirring of annoyance, but he had spent his temper and wondered if she was deliberately trying to arouse it again. If she was, she would no doubt succeed. He had never known a wench who could so easily draw his ire.

James was lifting Kate to his saddle, and Rothwell said evenly, "Did she tell you they have mounts?"

"She did," James said. "They left them at the foot of the hill yonder, through the woods. Seems they took a shortcut she knew and nearly stumbled headlong into that nest of vipers."

The hair on the back of Rothwell's neck fairly stood on end, and he said in measured tones to the woman in his arms, "Consider yourself warned, my dear, that if you ever, as long as you live, do anything like this again, I will make you wish you had never been born."

"As long as I live," she murmured. "Don't be a fool, Rothwell. With luck, we will scarcely lay eyes on each other again after you succeed in annulling our marriage."

His teeth grated together. She was baiting him, truly, but he would not allow her to infuriate him again. Silently, he carried her to his horse, and when they found hers and Kate's, and Maggie said stubbornly that she could ride alone, he did not argue with her. The ride back to Glen Drumin was a silent one, for not even James spoke again until they had ridden into the yard, when Kate announced that she had things to do.

"Now that it's safe again, I must ride over to the place and see that all is well there," she said in an offhand way.

"I'll go with you," James said.

"You've a poultice to make, and you should look after Ian."

"Then you will stay here. I have more to say to you."

"Very well."

Maggie stared at Kate, dumbfounded. Never in her life had she seen her submit to any man, let alone to one who so casually countermanded her decisions. But Kate did not even look irritated. Slipping down from her horse, she handed the reins to a lackey, and went into the house with James.

Rothwell dismounted, gave orders to the lackey to see to the horses, then turned to help Maggie. She would have liked to ignore him, but his unusual display of temper had unnerved her, and she was not by any means certain he would not attempt to carry out the worst of his threats if she pushed him too hard. So when he reached up to lift her down from her saddle, she did not object, but when he did not let her go, continuing to hold her where she stood, she looked up to find him regarding her with a quizzical expression.

"I suppose you have more to say, too," she said wearily.

"I do," he agreed, "but I think, just now, you ought to go up to your bedchamber and rest."

She swallowed the retort that sprang to her tongue, kept silent long enough to be certain of her temper, then said carefully, "I am not a child. Neither am I the fool you named me earlier. My wound is slight, and although having it seen to was a painful affair, I am quite capable of deciding for myself if I require rest, so, if there is nothing further, I have things I must do." She began to turn away, not wanting him to see how much her shoulder really hurt her, but he stopped her with no more than a touch of his hand.

"Maggie," he said gently, "I am sorry I shouted at you. It is not my nature to shout, but I was badly frightened."

She was singularly aware of his hand on her arm, and the gentle, nearly sensual note in his voice. Her pain forgotten, she looked into his face again, searching it for an indication of his feelings. She saw an intensity, a look that told her he was hoping she would believe him, but believing that he had experienced real fear was like trying to believe the same of Kate Mac-Cain.

"Why were you frightened?" She had meant to sound brusque, but to her own ears she sounded merely curious.

"I was dismayed to learn you were even nearby, and feared the worst when Kate said you were hurt. When James told me the wound was not serious, I ought to have been relieved, I know, but instead I just wanted to shake you. Why did you disobey me? And before you snap more nonsense about my not having the right to govern you, recall that your own father told you to stay behind."

Maggie bit her lower lip and looked up at him from under her lashes. "I fear, sir, that I do not always obey my father either. Papa often gives orders out of impulse, and when I believe what I'm doing is right, I ignore them."

"I would never have guessed that," he said dryly. "Will you answer my question now?"

"I went because I wanted to see Fergus taken, and because I knew Kate would go whether I did or not. We never expected to run into his men, and before you say we *ought* to have expected it, recall that you and Papa were also taken unaware. And, sir, though you insist that our being there made no difference, had

Kate not fired that first warning shot, you really might all have been killed. You do know that. You must."

"I do," he said. "If I denied it earlier, it was out of pique and plain aggravation with myself for not having assumed Campbell would behave like the scoundrel he was. I suppose I thought of him as a pawn of the Crown and nothing more, a considerable mistake to make, both for me and for your father."

In Maggie's experience, men did not generally admit when they were wrong, and she had not expected Rothwell to do so. It took the wind out of her sails, and she did not know what to say to him. She looked away, and the silence lengthened until he said, "You will get cold, standing out here. We had better go in. I hope there is not a great deal for you to do."

"Only to tell the servants Papa and the others will not be here for dinner," she said, "and to see how Ian is doing."

"I will come with you then," he said.

They walked in together, and though he did not touch her, Maggie was conscious again of his intensity. The sensation was almost tactile, and she knew he felt strong satisfaction at what had just passed between them. She knew it as if he had expressed himself in words to her, but she did not understand why or how she knew. Nor did she understand his feelings, or her own.

Dinner was a cheerful meal, for James's bread poultice had eased Maggie's pain, Ian was much improved, and Kate was in an excellent humor. Kate seemed to have forgotten she had ever disliked James, and they talked together throughout the meal as if they were old, even intimate friends. She was pleased with Rothwell, too, if only because he had dispatched Fergus Campbell.

Maggie was aware of Rothwell's steady, thoughtful gaze upon her from time to time. Not knowing what to make of it, and certain he would resist any request to look elsewhere, she tried to ignore the looks and succeeded only in becoming more aware of them. It was as if he touched her, though he sat across the table from her and could not have done so had he wanted to.

When dinner was over at last, Kate and James withdrew to seats nearer the fire, still talking easily with each other. Maggie envied them their casual camaraderie, and wished she could talk like that with someone. There had been times when she had talked so with Kate, but they had scarcely talked at all since her return from London.

Rothwell got up from the table when she did and when she sat down with some needlework, he moved to stir the fire, standing for a time, silently, staring into the flames. She was tired, her arm ached, and it was not long before her eyelids began to droop. When she pricked her finger, she set her work firmly aside and said she was going up to bed.

Kate smiled and nodded, and James said goodnight; but Rothwell, watching her with a lazy, speculative look in his eyes, said nothing, and she wondered what he was thinking. Turning away, she went upstairs slowly, knowing he was still watching.

She went first to Ian's room, and found the boy being tucked in by one of the maids, having eaten his dinner. He grinned at her. "They tellt me the laird got Fergus Campbell," he said cheerfully. "He's dead then, and a good riddance."

"He is, but it was Rothwell who killed him," she said.

"Aye, that's what I said," Ian said, nodding.

"But he is not—" She broke off, startled, when she realized that Rothwell had taken her father's place in the boy's mind. She remembered his telling her father to invoke his name if MacDrumin encountered any awkwardness over the arms his men had carried. They would have been fools to go after Campbell unarmed, and her father was not a fool, but she had wondered at seeing how well-armed they all were, and realized suddenly that MacDrumin must have been certain Rothwell would support them.

MacDrumin, she thought, had been mighty sure of Rothwell all along, and she wondered what the wily clan chief had been thinking. She went to her bedchamber and began to light candles from the fire so she could prepare for bed. Maria entered a few moments after she did.

"I did not send for you," Maggie said, smiling at her.

"No, your ladyship. My lord told me you had come up."

"Well, I'm glad he sent you," Maggie told her, "for I welcome your help. I had not realized how much one uses one's left arm, but I seem to want it for all manner of things. It is aching again now, and my right arm is exhausted."

Maria went efficiently to work, moving around the room with no more noise than a rustle of skirts and the rattle of items she picked up and put down. Maggie's flannel nightshift was whisked over her head and drawn carefully over her bandaged arm, and then, slipping gray mules onto Maggie's feet, Maria looked up and said, "If the pain is so great as to disturb your sleep, ma'am, I do carry a small bit of laudanum with me."

"That is kind of you, Maria, but I think not, and I

must say you don't seem the sort to take laudanum. You are not at all vaporish."

Maria got up and turned to fetch Maggie's hairbrush, saying, "I am quite fit, your ladyship, but occasionally, for pain, you know, I do take just a few grains dissolved in water."

Maggie grimaced. "If I have to take it, I prefer it in one of Papa's toddies, or a cup of strong tea, to mask the taste."

Shocked, Maria primmed her lips and said, "Tea is too expensive to be wasted in such a fashion." Draping Maggie's shawl over her shoulders, she unpinned her kertch, let her hair tumble free to her waist, and began to brush out the tangles.

There was not a sound to announce him, but Maggie knew without looking that Rothwell had come into the room. She waited for Maria to acknowledge him, but the brush strokes continued without pause. Maria had not heard him, nor could she see the doorway in the small glass on the table. Neither could Maggie, but she knew he was there, and the fact that he had entered her bedchamber as only a husband would was enough to stop the breath in her throat while she waited for him to speak.

Rothwell stood silent in the doorway, watching, wishing Maria would move to her left so his view of Maggie's beautiful hair would be unimpeded. A golden cloud of soft waves, it glowed in the light from the few candles in the room and the small fire on the hearth, and he found himself thinking of the way Lydia's bedchamber—or indeed, any room she was in—was always filled with light. His sister was a wasteful chit, but at the moment he would have liked very much to see the light of a hundred candles reflected on Maggie's soft, shimmering hair.

He had been drawn to this room by a force stronger than common sense, and when he had found the door ajar, he had pushed it open on what he told himself was no more than an impulse, but he knew now that he had intended to come here tonight from the moment she had taunted him with being no proper husband and wanting no proper marriage. She was wrong.

For a moment he thought neither woman had seen him, but then Maggie's rigid posture told him she knew he was there. Either that, or her arm was still hurting her. Just thinking of how near she had come to being killed sent tremors of fear through his body, but when she turned her head in response to a harder than usual tug of the brush, and he saw the line of her throat and her delicate profile, desire swept the other feelings away. He wanted her. She was his wife, and he wanted to feel her soft skin beneath his fingertips, to touch her breasts, her hair, her lips. His breathing quickened, and his body stirred with hunger for her. He wanted to hold her, protect her, seduce her.

His voice sounded gruff, unnatural, when he said suddenly, "Stir up the fire, Maria. It's damnably cold in this room." The words spilled out without thought, and he realized they were ridiculous. It was anything but cold in the room.

Maria started at the sound of his voice, but when Maggie did not, he knew he had been right. She had known he was there.

The tirewoman made a small curtsy and went to do as he had commanded, and still Maggie did not turn. He wanted to see her expression, but he waited until

Maria had put another log on the fire and coaxed more flames from it. Then he said, "Leave us."

She went without a word, and not until the door had shut behind her, firmly this time, did Maggie speak. Turning on her stool to look at him, she said, "She had not finished, and I cannot do it myself tonight. You should not have sent her away."

"What else do you have to do?" he asked matter-of-factly, moving to stand behind her, but taking care not to cast a shadow where the firelight danced on her hair.

"I plait it," she said, "and tuck it into a cap."

"I can plait it."

She turned then, smiling. "Can you indeed? I'd not have thought it, but now I remember what you were like in London. You have changed here."

He was surprised that she seemed so much at ease with him in her bedchamber. He had expected a show of temper. "Did you believe I would continue to play the fop on such a stage, my dear? 'Twould be singularly inappropriate here."

"Fergus Campbell thought you one."

"That was his mistake."

She nodded, watching him, and her lips parted invitingly.

His voice sounded harsh to his own ears when he said, "Does your arm give you much pain?"

"No." She licked her lips.

"You must be exhausted."

"No."

Encouraged by these obvious lies, he said, "Stand up, little wife. I would have a closer look at you."

"You said you would fix my hair."

"I like it as it is. Sweetheart, I have been a fool."

She stood then, and he drew her closer to the fire,

where the air was warm. Her hair smelled of wood smoke and herbs. He liked the scent. Her lips were still parted, and he wanted to kiss her again, but he knew she had little experience of men, and that he should go slowly. That she seemed willing at all was more than he deserved.

Gently, he drew the shawl from her shoulders, revealing the white flannel night shift beneath it. The shift and the gray mules on her feet were plain, and he tried to imagine her in clinging silk with lacy trimming. Then he touched her arm, and the worn flannel sleeve was so soft that he stroked it, feeling her tremble beneath his fingertips. Her eyes were wide, but there was no fear in them, only wary anticipation. Holding her gaze, he moved his hand tenderly back up her right arm to her shoulder, then down the slope of her breast, barely touching her, enjoying the softness of the flannel and the arousing expectation of touching what lay beneath.

Softly, she said, "If you do what you intend, sir, an annulment will be difficult to procure."

"I don't want an annulment," he murmured.

XIX

Maggie moistened her lips again, feeling the warmth of his hands on her arms and the heat of the fire beside them. She knew he wanted her, and wondered if that was all it was, if he would change his mind again once he had his way with her. She knew many men were like that. Girls were warned about them from childhood. Never let a man have his way, for he will not want to wed a lass whose virtue is so easily taken.

But this man was already her husband. He had the right to command submission, and though he had not done so, his very presence in her bedchamber had been a declaration of his intent. She wondered if he would leave if she told him to go. Looking into his eyes, seeing raw desire there, she doubted if he would. Oddly, instead of stirring fear, the thought stirred a response in her own body like an awakening flame. His touch ignited feelings she had never experienced before with any man, and she knew she did not want him to go. When his hand moved from her shoulder to the slope of her breast, a tremor shook her from tip to toe, but she made no move to stop him, nor did she want to. She wanted to know what he would do next.

She understood coupling. She knew how children

came to be made. But she knew next to nothing about seduction, and clearly Rothwell knew what he was doing. That thought made her wonder how many other women he had done such things to, and it was with a strangely detached air that she let his hands wander at will, even when one moved to unfasten her shift and slip it off her good shoulder, taking care not to hurt the other. The shift slid down, catching on her hardened nipple, revealing the softness of her breast, and her breathing quickened. Her senses wakened to his slightest movement, and fatigue and pain became dim memories.

Rothwell put a finger under her chin and tilted her head up, making her look into his eyes, much as he had done before, but his expression now was nothing like the other times. "You are beautiful," he murmured. "I want to see all of you." But he did not move. He continued to look at her, his gaze searching, hypnotic, as though he would look into her soul, so penetrating in fact that she did not doubt for a moment that he knew she would make no effort to deny him. Softly, his voice like warm velvet, he said, "I don't want to hurt your arm, sweetheart. Take off your shift for me."

Fascinated by a sudden, overwhelming urge to submit to him, she obeyed without looking away from that penetrating gaze, and he watched her, not offering to help even when the left sleeve caught on her bandage. She managed to free it, and with a final whispering hush the shift slid down over her hips to fall in a crumpled heap around her ankles.

"Step away from the gown," he murmured. "Out of the mules, too. I want to see you dressed in nothing but firelight."

Her body tingling, she did as he asked, stepping a

little away from him in the process. The warmth from the fire was like a caress on her naked skin.

"By heaven, you are beautiful," he murmured. "Now, come here to me."

His leather waistcoat was open, revealing his white shirt, but he still wore his coat, so she said demurely, "Is it not necessary for both of us to remove our clothes, sir?"

"Oh, yes," he said, catching both her hands and drawing her gently nearer when she hesitated. "I'll show you how we go about that part in a moment, but first I want to taste you, little wife. I have wanted to do this again for hours."

She did not wait this time for him to tilt her chin, but willingly turned her face up for his kiss, and when his lips met hers, she felt the fire down to her toes, but this time it flamed from within her, stirring torrents of heat all along its course, and when his arms went around her, she melted against him. Hearing him moan, she sighed with pleasure. His tongue touched her lips then, parting them, and she welcomed its entrance, teasing it with hers, delighting in each new sensation as he began her lessons.

His kisses deepened, and he caressed her with his hands. For a time she was lost to everything but the feelings he created wherever he touched her. But when he paused, kissing first her lips lightly and then the tip of her nose, his hand on her back reminded her of her nakedness and his own state of being still clothed, and she murmured, "It is not fair, sir, for you to remain guarded against my touch. I want to explore your body as you explore mine."

"Do you, sweetheart?" He kissed her lips lightly again, a butterfly's kiss, and she remembered he had used the endearment before. She had paid it little heed then, and did the same now, certain he was merely exercising a husband's rights, that he felt no more than his physical need for her. For the moment though, that was enough. She wanted to know more about such things.

She stepped back again, and when he made no attempt to prevent her, she tilted her head to one side and said imperiously, "Your coat is in the way, sir. Take it off."

He put his hands on his hips instead, looking sternly at her. "Do you dare to give me orders, wife?"

She grinned saucily. "Did you think I would not?"

"Nay, I fear that I shall live under the cat's paw." He shook his head and sighed. "I never knew such a stubborn wench."

Pretending astonishment just as she was sure he had pretended displeasure, she said, "Do you think me more stubborn than Kate MacCain?"

Chuckling, he retorted, "I do not, nor will you be allowed to become so. To that end, I will not agree to take orders from you tonight, sweetheart. I prefer to watch you obey mine. Now, come and remove this coat of mine, and mind you do it carefully. It may be meant only for country wear, but it is a fine garment nonetheless, and I'll not have you throwing it on the floor in a like manner to the way you treated your shift."

She glanced down at the puddle of flannel on the floor near her feet and shook her head. "Very untidy."

"You are dallying, wife. Do as you were bid."

Approaching him, she felt the fire leap again in her body and wondered that such a sensation could be caused merely by allowing herself to be ordered about like a servant. She was enjoying herself, and she could tell from his expression and the way he stood that he was enjoying her, too. Was this what it was to be wanton? It did feel wicked and was no doubt the sort of thing Puritans carried on about when they spoke of the evils of the flesh, but it was most pleasant, and she did not think God would allow such a pleasurable thing to be true wickedness.

His coat fitted him tightly across the shoulders, and it hurt her arm to tug on it, but she ignored the pain until a heedless motion brought a twinge sharp enough to make her gasp.

Rothwell turned at once with a rueful look in his eyes. "I thought you said your arm no longer hurt. Let that be a lesson to you not to lie to your husband. I will do the rest."

"No, let me. It was no more than a twinge, and I like doing it. My arm burns, but truly it does not bother me unless I move so that it rubs the bandage. It is only an abrasion."

"I saw your wound, Maggie. It was more than an abrasion, and James still worries about infection."

"Well, Papa does not," she said, smiling at him. "Not after the whisky was poured over it. He really does believe the spirit cures anything that can go amiss with a body, and it is true that few people hereabouts suffer infection, except with truly nasty wounds, the kind that go deep and fester from within."

He looked skeptical, but when she insisted, he allowed her to continue, helping when he could and clearly delighting in giving her more orders to follow. Soon, he was as naked as she, and Maggie felt suddenly shy. She had seen naked men before, but never one so splendidly constructed. He was magnificent. The muscles of his arms, chest, buttocks, and thighs were large and clearly delineated, and the dark hair on his chest was thick, crisp, and springy to the touch. His stomach was flat and taut, and a line of hair led straight from his navel all the way to—

"Do you like what you see, sweetheart?" he asked, breaking into her thoughts and bringing more fire to her cheeks.

She looked up quickly, flushing more deeply, and said, "You are very large there, sir, surely too large to . . ."

"To what, little wife? How much do you know about such things? Do you know what I mean to do?"

She nodded, again finding it difficult to breathe properly. "In faith, sir, I know what is supposed to be done, but I cannot think you will succeed. Surely, I am not so . . . so large inside as to accommodate all . . . all of you."

"Not all, Maggie. Only a small part of me."

"That part," she said, pointing, "is not small."

He grinned. "I believe I will keep you."

"Will you, sir?"

"Aye, and my family calls me Ned, sweetheart. You may do so as well. I would like to hear you say it."

"My mother called my father her lord till the day she died," she told him thoughtfully.

"Say my name, Maggie. I want to hear you say it."

"Very well . . . Ned."

"Good lass. Now come and kiss me again."

She obeyed, and feeling her skin against his brought new sensations that electrified her. She savored every touch, every movement he made, and when she sighed with pleasure, he chuckled again, a sound she was coming to like very much.

"I'd like to take you right here on the floor," he said.

"Then do so," she replied. "My body cries out to be touched, sir, so why have you stopped? Touch me some more."

"Ask me nicely," he said, and there was laughter in his voice. "I think I would like to hear you beg me, little wife."

"Would you, sir?" Briefly she considered the notion, then said, "I daresay you *would* like it, but much as I seem to enjoy submitting to most of your whims, I do not believe I can submit to that one. A MacDrumin begs favors from no man."

"You are a proud woman, Maggie, but you are no longer a MacDrumin. Your proper name now is Margaret Carsley, fourth Countess of Rothwell."

"Not unless I will it so," she said, grinning. Since I am the daughter of a chief with no son, it is my right to keep my own name. I need not take my husband's. In fact," she added, enjoying herself, "you might take the name MacDrumin. You are allowed to do so, having married me."

"We can discuss such matters at a more appropriate time," he said, surprising her. She had expected outrage.

"I fear that inside I shall always be pure MacDrumin, sir."

"How are you commanded to call me?"

"I think I will call you Edward if I am to use your name. 'Tis unbecoming in me to address you by a nickname."

"Edward will do. No one else calls me so. Now, to punish you for your impertinence, I will teach you that you can do anything if the motivation presents itself. Get into bed."

Disappointment surged within her, but she would not give into him so easily. "I will be sorry to end this," she said sadly, "but I cannot beg, Edward. It is not in my nature."

He chuckled again. "We are not ending this, Maggie, not for a long while, but if we continue where we are, I *will* take you here on the floor, and although the fire burns well now, by the time we finish, those ashes will be stone cold, and come morning, the servants will find two icicles lying on the hearth. Now do as I bid you, and I will put another log on. I want to watch your reactions for as long as I am able, and I cannot do so if the fire burns low too quickly.

The moment she moved away from the fire's warmth, the air felt icy cold, and she hurried to get beneath the covers, then lay there and watched him with an increasing sense of pleasure. He seemed unconcerned with his nakedness, not at all shy but sure of himself, moving the same way he did when he was clothed. Watching him fascinated her, and she thought she was not at all nervous, until he straightened and began to walk toward the bed.

He pulled back the covers and stood to one side, letting the firelight play on her body, looking silently down at her.

"Are you getting in?" she asked. Her voice was low, little more than a whisper, and to her, it sounded like a stranger's. When he did not reply at once, she said softly, "Edward?"

He smiled then. "I do like the sound of my name on your lips, little wife, and I like the glow of firelight when it dances on your skin. You have very smooth skin."

She was still, watching him, conscious of his gaze, waiting, saying nothing at all.

Slowly he climbed into bed beside her and took her in his arms, being careful of her injury. He felt warm against her body and large, filling her small bed. A candle guttered with a sputtering sound, and a log shifted on the hearth. The light was behind him now, his head like a big shadow, coming nearer.

His lips touched hers, gently, then more possessively, and then his hands began to roam over her body, touching her, caressing her everywhere until her skin was afire again and she felt as breathless and exhilarated as if she had been running uphill toward the sunrise on a winter morning. Slowly at first, then with more assurance, she began to follow his lead, to touch him and caress him the way he was touching her, and when his lips released hers, she tasted other parts of him, satisfying curiosity whenever it stirred.

When his hand moved between her legs, she went still again, all her senses sharply focused on what he was doing. He kissed her gently and said, "I will try not to hurt you, but there will be discomfort the first time. That is only natural."

When she said nothing, waiting tensely, he began to caress her with his fingers till her body leapt in response and her tension vanished as if it had never been. When he entered her, she cried out, for he had been right and there was pain; but he was as gentle as anyone could be, and the ache was bearable. He began to move faster, and she knew he was rapidly giving in to his own passions. And when he was spent at last, he lay atop her for a few moments before he said, "Am I too heavy?"

She had to swallow before she could speak. Then she said only, "No." As big as he was, he did not feel heavy, and though her arm ached fiercely again, she did not seem to care. She did not know how to explain how it felt to have him atop her. She knew only that she did not want him to move yet. She liked the sensations he stirred in her body.

He taught her more before they slept, though he

seemed to have forgotten his promise to teach her to beg, and she enjoyed every moment. She fell asleep in his arms and awoke there in the morning, attacked instantly by second thoughts, and not by any means sure she had done the right thing by submitting to him.

He bade her good-morning, and got up at once, telling her that they would henceforward sleep in his bed, where there was more room for a man to move; and MacDrumin, returning midmorning to be greeted with the news that Rothwell and Maggie had spent the night together, expressed no qualms about it whatsoever.

"Well done, lad, well done, and about time, too!" He grinned at Maggie, and knowing he was well pleased with her, she wished she might be as sure of the union as he was.

For the rest of the week, it went well. Finding that Rothwell was determined to learn as much about Glen Drumin as any man could who had not been born and raised there bolstered her good opinion of him. He was kind to her, and he taught her much more in bed—his bed now, for it was indeed much larger—delighting and stimulating her, and easing her fear of the future merely by being gentle and kind.

James was clearly as pleased as MacDrumin was about the new arrangement, but Kate seemed more uncertain and, in consequence, her attitude toward James altered yet again. When Rose MacCain and Granny had been properly buried, and Ian was out of bed and healthy again, Kate insisted that she and the boy should move back to the MacCain place.

"Now that Fergus Campbell is no more, and his minions sit in the Tolbooth, we will not be molested again," she said.

James argued with her, but when word came that a

new bailie had already been appointed for the area, and one moreover who intended to see that the excise officers collected every penny due the Crown in whisky duties, Kate tossed her head, announced that she and Ian would be safer at the MacCains' than at Glen Drumin House, and threatened to depart that very day.

"Your reasoning is faulty," James said flatly. "Anything can happen to a woman and child alone at the head of the glen."

"I will do as I please, James Carsley. Rory and Dugald can take up residence nearby if it becomes necessary."

"Rory and Dugald," James said, "take their orders from Ned."

Kate stayed, but her temper did not improve.

They saw nothing of the new bailie for several days, but Rothwell made it plain that, bailie or no bailie, he intended to see changes made at Glen Drumin before long.

"Manufacturing whisky illicitly is too dangerous," he told MacDrumin one morning over a late breakfast, "and since you flatly refuse to pay the duties—"

"I have told you, lad," MacDrumin said, " 'tis no more right and proper that we should pay duty on a product we produce in the Highlands than that a man who grows corn in Gloucestershire or one who mines tin in Cornwall should have to do the same."

"He is right, Ned," James said, nodding.

"Nonetheless, that is the law," Rothwell said, and Maggie heard the note of finality in his voice. "The men must be encouraged to seek other sorts of work."

Maggie said indignantly. "You are very high-handed today, sir. The men of this clan will not change their ways merely to suit their English overlord, but just what sorts of work have you decided it will be proper for them to seek?"

Looking from one person to another, Rothwell said quietly, "I don't know yet, but people here in Glen Drumin simply cannot continue to exist as they did before the uprisings. That much is obvious to the meanest intelligence."

"Thanks to the English," Maggie said bitterly.

He gave her a rueful smile but shook his head and said, "We will all do better to learn to live with the changes they have wrought here, and to profit from them."

" 'Lord Zeus, listen to the little bird's voice,' " Mac-Drumin said with a snort. "Just how would you advise us to do that, lad? We've no money, and the land will support sheep on the high slopes or barley down below but little else."

Maggie could see that Rothwell did have a plan and was uncertain of how it would be received. He said, "Even in the past your people remained poor, Mac-Drumin, with little to call their own. I believe I know how they all might prosper in time."

"If you do, lad, let's hear it. I confess, I've thought and thought over the years without coming up with a thing that would work—other than selling the whisky."

"You do not have the resources for this plan, but I do, and I am willing to do what I can to help." He glanced at Maggie, and she saw warmth in his eyes even before he smiled at her.

"What is your plan, sir?" she asked more gently.

Taking a deep breath, he said, "I propose to frank the men while they seek work, until they are well enough established in new homes to look after their wives and children. The details remain to be worked out, of course, but it seems to me, the only thing preventing any man of the glen from going to a seaside town where work is plentiful, or setting himself up as a farmer in the lowlands, where the earth is much more fertile, is mere money."

"Mere money," MacDrumin said thoughtfully. "Aye, lad, mere money could do a lot to help my men and their families. Have you really got enough for all of them?"

"I don't propose to support them all in grand style," Rothwell said, responding sharply to the note of sarcasm in MacDrumin's voice. "I suppose I must sound like a popinjay, offering to throw money about to solve your problems. I am not doing that, I promise you, but any man who agrees to go elsewhere can depend on me to frank his move and to transport his family to him when he is ready for them. I'll look after the families, too, until they can be moved. No man can say fairer than that."

" 'Tis fair," MacDrumin agreed, "and most generous."

Maggie had heard enough. "It is nothing of the kind," she said. "I never heard of anything so barbarous in all my life. How can you be so arrogant, Rothwell? Have you no heart at all, or just an English one?"

"I thought you would be pleased," he said. "The offer is a generous one."

"You offer to uproot every man of our clan, ship him off to the coast to fish, or down to the lowlands to grow crops like a border ruffian, and you call that generous! Think of what you are saying! You cannot simply move people about like pawns on a chessboard, as if they had no other ties."

"I have said I will move their entire families," he replied. "What other ties could there be?"

"Our people are as attached to their land as they are to their families," she informed him. "You see only the land, not the people! What can it matter to men if you move them, you ask? Would you leave Rothwell Park and move everything you own to Scarborough or Newcastle because someone told you to do so?"

"It is not the same thing!"

"Is it not? Well, I'm glad to find out what sort of man you are. I just wish I had done so a week before now!"

"And just what do you mean by that?"

She heard the warning note in his voice but ignored it. "I mean, my lord, that now that I know you for what you are, I'll have nothing more to do with you, and if the good Lord is half as intelligent as He is supposed to be, I shall very soon discover that you have not succeeded in impregnating me with your English seed. As soon as I know that for a fact, you can get on with your annulment or your divorce, for I will have none of you!"

He was on his feet now and so was she. He said grimly, "Leave the room, Maggie. We'll not discuss such matters at the tops of our voices in your father's hall."

"I've said all I want to say, but I'll say *what* I want, *where* I want," she retorted, "and you'll not stop me, Rothwell. Women of the Highlands do not leap to obey masculine commands like the women of London do."

"Then, by God, one of them will very soon learn to do so," he growled, reaching for her.

"Don't you dare touch me," she said, stepping back and watching him warily. "You've no right!"

He glanced at MacDrumin, who was watching the scene with avid interest, and said grimly, "Do I not have every right to teach my wife a lesson in conjugal obedience, MacDrumin?"

"Aye, lad, you've every right to take a stout switch to the saucy lassie's backside. However," he added with a thoughtful air when Rothwell took another step toward Maggie, "the lass having never learned what you English call proper submission to a man's will, has a will of her own when all's said and done, so if you do beat her, I'd warn you not to sleep too deep any night soon, lest you waken on a cloud in God's own heaven—assuming, of course, that you've earned the right to go to heaven and won't be sent the other way when you seek entrance at the pearly gates."

Rothwell grimaced but made no further move toward Maggie.

James hid a smile, looked down at his empty plate, then suddenly scraped his chair back and got to his feet, saying with an air of false alacrity, "By heaven, I nearly forgot Dugald promised to take me with him today to see the new bothy. I've a mind to paint a still life," he added with a twinkle, "when I finish the picture I've been working on."

MacDrumin chuckled, and when Rothwell relaxed, Maggie smiled at James. "Beware the new bailie, sir," she said.

"Aye, we will."

When James had gone, Rothwell looked at Mac-Drumin and said, "Is this new fellow really likely to cause trouble?"

"He might. They say he's an inquisitive sort, putting his long nose into places where he's like to get it snapped off."

"Then whilst he's about, tell your people to stay clear of him and the bothies as well. I don't want more trouble here."

"Faith, lad, we've orders to fill and a shipment to get on its way to Edinburgh. We dealt easily with Fergus Campbell for five years, and this new chappie will be less experienced and more easily led by the nose."

Maggie left them to their argument, glad to slip away and certain that in this instance, whatever Rothwell might say, her father would prevail, for the men of the clan were accustomed to following his commands and, where the whisky was concerned, would not be quick to take the earl's side against him. She went about her usual duties but took time to move her things from Rothwell's bedchamber back to her own, keeping an ear cocked for his voice or his step so that he would not come upon her unawares. When Kate, looking glum, told her sometime later that he had gone out with MacDrumin, she was oddly disappointed.

"You're a bit gloomy," Maggie said, "Is Ian sick again?"

"No, only chafing at being kept in, but James said he must rest a day longer, so he will. What the devil am I to do, Mag?" She looked away, biting her lower lip, then looked back and blurted, "I want to turn my hand to the whisky with the others, but Dugald and them won't agree, and I don't know how to make them change their minds. But what else is there if I give up going for coaches as, I see now, I must? I won't bake bread!"

"Rothwell will say that you ought to move to the seaside, to take up mending nets for fishermen, or some such thing."

"Aye, well, he's daft is all," Kate said flatly. "I'll not move to the sea, but if he wants to take me to London and set me up in grand style, I'll go right gladly, and take Ian with me."

"I doubt it's Rothwell you want to set you up, but you don't want Ian loose in London," Maggie said with a weary smile.

Kate bristled at her first words but forgot her posturing when Maggie described what she had seen in the city's streets, and how she had been tricked. "It sounds a fearsome place," Kate agreed with a sigh, "but what is to become of us then, Mag?"

Maggie could not give her an answer. She thought James might have a suggestion, and was certain he was responsible for Kate's decision to give up robbing English coaches, but she was just as certain that a man in James's position would no more think of taking a wife from the Highlands than Rothwell would of walking naked through the streets of London. And even if James might think of marrying her, Rothwell had it in his power to stop him. Kate would not consider another relationship, but even she would agree she was not suited to be the wife of an English gentleman, even if she was falling in love with him.

Kate left, murmuring that she ought to go to Ian, and Maggie, noting that it was nearly four, went to her bedchamber to change her gown for dinner. Maria was waiting. Seeing a fresh bruise on her cheek and feeling no charity toward men just then, Maggie said sympathetically, "What happened this time, Maria?"

"Nothing, your ladyship." Maria turned to pour fresh water from a ewer into Maggie's basin so she could wash her face.

"Perhaps a cold cloth would help."

"I've put some of my lady's distillation on it, ma'am. She gave me some of what Master James made up for her." When Maggie looked surprised, Maria added hastily, "My lady thought the Highland air would roughen my skin, ma'am."

"H-how kind," Maggie said. Conversation languished after that, but she was soon ready to go downstairs. When she did, she found Rothwell waiting for her, alone.

"Where are the others?" she asked, eyeing him warily.

He smiled, giving rise to a hope that he had forgotten their earlier debate, and said, "Your father has not returned. James has, but he rather foolishly began to put some sort of last coating on his picture and doesn't want to stop now till he's done, and Kate ordered her dinner served in Ian's bedchamber. She said the boy was too tired to come down. I think she is overcautious, fearing James will be displeased if Ian becomes ill again." He paused, then added evenly, "I have told the servants to let us serve ourselves. Will you sit down?"

"Aye," she said, suiting action to word, but her wariness returned. "How did you spend your day, sir?"

Taking a seat on the bench opposite her, he said, "I walked with your father for a time, and then roamed about on my own, thinking about a number of things."

"Did you?" She watched him closely.

"I did, and when I returned, I discovered that my wife had removed all sign of her presence from my room."

"I meant what I said earlier," she said quickly. "I mean to sleep alone from now until you depart, for I want to help you end this ridiculous union of ours. We are not suited."

"Whether we are or not," he said calmly, "you are still my wife and must obey me until the situation is altered. I have thought about what your father said when I warned you earlier to have a care for how you spoke to me, and lest you begin to think I fear your temper, let me tell you now, for your own sake, that I do not fear you, nor ever shall. I am accustomed to having my orders obeyed, sweetheart, and that will not change. You will sleep with me, in my bed, and that is that."

She tossed her head. "I remind you, sir, that there was not one word in that peculiar marriage ceremony of ours about wifely obedience. I will spend this night and all that follow it in my own bedchamber, and you will not step a foot inside it."

"By God, Maggie—"

"Look who I found wandering about the glen," MacDrumin said cheerfully from the doorway, startling them both. His companion was a rather stout little man, amazingly red of face, and seeing their startled looks, MacDrumin added smoothly, "This fellow here is our new bailie, and I've promised him a chopin of the finest whisky in Scotland to drink with his dinner."

Maggie got up quickly, saying, "Come in at once, the pair of you. James has not had his dinner yet either, Papa. I'll send for him to join us and order more food for you all." She avoided meeting Rothwell's eyes.

"Do that, my dear," MacDrumin said, "and order plenty of whisky as well, for poor Goodall here means to search the rest of Glen Drumin after he dines. Some lying mischief-maker has told him we've a host of illegal stills hereabouts, and though I've explained that we've only the one for our own use, as allowed by law, he insists he must do his duty and search the whole glen."

XX

Rothwell watched with amusement while Maggie scurried about, calling orders to the servants and making a great thing of extending MacDrumin hospitality to the new bailie. The earl knew she was grateful for the interruption and believed, erroneously, that it had saved her from having to submit to his commands. He could be patient, however, for no matter how long she lingered she would have to go upstairs before the night was done, and when she did, they would have it out, and she would lose the battle.

The new bailie seemed to be the antithesis of Fergus Campbell, for he was a plump little fellow with a serious look, seemingly without bluster or spirit of any sort. His manner was deferential, becoming even more so when he was presented to the earl, and for the first time since Rothwell's arrival in the Highlands, he felt a nearly overwhelming urge to resume the foppish manners that served him so well in London. He resisted the urge, but his tone was silky smooth when he acknowledged Goodall's introduction. "You are an Englishman, sir," he said.

"Oh, yes, my lord, that I am," the bailie agreed. " 'Twas thought by many that 'twould be ill-advised to assign another Campbell, or even a member of the MacKenzie tribe, after that dreadful business that transpired here some days hence."

"To appoint a different sort of man is certainly a tactful gesture," Rothwell agreed. "Fergus Campbell was not well beloved in these parts."

"I doubt I shall be loved much more, my lord," Goodall replied with a steady look. "I intend to do my duty."

"As you should, sir, as you should."

MacDrumin chuckled. "Faith, Mr. Goodall, we do not despise a man for doing his duty, only for enjoying it in the fashion favored by the late, most unlamented Campbell. But then, sir, I'll wager you will not physically attack our lassies or ambush good men who are merely going about their lawful business."

"Goodness, no," Mr. Goodall said, clearly aghast at the thought that he could be guilty of either transgression. He looked at Rothwell and said diffidently, "You are English, too, my lord, or so I was informed, but I was also told that you had taken a Scottish woman to wife. Pray, what is your exact position here, if I may be so bold as to inquire?"

"I own the Glen Drumin estate," Rothwell said lazily.

"But I was told 'twas still Lord MacDrumin who—" Goodall glanced at MacDrumin, then looked quickly back at Rothwell, clearly flustered. "That is to say, my lord, I fear that even in the face of an English nobleman's owning this estate, I must nonetheless insist upon searching for any illicit stills."

"Do what you will, Goodall," Rothwell said with a dismissive shrug. "I am persuaded that no one will interfere with you."

MacDrumin nodded and said, "To be sure, that is

quite true, for there can be no cause, after all. Come sit by the fire, Goodall, and warm your innards with a bit o' whisky. I'll pour it out for you myself.'' He proceeded to do so, in a tall chopin, then watched confidently when Goodall took his first taste.

The bailie sipped, sipped again, then sighed and said, ''A tolerable brew, my lords, most tolerable indeed.''

Exchanging a look with James, Rothwell relaxed, expecting to enjoy whatever was coming.

''Aye, 'tis tolerable,'' MacDrumin agreed. ''Let me add a wee bit more, Mr. Goodall. Come, lads,'' he added with a gesture to Rothwell and James, ''pour yourselves each a mug. We cannot let our guest drink alone. Maggie, lass, have you food for us yet?''

''Aye, Papa, I have,'' she said, still evading Rothwell's gaze whenever he tried to catch her eye. ''We've sheep's head broth, leg of mutton in caper sauce, black pudding, and a pair of fine roast pigeons. 'Tis excellent fare for weary men.''

''Leave us the jug, lass,'' MacDrumin said as he, James, and Goodall took their places at the table. ''I will propose a toast, lads, to Mr. Goodall and to prosperity in his new grand position. Drink up now, everyone, drink up!''

''Thank you, sir,'' Goodall replied in his turn. ''I shall drink to your health.''

''To the Highlands,'' MacDrumin said when they all began to lower their mugs.

''To the king,'' Rothwell murmured, eyeing MacDrumin with amusement.''

''To halcyon days,'' retorted that gentleman, grinning.

''To our host,'' Goodall said next, not to be outdone.

"To women," James said, "bless their foolish hearts."

"Aye," MacDrumin said approvingly. "How they do get around us. 'Can't live with them, or without them!' "

The toasts continued, and before the newcomers had even begun to eat, two of them at least had emptied their mugs several times over. MacDrumin soon bellowed for more whisky.

"To a fine dinner," he said when the mugs had been refilled.

"I will certainly drink to that," Mr. Goodall said, beaming now. "To your cook!"

"Aye, to the cook," MacDrumin repeated. Sometime later, he said casually, "You know, lad, I've been thinking that it's darkening far too quickly for you to make any proper search tonight. You'd be well advised to have a good night's sleep and finish your task in the morning."

Goodall nodded sagely and drained his mug. "I believe you are right about that, sir. Is that jug empty again?"

"Nay, lad, have another nip." MacDrumin poured.

Maggie, who had been sitting with them, watching the proceedings in evident fascination, got to her feet at last and said in an offhand way, "I will bid you a pleasant good-night now, everyone, and take myself along to bed."

"An excellent notion," MacDrumin agreed, "but before you retire, lass, have them make up the bed in your old bedchamber for Mr. Goodall."

"How very kind of you," Goodall said, his words slurring.

" 'Tis naught," MacDrumin replied, "but I see that

your mug is empty again, sir. Permit me to rectify the matter."

"Papa," Maggie said firmly, "I will gladly order a room prepared for Mr. Goodall, but I mean to sleep in my own bed."

"Nonsense," MacDrumin retorted. "You'll sleep with your husband, lass, and let Mr. Goodall have the next best chamber. Our other guest chambers are right drafty and cold on a winter's night. What's more the *view* is best from yours."

"The west corner chamber—"

"Whisst now, not another word." MacDrumin's tone hardened. "Would you be inhospitable to a guest, lass?"

Flushing, she denied that she was being any such thing, and when Goodall protested that any dry nook or cranny would do very well for him, Rothwell took a hand in the conversation at last.

"You will do as your father bids you, sweetheart. I'll come upstairs shortly."

She hesitated, glaring at him, until MacDrumin said impatiently, "Oh, go along with you, lass. We'll none of us be long now, but I do want a word with Ned before he goes up."

Maggie looked at him in surprise, and Rothwell realized it was the first time MacDrumin had called him Ned. Again, he caught James's eye, and saw that his brother was considerably amused. James had not refilled his mug nearly so many times as MacDrumin or Goodall had done, or even himself, though Rothwell had less than half what the others had drunk. James looked merry enough nevertheless, and Rothwell had no doubt that his irrepressible brother was enjoying himself hugely.

Maggie tossed her head, but she went, and when she

had gone, MacDrumin made a small sign to James, who promptly engaged Mr. Goodall in conversation. MacDrumin got up to shout for more whisky, signing to Rothwell to go aside with him and saying in a lowered tone when he did, "I wanted him in Mag's room because I mean to have a little sport with him. Do you recall what I told you once about how we rid ourselves of another fool excise man?"

"The dummy in the tree," Rothwell replied promptly, "but surely you won't try anything so crude with Goodall. He is too unimaginative to be frightened off by primitive hints of danger."

"No bailie is unimaginative," MacDrumin growled. "Every one is a damned nuisance, and when we're lucky enough to find one who is a fool, it would be a crime to ignore the fact. But the lad coming alone like he did, and over the ridge instead of keeping to the track like a Christian, nearly stumbled right onto the ponies we were packing. I had to draw him off, but we cannot have him feeling so welcome that he drops in on us without warning whenever he's a mind to taste our whisky, can we?"

"Perhaps not, but tread gingerly, MacDrumin."

"Och, and don't I always? I'll have a wee word with James next, so he can slip out and tell Dugald and the lads it'll be safe to nip the consignment out of the glen tonight."

Noting that MacDrumin's words were no more precisely spoken than those of his guest, Rothwell said no more, believing both men would soon be too inebriated to get into trouble. He went back to the table long enough to finish the last few drops of whisky in his own mug, but when MacDrumin moved to refill it, he put his hand over the top.

"No more for me. Maggie's waiting."

MacDrumin chuckled. "Aye, she is and all. Take a good stout targe wi' ye, lad, lest the lass has armed herself. James, lad, a word with you, if you please," he added.

"I thought Highlanders were forbidden to take up arms!" Goodall was clearly surprised and not too pleased.

To deflect his attention from MacDrumin and James, who had moved a few feet away, Rothwell smiled and said, "I doubt any government has discovered how to disarm the fair sex, Goodall. MacDrumin refers only to his daughter's temper. Like most women she is armed with sharp claws and a sharper tongue."

When Goodall nodded, sipping thoughtfully, James laughed and said, "They breed fiery women in the Highlands, Goodall, as you will discover if you remain here long. I've met one myself who will snatch off my head if I do not make good my promise to take her out walking this evening. Since you have all decided to remain within by the fire, I pray you will hold me excused now, and wish me well, for wee bonny Kate has a temper far greater than our Maggie's, and since she had been containing her soul in patience this past hour and longer, waiting for me, she may well be primed to explode by now."

"Aye, lad," MacDrumin agreed, "that lass will rip off your arm and beat you with the bloody stump if you've put her out of temper. You had better take one of the stouter lads upstairs with you for your own protection."

"I doubt any of them would agree to bear me company," James said, grinning. "They're all downright terrified of her."

When Goodall looked from one man to the other in confusion, Rothwell took pity on him, saying lightly,

"They exaggerate, Goodall, as I am sure you must perceive."

"Yes, my lord, no doubt." He swallowed the last of his whisky too quickly, choking on the heady brew until MacDrumin pounded him on the back, nearly unseating him.

"Have a care, lad. Men have suffocated in just such a manner. Have another drink." MacDrumin poured it for him.

Rothwell bade them good-night and followed James, who paused near the stairs and muttered, "I hope she isn't angry with me."

"Scared of the wench, Jamie?"

"Stimulated, brother, not scared. She's a wonder, is Kate, and will be glad to be included in my little venture tonight, but she may have expected me upstairs sooner than this."

"You like her." He made it a flat statement of fact.

"I do." James's look challenged him to disapprove.

Rothwell grinned at him. "I wish you well of her. She is like to murder you, and it will be no more than you deserve."

Chuckling, James turned and they went upstairs together. Rothwell left him at Ian's door and went up to find Maggie, thinking as he approached his bed-chamber that he was most likely going to have to search for her, and wondering just how angry she could make him if she set her mind to it. To his aston-ishment, she was waiting for him, but she was not alone. She wore her thick chestnut-dyed mantle over a pale pink flannel shift, and Maria was brushing her hair.

"Leave us, Maria," he said.

"Don't go, Maria," Maggie said sharply. "I wish to have my hair properly plaited before I retire."

"Yes, your ladyship," Maria said, continuing to brush.

Rothwell said gently, "Must I put you out, Maria?"

Her dignity undiminished, Maria made him a stiff curtsy and left the room.

Maggie bit her lower lip, then said thoughtfully, "It is a wonder to me how a servant who was supposedly provided for my use ignores my every command."

"If she does indeed do any such thing, you have only to tell me. I will see that she obeys them forthwith."

She sighed. "You know perfectly well what I mean. Maria is not a servant I would choose for myself if I truly wanted to have someone at my constant beck and call, but she does obey my commands well enough when *you* are not at hand."

"I am glad to hear that. She will also obey *my* commands when I *am* at hand, or she will be very sorry that she did not."

She looked directly at him then, clearly hearing the note of authority he had intended for her to hear. There were roses in her cheeks. The flickering light from the fire and from the candles on the dressing table and chest, recently added to the room's stark furnishings, gave her complexion a rosy golden warmth; and her long, thick, tawny hair gleamed brightly with a million flaming highlights. He felt his body stir with desire for her, but ruthlessly repressed the feeling. He had things he meant to make plain to her before either of them was much older.

She licked her lips and watched him, the long silence clearly disturbing her. Finally she said softly, "I think you no longer speak of Maria. If you are angry with me, I wish you will say so. You commanded my presence here tonight, and I have obeyed you, but I have not changed my mind. I want you to end this crazy union of ours as soon as you return to London."

He wondered at the lack of response in himself. Had she said such a thing weeks before, he would have been grateful. And since he had long since decided he no longer wanted annulment or divorce, her words now ought to disappoint him, but they did not move him one way or the other. If he felt anything, it was slight amusement. Was he so cocksure of himself? Of her? If either was the case, he must be a knave.

She moistened her lips again. They were parted now, expectantly, but what did she expect? His body stirred again, and he said quietly, "I no longer want to end our union, Maggie. I thought I had explained that quite clearly."

"But it's wrong," she said sadly. "We are too different. You have been kind this past week, to be sure, but this morning I realized our union is as misbegotten as the union between our two countries. Our traditions are different, and so are the things we think most important. Like should marry like, Edward, and no one should be forced to marry. You were tricked into this marriage. No man could want that."

"Nor any woman. It is not the manner I would have chosen, but I have become accustomed to seeing you each day, to watching for your smile and listening for your voice. I won't willingly give up those pleasures now. As to what we have in common, I believe there are many things. We can laugh and love together—"

"Aye, I know you like that last bit, but it is not enough."

"There is much more," he said. "I have never been tempted to propose marriage to any woman before, for I found most of them manipulative and greedy, wanting only to marry my wealth and position. But you don't care for either one, and although you too frequently speak without even a moment's thought, I admire your honesty and your courage, and—"

"And my temper, sir? Do you enjoy that as well?"

"Not so much, and it is that of which we will speak next."

"Will we, Edward? I daresay you want only to speak of what I did to anger you, not of what you did to anger me. What if I do not wish to listen to you?"

"It is still my right to command you, sweetheart." She had not moved from her stool, and he stepped toward her now, watching to see how she would react. "You must learn to obey."

Her eyes widened, and she said quickly, "I never vowed obedience, not to you or to any man."

"Stand up, sweetheart," he said gently, standing very near her now, towering over her. "Let us measure our length and breadth, one against the other, and see which of us has the greater likelihood of enforcing a command."

"Don't be nonsensical," she snapped. "I know you are bigger than I am, and I don't doubt that you can force me to bend to your will, but Papa was right, so if you would sleep safe at night, you had best recall his warning."

Rothwell shook his head reprovingly. "I've told you before that I don't respond well to threats, sweetheart, certainly not to idle ones, and I've already said I do not fear you. Do you really expect me to believe you would attack me in my sleep? Come now, look me in the eye and tell me that is something I need fear. You are not one of the murderous Campbells, Maggie, and this is not Glencoe, so I am as safe from you beneath this roof as Goodall or anyone else who seeks shelter here."

She gasped and went white with shock. "How dare you!"

"Is the comparison not an apt one?"

"You *know* it is not."

"You must forgive me then. I thought you were the one who suggested it. Perhaps I misunderstood you."

There were tears in her eyes now, and he was sorry to see them there, but he would not apologize for his words, nor would he make this easier for her. She had been allowed for far too long to speak her mind without thinking first of consequences.

She was silent for a moment, gathering herself. Then she said through a small sob, "I hate being likened to a Campbell, but I suppose I deserved it, and much more, for even suggesting such a terrible threat. I will do whatever you ask of me."

His lips twitched, and though he controlled his amusement before it could become evident to her, he knew better than to believe she had submitted so tamely. For the moment she might believe he had the upper hand, but it would not be long before she began to plot ways and means of being even with him. Nor did he want that part of her to change altogether. He wanted only for her to learn to think before she blurted out the first thing that entered her head. He said provocatively, "First I want you to stand up as I asked you to do sometime ago, Maggie."

She looked uncertain, but when he did not smile or speak, she got slowly to her feet. "Rothwell, I—"

"Edward."

"Yes, of course. Edward, if you mean to punish me, I—"

"You defied me earlier, did you not?"

"Defied you?" She would have stepped back but the stool prevented her. "I am sure I never actually—"

"You declared that you would sleep alone, and you said it after I commanded you to sleep with me. Defiance, surely."

"It was but a difference of opinion, sir."

"It is not right for a woman's opinion to differ from her husband's, little wife. Surely your father explained that fact to you at one time or another."

"He did not."

"Well, he ought to have done so. We would not have suffered through such an unpleasant dispute this morning if he had."

"This morning?" Her eyes flashed, and he could see that her recovery would be swift. "Do you dare to insist that I agree with your stupid plan to uproot our people and send them off to live in the lowlands, or by the sea?"

"Your disagreement did not displease me so much as the manner you chose to express it," he said, suppressing a surge of annoyance even now at her choice of words. "You have been rude, defiant, and disobedient. Do you deny any of those things?"

She opened her mouth instantly with the clear intention of doing just that, but he caught her eye and was satisfied to see her swallow the words that had leapt to her tongue.

"Very wise," he said. "You are indeed an honest woman, I believe. Now, answer my question, and do so in a civil manner."

He could almost hear her teeth grate together. She said, "I suppose I am all the things you just said, so I cannot imagine why you insist you no longer want annulment."

"Perhaps it is because I have come to believe that you have other attributes a man looks for in a good wife," he said. "A saucy tongue can easily be mastered."

"I doubt you can do it, sir, any more than James will teach Kate to behave like a butter-tongued Englishwoman."

"The cases are different, sweetheart. James has no legal right to command Kate's obedience. But you," he added, "will soon learn that I mean to command yours."

Again she tried to step back, slipping sideways to avoid the stool, but he caught her arm, hoping it no longer hurt her, and held her tightly.

"Let me go, Rothwell."

"Look at me." He could read her thoughts more easily when he could see her eyes. "Are you afraid to look at me, Maggie?"

Her chin came up, and there was defiance in her eyes, and something more, a challenge, provocation. "I do not fear you, Rothwell," she muttered.

"Edward," he reminded her. "You keep forgetting. But perhaps you do it on purpose to annoy me. Ah, yes, I see by the look in your eyes that is just what you do. Naughty wench, I believe you deserve a lesson in how to please a husband."

Her lips parted again, and though he could tell by her expression that he had not frightened her, there was tension between them now, an electricity that was nearly palpable. It was all he could do not to sweep her up into his arms and carry her to the bed. It required a will of iron to resist the temptation, but he had other plans in mind for tonight.

He eased his grip, pleased when she did not pull away. He was learning to read her well, and he knew that curiosity was now uppermost in her mind, that she was waiting to see what he would do. With his free hand he touched her cheek and, hearing her quick intake of breath, drew his finger to the delicate line of her jaw and along to her chin. She was very still, watching him, her gaze not wary anymore but sensual, her reason suspended. Her little pink tongue darted out, damping her lips invitingly, but again he resisted temptation, wanting to arouse her more, to teach her a lesson they would both enjoy.

He felt the soft material of her mantle beneath his hand, and soft though it was, it was an impediment. Gently, slowly, his other hand still at her chin, he eased the mantle from her shoulder, feeling her tremble when the air, barely warmed by the fire, touched her bared skin. The mantle slid to the floor.

Her right hand touched his waistcoat, then drew back again, and he said, "Ah now, that was good, sweetheart. You await my permission, as a good wife should."

Anger flashed in her eyes. "I did no such thing!"

"Then why draw back, if not because you knew you ought to await my command?"

"I don't even know why I touched . . . That is, it was no more than an impulsive gesture. I don't want to touch you!"

He sighed. "And to think that not ten minutes ago I commended you for your truthfulness. Maggie, Maggie, what am I to do with you?"

"Nothing!"

"Very well." He released her.

"Oh!" She raised her hand, instantly thought better of it, and let it fall again, glaring at him.

He nodded. "You are learning to think before you act, sweetheart. There is hope for you yet."

This time when her hand flew up, he caught it and pulled her hard against him. "Kiss me, little witch. I was but testing you. This lesson has scarcely begun."

Her lips were hard beneath his at first, defensive, unyielding, but when his hand moved to her breast, she moaned softly against his mouth and her mouth became more compliant. It was all he could do not to take her then, but he wanted more from her, and he was determined to get it.

His hands were swift, adept, and when her fingers moved to his waistcoat buttons again, he helped her. Soon their clothes lay scattered on the floor, yet despite the chill of the room, Maggie's soft skin was hot to his touch. She sighed when he lifted her into his arms and, with her head against his shoulder, breathing softly, her warm breath tickling his ear, she said, "Do you really think you can tame me, Edward? I must tell you that so far your notion of punishment does not march with mine."

"We'll see, little wife, we'll see." He lay down beside her on the bed and caught one of her nipples between his teeth.

Maggie gasped when she realized how easily he might hurt her, but the sensation passed in an instant, replaced by another, more stimulating one. He was skilled at igniting responses from her body, and she wanted him to take her quickly. She had expected him to give her orders again, had even looked forward to the experience, for deny it though she did—and frequently—she enjoyed the feelings his dominance aroused in her. But when he gave her no orders, she could scarcely protest. Nor could she wait for him now. She stirred impatiently.

He kissed her breasts and her stomach, his kisses light and teasing, tracing patterns on her skin, drifting lower; but when she moved beneath him, urging him to be more ardent, he soothed her instead, moving his hand up to stroke her right breast, kissing her there again. The heat between her legs increased, flaming, till she thought it would consume her. Slowly, his hands moved lower again, stroking, caressing, playing with her body until it began to respond to every move he made with a will of its own. And when she tried to reciprocate, to tease him the way he was teasing her, he caught her hand and said gently, "Not yet, sweetheart. It is still your turn."

"Edward, please." The words came with a gasp before she knew she was going to speak them.

"What?"

"God in Heaven, don't stop! You're tormenting me."

"What do you want me to do, sweetheart? Tell me."

"I . . . I don't know the right words. I thought you would just do what you've done before. I can't bear it when you tease me like this."

"The more your body wants mine, the more pleasure there will be for both of us. Of course," he added provocatively, "if you were to beg me to do certain things, specific things, you might convince me to speed this up a bit."

"I will never beg you for anything," she said between gritted teeth. But before he let her sleep that night, she did beg, and she knew then that he was punishing her just as he had promised he would. But by then, she did not care a whit.

She slept deeply, stirring only once when her foot encountered a chilly spot where Rothwell ought to have been. Thinking he had gone, she struggled to waken, only to feel the bed shift with his weight, and then she was in his arms again. Snuggling against him, she drifted back into deep sleep.

When she awoke the next morning, she slipped carefully out of bed, trying not to waken him and thinking that in his sleep he looked rather more like an unruly boy than an English earl. The thought brought a smile to her lips as she scrambled into her dress. Taking time only to brush her hair into a twist and pin her kertch in place, and to don her mantle against the chilly stone halls, she slipped out of the room, meaning to go to the kitchen to be sure that a lavish breakfast was being prepared for the men who had taken too much drink the previous night.

Passing her old bedchamber, she heard the latch click and slowed, thinking Mr. Goodall might want her to summon a servant to aid him in dressing. The door was flung wide, and Goodall stumbled from the room, his face white with shock. "Outside," he gasped, his teeth chattering together. "Look out the window! Someone's hanged a man out there!"

XXI

Goodall was holding his head, and he looked extremely ill.

Maggie said, "There can be no one out there, sir. It must be a figment of your imagination."

"That is no figment, I tell you!"

"But it must be."

From behind her, Rothwell said in the bored tone she had heard so frequently in London, "Dear me, my lady. Pray, forgive her, Goodall. These Highlanders, you know, are rather callous about human life."

"Edward!" Maggie whirled, but her anger was forgotten in her astonishment to see him garbed in a brilliant red brocaded dressing gown and holding a long-handled, gold-rimmed eyeglass. He had not used one for weeks.

He went on blandly as if she had not spoken, "So many deaths, you know, since the Uprising. I think they simply take them in stride now and that is how she has come to forget so quickly the fate of one of Fergus Campbell's tame excisemen who chanced to wander into Glen Drumin. It was an unfortunate accident, of course, or so I was told."

Goodall shook his head. "My lord, you cannot have

seen what I saw from yonder window! 'Tis a corpse a-swinging from the branch of a tree not fifty yards away!"

"Indeed." Rothwell lifted his eyeglass and peered through it at Goodall. "But no doubt, after last night, your vision is not as clear as it might be. I was told the man had stumbled and caught his neck in a vine. Dreadful, but scarcely actionable."

"But they haven't taken him down!"

"An oversight, I'm sure. Perhaps you would like to do so. I daresay it will be good practice for you, you know. In your new position, you are likely to encounter a body or two, are you not? And this one should not be too bad. Not much worse than venison that's been properly hung, when all is said and done."

Goodall clutched his head, and Maggie, concealing both her astonishment and increasing amusement, said gently, "Let me fetch a servant for you, Mr. Goodall. You will want your breakfast."

With a strangled sound, the bailie turned and fairly threw himself back through the bedchamber doorway, and Rothwell said with a twinkle in his eyes, "I think the man wants a basin more than he wants a servant, sweetheart. Come away from his door so you won't be offended by noises from within." He drew her gently back toward his own bedchamber.

"You were dreadful," she said, trying to hide her laughter.

His eyebrows flew up in astonishment. "This accusation from MacDrumin's daughter? I thought I was magnificent, as good as the old man himself, although I still have my doubts as to whether his plan will work in the end."

"This was his notion then. I did not think it was yours, but there isn't really a body out there, is there?"

"No, but not for lack of wishing for one. Your resourceful sire observed that it was a pity we hadn't thought to keep Fergus Campbell's body above ground for just such a purpose. However, he—your father, that is—was in no shape to argue for long with James and me, when we insisted upon using a stuffed dummy rather than digging Fergus up again."

"James and you? Then you did get up in the night. I missed you, but before my thoughts cleared—"

"You missed me?" Again the eyebrows went up, and with an exaggerated gesture he raised his quizzing glass to look at her.

"Put that thing down. You look ridiculous, sir. I hope you do not mean to parade around this house in that outlandish dressing gown. It fair makes me blush to look at you."

"I like your blushes, sweetheart. Come and kiss me, and I shall decide whether to dress properly yet or not."

"I must find a servant to help Mr. Goodall."

"Hang Mr. Goodall. Chelton!" he shouted, and when Chelton came running, Rothwell said, "See to Goodall, will you? I'll shout again when I want you."

"Yes, my lord."

To Rothwell's delight, Maggie made no objection when he drew her inside his bedchamber again, and it was some time after that before they descended to break their fast. There was still no sign of Goodall, nor had Rothwell found it necessary to shout again for Chelton to help him dress, for Maggie had served him.

MacDrumin, whom they found consuming a large breakfast, looked chipper and exhibited a hearty appetite, though he had surely taken as much drink as the bailie. When they explained Goodall's condition, he grinned impudently and shouted for a man to go up and see if Chelton needed assistance. "Don't go and let Goodall die on us now," he called as the man hurried up the stairs, adding in a lower tone to Maggie and Rothwell, " 'Twould be a pity to have wasted all that whisky only to have to do it again when they send us a new chap."

"Papa, for goodness' sake," Maggie scolded. "What an awful thing to say!" But when she looked at Rothwell, he saw mischief in her eyes. She said, "To think that Papa should provide evidence for your wicked comment to Mr. Goodall about our so-called Highland disregard for human life!"

MacDrumin demanded an explanation, and while she unfolded the details of their encounter with Goodall, Rothwell watched her, thinking again that he enjoyed studying the quick changes of expression on her face and looking for the twinkle in her eyes and the lurking smile on her lips. He liked MacDrumin, too, which no doubt accounted for his uncharacteristic behavior the previous night when, having wakened with a sense of unfinished business, he had dressed again and gone down to the chilly hall to find the bailie snoring stertorously on a bench before the fire and MacDrumin attempting unsuccessfully to wake him to get him to bed. The chief had seemed pleased to see Rothwell and had muttered in what he had no doubt meant to be a low voice that he had laid the groundwork but there was still much to be done.

" 'Tis a pity we haven't got a real body," he had said then. "We ought to have kept Fergus."

"A dummy will do, if anything will," Rothwell said firmly.

"Aye, I expect it will. Well, I've clothing and such,

but it requires to be stuffed, and I'm not so sure I can hang the thing m'self, for my head is spinning just now, but I don't know where everyone else has gone."

"Since it is well past midnight," Rothwell had told him, "no doubt they have gone to bed."

"Faith, I did tell them to go, for I didna want anyone being helpful and telling the fool I was spinning yarn when I recounted a tale or two of the olden days, so that's all right, but you'll have to help with the business now, if you will be so kind."

Fortunately, since Rothwell had not been sure that he would be able to manage MacDrumin and get Goodall safely to bed, James came in shortly afterward from the north parlor, where he had retired to think, he said, after seeing Kate safely to her bedchamber. Between the two of them they had got Goodall upstairs and then persuaded MacDrumin to leave the rest to them; for, as Rothwell had expected, James entered with enthusiasm into the notion of playing a prank on the bailie, an attitude for which the earl had felt obligated to take him to task once they had stirred up the fire and begun stuffing their dummy.

James, unabashed, only grinned at him and recommended that he put a bit more straw into the sack they were to use for the head. "Don't tell me you aren't enjoying this, Ned, for I won't believe you. I tell you, too, I've never known you to be so human as what you've been these past weeks. Highland life agrees very well with you."

"Does it? I'll admit I like it well enough." Seeing another question hovering on James's tongue and certain he was about to ask why they had lingered in Glen Drumin so long, he said quickly, "How went your evening? You appear to have returned with all your parts intact at least."

James chuckled. "Aye, she was pleased with me for taking her along. MacDrumin's been telling her she cannot go back to the old place, and Dugald and her lads agree with him, which she's been taking hard. It was bad enough for three women and a child to live there. It would be utter nonsense for one female and a boy to do so, and I told her so myself."

"And still you came away with all your parts intact? There are men hereabouts who would like to know your secret."

"There is no secret. I know Kate can take care of herself, but I can see that she's heartily sick of it, too. I told her she ought to let someone else take on part of the burden for her." There had been no doubt about the challenge in James's voice then, and Rothwell had found himself hoping that his brother did not expect to take the pretty vixen back to London with them, as some sort of souvenir of his journey.

Maggie's stifled laughter interrupted his thoughts, and he looked up to see Goodall on the point of descending the stairs. The man still looked much the worse for wear and was leaning heavily on Matthew's arm, but he looked determined, too.

MacDrumin leapt to his feet and hurried to meet him, saying in a tone of deep concern, "My dear sir, I hope you haven't taken an illness under my roof. Let me send for a toddy!"

Goodall clapped a hand to his mouth and looked beseechingly at Chelton, who said, "He does not care for anything now, your lordship. He already suffers from a surfeit of whisky, I fear."

"Faith, there is no such thing," MacDrumin said flatly, taking Goodall's arm and drawing him inexorably to the table, where Maggie obligingly scooted down her bench to make room. Shouting to a maidservant to fetch him sugar, boiling water, whisky, and the other things he would require to mix a toddy, Mac-Drumin did his best to soothe Goodall's protests, saying, "Nay, sir, you'll soon be feeling much more the thing, I promise you. There we are," he added a few minutes later when the maid returned with the objects he had requested.

"Making a good toddy is an art," he said, arranging the items with care. "First we want three squares of loaf sugar dissolved in boiling water . . . so . . . then a wineglass of whisky. Stir the whole with a silver spoon, add a glass of boiling water, and now, to crown this liquid edifice, we top it with a bit more whisky, stir it again, and there you go, Mr. Goodall. Drink that with slow and loving care."

"Go on, Mr. Goodall," Maggie said encouragingly. "Papa's toddies are famous throughout all Scotland."

"They are," MacDrumin agreed complacently.

Doubtfully Goodall peered into the tumbler, from which a cloud of fragrant vapor was rising. He sniffed, then sniffed again, then lifted it to his lips and sipped carefully. His expression cleared a little, and he glanced at MacDrumin with near approval. "This is rather good, sir."

"Rather? Faith, you'll never taste better, and a good toddy will comfort anything that ails a man. Why, the only cure for a feverish cold hereabouts is to take your toddy to bed, put your hat at the foot of it, and drink toddies till you see two hats."

Goodall winced, took another sip, and said, "I'll admit my head begins to feel like it might stay attached to my body, but I cannot say I am looking forward to getting on a horse today."

"And haven't I been telling you there's no cause to do any such thing?" MacDrumin said cheerfully.

"You're welcome to stay another night, lad, or as many as you like. There's more good whisky to be drunk, after all."

Goodall winced and looked around, and Rothwell saw wariness come into his eyes again even before he said, "As to that, Lord MacDrumin, I must be on my way. I've other glens to visit, after all, and while I'm certain I shan't find anything amiss here, I'm a man who believes in doing his duty."

"And so you shall, sir," MacDrumin agreed. "Would you like me to send a pair of my lads along with you to see you don't fall off that horse of yours?"

Goodall started to shake his head, evidently thought better of it, and said carefully, "No, thank you, I am not so bad off as that, I promise you. I shall do well enough on my own."

They saw him ride out of the yard less than a quarter hour later, and Rothwell said with mock sternness to MacDrumin, "I told you your little prank would not frighten him off."

"So you did," MacDrumin agreed, but his eyes were twinkling with devilment. "The man puts a good face on it, I'll grant you, but if you think he will dally in Glen Drumin today, I will be happy to fix a wager with you."

"You think he will not search?"

"I know he will make a grand show of riding through the glen. But if he strays from the main path after what he saw from his window, I'll own myself astonished. Not only will his head begin to ache again as soon as the first effects of the toddy leave him, but if the sight of that bag of straw hanging from a tree branch was enough to make him sick to his stomach, the memory of it will tease him for many a long day. And in any event, he won't find anything today even if he does search. By the time our Mr. Goodall had begun his snoring last night, the train was well on its way. He won't find a thing today."

Rothwell was amused, but the incident reminded him rather forcibly of the dangers still inherent in MacDrumin's illicit operation. It occurred to him again that, since the land was legally his and the tenants living on it his responsibility, their involvement in something so blatantly illegal was dangerous not just to themselves but could also prove to be extremely embarrassing, if not worse, to him.

The knowledge did not frighten him. He was a powerful man and did not doubt that he could find a means of extricating himself from any predicament arising from MacDrumin's activities; however, he was not so certain that he could protect MacDrumin in the event that the extent of his smuggling should come to light. Something had to be done long before then, if only to protect the wily old reprobate from the consequences of his actions.

In the next few days they learned that Mr. Goodall was attending to his duty elsewhere; James spent more and more time supposedly sketching or painting—but most likely, in Rothwell's estimation, with Kate Mac-Cain and Ian; and Rothwell himself tried more than once to convince MacDrumin to put an end to the illegal operation and to urge the men to seek other, strictly legal employment. All he accomplished, however, was to discover the extent of the MacDrumin temper.

When he realized at last that the fiery chief really would prefer to die rather than pay a cent of government duty or tax on his whisky, Rothwell was tempted to point out that the decision was not really MacDrumin's to make at all. Nor was it really MacDrumin's place any longer to decide what his men should or should not do about their future security. But these thoughts entered his mind only to be swiftly dismissed.

Not only had MacDrumin made it plain that though he recognized Rothwell's lawful authority he did not always choose to bow before it, but for once in his life Rothwell was loath to make his power felt. He liked MacDrumin, and he liked the people of the glen. They were fighters and survivors, as unlike his Derbyshire tenants as they could be but increasingly as important in their own right. The men and women of Glen Drumin were people he had come to care about, people he had begun to think of as his friends. He knew James felt the same way, and whatever other changes the future held, he did not want that state of affairs to alter for either of them.

Maggie's demand to know if he would submit tamely to an order to uproot himself rather than stay to protect his home had not only struck a nerve but the image had lingered and grown. He knew that she had been right, that a man was inclined to grow as attached to the land on which he had been born as to the family that had produced him, or the one that he in turn produced. The thought that he would someday have a son strengthened these new beliefs, for he knew he would want his son to take the same pride in the land belonging to the Carsley family as he did.

But in order to keep the people of the clan on their ancestral lands, he would have to think of a way that was both legal and profitable. Smuggling, though profitable, was not an acceptable path to prosperity, but he doubted there were many, if any, profitable crops that would grow in the unforgiving Highland soil, and he was by no means sure that any cash crop would flourish there. That thought stirred others, however, and a germ of an idea took root and began to grow.

While considering his primary dilemma, Rothwell also thought more than once of the real reason he had come to the Highlands. To remember now that he had ever even had an ulterior motive was difficult, but he knew that Ryder was waiting—impatiently, no doubt—to learn all he could tell him about Jacobite activities in the area. In fact, he had nothing to tell. Though the men of Glen Drumin were Jacobite sympathizers and might well be running information along with their whisky, he had seen no sign of it, or indeed of any activity other than whisky-making. Moreover, he was as sure as he could be that even if he did encounter evidence of other activities now, he would not pass it along unless a new uprising appeared imminent.

At last he decided it would behoove him to sit down and write to Ryder to explain that he could not help. He tried to couch his periods in a form that made them sound at least as if he took the matter seriously, but even that much was hard, and in the end, he did not send his letter at all, for before he had arranged for a man to take it to Inverness, from whence it could be carried post to London, a letter arrived from Ryder by special messenger, the contents of which put Highland Jacobites, and even whisky-making, straight out of his head.

Maggie, having learned that a special messenger had arrived, went in search of Rothwell and found him in his bedchamber, letter in hand, looking both solemn and annoyed. He looked up when she entered, and she thought there was a measuring look in his eyes, as if he wondered what he ought to tell her.

"Ian said a messenger had come, sir. Not bad news, I hope, though in my experience, bad news comes more swiftly than good."

He smiled. "Your experience is apt, sweetheart. There is little you will count as good news in this letter, I think."

"May I ask who sent it?"

"Sir Dudley Ryder," he said.

"The attorney general?"

"Yes. He writes, by the way, that Charles Stewart has returned to the Continent, that in fact, he did so less than a week after Lady Primrose's masquerade. There was no real support to be gained for his cause, I'm afraid."

Maggie sighed. "I am not surprised to hear that, for I saw as much for myself. Too many people were like your sister, Lydia, thrilled to think themselves part of a secret conspiracy but unwilling to exert themselves to help."

"The Pretender's cause would not have prospered in any case," he said gravely. "For all that some members of the government still leap in alarm whenever Charles makes the slightest move, there is no good reason for them to do so."

"Are all his supporters so powerless?"

"Not powerless, exactly, but the carnage at Culloden and the brutalities of Cumberland's raiding parties afterward weakened the ranks here in Scotland, certainly, and what those things did not accomplish, the struggle for economic survival soon will."

"How can you say that much and still insist that the English government is not to blame for our ills?" Maggie demanded.

"I have never said the government bears no share of the blame," he said gravely. "The men at Westminster were badly frightened by this last uprising, and they resolved never again to be threatened by supporters of the House of Stewart. I do think they went too far in their political war against the clans and against your ancient way of life here in the Highlands, but Jacobites were especially numerous and strong here. That is why government troops were left in such substantial numbers to man the forts of the Great Glen, to overawe the inhabitants."

"We are not so easily overawed, sir, as you have seen for yourself." An unwelcome suspicion leapt to mind as she said the words, and impulsively she said, "Is that why you agreed to come here, to discover for your precious government just what the situation was like? Was that why you agreed to bring me home? I wondered, you know. You changed your mind so quickly." His silence was answer enough, and the chill that swept through her when she realized she had discovered something she had not wanted to know made her feel a little sick. "Have you been sending letters to Ryder all along, betraying Papa and our people to the English government? For by heaven, Edward, if you have—"

"I have not written before now but only because I lacked the means to get messages to London without anyone knowing," he replied with devastating candor. "I admit, however, that such a plan was in my mind when I agreed to come. I did not realize then how remote this glen is from the Great Glen, from Fort William and Fort Augustus, and in my ignorance I believed I would be able to arrange for someone in one of those places to carry information back to Ryder. That is certainly what he expected of me, and it is one of the points he makes in this letter, that I have been remiss in my duty. You can read as much for yourself if you like. I have no objection; however, there is something else I must tell you before you do."

Astonished that he would allow her to read a letter addressed to him—for even in the Highlands men did not generally confide business matters to their women—she said, "Go on then. I am listening."

"The time has come to return to London, Maggie."

An unexpected wave of disappointment surged through her, but she managed to maintain her air of composure, saying, "I never thought to hear myself say this, but I shall be very sorry to see you go. I think Papa will miss your company, too."

He shook his head. "Your father might miss me, but you won't, sweetheart, for you will go with me."

"To London? But Glen Drumin is my home, and since you own the land now, there is no reason it should not become our primary residence. I have no wish to live in London." She realized even as the words tumbled from her lips that she ought to have expected this ever since he had made it plain that he had no intention of ending their union. She was married to him and must by rights live where he lived. It seemed astonishing now that the fact that he would take her away from Glen Drumin had not so much as crossed her mind before this moment.

He was watching her, and she saw by his expression that he had read her feelings in her countenance, for a sad little smile touched his lips. He said quietly, "My life is centered in London. It has been for many years. You must come with me. I hoped you would want to come."

"I . . ." His sad smile stirred an instant urge to say what he wanted to hear, but she could not say what she did not feel. Though she had spoken the truth in saying she would miss him, the thought of living permanently in London dismayed her. She had gone there in the first place only to seek help for her people, and if she left now, she would be leaving them in much the same position as they had been before she went. But more than that, she did not want to leave her home. It was unthinkable to put the beauty of the Highlands behind her, and to replace it with the filth and noise of London, or even with the lovely view of the Thames from Rothwell London House. "I cannot go," she said at last. "I know that must vex you, Edward, but I simply cannot live in London. I would wither away there and die."

"You are not as fragile as that, sweetheart," he said, still in that quiet, patient tone, "and I am afraid the choice is not yours to make. Your position as my wife includes certain duties and responsibilities that you must not shirk."

She had a sudden mental vision of him the way she had first seen him, foppish and languid, dressed in the extreme height of London fashion, drawling at her, apparently only curious to know why James had invaded his library with a bedraggled female in tow. How much, she thought, they both had changed since that fateful day. But one thing had remained the same. Though she knew now that she cared about him—about the man he had become here in the Highlands, at least—and knew, too, that she stirred his masculine passions and he could delight her in bed, she was just as certain that she could never love the man she had known in London, nor he love her. Indeed, Rothwell could not love her at all, or he would understand her dread of leaving Glen Drumin.

"I won't go," she said flatly, trying to keep her tone

as quiet and patient as his, "and do not think you can force me to go, sir, for you will quickly learn how little your word really counts with our people." Tears sprang to her eyes, and she knew she was nearly as loath to force him to choose between London and herself as she was to go with him. He would certainly seek an annulment or divorce now, and his English Parliament would grant his wish in the twinkling of an eye. And that was something she no longer wanted in the least.

She expected him to become angry, and his lips and the muscles in his jaw certainly tightened ominously enough to frighten a lesser woman, but all he said was, "I warned you before that I do not take kindly to threats, Maggie. I would dislike very much to have to exert my authority here, but if you force me to do so—you or your father—do not think for a moment that I won't. I did not intend to leave so soon as this, for I was aware that you would not want to go, but certain matters at home have forced my hand."

"What matters?" she demanded, trying to ignore the shivers that his icy tone had sent racing up her spine.

"My stepmother and Lydia mean to be in London by Martinmas," he said, the chill in his voice no longer directed at her.

"So soon?" She calculated swiftly. "That's less than a fortnight from now."

"Yes. Fortunately, my stepmother must have chosen to confide her intent to one of her more garrulous bosom bows, and Ryder learned of it in time to send me this message, but although his messenger made excellent time and tells me the road from Edinburgh to London is relatively clear, it is unlikely that even by leaving at once we shall arrive in London before them."

"I am sorry that Lady Rothwell has displeased you, Edward," she said calmly, "but it can be no great thing, after all. You were concerned lest the news of Lydia's presence at the masquerade become public, but that cannot matter now, and though I know that it displeases you when the women in your life fail to obey your commands, surely it is not necessary for you to rush to London only to express your displeasure."

He grimaced. "The danger to Lydia now is as great as it ever was," he said, "perhaps greater. I have told you how frightened certain people in Westminster become when any Jacobite stirs. Those men know that the Pretender escaped again after strolling around London as if there were not even a threat to detain him, and Ryder writes that many are so upset there is even talk in Parliament of hanging all Jacobite sympathizers outright. While I do not believe widespread hangings will result, cases will be brought to court for the sole purpose of making examples of a few to suppress overt displays of sympathy by many more. I don't want my sister to become a victim of such an action merely because a few idiots are terrified of another Jacobite uprising."

"Then I do understand that you must go, sir, but I shall not, for I can think of no good reason to do so."

"There is every reason. That I have been in Scotland will be no secret. That I have acquired a Scottish wife may also be known. Certainly, Mr. Goodall had heard as much. If I leave you here, that action alone may be enough to make doubly suspect any action I make on Lydia's behalf if she encounters trouble."

"But won't there be danger to me as well?" Maggie asked.

"The fact that you are my wife will protect you, and that same fact is reason—" He broke off to say as MacDrumin strode into the little room, "I was just going to send for you, sir."

"Aye, and so I thought myself when I heard that a messenger had come, so I came to find you. Bad news, lad?"

"Personal business but serious enough to recall me to London," Rothwell said.

"We'll be saddened to see you go, and just when you were just beginning to appreciate the glen."

There was enough of a twinkle in his eyes to convince Maggie that he was not really sorry to see Rothwell go, and not wanting the earl to notice, she said quickly, "He wants me to go with him, Papa, but I will stay here, of course."

MacDrumin shifted his attention to her. "What's that you say? Nonsense, lass. A woman goes where her husband goes."

"But I don't want to live in London," Maggie cried, feeling suddenly as if the floor beneath her had begun to tilt beneath her feet. "I thought you of all people would understand!"

"I do, but you'll go with your husband, lass, and that's all there is about it. I'll take her away and talk to her, Ned," he added with a nod. "You'll have things you want to see to."

"I do," Rothwell agreed, "but there is one other matter that I want to discuss with you before I depart, MacDrumin, that has to do with the future of Glen Drumin."

Hearing a note of finality in his voice, Maggie looked quickly at MacDrumin, but the old man was regarding Rothwell with nothing more than simple curiosity.

"What exactly do you want to discuss?" he asked.

"I've given the situation here a great deal of thought," Rothwell said, "and I've come to realize how important it is for the people of your clan to stay together if it can be made possible for them to do so. I believe I can do just that, and in such a way that they can get out of the illegal whisky business and make even more money quite legally."

"And just how can you do that?"

"We are going to run sheep in the glen."

XXII

Though Maggie was certain that MacDrumin must be as appalled as she was at the notion of running sheep for profit in Glen Drumin, and would have been only too willing to list for the earl's edification all the reasons that such a plan was doomed to failure, he said only, "It might take more time than you think to develop a herd large enough to support the entire clan, lad."

Rothwell said, "The hill country here seems well suited to them, however. You simply haven't run enough sheep yet to produce an acceptable profit, but I can change that, and I mean to do so. There are excellent markets for wool and mutton."

Still maintaining what Maggie was certain must be an unnatural hold over his temper, MacDrumin said, "We can discuss it a bit more, I suppose, lad. How soon do you mean to depart?"

"We'll leave first thing in the morning."

MacDrumin chuckled. "Am I to suppose you will spend the Sabbath quietly at Laggan then?"

Rothwell's eyes glinted appreciation. "I've coaches to collect, and a coachman, but I may not spend any more time than necessary to collect them after what happened there. But I do take your meaning, sir. I mean to travel as fast as I can, and if that means traveling on Sunday, so be it. Maggie," he added, turning to her, "I do want to talk more with your father. Please tell the Cheltons and James to prepare to depart at first light. We'll take only what we can carry. The rest must be sent later."

Still stunned by her father's mild reaction to the notion of sheep replacing whisky in Glen Drumin, Maggie watched as the two men left the room together, and then, resigned to her fate, she went to do Rothwell's bidding. Having given the necessary orders to the Cheltons, she went in search of James, finding him at last in the north parlor, standing in front of his easel.

Pausing in the doorway, for she knew he disliked showing his work before it was done, she told him what had happened, and when Rothwell meant to depart.

"The devil take Mama, and Ned, too," James said. "I don't know that I'm ready to leave, but at least these pictures are done. Come and have a look."

She went at once, and when she saw the picture of the bothy with Rory, Dugald, and the others loading kegs on ponies in the foreground, she chuckled. "I like it," she said, "but I think your brother will not care for it much."

"Your father will like it. He'll like this one better, though, or I miss my guess." He took the first from the easel and replaced it with another. "Did I get it right?" he asked when she stared at it in amazement. "Kate suggested it. She said the laird had wished he could have a picture made of the scene and asked if I could do it, but I had only her memory and bits of my own to rely on for the faces. What do you think?"

Chuckling in appreciation, Maggie said, "Your magistrate is not nearly fat enough, and the Inverness court is not so much like the London one as you have made it, but you caught the look on Fergus Campbell's face when they opened that keg of rotten herring just as cleverly as if you had stood there and watched it happen. Papa will love it!"

His expression altered swiftly as she spoke, from a frown to concentrated thought to a wide grin of satisfaction. He said, "That's all right, then, and a good thing, too, because if I've got to leave in the morning, I must talk to Kate now. Did you tell Chelton to look after my gear?"

"I did." As he moved to pass her, she added impulsively, "Will you try to take Kate with you, James?"

"Egad, no," he said. "She would hate London. You ought to know that if anyone does." He was gone before she could reply.

Leaving the packing to Maria, Maggie went for a walk, not caring who might know she had gone alone, for she wanted to be by herself, to drink in the sights and the sounds of her home before she must leave it, particularly since she had no way to know when, or even if, she would return.

When she joined the others for dinner, the first thing she discovered was that the discussion between Rothwell and her father had grown a bit less civil in nature, for as MacDrumin took his seat at the table, he said bluntly, "I am not at all convinced about this sheep business, lad. I still think you would do the folks of Glen Drumin a better service if you would convince the fools in Cloud-Cuckoo-Land to alter their laws so that we can return to the best of the old ways, at least."

Taking his own seat, Rothwell shook his head with a weary smile, "Peace, sir, I meant no disrespect nor do I want another war of words with you. I know you want what is best for your people, just as I know that in the past you have done what you believed necessary to protect them and provide for them—"

"I could do a sight more to protect them had the government not done what it could to reduce my powers to zero," MacDrumin said acidly, "but when I can no longer sit in judgment when a crime has been committed, when in fact I must depend upon bailies who are worse than—Ah, faith, I've said it all before."

"So you have, but I wonder if at times you have not acted, at least in part, to vent your resentment of the situation. Do you not delight in pulling the government's tail, sir, in revenge for that reduction in power you just mentioned?"

"And if I do, what of it?" MacDrumin said gruffly. "They deserve to have it pulled."

Kate murmured, " 'Tis my opinion that what's done is done and best let be."

James smiled at her, and when Kate smiled back, Maggie was astonished to see the warmth of her smile. Suddenly aware of a new current running between the two, a tension, a new rapport that set them apart, Maggie recognized it with a sense of shock as a dawning intimacy. James looked the same as ever, but Kate seemed softer, less prickly, and much more genial and compliant. There were roses in her cheeks, and she looked healthier and happier than she had in a good long while.

If Rothwell noticed the change in her, he had the good sense not to comment upon it. Instead, he said pacifically to MacDrumin, "Kate is right, you know."

MacDrumin said bluntly, "I make it a point not to fight what I cannot change, lad, whatever you may think to the contrary, but running sheep will not support everyone like you think it will, and the work will interfere with what keeps us all from starving. As to resentment at having my powers reduced, you must have noted during your visit here that my powers in Glen Drumin have altered very little. 'Tis not on my own account that I act as I do."

In the silence that followed this declaration, Maggie saw James shoot a wary glance at Rothwell and realized that she, too, was concerned about how he would choose to reply. The silence lengthened, but MacDrumin's steady gaze did not waver. Finally, quietly, Rothwell said, "It is true that, as matters have transpired so far, you continue to wield a great deal of influence both over your people and over what might become of them in the future. In order to retain that influence, I suggest that you cease to rely upon continued defiance of the law to achieve your ends. I could state the matter more exactly, sir. I hope I shall have no cause to do so."

The silence this time was nearly tactile. Even Kate did not dare to break it, and Ian riveted his attention to the plate in front of him. A log broke and fell on the hearth, the sound like the cracking of a whip. Maggie jumped, but neither Rothwell nor MacDrumin appeared to have heard anything. They continued to look steadily at each other. Finally, MacDrumin said, "I suppose a few of the lads might look into pasturing, but I don't know where you think you will find enough sheep to make the business a profitable one."

James quietly got up and went to the north parlor.

"You can leave finding the sheep to me," Rothwell said. "Of course, if you know of a breed particularly suited to the area or learn of someone wanting to sell a good herd, you will use your own judgment. Consider also which crops besides barley grow well in

Highland soil that it might be to our benefit to plant. I believe there is a great deal of money to be made here by those who can discover how to use the land for profit."

"Perhaps you will prove right, lad," MacDrumin said, adding when James returned with the paintings, "but what's this, then?"

"A pair of parting gifts for you, sir," James said.

When MacDrumin saw the picture of Fergus Campbell and the herring, he laughed with pure delight and soon recovered his natural exuberance; however, Maggie encountered his gaze several times before everyone began to retire, so she was not surprised when he drew her aside and said to Rothwell, "I want a moment with my lass to bid her farewell. You won't mind, I know."

Rothwell smiled at Maggie and said, "Not at all, sir. I know you will miss her sadly."

"I will," MacDrumin agreed. He waited only until the others had withdrawn before saying, "I will miss you, lass, though Kate has agreed to remain here and see to things after you go. In faith, it's like another daughter she's become. I don't know how young James managed it, but she wants to be useful, and now that she's given up lying in wait for Sassenachs to rob, it will do her good to have plain woman's work to do. 'Tis a pity and all that you must live in London, but it will be for the best, I think. The wise learn many things from their enemies."

"I do not think Edward is our enemy, Papa."

"Aye, perhaps not, but you cannot teach a crab to walk straight, lass, nor an Englishman to think like a Scot."

"Please, Papa, do not fight him anymore. You cannot win."

"In faith, child, I shall not lose if you keep him safe in London where he belongs. I like the lad, but sheep? Still, what he does not see, he will not grieve over."

"But he will know if you do not follow his instructions, and indeed, Papa, he cannot mean to remain in London forever. You must do as he wishes. I could not bear being married to him if bad blood erupted between the two of you."

"Be easy, lass, I'll do what I must, but I'll not allow anyone hereabouts to starve whilst his lordship makes his plans and searches for sheep. Bah, sheep! Nasty, smelly creatures, and stupid, too. Our brave lads won't take kindly to being told they must become shepherds. Aye, and that's another thing your Edward don't understand, Mag. Our lads enjoy running whisky. They love the business, aye, *and* the danger."

"And you like tweaking the government's tail, just as he said you do," Maggie said, smiling at him. The twinkle in his eyes was response enough, but she felt her old fears rise again at the sight of it and said hastily, "Papa, do as he asks. I mean it, for if you are arrested and clapped up in the Tolbooth, I'll . . . I'll come home and snatch you baldheaded!"

He hugged her then and told her not to fret, assuring her that he would not be arrested, and though his words did little to reassure her they parted affectionately, and she went upstairs.

Kate startled her when she stepped out of the shadows and said, "Mag, dinna go to bed yet. I want to talk." When Maggie followed her into the small room that had become her own, Kate barely waited for the door to be shut before she said, "I wish you were not leaving so soon."

Maggie grinned. "You don't care about me, Kate

MacCain, so you can stop pretending. You did not grieve a whit when I went to London before."

"But I knew ye . . . you were coming back. This time I don't know how long you will be gone." Kate looked anxious, but Maggie still was not fooled.

"Dear Kate," she said, "I have seen how you look at James Carsley, and it is James you will miss, not me. Have you fallen in love with an Englishman, you daft girl?"

"I have not," Kate said instantly, turning away to stare into the empty fireplace. "I trow, I'd not know love if it stepped into this room and shouted at me."

"He is kind, is he not?" Maggie said gently.

"Aye, he is," Kate agreed, turning back to look at her rather searchingly, "and when he is by, Mag, a lass feels like one of those princesses you used to tell about, from the books you read at school, and he the knight on the white horse who would ride through peril after peril to save her."

"Good God," Maggie said, shaking her head and doing her best to hide her amusement, "you will make me ill with such talk, Kate. A knight indeed! What will you say next?"

Kate flushed but said firmly, "I only said 'twas how he makes me feel, Mag. How you do take a person up!"

"And has James said aught about saving you?"

"Dinna keep on about that now. I wish I'd never said it."

"I'm sorry I teased you," Maggie said, "but has James spoken at all about the future?"

"He said he means to look after me," Kate said simply, "and after Ian, too; and he will, Mag. For all that he is English, he is not one to promise and forget. I mean to wait for him."

"You cannot think he means to marry you, Kate," Maggie said gently. "His brother is an earl, after all."

"I dinna care," Kate said. "I'll take him as he chooses."

"Oh, Kate." Maggie hugged her. She could not wish for such a relationship for Kate, or for anyone, being certain that only heartache could come of it, but she could say no more about it without upsetting Kate or unleashing her volatile temper, so she changed the subject and sat talking a little longer before she left to prepare for bed. Rothwell was waiting for her, and soon put Kate's problems out of her mind entirely by keeping all her senses well engaged until they both fell fast asleep.

The following day when they were ready to depart, Kate was there to see them off, and Maggie noted how tenderly James kissed her and how fondly he tousled Ian's hair. Although she believed James felt no more than a passing fancy for Kate, there was nonetheless something in the relationship he had developed with her that Maggie found appealing and even envied a little.

The sky was overcast, and a light drizzle began falling when they reached the head of the Corriearrack. Looking down through the mist at the steep descent and the bleak rolling hills beyond, it was as if, Maggie thought, they had stepped through a door at the top of the world, where except for the jingle and thud of harness and hoof, all was solitude and silence.

She had been following James with Rothwell beside her, and the Cheltons trailing behind. When James drew rein, the others gathered nearer and Maggie heard a sharp intake of breath, and Maria said faintly, "I cannot ride down that dreadful road. Only look at it, as steep as a wall, all zigzags and cliffs with water flooding over it everywhere. We'll all be killed!"

"Don't be foolish," Maggie said sharply, having no patience today for the woman's affectations and alarms. "The Corriearrack is never hospitable, Maria, but you rode up; you can certainly ride down. I have done so any number of times and in all sorts of weather. It is not at all frightening."

"Not to you, perhaps," Maria said crossly enough to show that in her fear she had forgotten her usual stiff courtesy, "but we were not all bred in this barbarous place, you know."

"That will do, Maria," Rothwell said, silencing her. He scanned the road ahead and turned to Maggie, saying, "Are you certain it is safe for riders in this weather?"

Surprised that he seemed willing to accept her judgment, she nearly reminded him tartly that she had just said it was, but something in his expression stopped the words on her tongue, and she took a moment to consider before she spoke. Then, realizing that her annoyance with Maria might have made her speak hastily, she said, "I have no doubt that a confident rider would be safe enough. However, if Maria is frightened and communicates her fear to her horse, she may encounter difficulty. It would be safer, perhaps, if we all dismount and walk down."

He nodded as if her response accorded with his own judgment of the situation, and she read warm approval in his eyes.

Chelton said, "No reason to coddle Maria, my lord."

"Ned, if we put her between us, she will be safe enough," James said. "We won't always be able to ride three abreast, but I don't recall anywhere the road won't take at least two horses. It was constructed for the military, after all."

Maria said tensely, "I am sorry to be difficult, sir, but I shake just looking down from here. I cannot think how I would manage to ride down."

"Maggie is right," Rothwell said calmly. "It will be far safer for us all to walk down, and it will not take much longer. How long till we reach Laggan, sweetheart?"

"From here, several hours," she said, frowning at the sky. "We shall all be very wet by then."

"The sky is going to clear," he said, smiling at her.

She did not believe him, but he was soon proved right, for the clouds parted before they reached the foot of the pass.

Maria expressed her gratitude for their forbearance frequently and at length until her husband said curtly, "Have done, Maria. They'll think you're daft."

She was silent after that, mounting her horse without objection or complaint when the road leveled, and they reached Laggan shortly after noon, where Rothwell decided to push on to Blair Atholl. Maggie knew he was in a hurry to reach London, but to attempt nearly thirty-five Highland miles in a single day she thought utter lunacy. For a wonder, however, Maria said nothing, and although Chelton sighed audibly before he climbed into the coach with her, he too held his peace.

Rothwell and James, at Maggie's insistence, sat in the coach with her, and when they were settled and the coachmen had found a pace that pleased them and did not jostle their passengers beyond bearing, James chuckled and said, "Kate wanted to bet against our spending a night at Laggan. I'm glad I didn't take the wager."

"I half expected you to bring the pretty vixen along with us to London," Rothwell said.

"I'd have liked nothing better," James replied frankly, "but she would not like the city, and I thought it would be better to go home with you and make all tidy with Mama before presenting Kate to her."

Rothwell's brows rose slightly. "Do you intend to present her then? I should think it would be most unwise."

Frowning, James said, "Would it not be more unwise *not* to present my intended bride to my mother, Ned?"

Maggie gasped, but to her surprise Rothwell said only, "So the wind sits in that direction, does it?"

"It does. Have you any objection?"

"None that will deter you. I own that she is not the bride I would have chosen for you, but then nothing I have suggested in the past has ever met with your approval, so I daresay that one small point is of no consequence to you at all."

"None," James agreed, grinning at him and visibly relaxing.

Maggie said, "Does Kate know you wish to marry her, sir?"

"I have told her so. She does not believe me, however. It seems," he added, giving her a speaking look, "that certain well-meaning persons have taken it upon themselves to warn her against harboring thoughts of marriage. They have not said, mind you, that the word of an English gentleman ought not to be trusted, which one might expect, given the enmity they feel. They say instead that no English gentleman would consider marrying so far beneath his station."

"I see that you know I was one who warned her," Maggie said, "but, for all her willingness to flout rules and conventions, Kate does have a standard of conduct to which she holds true, and I did doubt that you would consider marriage. I doubted, too—for all that she says she will—that she would agree to live with you without benefit of wedlock."

James grinned again, apparently entirely at his ease now with the conversation. "So she told you she would take me any way I wanted her, did she?"

"Aye, sir, to her shame, she did."

"Well, when I told her I'd not want a jade who would agree to sleep with a man who was not her proper husband, she boxed my ears quite soundly."

"She did?" Involuntarily, Maggie glanced at Rothwell, recalling how he reacted to a threat of having his ears boxed.

He smiled lazily back at her. "I'd still not advise you to take up the practice, sweetheart."

"Faith, sir, do you pretend to read my mind?"

"It is not so difficult, you know. Every thought transfers itself instantly to your bonny eyes."

Resolutely, she turned back to James. "What did you do then, sir? I hope you did not put her across your knee again."

He chuckled. "No, I've learned my lesson about that sort of thing. I pointed out to her that she is now fully avenged for that earlier encounter and promised to return to her just as soon as I've smoothed things over with Mama."

Rothwell said wryly, "Do you really think you can do that?"

"I mean to try. I'll even stay at the house if you'll let me. That's how determined I am, though I confess I packed seven bottles of MacDrumin's best whisky to help me recuperate from the diatribes I expect to endure." He was silent for a moment before he added in the same relaxed tone, "We would like to live at Glen Drumin House, Ned, if you can stomach the notion and MacDrumin's agreeable. Kate really wouldn't like London, you see."

"But won't you miss the city, James?" Maggie asked, surprised that he could so casually speak of uprooting himself.

"I'm an adaptable fellow," he said. "Ned calls it being marked by erratic inconstancy, but the fact is, I'm fond of the Highlands, and no one in the glen will give a thought to whether Kate is a suitable wife for me or not. They think I'm some sort of magician just for having tamed her. More to the point is that I feel at home there, and needed, too. I mean to spend a good deal of my time at home with Brockelby, learning as much as I can from him before I return."

"You are entirely welcome to live at Glen Drumin House," Rothwell said. "I'll be glad to have you there in fact, for I think you may be more receptive to some of my ideas for improving things there than MacDrumin is, unless you fancy setting yourself up as a doctor of some sort instead."

"I don't, but one never knows when knowledge will be useful, and it seems foolish not to advance my skills when I have the opportunity." He was silent for a moment, then added, "You know, Ned, I have been so taken up with my own problem with Mama that it occurs to me only now that yours is far more imminent."

When Rothwell did not reply at once, Maggie glanced at him and then back at James before saying, "Do you mean me, sir? I own, I have been listening to the pair of you talk about London with increasing dread, but I thought it was only that I have no more fondness for the city than Kate does and shall have so much less freedom there. I didn't think of Lady Rothwell." She looked at her husband. "She will not be at all pleased by our marriage, will she?"

James choked back a laugh, but Rothwell gave him a quelling look and took Maggie's hand in his much larger one. He gave it a reassuring squeeze and said quietly, "She will become accustomed to the notion soon enough. She is not a stupid woman."

"I hope so, sir," she said, but her thoughts continued to dwell on Lady Rothwell's likely reaction until she could not think of anything else, and by the time they reached the inn at Blair Atholl, all she could think about was how quickly she could manage to get back to Glen Drumin.

Hoping Rothwell was too concerned about Lydia's being loose in London to take time to pursue her, Maggie decided to make her escape before they had gone any further and to enlist the aid of the innkeeper, whom, despite his present obsequiousness and earnest assurance that his establishment was wholly at their disposal, she believed to harbor a typical Highland distrust of Englishmen. The notion of returning to Glen Drumin having thus taken hold of her mind, she gave small thought to anything else, taking little part in conversation during the excellent meal that was served to them before they all went up to bed.

Chelton served them, as he had on their previous journey, and Maggie saw that Maria was also in attendance, for once when Chelton entered, he looked annoyed and she heard Maria's sharp voice from the corridor, evidently taking someone there to task.

Rothwell, looking at Chelton, raised his eyebrows just a little, and the manservant said hastily, "She's getting above herself again, my lord. Says she don't like this and don't like that, but I'll soon straighten her out."

Rothwell said gently, "I want to see no more bruises, if you please. Do you take my meaning, Chelton?"

Chelton flushed, nodded, and said, "Yes, your lordship."

Maggie wanted to cheer. When Chelton had gone away again, she said, "I did not think you had noticed, Edward."

"I notice many things," he said. "You look tired, sweetheart. Shall I tell Maria you are ready to go upstairs?"

"Aye, sir," she said, trying to think how she would manage to slip out of the bedchamber she shared with him to make her appeal to the innkeeper. The feat proved even more difficult than she had imagined. She could not avoid Maria, for if she refused her assistance, the woman would stay in the kitchen, and she could not do a thing while Maria was with her. Nor, she discovered, could she leave the room after Maria was dismissed for fear of encountering Rothwell on his way up to bed. She would have to wait until he slept. She only hoped she would be able to stay awake until then.

When the earl came into the room a short while later, he seemed tired, too, and even in the dim light cast by the fire and a few candles, he looked pale and lacked his usual energy.

She watched from the bed while Chelton helped him undress, and when the man had taken his departure and Rothwell moved slowly to snuff the candles, she said, "You look tired, sir."

"It has been a long day, has it not?" he said, moving toward the bed with the firelight behind him. His voice sounded strained, and she wished she could read his expression.

She wondered if he had sensed her feelings, if perhaps he had somehow guessed she meant to leave him. But when he lay back against his pillow without so much as kissing her good-night, she remembered his odd illnesses during their previous journey. Her compassion was stirred. "Are you feeling sick again, Edward?"

He sighed. "I own, sweetheart, the food at your Scottish inns does not seem to sit well with me, but my stepmother would no doubt say I was just feeling bilious and recommend a dose of salts or something equally unpleasant."

"It does seem odd that only you should be affected," she said. "We have all eaten much the same things, after all."

"One frequently finds bad food while traveling, however. No doubt I have simply been more unlucky than the rest of you."

"Shall I call for someone to fetch James?"

"No, no," he said. "There is no cause to disturb him. A little sleep and I will recover."

The answer was reassuring, particularly since she did not think she could leave him if he were ill. She realized that she did not really want to leave him at all, that she would much rather he return to Glen Drumin with her and leave James to look after Lydia in London. Sighing at the thought, she snuggled against him, listening for the even breathing that would tell her he had fallen asleep. Perhaps, she thought, if she were to leave him a careful explanation of her reluctance to face not only the dowager but the host of others in London who would despise her merely for being Scottish, he would understand at least why she had turned back, and would not be too angry with her.

Thoughts chased each other through her mind while she tried to decide what was best to do, until she suddenly realized that although his breathing was a bit more ragged than was normal, it had altered to the steady rhythm of a sleeping man. Slowly she inched her way to the edge of the bed and sat up, sliding till her toes touched the cold floor. Then, moving as silently as she could, she found clothing and dressed herself by what remained of the firelight and, carrying her shoes, tiptoed toward the door.

"Maggie, don't go."

His voice was low, but it stopped her in her tracks. She turned. "I must, Edward. London is no place for me."

"Your place is with me, little wife."

"Your stepmother will say that you were trapped into an unsuitable marriage, and she will be right."

He murmured, "I did not know you were a coward, sweetheart."

She stiffened, but honesty compelled her to admit that he was right to name her so. Relaxing, she said, "Very well then, I will go with you, but I fear we will both be sorry."

He sat upright in the bed, holding out his arms. "Come here, sweetheart, and I will show you—" Breaking off with a sharp cry, he doubled over and gasped, "Get James. Hurry!"

XXIII

Terrified, Maggie flew to the next room, shrieking James's name as she flung open his door. He wakened at once and quickly followed her back to Rothwell with his satchel in hand. When he saw what condition the earl was in, he ordered Maggie sharply to send for Chelton and to rouse someone to produce chamomile tea.

"Then take yourself off," he added before she was out the door again. "You cannot help here."

Her terror nearly closed her throat, but she forced herself to speak. "I'm staying, James."

"No, you are not," he said, glancing at her impatiently. His expression changed then, and he said more gently, "He is not going to die, Maggie. I won't let him. Now go. Ned won't want you here, for I'm going to dose him with ipecac as before, and if that don't answer the purpose straightaway, I mean to give him a good dose of rhubarb. I promise you, when their power takes hold of him, he won't want you around. Tell Chelton to bring a basin, several in fact, for I hope the one that is here now will need to be emptied by the time he gets here."

"Go, Maggie," Rothwell said, his voice weak but

nonetheless commanding. "James will look after me." There was sweat pouring down his face, but she waited to see no more, hurrying in search of the landlord and Chelton and, she hoped, something to do to keep her mind occupied so that it would not dwell upon what James was doing and whether or not he would succeed.

In the bustle that ensued below stairs, she soon saw that she would be more hindrance than help. Not wanting to stay in the coffee room alone, she spent the next two hours in James's bedchamber. Maria had come upstairs with Chelton, offering to do what she could to help, but James had sent her away again, and Maggie did not want her.

Maggie could not sleep, however, and by turns paced the floor or stood staring blankly into the fireplace, wondering what Rothwell could have eaten that the rest of them had not, or what it was in Scottish food that so violently disagreed with his constitution. He was certainly not a man who was inclined to be sickly, and it seemed most peculiar to her that he should react so violently to any ailment. Could someone be trying to poison him? But who? It had to be someone who gained access to him only outside Glen Drumin, for he had never been sick there, and they had encountered no interested strangers on the road.

James came to her at last, and he was smiling. "He'll do now," he said. "I did have to resort to the rhubarb, so he's exhausted, but he'll sleep now, for he is much better."

"What caused this illness?" she demanded. "Surely, it is not just our food here in Scotland that makes him sick, for all he says one frequently encounters bad food when traveling."

James grimaced. "I don't know. Some people have

odd reactions to certain foods, but they usually know what makes them ill, and they know long before they reach adulthood. We've been served things here in Scotland that we don't eat at home, but Ned always seemed to have a stomach of iron before now. The symptoms are odd, too. At first, he was just queasy after he ate. The next time he was sleepy. This time, he was lethargic at first, then nauseated, and then he had that awful, sharp pain."

"Could . . ." She swallowed. "Could it be poison?"

He grimaced. "Don't think I did not think of that, but if you are thinking I might have—"

"No, no," she protested. When she saw he was not convinced, she said bluntly, "If you wanted him dead, James, you would have just let him die. You would not have saved him."

"Well, that leaves the Cheltons," he said, "which is absurd, since they could have murdered him any time these past twenty years, had they wished to do so. And if it is poison of some sort—or Scottish food, for that matter—why was he never ill at Glen Drumin? He wasn't, you know, not once."

"I know." She thought for a moment, then said, "Could it be that this illness strikes him only when he is particularly tired? We're all much more so than usual tonight."

James shrugged. "I suppose that is possible. It's also possible that Ned is right and he simply ate some bad food the rest of us avoided. Heaven knows I was so tired I don't recall what I ate, let alone whether we all ate the same things."

"I don't recall either," Maggie admitted.

"Well, whatever the cause, we must hope it does not happen again," he said. "I've used my supply of ipe-cac, and the rhubarb and several other remedies as well. What I didn't use in the glen, I finished tonight, and at this time of the year I shan't find much of anything growing naturally. I didn't even have a composer to give him after his trial tonight and had to make do with mine host's chamomile, though I added a generous dose of your papa's excellent whisky. I'll get more supplies when I see Brockelby, of course, but if anything else should happen to Ned, I'll be hard-pressed to do more than give him whisky next time."

She smiled wanly. "Papa would insist the whisky's enough to cure anything that ails him. May I go to him now?"

"Aye, but don't expect him to talk much. He was already asleep when I left. I sent Chelton on to bed before that and sat with him until I was certain he would really rest."

She thanked him and went quickly to see for herself. The fire had been built up and someone had boiled herbs in a pot over the fire, for the room was redolent with their fragrance. She realized that it had been done to cover more unpleasant odors, and was grateful to James for his thoughtfulness. Rothwell lay sleeping, his breathing normal now and deep, his expression one of peacefulness. Smoothing his hair back from his forehead, noting that his brow was cool, she stood watching him for a time, conscious of a sense of gratitude that went far beyond thought of herbs or of James's consideration or even his skill. All desire to return to the glen was gone. Whatever lay ahead, she would face it, certain that Rothwell would do what he could to protect her, and realizing now that, had she run away, not only might he have succumbed to the mysterious illness but she would have been leaving him to face his stepmother's acid tongue alone.

Slipping out of her clothes, she crawled into bed

beside him clad only in her chemise, snuggling close and relaxing, asleep almost before her head touched the pillow. When she awoke the next morning her head was not on the pillow at all but rested in the hollow of Rothwell's shoulder, one ear and cheek against his chest, where she could hear the deep, steady beat of his heart. A comfortingly muscular arm embraced her, and beneath the covering, a large hand rested lightly on her naked hip.

He said, "Good morning, sweetheart." The hand moved, stroking her hip. "Where is your nightshift?"

"I slept in my chemise," she said. "It is rucked up around my waist. Are you completely well again, Edward?"

"I am hungry. That must be a good sign." He stirred, coming up onto his elbow, turning her slightly so that she lay on her back, looking up into his face. He looked his usual self, and his eyes gleamed with purpose. His free hand moved to the ribbon tie nestled in the lace trimming of her chemise, and a moment later her breasts were bared to his touch.

She sighed with pleasure when he caressed her, smiling up at him. "Are you sure you are not too weak for this? After all you endured, I'd think you would want your breakfast first."

"I long only for the taste of you, my sweet." He kissed her nipples and his hand crept lower, urging the twisted folds of her chemise out of his way.

A sharp rap on the bedchamber door startled them both, and Rothwell whipped the coverlet swiftly back over her. "Who knocks?" he demanded. "Go away."

The door opened without further ceremony, and James, with laughter in his voice, said without looking in, "I hope you are both presentable, for I have ordered breakfast to be served to you here in less than a quarter of an hour. May I enter?"

"Yes, damn you," Rothwell said, his tone nearly a snarl. "You take a deal of initiative upon yourself, my lad."

Peeking around the door, James chuckled and said, "Consider it my medical opinion that you ought to eat before . . . before we depart, and it is your own fault beyond that for ordering me to make sure our departure was not delayed beyond eight o'clock."

Maggie, clutching the quilt to her breasts, leaned up on an elbow and said anxiously, "Should he eat anything else here?"

"Never fear," James said, still smiling. "I have ordered boiled eggs served in their unbroken shells, toast, and coffee, and Maria has promised to make the coffee and toast with her own capable hands. Chelton clearly thought that was going a bit far, but she stood up to him for once, and when she insisted, he was compelled to agree that so long as the pair of them watch every move that is made, nothing that Ned is not accustomed to eat will be served to him. Indeed, Maria seems determined to keep him safe all by herself if necessary, for she has announced that she will keep a sharp eye on his food preparation until we reach London. So I think we can all rest a bit easier, don't you?" He grinned again. "Now, shall I tell them you prefer to wait a minute or two for your breakfast, or may they bring it up now?"

"You win," Rothwell said with a grimace. "Tell them to bring it." He looked ruefully at Maggie when the door had shut and murmured, "We'd best make ourselves presentable to eat, I suppose, sweetheart, but I think I'll plead exhaustion at four o'clock today. It will be nearly dark by then in any event, and I've a desire to spend some uninterrupted time with my wife."

"Have you, sir?"

"I have. I am very glad you did not leave last night." The look in his eyes was warm, and for a moment she fancied it was true love she saw; but he had no more cause to love her now than he'd had the day of their odd marriage, and he certainly had not loved her then. That her feelings had altered considerably in the meantime was a fact of which she was well aware, but she knew that females set more store by notions of love than men did, so that was no reason to think his had changed as well.

They traveled swiftly, and although they encountered occasional flurries of light snow, the weather continued to hold, and aside from a single repair to a wheel on the second coach, they suffered no particular delays. Maria kept her word about inspecting anything that was cooked for the earl, and they arrived in London at last, on Martinmas Day, without his having suffered any recurrence of his odd and unfortunate malady.

Despite the wicked pace, Maggie enjoyed their journey much more than she had the previous one. Not only did she enjoy being looked after and treated everywhere they stayed as befitted the Countess of Rothwell, but the men sat in the coach with her most of the way, and while James read or sat contemplating his own thoughts, she discovered that she liked her husband very much. A restful but also an amusing companion, he was as willing to describe for her amusement the great houses they passed, and their owners, as he was to take a hand of cards or just to talk. The days passed swiftly, and despite her weariness, she found that she was sorry when the journey was done.

It was nearly ten o'clock when at last the carriages rattled into the courtyard at Rothwell London House, but there were still lights at most ground-floor and first-floor windows, and the front door opened at once, spilling light onto the pavement.

"Mama and Lydia are certainly in residence already," James said. "The place would not look nearly so lively if they were not. Here, Frederick," he called out the coach window to the footman looking out to see who had arrived, "have some of the lads collect our portmanteaux and look after these coaches."

"Mr. James, is that you?"

"Aye, and his lordship," James replied, opening the door and jumping out. Putting down the step for the others, he added, "Make haste, her ladyship is well nigh fainting from fatigue."

"Her ladyship? But, Mr. James, their ladyships have both gone to Lady Ordham's Martinmas ball and did not anticipate returning before midnight. Has one of them fallen ill, sir?"

For a moment, James looked bewildered, and before he had regained his senses, Rothwell, descending from the coach in his wake, said matter-of-factly, "Mr. James speaks of your new mistress, Frederick. Come, sweetheart."

Taking the hand he held out to her, Maggie stepped down from the coach, feeling suddenly shy and wondering how his servants would respond to her new estate. She was grateful to know Lady Rothwell was not at home, if only for a short time longer.

Frederick was staring at her. "Miss MacDrumin!"

James chuckled, as Rothwell drew her closer and

said, "You may felicitate me, Frederick. She is no longer Miss MacDrumin but my own countess."

The word passed swiftly, and it seemed to Maggie that in the next few minutes every member of the household was determined to catch a glimpse of her. To her relief, every one of them seemed sincerely delighted by the news.

When she came to a standstill in the middle of the hall, looking around in something of an exhausted daze, Rothwell smiled at her and said, "Thinking of changing things already, my sweet?"

Starting a little, she stared at him. "Why would I be thinking any such thing, sir?"

"It is no more than your right. Most wives change things."

She grimaced. "I daresay Lady Rothwell will have something to say about that."

"Not much, I should think." He turned to the footman and said in his languid way, "Ah, Frederick, do not say anything to their ladyships about my new countess. I want to break my delightful surprise to them myself."

"Yes, my lord, to be sure. And which bedchamber shall we prepare for the new Lady Rothwell, if you please, sir?"

"My own mother's room," Rothwell said softly. Looking at Maggie, he explained, "My stepmother preferred another chamber, and I think it is time my mother's room was occupied again."

Maggie felt a surge of relief, for in the moment between the footman's asking the question and Rothwell's answering it, she had feared he would say she must take the dowager's chamber, and she was as certain as she could be that she would not have had sufficient nerve to do so. His solution was much better.

"Are you hungry, sweetheart?" Rothwell asked. "Shall I tell them to bring food to the library for us?"

"Presently, perhaps, but I think I will change my gown before I eat," she said. "I do not want to meet your mama and Lydia whilst I am still so travel stained."

"They are not likely to return before midnight," he said. "Surely you would prefer to go to bed before then."

"No," she said more sharply than she intended. When he frowned, she added hastily, "I would not sleep, sir, for imagining things." She could say no more with the servants so near at hand, but he understood her, for he nodded.

"I'll take you upstairs myself," he said. "Frederick, order a bath for her ladyship. Do you want Maria, sweetheart?"

"No, thank you, sir. She is no doubt as tired as I am and will be wanting her bed. Any maidservant will suffice."

He gave the necessary orders and Maggie soon found herself alone with him in a very pretty bedchamber.

"This room adjoins mine through that door there," he said, smiling at her. "My stepmother's chamber adjoins my dressing room, but that need not concern you, for the door between has long since been blocked by a chest. Do you like this room?"

She nodded. It was larger than the one she had occupied previously, with rose-colored hangings and warm, colorful rugs, and she liked it very much. Why did your stepmama take the other room in preference to this one, sir?"

"I don't know precisely," he said. "I was a child at the time, but I believe the decision was my father's. He married her for her money, you see, and to secure the succession. He was not an affectionate man, but I think he cared for my mother. Perhaps the comparison between them, here, was too stark for him."

Maggie's bath was soon ready, and he left her to the ministrations of Tilda, who had come at once, delighted to welcome her back to London and saying she could imagine no good reason for anyone else to wait upon her.

"We arrived three days ago, my lady," she said cheerfully, "but no one thought his lordship would be here. What a surprise he's got for them, to be sure."

Maggie hoped Lydia had not yet managed to fall into any scrapes, but she forbore to question Tilda further, being certain the woman would not divulge such information, if she knew of any.

Both men were in the library when she returned, and rose to their feet at her entrance. They too had changed out of their travel dress to more elegant attire, and Rothwell raised his quizzing glass and looked her over from top to toe in very much his old manner, but she detected a twinkle when he drawled, "That rig is becoming, sweetheart. I do not recall seeing it before."

Maggie looked down at the wide-skirted blue dimity gown and smoothed the lace ruffle on one sleeve. "It is one of those that was ordered made for me before we all left, and Tilda said when Lydia learned it had been delivered, she meant to have it sent to me. I'm glad she did not do so the minute they arrived," she added as she sat down in a chair near the desk.

James said thoughtfully, "I'd like to know who was Ryder's source of information. He appears to have been deuced accurate."

Rothwell said, "No doubt it was one of your

mama's friends—Lady Ordham, perhaps, if they are dining with her tonight."

"But Mama don't correspond with that old trout," James protested. "She don't even like her much. Says she's the sort to put sugar in her tea," he added with a mocking grin. "Makes me think the better of Lady Ordham, myself, but I know you won't agree. Might not Lydia have told someone?"

Rothwell shrugged. "She might, but I cannot think who she knows who would have confided such information to Ryder."

Frederick and a maidservant entered with the refreshment the earl had ordered, and conversation became desultory until sounds of impending arrival were heard in the courtyard.

Rothwell got up to open the library door, and in the brief moment before he blocked her view, Maggie glimpsed Lady Rothwell and Lydia as they swept into the hall, attired in elaborate gowns and wearing ostrich plumes in their well-powdered coiffures.

Lydia was saying, "But I don't understand any of them, Mama. That absurd chit is quite dreadfully bookish and not even—" She broke off, gaping at Rothwell.

"Welcome home, ladies," he drawled. "I trust you have enjoyed a pleasant evening."

Lady Rothwell stared at him but collected herself swiftly, saying in a sharp aside, "Close your mouth, Lydia," then adding smoothly, "I must suppose you are a trifle surprised to find us in town, Rothwell, but finding country life insupportable at this dismal time of year, we decided to return. And not before time, I might add, for Lydia has already learned that in her absence another young woman has taken the eye of the most eligible gentlemen in London. She is most put out with you. Indeed, I cannot say how delighted we are that you have returned."

"In truth, I must suppose you cannot," he replied suavely, "but perhaps you can think of something more appropriate to say when I inform you that you are to wish me happy. May I present my countess." He stood aside, revealing Maggie.

She found herself looking directly at the dowager. For a long moment the woman stared at her, stunned, before anger flamed in her eyes and, turning to Rothwell, she said furiously, "Have you taken utter leave of your senses?"

"I have not," he replied calmly.

Lydia, too, had been staring at Maggie, but she smiled now and said shyly, "Is it true? Are you really married?"

Maggie nodded, still watching the dowager, who said suspiciously, "Even from the wilds of Scotland news of such an event as the wedding of the Earl of Rothwell must have been thought worthy of publication. Why have we not heard so much as one word of a wedding being either planned or celebrated?"

James stifled a choke of laughter, but Rothwell said calmly, "Since you have no idea when we were wed, madam, I do not know why you think the news ought to have preceded us, but if you will step into the library, we can certainly discuss the matter."

But although she swept haughtily past him into the room, followed quickly by Lydia, she had not missed James's reaction; and Maggie, feeling fire in her cheeks, was aware of a shrewd glance cast her way as well before Rothwell shut the door. She looked imploringly at him even as the dowager said imperiously, "There is something odd about this, for all you pretend there is not. There was nothing loverlike in your behavior before you went to Scotland, Rothwell. If one was concerned about this woman's trapping anyone, it was James for whom we feared; but now you expect us to believe a wedding had taken place. I don't believe it. Indeed, I daresay the truth is you seduced the wench and brought her back to London, thinking us safely in Derbyshire; and now, astonished to find us here in town, you have simply said the first thing it entered your mind to say in hopes of sparing Lydia's blushes. Fine doings, sir! Find doings indeed."

"That will do," Rothwell said, the ice in his tone chilling even Maggie. "I will not tolerate any insult to my wife."

"If I truly insult you, show me your marriage lines, sir, for I shan't believe in them until I have read them for myself."

The silence that fell then was a pregnant one. Maggie's cheeks burned, and she could see that neither James nor Rothwell was anxious to reply. With an odd sense that she was putting her head into a hangman's noose, she said, "You must tell her the whole, Edward. Maria or Chelton will do so if you do not."

He nodded and proceeded to do so; however, if he had hoped to calm his stepmother's fury with an explanation he soon discovered his error. Although she heard him out in stony silence, when he had finished she said flatly, "I have never heard anything so disgraceful in all my life. Such a marriage cannot be legal, but if it is, it must certainly be annulled."

A frisson of fear shot through Maggie, but Rothwell said, "No, madam, it will not be annulled, and you do yourself no service by taking this attitude, I promise you. I can allow for your shock, but I suggest you retire at once and give thought to your position. I will not allow you to treat my wife unkindly."

The dowager folded her lips tightly together, but it was clear that his words had only increased her fury. When he opened the door for her, she stormed from the room, head held high, skirts arustle, and ostrich plumes flailing.

Rothwell, still holding the door, looked at Lydia, but though she bit her lower lip, she made no move to obey his unspoken command. When it became apparent that he meant to wait, she said, "I know you are vexed with us, Ned, but indeed, it was horrid in Derbyshire, for Mama was cross with everyone and I missed my friends, and now everything is in a mess, so please don't be too angry with me. I . . . I'm glad you married Maggie, however it came about." She looked at Maggie and smiled through unshed tears. "Now I have a sister. Brothers are very nice, in their own way, but a sister will be much nicer."

Rothwell's expression softened, and as he closed the door again, he said, "If you can find it in your heart to be kind to Maggie, puss, I might even be glad you came back. As I recall the matter, however, I had excellent reason to send you home."

"You did it out of temper, sir," she said with a sigh, "and indeed, I suppose you had cause to be vexed, but it has spoiled everything now, or very nearly."

James said lightly, "Did I hear Mama say your star had been eclipsed? Who is this diamond who dares cast you in the shade?"

She grimaced. "I don't understand it, for Ophelia Balterley has not got the least sense of fashion and actually reads books—not the sort one likes to read, but fusty ones written in Greek and Latin, for she was educated with her brother, of all dreadful things. Yet they are, all of them, quite mad for her."

Rothwell drew a chair forward for her, saying as she

sat down, "May we take your dismay to mean that Lord Thomas Deverill has turned his eyes in the paragon's direction?"

Lydia tossed her head and said, "I'm sure I don't care what Thomas does, but considering that he once tried to hang himself with my hair ribbon only because I failed to wear a posy he'd sent me, Ophelia *must* have cast a spell over the awful man."

"What is her portion?" James asked, glancing at Rothwell.

"Balterley is extremely well to pass, certainly, but he does have a son," the earl replied.

Lydia sniffed. "They say Lord Balterley has arranged to divide his private fortune equally between them. 'Tis very odd."

"Damned odd," Rothwell agreed, "but therein lies the reason for her extreme popularity, my pet. She will inherit a fortune much larger than any portion you will receive, so there must be any number of men in London clamoring to get their hands on it."

"If you had not sent me away," Lydia said, "this would not have happened."

"If that is true," he replied, "you will soon have them all at your feet again, including young Deverill."

"Well, but though I wrote to say we were coming, he did not seem cast into transports to see me tonight," she sadly, but when the full meaning of his words struck her, she perked up at once. "Do you mean to say you won't send me back to Derbyshire, Ned? Oh, pray do not! I promise I won't do anything you don't like."

"To quote my dear stepmother," Rothwell said dryly, "I cannot tell you how reassuring I find those words, puss."

Maggie and James chuckled, but Lydia took no offense, saying earnestly, "I know you don't believe me, but I mean it, and oh, Ned, if you are disposed to be kind, please say we can go to the winter ridotto at Ranelagh on Friday. Mama said I could go, but the moment I saw you, I was certain you'd forbid it. Everyone will be there. Please, *dearest* Ned, say we may go."

Rothwell looked thoughtful for a moment, then said, "I think we all ought to go. I've a mind to see this heiress for myself."

Lydia laughed. "You will see her, that's certain enough, for Mama has already decided that James is to marry her, so she is certain to present him to her notice. Lady Portland's niece has gone home until February, so there is no hope for you there at present, dear James, but Mama believes you can easily cut out all the others with Ophelia." She sighed a little forlornly, adding, "I only hope you can."

"The devil fly away with Mama," James snapped.

"James!" Lydia's hand flew to her mouth.

Rothwell's eyes gleamed with amusement. "Easy, lad. You have shocked your sister. Apologize to her, if you please."

"But, Ned, if Mama is determined, it will make it much more difficult for me to—" He broke off, looking quickly at Lydia.

Her eyes widened. "More difficult to do what, James? Tell me." When he remained silent, she turned to Maggie and said, "Do tell me! I hate it when people keep secrets!"

Maggie looked at Rothwell, who said smoothly, "There are no secrets to tell you, puss. James is only fretting because he promised to help smooth the way for Maggie with your Mama, but I can look after my own wife perfectly well. At all events, I begin to look forward to this ridotto of yours. I daresay we shall all enjoy it very much indeed."

XXIV

Having sent Maggie upstairs with Lydia, Rothwell poured more wine for himself and for James, and said casually, "Might your friend Deverill be acquainted with Ryder, do you think?"

James's thoughts had clearly been elsewhere, but as he took the glass Rothwell handed to him, he said, "They know each other, certainly, but I should not have said they were particularly well-acquainted. Why do you ask?"

"Because Lydia said she had written to apprise Deverill—most improperly, I might add—of her return to London."

"Naughty of her, I agree, but what—Egad, you think he might have been Ryder's informant. I suppose it's possible, but I can't think why Dev would confide such information to Ryder, and it don't signify anyway. What's done is done. My only concern is to keep Mama from trying to foist that damned heiress onto me for a bride."

"I should think she would have trouble trying to foist any bride onto you, dear boy, and certainly the young woman's family will have something to say about it."

James shrugged. "One might think so, but you know as well as I do, Ned, that Mama makes life damned uncomfortable for me whenever she thinks I'm running counter to her wishes."

"Just now she ought to have her plate full, just trying to get used to the notion of my marriage."

"Well, you don't know Mama as well as you think you do if you believe she can think of only one thing at a time. I can just imagine what that ridotto will be like, with her determined to fling me under the nose of this damned heiress just when I wanted to cozen her into seeing things my way for once."

"I will help all I can with your mother, James, but when we are at Ranelagh, I want you to watch Lydia and keep your ears cocked for information about any Jacobite activity, or the lack of it. I want to hear that some new scandal has taken the public mind off the notion of spies in our midst, for I'll not rest easy until I am convinced that damned Primrose masquerade has been forgotten. I mean to see Ryder tomorrow, and I'll discover from him just how much danger still exists, but even if he should tell me there is none whatsoever, I want you to make certain Lydia keeps silent about her presence there."

"Maggie and I were also at the masquerade," James reminded him soberly. "Dev was, too, for that matter."

"I know that, of course, but I hold no brief for Deverill and I hope you and Maggie are both sufficiently aware of the danger to mind your tongues. Lydia is another matter."

"Tell her then."

"No, for I would only put the notion into her head, and once it's there, she would be quite unable to hold her tongue. She probably has said nothing as yet. Her thoughts seem to dwell only on possible spells being cast by Lady Ophelia Balterley."

"I'll do what I can to watch her at Ranelagh," James said, "for all the good it will do."

Rothwell was grateful to him, and had cause the next day to hope James would have more success than he anticipated, for, when the earl met with Sir Dudley Ryder at the office that gentleman used near the House of Commons chamber, to report on his visit to the Highlands, the news Ryder had for him was not reassuring.

When Rothwell explained that he had uncovered no impending threat to British peace in the central Highlands, and then deftly and rather hastily turned the subject to London Jacobites, Ryder said with a sigh, "Charles Stewart's departure ought to have ended all that, but a few of his more dedicated followers have been a bit of a nuisance, and a few outraged fools in Parliament, who ought to know better, keep looking for Jacobites under their beds. Thus, the official position is still that support for the Pretender equals treason to the Crown, and will be punished by death. No one has actually been executed yet, but that doesn't mean no one will be." He paused, and when Rothwell did not reply, he added, "You passed very quickly over your exploits in Scotland, my friend, but you must know I am curious to know if I was right when I said your people might be smuggling whisky. You did not say what you learned about that."

Rothwell smiled. "You may take it then that there is nothing to say."

"Or nothing you wish to say?"

"As to that, there *is* one thing I should have told you at the outset of this conversation. I am married."

"Good lack, you certainly should have told me! But

how can this be? Who is she, and why in the name of all that's holy did we hear nothing of your impending nuptials?"

"You and my stepmother," Rothwell murmured, "ought to get on far better than you do. Both of you have very suspicious minds."

"Lady Rothwell does not approve?"

"She does not. You see, I married MacDrumin's daughter."

Ryder's eyebrows shot upward. "I comprehend now why you are so interested in London's attitude toward Jacobites, my friend. Guard her well."

"I intend to do so, but there is no cause for concern there. Her father was never successfully implicated."

"Not implicated, perhaps, but he was certainly suspected. What of your delightful sister? Does she approve this marriage?"

"She does," Rothwell said, "but that brings to mind another small point that I intended to raise with you. How well are you acquainted with young Lord Thomas Deverill?"

He was watching Ryder closely when he asked the question and was satisfied when his friend seemed to hesitate before replying. The hesitation was small, no doubt unnoticeable to someone who did not know Ryder very well, and his tone was perfectly calm and self-assured when he said, "I know who he is, of course—the Marquess of Jervaulx's younger son— and I think you have mentioned him to me before. He is the young idiot who has been making such a cake of himself over Lydia, is he not?"

"You know perfectly well that he is, although he seems to have found a new quarry for the moment. You disappoint me, Ryder. It would have been much better to say you knew him well, a perfectly simple statement of fact and not nearly so damning."

"What are you saying, Ned?" He looked uncomfortable.

Instead of answering directly, Rothwell said thoughtfully, "I think you should encourage him to return to the Continent to extend his . . . shall we say his grand tour?"

"Good lack, why should I do any such thing?"

"You see," Rothwell said gently, "Deverill was the only one who knew of my stepmother's intended return to London."

"Was he? I should have thought she would tell her servants at least." When Rothwell remained silent, Ryder grimaced. "I suppose your people have standing orders always to keep your London house in readiness for your arrival."

"They do. Nor would I accuse you of quizzing my servants, in any case. Has he been your mysterious source all along?"

"Curse you, Ned. Even between these walls I do not mean to gratify you by saying any more, but I will do what I can to keep him out of Lydia's way. Though if another young woman has drawn his regard, perhaps there is no real cause to do so now."

"That young woman is said to be quite intelligent," Rothwell said evenly. "I doubt she will encourage anyone as idiotic as Deverill pretends to be. Moreover, his behavior upsets Lydia."

"More and more you convince me, damn you," Ryder said with a sigh. "He won't go to the Continent, says it don't amuse him anymore, but perhaps I can induce him to go home to Cornwall for a few months, at least until this last burst of fury dies away."

Satisfied, Rothwell turned the subject again and

thought no more about young Deverill until he encountered him at the Ranelagh winter ridotto the following night.

On Friday night the Chelsea Road, which was the
main approach to Ranelagh Gardens from London,
was so thronged with chairs, carriages, and pedestrians from St. James's Park who had joined the cavalcade on the road at Buckingham gate that the bumpy
journey took twice as long as it should have. By the
time the two carriages bearing Rothwell's party arrived at the gate, where a guinea for each occupant
was demanded for passage into the gardens, Maggie
was regretting her decision to wear a warm cloak over
her gown and silk domino, and feared there would
soon be rivulets of perspiration running through the
dusting of powder her new maidservant had applied to
her complexion.

When the carriages paused at the gate, she gasped in
delight at her first view of the garden's interior. Directly in front of them was a huge round building with
lighted windows around the top story that made it
look like a giant's lantern. Around it, paths and the
carriage drive were lighted by lamps swinging from
poles and tree branches, and people strolled along
them despite the cool night air. The sound of French
horns echoed on the wind from the river, and an orchestra was playing nearer at hand.

Staring in wonder, Maggie said, "Are all the public
gardens in London like this one?"

Lydia chuckled. "No, indeed. Vauxhall is more a
woodland paradise, but amusements there all take
place out of doors, so it is for summer only. Ranelagh
is only a vast assembly room set in a pretty garden, but

we can enjoy it all year. Look, we are driving toward the Thames now, and you can see the lights reflected in the water and hear horns from the barges. If some people," she added with a speaking glance at Rothwell, "had not been so concerned about taking a chill, we might have come by barge tonight, and we could have been dancing by now."

"That is Ranelagh House on the left," Rothwell said as if he were merely taking up the thread of her narration. "It was the home of the man who left the gardens to the city of London. The main entrance to the Rotunda is there on our right."

The carriage door was opened a minute later, and the steps let down. James and the dowager joined them from the other carriage, and Maggie soon found herself inside the huge building she thought looked like a giant's lantern.

Lydia caught her eye and, speaking close to her ear in order to make herself heard above the din, said, " 'Tis like an enchanted palace, is it not?"

Maggie nodded, though she would not have chosen such a description. They were in the middle of a vast amphitheater at least fifty yards in diameter, its painted and gilded decorations as bright and gaudy as they could be. A double tier of boxes separated by ornamented pilasters lined the walls. In the center stood a magnificent orchestra platform, its elaborate canopy rising all the way to the roof, and the whole scene was lighted by a vast number of candles enclosed in crystal glasses.

Groups of persons attired either in fancy dress or in silk dominoes, and wearing or carrying loo masks, were seated in boxes or strolled in a veritable parade, circling the orchestra. The magnificent fabrics, gold and silver lace, lavish embroidery, and precious stones of their colorful costumes added much to the splendor of the scene. All manner of refreshments appeared to be within call—although Maggie had heard James say earlier with some bitterness that there would be nothing to drink except tea—and music vied with noisy conversation for predominance.

Maggie's eyes were dazzled and within minutes her head felt giddy from the din. She had the odd notion that more than one orchestra was playing and that no one else inside the huge chamber was paying heed to the music at all.

For a time it seemed as if the merrymakers had come merely to drink fine imperial tea or to walk in a circle round the room, looking at each other, and being looked at in return, but once Rothwell got his party settled in the box he had reserved for them and Maggie had sipped a bit of her tea, she was able to sort out the activity around her more rationally. Whether it was that the sides and ceiling of their box helped reduce the din from the central part of the room, or just that her senses had stopped reeling, she did not know, but she could hear a man singing and saw that a number of persons actually appeared to be listening to him, apparently undisturbed by the incessant conversation.

"I do not think much of this tea," Lady Rothwell said suddenly, her commanding tones carrying easily above the noise. "It is no more than weakly flavored hot water."

Lydia grinned at her. "It is certainly not so flavorful as your prized Bohea, ma'am, but at least there are lemons, and perhaps we can get some sugar for James." She had taken off her mask and sat viewing the parade of strollers as they passed by the box, nodding and smiling to those she knew and conversing happily with anyone who paused nearby.

Maggie privately agreed with Lady Rothwell that the so-called tea was no more than tepid water to which a few—a very few—tea leaves had been added, but she had begun to enjoy herself, and when Rothwell stood and suggested that they join the strollers, she arose with alacrity to accompany him. James and Lydia being content to sit for a time with the dowager, Maggie picked up the ivory and lace fan Rothwell had given her that evening, and placed the fingertips of her other hand on his arm, thinking how well her soft blue silk domino complimented his outfit of silver-gray and pale pink.

The earl was not wearing a mask, and when he asked her to remove hers she realized that he wanted them to be seen and recognized. In the next hour, a number of persons stopped to talk with them and as he proceeded to make her known to each one, introducing her as not only his countess but the daughter and only child of a powerful Scottish chief as well, she became steadily more certain that he had some purpose in mind that went beyond merely making her known to his friends.

When he introduced her to the Prince of Wales, she was sure of it. The prince was strolling with his wife and members of their extensive entourage. He bowed gracefully over Maggie's hand after she had made her curtsy, and made her a pretty compliment when he drew her to her feet again. Augusta, Princess of Wales, was also remarkably condescending.

"Did one hear Rothwell say you are from Scotland, Lady Rothwell?" she asked graciously when the prince turned to address a comment to the earl.

"Why, yes, madam, I am."

"Not from one of the more difficult parts, one trusts."

Before Maggie could think of a suitable response, Rothwell, who had evidently kept at least one ear on their exchange, said smoothly, "My wife is the daughter of a powerful clan chief, madam. MacDrumin of MacDrumin has done much to stimulate a vastly increased English presence in the Scottish Highlands."

"Indeed," replied the princess, "how very admirable, to be sure. You must call upon us at Leicester House, Lady Rothwell. We shall be most pleased to receive you there."

"Edward, are you mad?" Maggie demanded when they had moved on. "How dared you say such a thing about Papa to her highness!"

"I spoke only the truth, sweetheart, and my purpose was well served. The prince and princess are not always in good odor with the king, but their friendship must always be an asset."

"Are they indeed your friends, then? I confess, I—"

"I have been known to agree with the prince from time to time. I have also disagreed with him, however, and he does not take kindly to criticism. Nonetheless, I am useful to him and therefore am not to be offended. You see, being extravagant, he frequently finds himself in difficulties to which neither his father nor most members of Parliament can be induced to turn a sympathetic ear. I have, at times, been disposed to be, if not sympathetic, at least more generous than they are. I also sometimes play tennis with him. Good God," he added, raising his eyeglass and peering across the room, "what is she doing now?"

Following the direction of his gaze, Maggie saw that Lydia had gathered a court of youthful and very exuberant admirers and appeared to be having the time of her life.

"She is just enjoying herself," she protested when she found herself being propelled hastily back toward their box.

"That chit has no more sense than the good Lord bestowed upon a garden rake," Rothwell muttered, his words carrying to her ears only because she strained to hear him. "She thinks even less than you do before she speaks, and I don't want her blurting something we'll all regret. Moreover, there's Deverill hovering over her again, no doubt whispering nonsense in her ear."

"If he is whispering in this din, sir, she does not hear him," Maggie said. But thinking she understood his reasons for intervening better now than he did himself, she made no further protest, and they made their way through the crowd to the box, where Lydia greeted them with delight and presented the solidly built but elegantly dressed young woman who stood across the barrier from her, with Lord Thomas, as Lady Ophelia Balterley.

Maggie acknowledged the introduction politely and regarded Lady Ophelia with no little curiosity, but there was no way to encourage the young woman to tell them much about herself, for the chatter around them had grown too loud and too merry for such an exchange of politeness to take place. Finding herself momentarily separated from Rothwell by the others, she looked for someone she knew to speak to, and finding no one near at hand, moved toward the box entrance, meaning to go in and sit down.

James pushed past several others to assist her, and Lydia, still chatting across the barrier with the others, obligingly moved her wide skirts so that Maggie could get to a chair. Lady Rothwell was leaning over a side panel, fanning herself and talking with a woman of her own generation in the next box. She ignored Maggie, who sat back, fanning her own cheeks and watching the others. No sooner did she begin to relax, however, than she heard Lydia say indignantly, "But what can it matter if Thomas *was* there, Freddie? I was at Lady Primrose's masquerade myself, so if being there makes Thomas a dashed sneaking Jacobite, as you say it does, why then, it makes me one too—so there!"

A sudden appalling stillness fell upon the group, as though the noise around them had stopped altogether, and no one knew what to say next or where to look. The moment had begun to lengthen uncomfortably when Lady Ophelia said calmly, "Well done, Lydia. In a better-run world—which is to say in a world run by intelligent females instead of by idiotic males, as this one is—one's casually innocent observations would not be instantly snatched up and twisted into incriminating declarations by persons intending nothing more than to make mischief. You may escort me back to my chaperon, Thomas, if you please. She will no doubt be wondering by now what has become of me."

If Lydia was not at all pleased to be rescued in a fashion that included the removal of Lord Thomas from her orbit, no one but Maggie noticed, for into the space created by their departure spilled a veritable cacophony of outraged exclamations.

"Egad, who does that impertinent chit think she is, suggesting that the world could be better run by females?"

"Someone ought to take her firmly in hand and explain the facts of life to her is what I say."

"Downright brazen, that's what she is."

"Just goes to show what comes of educating

females; they get above themselves and forget their proper place in the world."

"Outrageous, simply outrageous! How much did you say her portion will be?"

The discussion became even livelier then than it had been before, but Maggie noticed that others departed in the wake of Lady Ophelia and Lord Thomas, and melted into the crowd. She hoped there was no one among them iniquitous enough to repeat Lydia's absurd confession where it might do her harm.

Trying to catch Rothwell's eye, she saw that he too was searching the crowd. She was not certain at first if he had overheard Lydia's declaration, because certainly the din around them had not really suspended itself as it seemed to have done, but had continued throughout the awful moment. But the more she watched him, the more she became certain that he had heard it, and that its potential consequences disturbed him profoundly.

She was unable to speak to him at once, because though he turned toward the box, he was intercepted by a woman who held her loo mask on a stick and flirted with him from behind it. He responded with what appeared to be his usual grace and aplomb, and it was some time before he attempted to move toward the box again. By then Lydia, accepting an invitation to dance, had gone off with a young sprig of fashion dressed up as Little Boy Blue.

Making his way purposefully to Maggie's side, Rothwell sat down in the next chair and said in a voice that carried to her ears alone, "Do you think you can contrive to become ill in the next half hour or so, sweetheart?"

"Do you think she has endangered herself, Edward?"

"I certainly don't care to linger long enough to discover that she has," he said, still in that low but carrying tone. "If there should be an attempt to arrest her, I prefer it to take place at my own house, not in so public a place as this is."

"But it is absurd to think anyone could really mistake dear Lydia for a Jacobite," Maggie protested. "She does not even know the meaning of the word, Edward. She wants only to be associated with what she believes was a romantic cause."

"I know that," he said tersely, "but if you think that will make a difference to anyone sent here to find her amongst this lot, you much mistake the matter. She will be fortunate if the agent himself is educated enough to know the definition of the term. It is more than likely he will not, that he—or they, for that matter—will simply be carrying out orders issued by someone else. Now, can you feign an illness, or must I play the ogre?"

Since she was rapidly getting a headache from the noise if from nothing else, she agreed that she could oblige him without difficulty and asked if he wished her to do so at once.

"No, I want you to wait a few minutes at least, so that our going will not instantly be associated with Lydia's comment. She will probably be safe enough until Monday, unless someone behaves in a most energetic manner, and by then I shall have had an opportunity to speak with Ryder, who may well be able to head off any attempt to embarrass me through my sister."

Unfortunately, Maggie's headache was not sufficient to convince either the dowager or Lydia to curtail their evening, since both ladies pointed out with indignation that, since their party had come in two carriages, they could simply remain at Ranelagh with James while Rothwell took Maggie home. And when James, responding to a look from his half-brother, promptly said he had no intention of remaining at their disposal for the entire evening, and intended to leave soon himself, he succeeded only in diverting the dowager's wrath from Rothwell to himself; so, in the end it was necessary for the earl to exert his authority, which did little to soothe anyone.

By the time Maggie was able to retire for the night with her husband, her headache was raging. The dowager had not minced words in her disgust with what she chose to call Rothwell's arrogance in ordering others' comings and goings to suit himself. Since her diatribe began the instant it was made known to her that he would brook no argument, it was only with difficulty that they were able to get to the carriages without drawing the very attention that Rothwell was endeavoring to avoid; and, since she chose to rain words of displeasure upon James, her sole companion on the journey home, informing him not only that his half-brother took too much authority upon himself but that James himself had displeased her by not being more conciliating toward Lady Ophelia Balterley when he had had such an excellent opportunity to bring himself to her notice, it had become a near-run thing with him. He confided to Maggie and Rothwell later that he had very nearly told his doting mama that he had no intention of trying to win over the Lady Ophelia but in fact had decided to marry a wholly ineligible female from the wilds of the Scottish Highlands.

Curled up in Rothwell's arms at last, Maggie soon realized that her headache was dissipating, and after some considerable attention from her husband, it disappeared entirely.

"You know," she said thoughtfully when Rothwell moved to kiss her good-night yet one last time, "I believe you have shown me a much better cure than whisky, Edward, for I have never known even one of Papa's most potent toddies to cure a headache, and you have sent mine right away out of my head."

"I'm a devil of a fellow, sweetheart," he murmured, kissing her again. "You would be surprised by the extent of my powers."

She chuckled, but she had no cause to doubt him. He had surprised her more than once in the past weeks, not least the first night she had spent with him in this very room, when he had taken obvious delight in describing to her the history of the two absurd portraits of Adam and Eve flanking the fireplace, where they could best be viewed from the huge master bed.

Though she had expected him to revert the moment the carriage wheels struck the cobblestones of London to the foppish fellow she had first met, he had not done so. He had certainly donned city attire—his worst enemy would never call him shabby or unfashionable—but there was a new air about him now, and she knew it was not all due to his concern for Lydia's safety.

Indeed, any danger to Lydia must have existed only before he was not present to protect her, for certainly, with his many friends and acquaintances amongst the rich and powerful, his half-sister must be well protected.

She let her thoughts drift back to Ranelagh, where she had greatly enjoyed strolling around the Rotunda on her husband's arm, drawing attention from everyone they met. There had been exclamations of disbelief, but many felicitations as well, and everyone they met had treated her with respect, even with some affection, as though they would accept her into their midst only for being Rothwell's wife. She had enjoyed that as much as she had enjoyed being treated as a countess when they traveled. Oddly, she was finding London less irksome than she had expected.

XXV

The following morning, to everyone's surprise, the dowager joined them in the breakfast parlor at what was for her a most unseasonable hour. That she had been up for some time became evident when she announced that she had sent cards to Lady Ophelia Balterley and the aunt who was being kind enough to chaperon her, inviting them to enjoy some of her prized Bohea at Rothwell House that afternoon. Hearing this news, the other four people at the table stared at her in varying degrees of dismay.

Maggie, though not displeased by a chance to further her acquaintance with the astonishing Lady Ophelia, knew that neither Rothwell nor James would welcome her company and held her tongue.

Lydia was not so wise. "Mama, what can you be thinking!" she demanded. "Surely, you do not want me to make a bosom bow of Ophelia Balterley. I never have the least notion of what to say to her. Her notions are all so peculiar!"

"You must not always be thinking only of yourself, my dear," Lady Rothwell said. "You will do better to appear to be kind to the young woman than to snub her, for to do the latter is to encourage gentlemen to choose sides, and one cannot always be certain they will choose wisely. In any event, it is as much your duty to further dear James's cause as your own."

Dear James sat stiffly at hearing these words, and said hastily, "I wish you had not invited Lady Ophelia here if you do so in my behalf, ma'am. That suit will not prosper."

"If you mean to say that you are not enamored of the young woman, dear James, that does not signify, for emotions do not enter into such matters if one is wise. Furthermore, you will be guided by me, if you please, for I know what is best for you."

"Damnation," James snapped, "you know nothing of the sort. And it is no use looking daggers at me, Ned, for I won't apologize. At least, I will apologize to Maggie and to Lydia, but not to Mama. You are stepping way beyond the mark, ma'am. I'll be da— That is, I won't have you telling me that I must marry some young chit scarcely out of the schoolroom, or anyone else for that matter."

"Little Ophelia does have a lamentable habit of flaunting what she believes, no doubt inaccurately, to be an education equal to that of any man, but she will learn better in time."

"I don't care if she does," James retorted, "and as for being inaccurate, let me tell you that if I may judge by the astute remarks she made last night, she has an understanding beyond that of any gentleman of my acquaintance. I believe I acquitted myself well in school, but I have not read half of what I must suppose that young woman to have read. Not that her education would repel me if I were interested in pursuing a closer acquaintance, for it would do nothing of the sort, but since I have no intention of pursuing such an acquaintance with anyone at all in Lon—"

"Easy, James," Rothwell said warningly.

Maggie, hoping to make it easier for James to recover after what she too believed to have been an unintentional slip, said quickly to Lydia, "If your mama has invited guests to join us this afternoon, perhaps you will be kind enough to help me select a proper gown to wear. I am still not well enough versed in the current fashions to be certain that I can choose wisely."

Before Lydia could reply the dowager said acidly, "How can you say you have no such intention, James? It is imperative that you marry wisely, as I think you know only too well. Not only are you your brother's heir apparent, but—"

"What rubbish!" James did not attempt to conceal his exasperation. "Not only is Ned married now, and to a perfectly healthy young woman who may be counted upon to produce a good many offspring, but—"

"That union will be temporary, as I have already made plain," the dowager said flatly. "It is a most unsuitable alliance—for call it a marriage I cannot and will not—and Rothwell simply must rectify the matter."

"I intend to rectify it," Rothwell said, his tone nonetheless ominous for all its gentleness.

Maggie looked at him quickly, fearing that somehow the dowager had convinced him of his error. When he smiled at her, however, she relaxed.

The dowager said, "I am glad to hear you say so, but if you intend to speak with your man of affairs today, I hope you will do so before this afternoon so that you can be present when Lady Ophelia comes. To take tea in the house of the Earl of Rothwell with his lordship in attendance must make a greater impact than if she is merely entertained by his stepmama, and if she is to comprehend the exalted position to which she might one day find herself elevated—"

"By the Lord Harry, Mama, what nonsense will you spout next?" James demanded, growing red in the face. "There is not the remotest chance that I shall—"

The dowager cut in again without hesitation, "There is every chance that such a thing could come to pass, my dear James; however, you mistook my meaning. I was careful to say only that she ought to be aware of the possibility, which, I might remind you, grows more likely the longer Rothwell goes without making a suitable marriage. Since he has apparently come to his senses, however, and means to set this young woman aside—"

"I mean to do no such thing," Rothwell said, "as you would have realized by now, ma'am, if you paid heed for two minutes to anyone's words but your own. When I said I meant to correct the matter, I meant that I will apply to the Archbishop of Canterbury for permission to be properly remarried in the Church of England. By law, since the marriage is legal in Scotland, England must recognize it as well, but I am only too willing to agree it is unusual. Not only will the Church be better pleased if we reunite with its blessing and approval, but you can then have proper marriage lines to put with your genealogical book."

His stepmother bowed to the inevitable, saying, "In that event, it is even more important that James pursue a marriage that will see him well-settled. He cannot want to be always hanging on your sleeve. Therefore," she went on, turning to fix a gimlet eye on her son, "I want to hear no more foolish talk from you, sir. You will do as you are bid."

James straightened, his temper under what appeared to Maggie to be the most rigid control, his voice unnaturally calm when he said, "I must disappoint you yet again, ma'am. No, pray do not speak, but listen to what I tell you. I meant to approach this matter carefully, in order to make you see how very well I have done for myself, but I see now that such a method will not serve. No, Ned," he added, holding up a hand when Rothwell moved to speak, "I have never been good at deception, or very tactful, for that matter. I must just speak my piece straight out. Mama, I am not going to marry a woman chosen for me by you or anyone else. I am going to marry one I have chosen for myself."

"Well, if you do not like Lady Ophelia," the dowager began, apparently deciding to be reasonable, "then I am sure we can find someone who will suit you bet—"

"I have found her."

"What?"

"I am going to marry a girl I met in Scotland."

The dowager clasped a hand to her heart and said in failing accents, "Not another Scotswoman!"

No one could pretend that the ensuing discussion was pleasant for anyone, but when James got to his feet at last, announcing that he had errands to attend to, there was only one person in the room who was not convinced he had come off with the honors. The dowager made one last attempt to carry the day, saying bitterly that she could not imagine what he could have to do since he had done quite enough already.

James said, "I want to collect supplies for my painting from the Bridge house and see that all is in order there. I had intended to remain at Rothwell House for a time, and I believe I will, even now, since Ned has said that I may, but Dev said something last night about paying a visit to his family's estates in Cornwall, and I want to make certain he does not leave Mrs. Honeywell without proper means to look after things there for us until I decide what is to be done about the house."

"But you will return here this afternoon," the dowager said. "I insist, James. You will displease me very much if you do not.

"I will do my best to join you, ma'am, but only if I can be sure you have understood me, and with your permission," he added quickly, "I will invite Brockelby to join us as well. I mean to call upon him, in any event, and his presence will make the gathering here a little less pointed, if I may say so."

"Very well," she said with a sigh, adding tartly when Rothwell also got to his feet, "Are you going out too?"

"Certainly, I am. I have a number of things to do. But," he added, smiling again at Maggie in a way that warmed her to her toes, "if you are entertaining this afternoon, ma'am, I will gladly lend my presence to the occasion."

"Three o'clock then," the dowager said. "Pray do not be late, Rothwell."

Maggie, realizing that he would go upstairs before he left the house, got to her feet, excusing herself hastily to the others, and moved quickly to accompany him from the room. He let her precede him, then took her hand and placed it in the crook of his arm as they ascended the stairs. When they were beyond the sharp hearing of the servants in the hall, she looked up at him and said, "I knew she would be displeased by our marriage."

"She is furious, sweetheart, but it will do her no good."

"Do you really intend for us to be married again?"

"I do. Would you like a huge wedding with all of London present, or would you prefer a quiet ceremony?"

She smiled. "I will do as you wish, but I think you know what I would prefer."

"I do, and so it will be. I've no wish to pander to public curiosity." He gave her a little hug and added, "I am sorry to leave you here today, particularly after that scene, but with James out of the house, I daresay she will turn her attention to her tea party. In any event, I must seek out Ryder in order to make certain that Lydia stands in no danger."

"Have you spoken to her?"

"In all honesty, I do not know what to say to her," he confessed. "If I order her to say nothing about Jacobites, she will think of nothing else, and the words will spill from her tongue again just as they did last night, for a more heedless chit I've never known."

"More heedless than I am?" She watched him from under her lashes, and was glad to see him smile again.

"Much more," he said.

"Well, sir, I think you wrong us both," she said.

He laughed and gave her another hug, but he did not linger once he reached his room, and since the noble Fletcher was once again in command of his attire, when he left, his appearance was precise to a pin. But Maggie noted that the languid air he had once affected with such regularity was gone, and there was a spring in his step. He did not so far forget his dignity as to twirl his cane when he walked, but she knew he was a happier, more purposeful man than the one she had first met.

When Lydia joined her in her bedchamber a quarter-hour later, bursting to discuss the morning's events, Maggie made no effort to divert her thoughts, studying her instead, certain Rothwell was mistaken in his half-sister's ability to understand the gravity of what had occurred the previous night. Having seen that Englishmen tended to think females somewhat less intelligent than themselves, and realizing that even the best of them were subject to odd prejudices, she listened to Lydia's exclamations and prophesies with but half an ear while she decided what to do. When she had, she cut the younger girl off mid-sentence to say, "Look here, Lydia, you did a very stupid thing last night."

Her mouth agape, Lydia stared for a moment, speechless, before she said, "I don't believe you heard one word I said, Maggie MacDr—That is to say . . . What did I do? I know something happened to vex Ned, but he never said what it was, and Mama would have it that he was merely being contrary, but he wasn't being, was he? What was it?"

"You announced to all and sundry that you had been at Lady Primrose's masquerade," Maggie said flatly.

Lydia frowned. "Lud, I know I said that, but what difference can that make now? Good gracious, Maggie, that ball was nearly two whole months ago."

"Nevertheless, Edward says Jacobites are still being condemned to death as traitors, Lydia, and since a good many of the people who care about such things evidently have at least a strong suspicion that there were many Jacobite sympathizers, if not actual Jacobites, at that masquerade, you associated yourself with them by announcing that you were present."

"But there were innocent bystanders as well," Lydia protested. "Why, Thomas was there, and James, and they are not Jacobites. And you were there, too, and while you may have been a sympathizer, I am persuaded you never took up arms against the English or incited anyone else to do so. And even if you did, the danger of another uprising is long past. Sir Dudley Ryder told Mama and me that much when he called upon us the day after we arrived in town. He was just making conversation, of course, but I distinctly recall his saying that, so what can be the harm in talking about the stupid masquerade now?"

"Would you tell anyone that I was there?" Maggie asked.

"No, of course not, because—" She broke off, coloring.

"Just so," Maggie said, certain now that she was doing the right thing and hoping she could convince Edward later that she had not, once again, merely spoken without thinking. "I will spare your blushes, Lydia. You would keep silent because you think people would more readily believe me a dangerous Jacobite than those same people would believe the same of you. True?"

"I do not believe you are dangerous," Lydia said flatly.

"But it does not matter what you think," Maggie pointed out. "What matters is the perception other people have, and the fact that you realize that I am at greater risk than you are, should my presence at the masquerade become known, only shows that you understand that perceptions are as important as fact. I daresay even Edward's power is not so great that it would protect me, because prejudice against Scottish persons is still too great in this city for him to overcome it. But your declaration last night may prove to be a great embarrassment to him, even if you do not find yourself in actual danger. You must take care in future, my dear, to make no more such declarations."

Lydia was silent, but Maggie knew there was no need to say more, and at last, the younger girl said quietly, "I was foolish, wasn't I? No wonder Ned was so vexed. Why did he not say all this to me himself? No, don't tell me," she added when Maggie hesitated. "I can imagine. He thought he had only to forbid me to speak and I would suffer a constant compulsion to say what I had been forbidden to say. You need not look so sympathetic, Maggie. He had reason to be concerned, for I have often reacted in just that fashion. I promise you, however, that I will take care this time. I am not a fool, you know, even if I am not so overeducated as Ophelia Balterley."

"I know you are not a fool," Maggie said, but she knew that Lydia had grown up quite a lot in just the past few moments.

They spent the next half hour choosing gowns to wear that afternoon, only to learn several hours later that the two ladies who were to have been the dowager's chief guests had been forced, due to a previous engagement, to decline her invitation. Since Lady Rothwell considered any offer to share her extremely expensive Bohea the height of gracious generosity, neither Maggie nor Lydia was at all surprised to learn that she took their reply as a personal affront.

"We need not have had the Bohea at all," she said with a sniff, "but here is James bringing that Dr. Brockelby and no doubt promising him Bohea, and so we shall have to have it out."

"Dr. Brockelby is a very kind gentleman," Lydia said.

"I never said he was not. But to think of giving my precious Bohea to a professional man! He is very nearly in trade, my dears, but no doubt that is what James admires."

"Mama," Lydia said, "I won't let you abuse James anymore today. You would be very much distressed if he refused ever to visit us after he is married, so you must not persist in condemning his choice of a bride."

"I am very sure I shall not condemn his bride, my dear," Lady Rothwell said calmly.

Maggie was not so sure, but since she knew that nothing she could tell the dowager about Kate Mac-Cain would relieve her concerns, she held her tongue. In the event, they were not to be restricted to only one guest that afternoon, for Rothwell, having been unable to run Sir Dudley to earth, informed his family upon his return that he had left invitations for him wherever he might be likely to find them and believed the attorney general would honor them with his presence just as soon as he encountered one.

"He was not at his lodgings," Rothwell said when he joined the three ladies in the grand saloon, where the dowager had decreed they would take their tea. "I visited his office and numerous other places, but his man was not certain where he was to be found, so I finally decided I'd do better to await him here. Where is James?"

When Maggie said with a welcoming smile that they had not heard from him yet, Lydia laughed and said, "He may not even come, you know. Once he finds himself amidst paints and canvas and dirty old rags, he forgets everything else. I daresay he is painting a picture and has quite forgotten Mama's tea party."

The dowager, signing to the footman to bring in her tea chest, said complacently, "It does not signify now, in any case, since Lady Ophelia and her aunt were unable to honor us with their presence. I am sure I do not know what can have been so important as to have kept them from joining us to enjoy this very fine tea."

She took the small key from around her neck and unlocked the tea caddy, saying, "Leave it on the table beside me, Frederick, and bring in the tray. We will not wait for Mr. James." When the tray was set before her, containing the silver pot of boiling water, the matching silver teapot, and the delicate porcelain tea service that presently enjoyed her favor, she proceeded to brew a carefully measured amount of the precious tea. "Now," she said graciously, as she replaced the lid on the teapot, "while that brews, perhaps you will entertain us with some account or other from your recent journey, Rothwell. I am sure Lydia and I would be most interested, and perhaps your wife can tell us something about her home there."

If Rothwell was as surprised as Maggie was to hear this request, he did not show it but said only, "I could tell you a great deal of what I learned there, ma'am, but I daresay you will be content with a brief account. Conditions in the Highlands are difficult, in no little way, I regret to say, because of the way our soldiers have behaved toward the inhabitants there."

"But surely," the dowager said, casting a superior glance at Maggie, "our enemies cannot expect to be treated as well as our friends are treated. You will forgive me for speaking plainly."

"It is I who will speak plainly," Rothwell said. "As you know, numerous large estates owned by chiefs who supported the Pretender were confiscated and awarded to others in an attempt that is most diplomatically described as an effort to modernize the estates and civilize their inhabitants. In point of fact, however, the result has been a disaster for too many people."

"I am sure you are an efficient landlord, Rothwell."

"I *was* a devilish poor landlord, but I hope to be a

better one," he said, smiling at Maggie. "I've already begun what I hope will be a prosperous venture for everyone in the glen."

"How too utterly fascinating, I'm sure," the dowager said, beginning to pour out the tea. She handed small porcelain cups to Maggie and to Lydia; and then, as she poured Rothwell's, she said, "I have added sugar, just as you like it, though I cannot think why you men want to adulterate such a fine blend as this."

Both Lydia and Rothwell spoke at once.

"I don't take sugar."

"Mama, really, it is James who likes sugar, not Ned."

The dowager looked dismayed. "Oh, how vexatious! You are perfectly right, but 'tis a pity to waste it when it is so dreadfully dear. I don't suppose . . ." She paused hopefully.

Rothwell sighed and held out his hand to take the cup. "Very well, ma'am. James insists that it improves the taste, so do not throw it out, I beg you. I am sure I would feel guilty for weeks if I were to make you do something so extravagant."

"Yes, you would," Lydia said, grinning at him. "She would make sure that you did."

"I am sure I should do nothing of the kind," the dowager said so archly that Maggie was certain that had she held a fan instead of a dish of tea, she would have flirted with him over its folds. Such behavior seemed odd, but when the dowager went on at once to inquire if Scottish customs were as peculiar as she had heard they were, she bristled at once, deciding Lady Rothwell was merely being rude and annoying, and nothing more.

Conversation lagged after that, even Lydia finding it

difficult to infuse cheerfulness into what seemed to be an attempt on the dowager's part to put Maggie firmly in her place. Rothwell, rather than putting an end to such tactics, seemed only to respond to questions as they were put to him, and Maggie began to wonder if he was feeling quite the thing. It did not seem like him to let his stepmother enjoy such a free rein.

When Frederick entered a few moments later and moved as if to speak quietly to the earl, the dowager said, "What is it, Frederick? Have James and Dr. Brockelby, or Sir Dudley, arrived? You ought to have shown them in at once. A family party like this one can be just too dull for words."

Maggie agreed with her, and Lydia's expression made it plain that she did, too, so neither expressed surprise when Rothwell said, "Yes, what is it, Frederick? It cannot be Master James, for he would have come straight in, but if you are keeping Sir Dudley kicking his heels in the hall, I won't thank you for it."

"No, my lord. It is a pair of . . . of persons, sir, who desire to have speech with you. That is, they actually demanded speech with Lady Lydia, my lord, but knowing what was right, which they clearly did not, I told them I would announce their presence to you, sir, which I would have done without—"

"Yes, yes, Frederick," the dowager said, "but since you have now whetted our curiosity, you must bring these persons who inquired for Lady Lydia straight in here. Sit where you are, Rothwell," she added when he began to get up. "You may think you call the tune, sir, but where my daughter is concerned, I demand to know what is going forward. Show them in at once, Frederick."

The footman glanced at Rothwell, who nodded wearily. Maggie, looking narrowly at the earl, was certain now that he was not himself. Not only was it unlike him to allow his stepmother to order things as she chose, but Maggie was sure his countenance was paler than it had been only moments before.

The two men who entered a short time later in the footman's wake were plainly not gentlemen. In fact, Maggie realized, even before the taller of the two announced that they were agents of the law, that they looked very much like the constable's watchman she had met her first day in London.

Lydia gasped and looked frightened. The dowager looked down her nose at the pair and said only, "Indeed?"

Rothwell said in an expressionless tone, "State your business."

"Yes, your lordship. I was about to do that very thing, your lordship. In point of fact, your lordship, we have come to question one Lady Lydia Carsley, having it on good authority that the young lady was one of those present at a most dubious event, consorting—if I may take such liberty to say so—with most suspicious persons, and we have been sent to discover what she can tell us about that event, and those persons."

Maggie's mouth felt dry, but despite her own fears she saw that the dowager, too, was becoming increasingly alarmed.

Lydia said indignantly, "I do not know who you are that you dare to question me, but I have no objection to telling you that I don't know what in the world you are talking about."

"About a masquerade, miss, at a house in Essex Street known to have been visited by Jacobites." He said the last word in much the same tone, Maggie thought, as he might have said *vipers* or *messengers of Satan.*

The dowager's posture was upright at all times, but upon hearing these words she stiffened like a poker and said in outraged tones, "You dare to accuse my daughter of consorting with . . . with—Get out at once! Rothwell, I demand that you prevent this outrage."

"They only want to ask questions, Mama," Lydia said. "I am sure I shall be happy to answer them. I have already said I know nothing at all to tell them, and that is the plain truth."

"Well, of course it is the truth," the dowager said angrily. "How can you possibly know anything about a masquerade in Essex Street of all places. You have attended no masquerades except for the ridotto at Ranelagh last evening."

"Well, in point of fact, ma'am, I *was* at the party in Essex Street, but my presence was completely innocent, I assure you."

"You!" Lady Rothwell leapt to her feet and pointed dramatically at Maggie. "You are to blame for this. How dare you try to lure my daughter into your treasonous endeavors! This is the one you want, my good man. This woman is Scottish! Her father is a Highland chief who no doubt led his men against our valiant English soldiers in that traitorous uprising, and she is no more than a branch from the same family tree. If there is a Jacobite in this room, it is she, not my innocent daughter!"

Maggie, shocked to her toes by the accusation, for she had not expected even Lady Rothwell to attempt so blatantly to throw her to the wolves, arose as if she had been a puppet on strings, staring at the dowager in astounded disbelief. She barely felt the hand that gripped her arm or heard the spokesman say, "You'll be coming along with us for questioning, young woman, and if your answers ain't satisfactory, we'll know what to do next. Ain't been no female Jacobites hanged as yet, but far as I knows it, being female don't save no one from the noose."

"No!" Rothwell, aroused to fury at last, leapt to his feet, took a step toward the man daring to lay hands on Maggie, and collapsed to the floor.

"My God," shrieked Lady Rothwell, clasping her hands to her bosom, "the wicked Jacobites have poisoned the Earl of Rothwell!"

XXVI

Maggie tried to run to Rothwell, but the taller constable caught her by the arm, saying harshly, "Oh, no, you don't, wench, not when you're the one most likely responsible for his collapse. I don't say it's poison, mind you—not without the doctor says so—but it can't do any man no good to learn he's harbored a spy in his house, let alone a high and mighty lord like that'un. You just come along with us now."

"But he needs help!" she cried. "Oh, Lydia, send someone at once to find James, or send for Dr. Brockelby."

"But what is wrong?" Lydia demanded. "Ned is never sick."

"Don't chatter! Just go at once and send Frederick to—Oh, thank God!" she exclaimed when, trying yet again to jerk away from the constable's clutches if only long enough to ring for the footman, she saw the door from the stair hall open and James appear on the threshold. "James, Edward's sick again!"

"What the devil?" James demanded. Then, evidently just at that moment seeing Rothwell lying in a crumpled heap on the floor, he turned and cried, "Brockelby, in here. Quickly, man!"

Hearing a gasp from the dowager, Maggie saw at once that she was looking gray, and remembering the dreadful accusation the woman had made against her, wondered if something might actually have been in the tea that would make them all ill. That thought stimulated a second, more terrifying one, and when the constable, still keeping a tight grip on her arm, began to pull her toward the doorway, she said urgently, "James, listen to me!"

But he was speaking to a stout gentleman in a red coat, who she realized with profound relief must be Dr. Brockelby. Not only did he carry the gold-headed cane of his profession but when he doffed his hat upon entering the room, Maggie saw that Frederick, entering behind him and reaching to take it, handed him a black leather satchel. James glanced at her when she called to him again, but his attention was divided between the fallen Rothwell and the doctor, and he said, "One moment, Maggie. Let Brockelby have a look at Ned first. And get all these extra people out of here, will you?"

"We'll just do as the man says, wench," the constable said, pulling her aside so the doctor could pass them. "His lordship's in need of a doctor, and he don't need the likes of you lingering about. You come along with me, like I said, and we'll get you all sorted out in a pig's whisper."

"But you don't understand!" she cried.

Lydia, hearing her, leapt up and ran to her side. "Let her go, you fool. This is my brother's wife you are manhandling. She is the Countess of Rothwell. Unhand her, I say."

"A likely tale, that be," declared the constable. "Now, don't you go a-worritin' me or spinning me no tales about his lordship taking up with the Scotch, for

I'll not believe a word of it, my lady. You've already gone and cost us a deal of trouble, and I've a notion I ought to be asking you a lot more questions, but since his lordship has fell by the wayside, so to speak, I'll just be a-taking of this Scotch wench along to the magistrate's office until I've spoke with them what sent me."

"Now, look here," Lydia began, but Maggie, terrified for Rothwell, cut her off.

"Lydia, forget about me. I will come to no harm. But tell James about the sugar in Edward's tea, and tell him I'm certain now the other times were not accidents. Promise me you will tell him that, Lydia, and don't let anyone but James or the doctor give Edward anything to eat or drink! I . . . I think . . ." But she could not speak the horrid thought aloud, not to Lydia, who looked at her now as if she were crazed, not even to James. She could only pray that between them James and Brockelby would save Rothwell. Taking a last look over her shoulder at the tableau she was leaving behind, misting now beyond a curtain of tears, she saw that Lady Rothwell stood as stiff and still as though she had been carved out of stone, and she hoped that Brockelby, who looked more like another aristocratic fop than any doctor she had ever seen, was no more a fop than Rothwell was and knew as much about his business as James thought he did.

Making no further protest lest she merely delay them in helping Rothwell, she let the two constables take her through the stair hall to the entrance hall, past curious, whispering servants, and out the door to the courtyard, where a shabby coach awaited them. Making no effort to stem the tears now streaming down her cheeks, blindly allowing the men to take her to their coach, she forced her mind to focus on prayers for

Rothwell's recovery and on reassuring herself that she could trust James, that no matter what, both James and Lydia cared more about Rothwell than either had revealed when she first met them, that they loved him almost as much as she did. They would not let him die. As she was hustled into the shabby coach, she recited to herself like a litany that Lydia would tell James about the sugar, James would tell Brockelby what had happened on the road, and Brockelby would know exactly what to do to save the earl.

She required no lengthy reflection now to know who must be responsible for Rothwell's illnesses. Remembering that Maria had carried lotions and distillations given to her by the dowager, and that Chelton had seemed to control his wife with an iron fist, she remembered as well that Maria had once offered to give her laudanum, telling her she kept it to use for pain. Maggie had thought at the time that Maria used the stuff to ease pain caused by Chelton's rough handling, but she wondered now if the opiate had also come from Lady Rothwell.

Whatever the cause of Rothwell's present illness, she had no doubt now that he had been poisoned and no doubt who had poisoned him. Remembering that James had dismissed the possibility of the Cheltons being involved because they had shown no inclination to murder the earl before, she realized now that neither James nor she had considered that the Cheltons might have been acting for their mistress. Lady Rothwell had no doubt wished to take advantage of a chance to eliminate the earl in such a way that others would be blamed, to pave the way for her darling James to take his place.

Sitting stiffly against the tattered upholstery, shifting a little to make room for the larger constable to sit beside her, and moving her feet to let the second man take the seat opposite them, she tried otherwise to ignore the two men, telling herself she was not afraid. Indeed, she hoped she was not concerned about herself at all, only about Rothwell, for whatever came to her, the most important thing was that he must not die. He would do what he could for her when he was well again, and even if he did not survive—a thought too dreadful to contemplate—Lydia would surely enlist the aid of Sir Dudley Ryder; although, of course, the possibility did exist that everyone at Rothwell London House would by then be too distraught by the death of its master even to remember her existence.

The possibility also existed that Lydia would think it silly to tell James about Rothwell getting sugar in his tea. Maggie wished she had been more specific in her accusations; however, there was also a chance—a remote one, she hoped—that James and Lydia both were more selfish than she thought they were, that James desired wealth and position enough to allow his half-brother to die. As the coach began to move and she found herself wondering what MacDrumin would do if she were in fact actually hanged as a Jacobite, she recognized in that maudlin thought, if not in the ones preceding it, an increasing tendency to fall into a pit of despondency. Ruthlessly forcing all such notions out of her mind, she began to collect her wits.

The coach lurched forward, and the horses pulling it were urged at once to a smart trot, so that when the driver was forced to rein them in quickly to avoid running into a chaise being driven through the gate from the Privy Garden as they approached, the passengers had to grab what they could to keep from being thrown to the floor. Maggie, clutching the window frame, looked out as the smaller vehicle swept by and found herself staring into the astonished countenance of Sir Dudley Ryder.

She heard a shout, her own vehicle paused after no more than another lurch, and the constables exchanged glances of puzzlement. The man opposite her could see more than she or her seat companion could, and he muttered with a frown, "Some nob, Cyril, a-jumping out o' yon chaise without it even done come to a proper stop." He blinked. "Only seen 'im oncet afore," he said, "but I've a mind that says I knows that cove."

"He is Sir Dudley Ryder," Maggie said quietly.

The tall man next to her said reprovingly, "Now, miss, you remember what I told her ladyship afore, and don't be telling me no more fairy tales."

"But it's him, Cyril," his companion said earnestly.

The coach door was yanked open, and Sir Dudley's face appeared. He said curtly, "What is going on here?"

"We've arrested a wicked Jacobite, yer honor, due to information received," the one called Cyril told him.

Maggie's first impulse was to shriek at Sir Dudley, to beg him to help her, to tell him she had been wrongly accused and that Rothwell was in deadly peril. But even as she opened her mouth to speak, she realized that she might say the wrong thing and make matters worse, both for herself and later for Rothwell. This man was after all the attorney general. It was his business to ferret out Jacobites and see them punished, and she could scarcely claim to be innocent of the charge. She had no idea what evidence might be presented against her, or indeed, what Sir Dudley already knew. These thoughts flitted through her mind in the blink of an eye, and she snapped her teeth together, waiting to see what he would say next.

He looked at her, clearly puzzled, and said quite calmly, "My dear, where is your husband? I collect that he cannot be here, or you would not find yourself in this predicament."

The two constables became noticeably still at hearing these words, and striving to match Sir Dudley's calm tone, Maggie said, "Rothwell fell suddenly ill, Sir Dudley, and in all the confusion that followed, these two men arrested me."

His stern gaze fell upon the constables, and he said grimly, "Do you know that this woman is the Countess of Rothwell?"

"We had just begun to suspicion that fact," Cyril said wretchedly, "but indeed, yer honor, an accusation were laid, and naught were said about the lady being no countess. Well, not nothing a sensible chap would believe."

About to explain that he spoke what was very nearly the truth, Maggie caught herself again and bit her lower lip, waiting to be asked if that was the case. Instead, Sir Dudley said, "Nonsense, man, you must have misunderstood, for I know this lady quite well, and I can assure you that she is no Jacobite."

"She were at that pestiferous masquerade, sir."

Maggie's spirits, which had begun to rise, flagged again, but she had underestimated Sir Dudley.

"Excellent," he said. "She can tell us more about who was present. As you must know, we've had a deal of trouble getting two persons to name the same names, so her ladyship may prove to be extremely helpful. Under the circumstances, I will assume that in the confusion caused by his lordship's illness you acted on an unfortunate misunderstanding. I'll sort it out myself, however, so you need not stay. Will you take my arm, ma'am?"

She did so and discovered that her hand was trembling. As they hurried back toward the entrance to the house together, Sir Dudley put his hand over hers and said urgently, "Is Ned really ill? How ill?"

Her emotions more uncertain than ever, Maggie's voice threatened to betray her, but she managed to say, "Very ill, sir, but James and the doctor are with him, so I hope that he . . . that is . . ." Striving to hold back her tears, she barely heard him when he said, "You behaved very sensibly back there, ma'am. That might have become a most dangerous situation. How came you to be arrested? Was there indeed a complaint laid against you?"

"Lady Rothwell," Maggie muttered wretchedly. "It may have been a misunderstanding. Indeed, I do not recall her precise words. She was distraught; she feared that Lyd . . . that is—"

"Say no more," he said, slowing so she could raise her skirt as they began to hurry up the steps. "If Lydia is in this, I know enough to guess the rest. In any event, I will see to it that you are not distressed anymore by this Jacobite business."

She looked up into his face, and, aware that the front door was open, and Fields stood beside it, she said carefully, "I must tell you, sir, that I will be of no assistance to you in . . . in the matter you spoke of a few moments ago."

To her astonishment, Sir Dudley grinned and said, "I don't doubt that, but whatever political games may be played by others, ma'am, I know you are no threat at all to England."

"Now, how can you know that, sir? You barely know me."

"Ah, but I know your husband, ma'am, and have done for nearly a quarter of a century. Good afternoon, Fields," he added before Maggie could think of a response. "What the devil is amiss with his lordship?"

Fields blinked at seeing Maggie, but to her surprise his expression warmed, although his tone was anxious when he said, "As to that, I do not know, sir, but Mr. James and Dr. Brockelby have taken his lordship up to his bedchamber."

Just then a clatter of footsteps sounded on the stairway, and when Maggie saw that it was James, the speed with which he was moving sent a thrill of terror shooting through her, and she rushed forward, crying Rothwell's name. James caught her and gave her a little shake, saying firmly, "Ned is fine, Maggie. Brockelby's methods acted much faster than my own. Ned says he is growing quite accustomed to having his insides turned out every which way. But what are you doing back here? Lydia told me what happened, and I was just on my way to find you and explain things to anyone who would listen to me. Ned would have gone himself, but Brockelby has threatened to sit on him if he tries to get up." He paused, grimacing, then added in a different tone, "This is the very devil of a coil, I must say."

Quickly Maggie said, "Sir Dudley rescued me."

James had been looking at her, but he looked up at the mention of that gentleman, whereupon Sir Dudley, who had been standing beside Fields, moved forward and said quietly, "I was glad to be of assistance to Lady Rothwell."

James exchanged a quick glance with Maggie and gave her shoulder a squeeze that might have been meant either to reassure or to warn before he stepped forward to greet Sir Dudley, saying, "You have our thanks, Ryder."

"I collect that I have come at a bad moment," Sir Dudley said. "If Ned is too ill to receive me, I shall understand, but he did send for me, you know, so perhaps . . ."

"But he will be delighted to see you, particularly since you have saved his wife from the indignity of being questioned by your voracious minions. She can take you upstairs to him at once, and I'll join you in a few moments. First I want a word with my mother—to reassure her as to Ned's condition—and then I must collect something to give Brockelby in lieu of a fee. Stupid fellow seems to think that because I invited him to take a dish of Mama's famous Bohea it would be a sin of the first order to accept his proper fee for saving Ned's life."

"Good lack," Ryder exclaimed, "surely, the case was not so dire as all that."

"No, as a matter of fact it wasn't," James said, shooting another glance at Maggie. "He just drank something that did not agree with him. But at the time, it frightened the liver and lights out of all of us, as you can well imagine."

"I can, indeed." He offered his arm again to Maggie, and said nothing until they reached the door to Rothwell's bedchamber. Then, as she put her hand on the latch, he said in a musing tone, "I wonder if Ned will confide the whole truth of this business to me or if I am meant to remain in ignorance."

Looking over her shoulder, she saw a twinkle in his eyes and, forgetting her resolution to think before she spoke, said frankly, "I don't know how much he will tell you, sir."

The sound of his chuckle as she opened the door was

reassuring, and she hoped that Rothwell would not have cause to blame her for speaking, yet again, out of turn.

He was sitting up against a pile of fluffy pillows, looking pale but talking amiably with Brockelby, who straddled a chair and leaned on his arms on the chair back. Seeing who had come in, Rothwell exclaimed, "Maggie, thank God!"

The doctor scrambled somewhat ungracefully to his feet, and made his bow, but Maggie ignored him and rushed to Rothwell's side. "Edward, are you truly well again?"

"I am." He smiled with warm relief, and he took her hand in his, giving it a hard squeeze.

"He is a trifle weak from his exertions, ma'am," Brockelby said, "but he will do well enough if he will but rest a bit."

"I'll see that he does," Maggie said firmly.

"And you, sweetheart," the earl said gently, "are you safe?"

"Yes, sir, thanks to Sir Dudley, I am."

He looked at Ryder, who had paused in the open doorway, watching the pair of them, and said, "I am in your debt again, Ryder, but I daresay you will collect, in your fashion."

Sir Dudley grinned at him. "I will. Ah, tell me, Ned, was all this why you sent for me?"

"In a way," Rothwell said, glancing at the doctor and back at Ryder. "I will tell you the whole presently, I expect, but for the moment I prefer to keep my own counsel."

"May one inquire as to the cause of your illness at least?"

Rothwell hesitated, but the doctor said, "An odd and most exaggerated reaction to tea, sir. Since no one

else became ill, and since his lordship does not customarily do so when he drinks Bohea, one's assumption must be that something other than tea got into the
cup, perhaps in the kitchen before it was brought out."

Fields, entering just then and clearing his throat,
startled the doctor, who turned and glared at him, but
his expression cleared at once at sight of the bottle of
whisky and glasses the butler carried on a tray. Fields
said, "With Mr. James's compliments, sir. He said I
should tell you, you would enjoy this more than
Bohea." After a pause, he added, "I assure you, sir,
nothing at all went into his lordship's cup in the
kitchen."

Before the doctor could discuss the point, Rothwell
said, "Fields, take Dr. Brockelby and Sir Dudley
downstairs and pour them all the whisky they want.
Just get them out of here."

Fields bowed, and the doctor immediately moved to
accompany him from the room, but although Ryder
seemed about to obey Rothwell's wishes, he paused
long enough on the threshold to say, "I trust you mean
to tell me the whole. To grant me a speaking part
without revealing the plot simply will not do, Ned."

Rothwell's eyes twinkled. "Knowing you have my
heartfelt gratitude must be enough for now, my friend,
although I will tell you—now that only Maggie can
hear us—that I sent for you because my chatty sister
made a verbal *faux pas* last night in the hearing of half
a dozen persons. Word of it evidently got to your
people, if not to you, since two of them had the effrontery to arrest my wife."

"But not, as I understand it, in mistake for your
sister."

"No, they were assisted in their decision, but that is
part of the bit I mean to tell you later. I assume since

you were kind enough to rescue Maggie, I need have no concern for Lydia."

"No, none."

There was a pause. Rothwell said, "Will you encounter trouble over this, my friend?"

Sir Dudley smiled and said, "Not much, I think, thanks to your countess's excellent good sense in saying absolutely nothing that can be repeated later to our embarrassment. Don't fret over this, Ned. I'll see to everything."

"Good man. Now get out. I want to be alone with my wife."

When Sir Dudley had gone and closed the door firmly behind him, Maggie felt nearly as shy as she had felt the first time she had found herself alone with Rothwell. He was looking at her now with both warmth and amusement, and she wanted only to hug him.

He pulled her down onto the bed beside him and said, "Would you like to climb under the covers? There is plenty of room."

She wanted nothing more, but she said, "I must not, not yet, but I'm so glad you are better. I've never been so terrified in my life as I was when you collapsed. I thought you had died."

"Would you have cared so much if I had, Maggie?"

"I would have wanted to die, too," she said simply.

"James said you just let them take you away. You ought to have made more of a push to tell them who you were."

"Would that really have made such a difference?" she asked, realizing he did not know the dowager had compounded her sins by accusing her of poisoning him. "It did not seem to signify when Lydia tried to tell them who I am, only when Sir Dudley did."

"I owe him a great deal," Rothwell said, stroking her arm. "You must have been very frightened."

She grinned at him. "Do you mean because Sir Dudley said I did not speak?"

"No, sweetheart, because the experience you have already had with our English law cannot have led you to have much faith in it. I presume that you held your tongue because you decided that keeping silent was the wiser course."

She raised her eyebrows. "You give me credit, sir."

"You said something earlier today that I have thought about rather a lot," he said. "You told me I had wronged both you and Lydia by not trusting you more. I realize I ought to have spoken with Lydia, and not merely assumed that to do so would be unwise. And in thinking about that, I realized that I have wronged you as well. You do speak out, sometimes without considering the consequences, but I have noted that you rarely say foolish things when you do. In fact, what I have liked best about you, aside from your more obvious assets, of course"—his hand moved to stroke her left breast—"is the fact that you are plain-spoken and direct. It seems absurd always to be taking you to task for that very asset. I do not doubt that there will be times in the future when your candor will annoy me again, but you have proven more than once—not least of all today—that you do know when it is wise to keep silent. A man can ask no more than that."

"I told Lydia why you brought us home last night," Maggie said, fairly blurting out the words in case they should make him change his mind about what he had just said.

"I ought to have told her myself. If I have learned anything from you, little wife, I hope it is that the female of the species is not always to be mistrusted. I had not thought that was how I felt, but what with living in the same house as my stepmother and being the target of every matchmaker in London, not to mention most eligible females—"

"Poor, poor Edward," Maggie said, her lips twitching.

He caught her by the shoulders and kissed her hard on the mouth, then held her away and looked at her suspiciously. "You didn't already tell Ryder what really happened, did you?"

"I still don't know exactly what happened. Do you?"

"I'll wager you guessed. I heard Lydia tell James not to let anyone give me anything to eat or drink. She said you had told her to tell him about the sugar in my tea, too."

"I thought you were poisoned," she said, "but perhaps if the doctor believes it was just something from—"

"Brockelby knows it was nothing of the sort. James had evidently told him as much before I came to my senses, but he said it didn't matter what it was, that since I had eaten it, the best way to deal with it was to empty my stomach. And that they surely did. If I can ever bring myself to forgive my stepmother for any of this, I'll never forgive her for the rhubarb, or the ipecac, or for whatever horrid thing Brockelby poured down me."

"I will never forgive her at all," Maggie said flatly.

He took her in his arms again only to release her when the door opened to admit Lydia, who clutched a damp handkerchief in one hand and looked as if she had been crying. She said, "It is dreadful downstairs. I told James that Mama had shrieked out some nonsense to those dreadful men about Maggie trying to poison you, Ned, and he has gone quite absolutely mad."

"Is that true?" Rothwell demanded, looking straight at Maggie. "She accused you?"

"She said Jacobites had poisoned you," Maggie said, "and since she had just accused me of being one, the inference was plain enough, but she was distraught, of course. Perhaps I ought to go downstairs and see what can be done."

She started to get up, but Rothwell held her. He said, "Where is Ryder, puss?"

"He and Dr. Brockelby came in while James was ranting at Mama, but he shouted at them to go into the library and drink the damn—dashed whisky, and they went away again. I could not get away so easily because Mama kept clutching at me, saying she didn't mean any harm, that if she had stupidly let some of her powders fall into your teacup and had even more stupidly allowed those awful men to believe Maggie was the daughter of a Jacobite when she actually said only that most Highland chiefs fought in the Uprising, she is very sorry. And she insists that she was very careful *not* to accuse Maggie of poisoning you. But James just went on shouting at her; and, since she also said she was quite certain that if God would but see fit to allow him to become Earl of Rothwell he would soon see that this proposed marriage of his is quite unsuitable, I think she *did* mean to do a great deal of harm. Oh, Ned, is that not a perfectly dreadful thing to think about one's own mother?" She began to cry again.

Rothwell said gently, "It is dreadful, puss, but it is not an unreasonable conclusion, considering the evidence. Did James by any chance discover what it was that she put into my tea?"

She dried her eyes, saying, "He did, but it was not Mama who told him. It was Maria. When Mama refused to reply to certain questions he asked, he sent Fields to get Maria and told her she would be hanged for murder if you died, because he would testify against her in court and say that she had tried and tried on the road to Scotland to kill you, and again on the way home. And Maria burst into tears and said she only did it the first few times, that she put nightshade into your food."

"Nightshade! Deadly nightshade? But that would have killed me at once, would it not?"

"So James says, and he thinks Mama *believed* it was deadly nightshade, only as it chances, the stuff he distills for her complexion is common English nightshade and not at all the same thing. And that, he says, is why it did not work when Maria put it in your food. In point of fact, he said, had he not added the juice of the berries to Mama's distillation, it would have been quite safe for you to drink. It was the berry juice that made you feel ill. Maria would have stopped when the stuff she added to your food only made you feel sick, she says, only Chelton made her try again, and he made her add some of the laudanum Mama had given her. She says she was afraid they would be caught and so she did not put in enough. And Chelton was so angry with her that he beat her. She told James they could do nothing at Glen Drumin House because the servants watched her too closely, and then she said you were so kind to her on the road—I don't know quite what she meant, and she did not explain that part—"

"We know what she was talking about," Maggie said quietly, remembering Maria's terror when they had begun descending the steep side of the Corriearrack. "Go on, Lydia."

"Well, she said she stood up to Chelton when he ordered her to put more of the stuff in Ned's food."

"She did," Rothwell said. "She announced to everyone within hearing that she would make certain I ate nothing that she had not fixed herself or watched being made. After that there was no way for them to accomplish their task without incriminating themselves. It seems I owe a great deal to Maria."

Maggie was not so certain. "Why did they do it?"

Lydia said, "Maria told us it was because she has always done what Mama told her to do, since she was quite young, but also Mama told Chelton she would turn him off without a character if he refused to do as she bade him. He is too old to find work elsewhere, especially if he were turned away from Rothwell Park. And too, Mama promised to pay him a great deal of money, though where she thought she would get a great deal of money I don't know. And now all she has accomplished is to infuriate James and to make me sorry she is my mother."

Maggie, feeling deep sympathy for Lydia, moved again to go to her, and this time Rothwell did not stop her. But as she put her arm around the younger girl, the door opened yet again, and Brockelby strolled in, a glass of whisky in his hand.

"I say, Rothwell, where the devil did you come by this stuff? Ryder says he don't know, and I'd have asked James, but he's still closeted with your stepmama and I did not like to disturb them, but I've never tasted better. I must have some."

Rothwell said, "That is private stock from my Highland estate, Brockelby. I'll gladly tell James to give you a bottle if you will take my sister back to the library with you now and pour her a glassful as a composer. My father-in-law declares the stuff can cure all the ills of the world, and while I will not say that much myself, I am rapidly coming to the conclusion that I must find a way to produce his product commercially."

Brockelby would have entered into a discussion of the best means to do that, but when Rothwell made a gesture toward the brooding Lydia, he collected himself and gently took her arm.

"I should go with her," Maggie said.

"No, sweetheart, we can trust Brockelby and Ryder to look after her for the present. Come here and—No, wait. Go and lock that confounded door first or we'll have James or someone else breaking in upon us. Then come here and sit down again."

"Should you not rest like the doctor bade you, Edward?" she asked anxiously when she had obeyed the first of his commands.

"No, I should not."

"Very well. We do have some things to discuss. You do know that neither James nor Lydia had any part in any of this."

"I know that, sweetheart. Now come back here."

She hesitated. "I do feel I must tell you at once that although I find I do not at all mind living in London with you, I simply cannot continue to share a house with your stepmama. I hope you will not expect me to do so."

"Good God, no," he said harshly. "She can go to the devil!"

"You cannot just turn her out of the house."

"No, and though she is guilty of attempted murder—yours as well as mine, thanks to that appalling accusation of hers—I don't want to produce an ugly scandal by turning her over to the authorities. What I will do is confine her to the dower house in Derby-shire, with Chelton to look after her and a few men I can trust to keep them there. Maria can do as she pleases. I will see to it that Chelton cannot harm her if she wants to remain with my stepmother." He added firmly, "But I don't want to talk about them anymore just now."

"I believe you, sir. You must be very—"

"Come here, Maggie." There was a new note in his voice that brought warmth to her cheeks and a tingling to a region much nearer the center of her body, but she went willingly to stand by the bed. He pulled his night-shirt off over his head, sending two buttons skittering under the wardrobe, and said, "Take off your clothes and get into bed."

She bit her lip to keep from smiling, then said, "It is too early, sir. Moreover, the servants will be serving dinner soon, and since I don't believe your stepmother will want to act as hostess, and Lydia is really too young to—"

"Take off your clothes, Maggie."

Obediently, she untied the ribbon at her bodice, but as she reached for the hooks behind, she said, "Do you really mean to produce Glen Drumin whisky commercially? How can you, since Papa flatly refuses to pay any duty or excise tax, and you said—"

"Whatever I said, I said before I knew there might be a market among those who can afford to pay as much for whisky as they pay for fine wine. Now that I do know, however, I'll find a way to sell it to them, even if I have to bribe someone to exempt Glen Drumin whisky from the damned excise! Now, get into bed."

She hesitated, letting her gown fall to the floor, enjoying the changing expression on his face as she did so. Her shift followed the gown before she said thoughtfully, "I am still not by any means certain that this marriage of ours can work, you know. We disagree on all manner of things, and while I know that you find me attractive and truly enjoy this sort of thing—"

"Damnation, Maggie, we are both strong enough to make this union work if we put our minds to it, disagreements or none, but if I have to get up to *put* you in this bed, I'll make you regret that you teased me this way." His last words lacked the strength of the first ones, which did not surprise her, for when she cupped her breasts in her hands midway through his threat and stepped toward him, she heard his breath catch in his throat.

"I think," she said provocatively, "that it would do you a great deal of good to learn to beg, Edward."

"You may think what you like, sweetheart," he said, reaching for her. "Come to bed."

She stepped back out of his reach and smiled. "You may begin by asking me more politely to join you in your bed."

Instead of coming for her as she had halfway hoped he would, he folded his hands behind his head, regarded her with lazy amusement, and said, "Have I told you that I love you?"

"No, but I guessed it, so do not expect me to tumble gratefully into your arms, sir, for in point of fact, I do not believe I have ever spoken those actual words to you either. If you want to hear them, you know what you must do."

"I will never beg you, sweetheart, so you might just as well put that notion straight out of your head. Now, come here."

This time she obeyed, for the air was chilly, but

when he moved possessively over her, she said sweetly, "I do love you, Edward, very much, but before this day is done, I will make you beg me, just as you once made me beg you."

"You won't ever do it, little wife."

But, to her credit, she did.

Dear Readers,

For those of you who always ask "How much of it is true?" I add this short note. The primary characters come from my own imagination—names, clans, and all. As to the rest, here are a few of the basic facts:

After the unsuccessful Jacobite Uprising of 1745 (the final attempt to restore the Stewarts to the British throne), the real tragedy for the Scottish Highlands lay not in the defeat of the clans but in what came afterward, when the English government followed its victory with a series of acts designed to prevent any risk of a Jacobite revival by crushing the Highlanders' spirit and destroying their very way of life.

The Disarming Act of 1746 imposed severe penalties for carrying or possessing arms and for wearing any tartan garment. The bagpipes were indeed prohibited as "instruments of war," and enforcers of these policies did include members of such non-Jacobite clans as the Campbells and MacKenzies, who cruelly used their privileged positions to settle old scores.

Lands of known Jacobite sympathizers were indeed forfeited to the Crown, then awarded or sold to absentee landlords who knew nothing and cared less about their Highland tenants. Later, the cult of the sporting estate gradually arose, and large areas that had supported many clansmen were given over to sheep with a handful of shepherds to mind the flocks, while the rest of the unfortunate inhabitants were evicted.

Bonnie Prince Charlie did visit London in September 1750. He did go to the Tower of London and to church. He also showed up at a ball given by Lady Primrose in Essex Street. I haven't a clue as to what he actually wore, but his character was unfortunately very much as I described it.

Between 1740 and 1824, whisky became the most

important industry in the Highlands. Illicit distilling was accepted by everyone as the only means of paying rent, and the extreme difficulty of collecting the unfair taxes and duties eventually defeated the government in the south.

In researching this book, I collected many tales of whisky smuggling, so nearly everything MacDrumin of MacDrumin does to outwit excisemen and bailies was done by someone at one time or another. And Rothwell's declaration that if nothing else works he will seek an exemption from the excise tax for MacDrumin is also based on fact. One distillery, Ferintosh, was actually exempted from the excise for over one hundred years. Other labels that trace their history to this period include Glenlivet, Laphroaig, Walker, and Seager Evans. The first legal Highland distillery, Glenlivet, was not licensed until 1824.

I hope you enjoyed *Highland Fling* and will look forward to reading *The Bawdy Bride* in September 1995.

Sincerely yours,

Amanda Scott

If you enjoyed HIGHLAND FLING,
turn the page for a peek at
THE BAWDY BRIDE,
also available from Zebra Books.

The Bawdy Bride

by

Amanda Scott

Prologue

October 1799, Derbyshire, England

So this was Hell. The once-noisy din of chatter and laughter from the next room that had gone on unceasingly despite her screams was muted now, growing distant, as if she heard it through earmuffs in a roaring winter windstorm. But it was not winter, and Hell was no place for earmuffs.

"Her eyes are open."

The voice floated over her, far away and fading, his words nonsense. Had her eyes been open, she would have seen him.

He said, "You oughtn't to have used such a heavy whip, your lordship. She's a small wench."

"I intended that she should fully comprehend the wisdom of remaining silent, now and forever more."

Even here and now, coming to her through airless, ever-thickening darkness, that low, purring second voice chilled and terrified her, but she would never keep silent. If God were in the mood to produce a miracle and snatch her to safety, she would tell the world all she knew about his bloody lordship. Not that God would do any such thing. He would not produce even a small miracle for such a great sinner as herself. Surely, Mary Magdalene had received not only her own share of such wonders but any share that might have come, centuries later, to a sister in sin. Unless she could manage somehow to escape on her own to tell the truth about him, the wicked man would go right on taking advantage of his lofty position to make others miserable.

Odd that with hellfire flaming through her body, threatening to consume her, she could still hear the crackling of the fire on the hearth, could still feel rough carpet beneath her cheek and the movement of the river tide below—and odder still that she felt cold. She had never known such pain, not even the many times her father had beaten her, determined to drive the devil out of her. He had warned her, so many times, that she would go to Hell. How pleased he would be now, to know he had been right.

She could not see the room anymore, though she knew its oppressive crimson elegance only too well. She could not see the fire either, for all they'd said her eyes were open. Instead, in her mind's eye, she saw a tiny golden-haired child laughing in church and being soundly switched then and there for her blasphemy, and an older child striving to memorize lines from a Bible she could not read and being beaten for forgetting. She saw a girl, free at last, going into service, wanting only to prove her worth, and the same girl learning her precise worth, learning that her father had been right all along.

A dizzy, spinning sensation threatened to overcome her, the same one she had felt when for no reason she had understood at the time, she had been turned off without a character. She knew the reason now only too well. Like others before her, she had been doomed, condemned to the *Folly*.

"She's stopped breathing, damn you!" It was the one who had so absurdly said her eyes were open.

"Mind your tongue, fool. Do you so quickly forget how to address your betters?"

Again the chill of that purring voice filtered through the heavy dark, cloud enveloping her, but how ridiculous for him to say she was not breathing. If that were so, she would be dead, unable to hear them at all. She could see a glimmer of light now in the darkness ahead of her. It widened, beckoning her nearer. Surely, there was sunlight ahead, and warmth, and love.

"Beg pardon, your lordship, I'm sure, if I've offended you," the first man said, and his voice seemed much farther away now. She barely sensed the irony in his words, barely heard him at all when he added, "Still and all, I tell you, the chit is dead."

"A pity, but she's no great loss. There are plenty more where she came . . ."

J

Thursday, April 10, 1800

Dear James,

I am to be married today. I stood in front of the glass this morning and introduced myself to my reflection as Lady Michael St. Ledgers but saw only Anne Davies, as always, looking too much like a child to be a bride. That one can still look so at the ancient age of twenty seems most peculiar, but since my hair is too fair and too fine to yield easily to fashion's dictates, and my body too waiflike to stir a man's desires (or so Beth tells me, and she should know), I can do nothing to alter the matter.

I thought, once I had met Lord Michael, I would feel differently about marriage, but I do not. He is large and, I suppose, rather handsome, but his demeanor is stern and his manner unyielding. I have seen him smile only once, and that was at Beth, who was flirting as usual. Tony does not seem to mind such antics, so their marriage lopes along peacefully enough. I hope mine will do likewise. I mean to be a good wife, James, for I know my duty, of course, and thanks to Grandmama's precepts and my experience here at Rendlesham, I am well trained for the position; however, since I have grown weary of constantly seeking compromise, and since I doubt that marriage can require less of that increasingly tiresome occupation than the single state requires, I must admit to certain qualms . . .

Lady Anne Davies paused, nibbling the end of her pen and absently stroking the small black cat curled in her lap as she tried to organize those qualms into words she could set to paper. Before she had done more than dip the nib into her inkwell again, however, the door to her bedchamber opened without ceremony and her maid, Maisie Bray, bustled in with Anne's wedding dress draped carefully over one plump, rosy arm.

Looking critically at her mistress, she said, "Beg pardon, my lady, I'm sure, but this be no time to be scribbling in that journal of yours. His lordship—which is to say your papa, not Lord Michael—wants to see you in his bookroom as soon as you be dressed, and it won't do to be agitating him, not today."

"I try never to agitate Papa, Maisie," Anne said calmly, "and if I do not write now, I do not know when I shall find the opportunity to write again." But she slipped the page obediently into the portfolio she kept for the purpose and, still holding the small cat, arose to put the portfolio into the carpetbag she would carry with her later in the carriage. Then she stepped to the window to take one last look out at her beloved gardens, just now beginning to show touches of springtime color.

The cat purred, and Anne stroked it while she gazed at her garden and the vast sloping sweep of velvet green lawn beyond. Behind her, Maisie said gently, "You'd best make haste, Miss Anne."

With a sigh, Anne put small black Juliette down on a favored pillow on the high, blue-silk draped bed, slipped out of her dressing robe, and stood in chemise and corset while Maisie flung the white muslin dress over her head. Maisie was careful not to disarrange Anne's hair, and once the gown was in place, while the maid fastened the golden ties at each shoulder, Anne gazed solemnly at her reflection in the cheval glass.

The gown was lovely, but she wished she might have had silver embroidered borders instead of gold. She had suggested that with her gray eyes and pale flaxen hair silver would be more becoming to her, but her mother had scorned such a notion.

"You are an earl's daughter, Anne, not a commoner," Lady Rendlesham had said tartly. "You are entitled to wear cloth of gold, and indeed, had Lord Michael's family not still been in half-mourning for the late duke, I would have insisted that you display your rank properly. But for such a paltry affair as this wedding will be, gold-embroidered muslin will suffice." She sighed, adding, "Why, when I was married, we had guests for three weeks beforehand at Belford. 'Tis the greatest pity Upminster had to die, else we might have enjoyed a truly splendid wedding."

Anne resisted the temptation to point out that had the sixth Duke of Upminster not died, the notion of marriage might not have occurred to his younger brother for some time yet. She said only, "There is still a Duke of Upminster, ma'am."

"A mere boy, and in mourning at that. He will not even be present at the wedding, for goodness' sake.

But others will, my girl, and you will not appear in paltry silver trimming."

And so it was that the gown's sleeves and hemline were bordered with gold. The close-fitting, high-waisted bodice was deep blue velvet, and a loose robe of white gauze, spotted and trimmed with a border and fringe of gold, lay waiting to be worn over the whole. Wisps of Anne's fine hair had escaped the carefully arranged coiffure over which Maisie had labored earlier; so, commanding her to sit again, the maid tucked them into place before fixing a small blue velvet cap to Anne's head and pinning her gauze veil in place at the back. Moments later, Anne stood, slipped her feet into blue velvet slippers, drew on her white gloves, and turned to leave the room.

"One moment, my lady," Maisie said. "You have forgotten Lord Michael's necklace."

The necklace, too, was gold, an exquisite chain with a pendant molded to resemble a rose and bearing a small diamond in its center. Anne liked it, and her elder sisters, Beth and Harriet, had assured her it was a perfect wedding gift.

Maisie fastened the necklace, then moved to take one last look at the full effect, and Anne was surprised to see tears sparkling in her eyes.

"What is it, Maisie? Is something amiss?"

"No, Miss Anne, it just makes me sad to think you are all grown up and will be going away to a brand new home, and all."

"Don't be a goose. You know perfectly well that you are going with me. Indeed, were it not for that, I think I would be paralyzed with fear, for I scarcely know Lord Michael, and I have never met a single member of his family. That he expects me to play mother to his brother's children is especially unnerving, I think. The poor things are bound to resent me fiercely."

"They will not," Maisie said stoutly. "For all that one's a duke before his time, they'll learn to love you like we all do."

"We will see," Anne said, smiling vaguely. "I must go now. Papa will be displeased if I tarry longer."

She left on the words, and hurried downstairs to the bookroom, grateful not to encounter any of her siblings on the way. Her five remaining brothers and sisters were present at Rendlesham for the wedding. Only James, the eldest and her favorite, was absent, but James was dead. He had died when she was nine, but she kept him alive in her memory by writing her diary as a series of letters to him. She had never told anyone about the diary, though Maisie knew she kept one, and no one else had ever read it. Even Maisie, much as she loved Anne, did not know how very alive James remained to her.

She found the Earl of Rendlesham pacing the floor in his bookroom, his ruddy face creased in thought, his large hands clasped behind his back, causing his waistcoat to gape over his stomach where the buttons strained. A cheerful fire crackled on the hearth, and through the tall windows, curtained with wine-colored velvet, sunlight spilled across the bright Turkey carpet; but his lordship looked more harried than cheerful.

"There you are," he said brusquely, pausing and straightening to glare at her. "What a time you have been! They'll be ready to begin the ceremony in a few moments."

"I'm sorry, Papa," Anne said quickly. "Dressing always takes longer than one thinks it will."

"Yes, yes, I suppose it does. Perhaps you had better sit down," he added, gesturing distractedly at a chair.

"Will you think me very disobedient if I do not?" she asked, smiling at him. "Maisie will be most distressed if I muss my skirt before the ceremony."

"Do as you please," he said. "The sooner this business is done, the better I shall like it. I've any number of other things I ought to be doing."

"Problems, Papa? Is there anything I can do to help?"

"Dash it all, I don't want your help, just your obedience. I don't want to hear any nonsense about this being a hasty affair, or about being afraid to go off alone with Lord Michael."

Anne looked at him in surprise. "But I have never said I would not obey you, Papa. Indeed, I know it is my duty to marry, particularly when such an excellent connection has been made available to me. I know how fortunate I am to make such a match, and if there is haste—though I have not complained of it—it is only because Lord Michael needs a mama for his nephew and niece."

Rendlesham shoved a hand through thick graying hair that he disdained to cover with a wig now that the price of powder had become extortionate, and said ruefully, "I suppose you haven't complained, but having listened to your mother—and to your sisters when they married—until I'd like to throttle the lot of them, I assumed your complaints would echo theirs. I ought to have known they would not. You are a good girl, Anne. Indeed, I do not know what we shall do here without you to make peace when the others choose to quarrel. But, as I told your mama, it is extremely rare luck to find any good match for a third daughter."

"Does Mama agree that Lord Michael is a good one for me?"

"Of course she does! Not only is he the son of a

duke, but the lad's got a respectable fortune of his own. Not a large one, mind you, but you'll be comfortable enough, particularly since you will live at Upminster Court, which is a ducal seat, after all."

"I know I will be comfortable, Papa. My own portion is respectable enough for comfort."

He did not meet her gaze. "As to that," he said, turning toward the fire, "I know you assumed you would retain a certain amount of control over your dowry, as I arranged for your sisters to do when they were married, but there has been a slight alteration in that plan, I'm afraid."

"Indeed?"

"Yes. Michael has some pressing problems—nothing that need concern you, of course, but I found it necessary to give in to certain demands he made regarding the settlements."

"I see."

"I do not suppose that you see at all," he said, turning back with a sigh, "but I believed I ought to tell you myself. I hope the news does not distress you unduly."

It did distress her, but she knew better than to express such feelings to him, or indeed to anyone in her family. They were all too concerned by their own needs to consider hers. She reassured him, as it was her habit to do, and agreed at once when he said they ought to join the others in the family chapel.

The group awaiting them was a small one, since only immediate family members and close friends had been invited to witness the marriage of Lady Anne Davies to Lord Michael St. Ledgers. Anne smiled at one familiar face after another, hoping she looked more collected than she felt as she walked at her father's side up the narrow center aisle.

Ahead of her, standing between her elder brother and the thin, elderly parson who was to perform the ceremony, stood her husband-to-be. She had exchanged only a handful of sentences with him, but when the ceremony was over, she would be his wife, subject to his commands until death parted them. The thought sent a shiver up her spine, but whether it was a thrill of anticipation or one of terror, Anne herself was not certain.

Dark-haired Lord Michael St. Ledgers towered over both Viscount Davies and Parson Hale. Lord Michael's broad shoulders were squared, his carriage that of a military man—which indeed, Anne knew he had been for some years. He was nine-and-twenty, nine years older than she was, and his stern demeanor made him look older. As Anne approached, his gaze caught hers and held it. His eyes were the darkest blue she had ever seen, making them look almost black until she got quite near him. They were set deep beneath his dark eyebrows, and the rest of his features were sharply chiseled. He looked for a moment as if he had been carved from stone, but suddenly, as if he sensed her increasing anxiety, she detected a barely perceptible softening in his appearance.

He did not smile, but his firm, well-shaped lips relaxed a little, and she felt herself relax in response. She had not expected him to woo her, for theirs was not a love match like her sister Harriet's with Alfred Crane, or a union arranged after long months of negotiation like Beth's to Tony. Beth, after all, as the earl's eldest daughter, her portion immense, had been the catch of the season the year she made her entrance to society. And Harriet, though a second daughter, had a wealthy godfather and her own vivacious demeanor to assure her of a good match.

Anne's marriage was not like either of theirs. Not only was she the earl's third daughter but she had formed no attachment to anyone during the two London seasons that had been granted her at her Grandmother's insistence. Moreover, Lord Michael had made it clear that he believed he had a duty to marry, and he was plainly a dutiful man. He was certainly not in love with her, nor she with him. She was merely the best bride he could acquire to serve as mother to his bereft niece and nephew, and one, moreover, who apparently met his financial needs as well.

The ceremony took less time than she had expected. When Lord Michael took her hand to slip a pearl ring on her third finger, she was surprised by how warm his hands felt. A moment later, Parson Hale presented the couple to the witnesses and everyone adjourned to the dining room for the wedding breakfast, called so despite the fact that it took place in the early afternoon. The next hour passed swiftly, and had Anne been asked what she ate or what she had said to anyone, she would have found it difficult to reply factually. By the time she hurried upstairs to let Maisie help her change her dress for the journey to Upminster Court, she felt as if she had been participating in a dream, and someone else's dream at that.

Less than half an hour later she was ready. Pausing only to pick up the carpetbag containing her portfolio, and to slip her small black cat inside, she hurried downstairs to make her farewells and to invite the various members of her family to visit her soon. Then, in what seemed little less than the blink of an eye, she found herself in a well-sprung carriage, next to her new husband, with her carpetbag at her feet. Her journey to Upminster Court and a brand new life had begun.

For the next several minutes, while the carriage

negotiated first the circular sweep in front of Rendlesham House and then the oak-and-rhododendron-
lined gravel drive leading to the main road, neither
occupant of the carriage attempted to speak. But when
Anne turned to look back as the carriage lurched onto
the high road, her companion said, "There is nothing
to see now. The second carriage will not follow at
once, you know."

She settled back into place, turning her head to look
at him as she said, "I wanted to take a last look at the
park, since I do not know when I will return."

"I thought you might be missing your maid. I must
suppose you have never been alone with a man in a
carriage before."

She had a sudden, uncharacteristic urge to tell him
she had been alone with all sorts of men, hundreds of
times, but she suppressed it, feeling heat in her cheeks
as she did. Such a wicked impulse was most unlike her.

He did not appear to notice her blushes, however, or
if he did, she supposed he attributed them to maidenly
modesty. He did not even seem to notice that she had
not replied to his comment. He was looking out the
window, not looking at her at all.

She was accustomed to silence, accustomed too, to
being ignored. For many years she had mediated her
siblings' battles and arguments, dried the younger
ones' tears and listened to all their complaints and
their dreams, even though they seemed to have no time
to listen to hers. From the instant she had known she
was to be married, whenever the demands of her various family members had grown tiresome, she had tried
to solace her feelings with the hope that she would at
least be more valued as a wife than she had been as a
sister or daughter. But judging by Lord Michael's air
of preoccupation, that would not be the case.

She said quietly, "I daresay our people will not be too far behind, sir. I have not met your man, but my maid is efficient and had little left to do. How long will our journey take us?"

"A few hours, maybe four. Upminster Court is located several miles west of Chesterfield on the Carlisle Road."

"My father said we would be living there. Is that right?"

He looked at her then and said gravely, "I suppose your father must also have told you that I am guardian for my late brother's children, one of whom is the present Duke of Upminster. I believe it best for him to grow up at Upminster, particularly since I am also his primary trustee and bear the responsibility for looking after his properties during his minority. Therefore, for the present at least, we will certainly live at the house."

"Those poor children," Anne said. "How dreadful for them to lose both parents within such a short period of time. Papa said your brother and his wife were taken within months of each other. Was it some sort of illness?"

"No."

When he did not elaborate, she tried another tack. "How old are the children, sir? What are they like?"

"Andrew is fourteen, Sylvia nine," he said in that same brusque manner. "As to what they are like, I cannot imagine that my opinion of them will aid you much in dealing with them. You are sure to form your own opinions once you meet them, after all, and you will meet Andrew at once, since he is at the house. Sylvia is presently residing with one of my sisters, but she can return whenever you like."

He looked out the window at the passing countryside again, and Anne, too, fell silent. The day having

turned blustery, the sun had been playing "All-hide"
with errant white clouds since shortly after the ceremony, but she had no wish to discuss the weather. And
since Lord Michael clearly had no intention either of
volunteering information about his family or of encouraging her to ask questions about Upminster
Court, she was at a loss. The thought of spending the
next two or three hours in close proximity with a man
who did not want to talk was a little daunting but not
nearly so daunting as the thought of spending the rest
of her life with him.

The carriage moved rapidly now, but it was well
sprung, and did not sway much, for which she was
grateful. She was a good traveler, but the day was still
warm, the road dusty, and she knew that were the pace
the sort to rattle her bones, she would develop a headache long before they reached their destination.

She made no further effort to engage him in conversation, entertaining herself instead by watching the
passing scenery, waiting for the time they would meet
houses and villages unfamiliar to her. The clouds grew
grayer, but the fields were green with new growth and
the hedges alive with birds and new color. She loved
the springtime. They passed through thick woodlands
of oak and silver birch, heavily populated with red
deer and grouse, and the carriage traveled across
lovely open moorland carpeted with bright new grass
and bushy dark-green heather.

They traveled as swiftly as the condition of the
roads allowed, and at Matlock, the red marls, gravel,
and sandstone of south Derbyshire began to give way
to limestone and gritstone, as the moors were replaced
by the steeper stone-walled hills and dales of northern
Derbyshire. Lovely midland moors and emerging

cornfields fell behind, giving way to harsher, higher grass country. The air was cooler now, and the wind-ravaged sky grew darker. Thunder muttered from glowering black clouds boiling up behind the Peaks to the north. At first the sound was barely discernible above hoofbeats and rattling wheels, but then the thunder groaned louder, belched, then roared to a crescendo, its echoes buffeting from rock to rock down the narrow valley. Anne became aware suddenly that the carpetbag at her feet was moving.

The first plaintive cry, she hoped, reached only her ears. Surreptitiously, she moved her foot gently, caressingly, against the side of the bag that moved. The resulting silence reassured her, but that silence lasted only while she continued to move her foot. When she stopped, there was instant complaint.

"What was that?" her companion asked.

Anne hesitated, unsure of how he would react to learning that the carriage contained a third occupant. Before she could think how to phrase the information, there came another clap of thunder, a yowl of protest from the carpetbag, and Lord Michael leaned down and picked it up. Without so much as a by-your-leave, he opened the bag and peered inside. To her astonishment, he laughed.

"What have we here?" he asked as Juliette's head popped up. The kitten looked at him, wide-eyed and trembling, then turned quickly, saw Anne, and with a mew of relief, leapt from the carpetbag into her lap.

Watching Lord Michael guiltily, Anne petted and soothed the kitten, saying, "I had to bring her, sir. She is accustomed to being with me, and I feared they would send her out to live in the stables if I did not take her away."

"Good Lord, of course you may bring her. She's a little beauty. Come here, cat." He held out a hand commandingly.

"She never pays heed to anyone but me, I'm afraid," Anne said apologetically.

He tickled Juliette under the chin, on the spot where the only white hairs on the little cat formed a lopsided triangle. The pointed chin went up obligingly, and Juliette began to purr.

"She will come to me," he said confidently, moving his finger along one side of the kitten's jaw toward an ear.

Anne watched, fascinated, as the kitten, ignoring the thunder now, pressed its head hard against the stroking finger, purring, clearly enjoying the attention of this stranger. When Lord Michael stopped, Juliette looked at him in indignation.

He wiggled the finger enticingly on his knee, then stopped. Juliette watched alertly. When he wiggled it again, the kitten put out a paw, halting it in midair when his finger again stopped wiggling. When the finger moved, the kitten jabbed, and when the finger disappeared suddenly between his legs, Juliette leapt from Anne's lap to Lord Michael's knee, reaching between his legs to attack. He played with the kitten for some time before, chuckling, he gathered it up and began to stroke its fur. Juliette purred, apparently perfectly at home, tucking front paws neatly beneath pointed chin. When he lifted the kitten to his shoulder, near Anne, it blinked twice at her, then curled into a ball and settled down, purring until it went to sleep.

Watching Lord Michael with Juliette, Anne began to revise her first impression of him, and when he turned suddenly and grinned at her, delighted by the kitten's acceptance of his friendship, she smiled back and relaxed. He might not be a talkative man, but he was not made of stone. Marriage to him, she decided, might prove rather interesting after all.